# The Owners Volume I:

## Alone

– CARMEN CAPUANO –

An environmentally friendly book printed and bound in England by
www.printondemand-worldwide.com

**Mixed Sources**
Product group from well-managed
forests, and other controlled sources
www.fsc.org  Cert no. TT-COC-002641
© 1996 Forest Stewardship Council

**FSC**

**PEFC**
PEFC/16-33-415

PEFC Certified
This product is
from sustainably
managed forests
and controlled
sources
www.pefc.org

This book is made entirely of chain-of-custody materials

www.fast-print.net/store.php

The Owners Volume I: Alone
Copyright © Carmen Capuano 2012

ISBN 978-178035-445-3

First published 2012 by
FASTPRINT PUBLISHING
Peterborough, England.
Printed by Printondemand-Worldwide

# Chapter 1.

It was the distinctive "EEEEKKBBRR," of his name being shrieked, which roused the sleeping boy. That initial piercing note, the shrill EE, jarred and jostled with the sharp consonant of the K, before being displaced by the thick and heavy guttural tones of the final letters. Each sound individually awful to hear, the combined effect was truly hideous and an assault to the ear drum.

Half asleep still, eyelids glued tight to one another, he fought his way to full wakefulness. His vision was blurred. Light deprived in their slumber, his pupils were too dilated to cope with the sudden light flooding into them and he was forced to blink rapidly just to focus. He had only a fraction of a second, to react to what he feared was coming.

"Please don't …" throat still clogged with sleep, his voice was almost unrecognisable, even to him.

Caught in his peripheral vision, the wickedly sharp talons looked even longer and fiercer than normal. Curved like scimitars, their ends honed down to razor sharp glistening points, they seemed to hover for a moment over his face, before journeying downwards toward his throat. All was silent and still now. Only the talons moved.

The drone of an insect outside served to shatter the silence, its thrum a seeming answer to the staccato drumbeat of his heart. Perspiration salted his face and adrenaline flooded his veins. He could feel his blood pumping, *almost hear* its rhythm, as it coursed through his jugular…even as the talons descended.

Swooping down in a rapid arc too fast for him to counteract, he at once perceived the beauty of the deadly implements in their gleaming blackness. As if in slow motion he watched, fascinated, as their lethal points impaled the sheet which covered his body, puncturing the material as if it had no more resistance than paper. And then tossed it to the floor.

"EEEEKKBBRR." Second time around, the noise was no less awful.

Distracted for a moment from the creature who stood before him, his gaze was drawn to the sheet, which had not at once fallen into a crumpled pile, as he would have expected, but instead retained some tension of shape, as though it now covered and obscured some other hidden monster.

"EEEEKKBBRR!" the creature cried once more, causing the boy's name to echo around in his head, finally bringing him fully awake and aware of his surroundings. That high-pitched almost electronic whine, fading into a clicking rasping noise, never failed to get his attention.

This time, the talons descended to his hair, ruffling it with a strange combination of irritation and tenderness.

Their lethal potential held in tight check, the sharp points scraped gently across his scalp in a rather pleasant way, bringing forth a set of shivers which tingled down the length of his spine. He rubbed his eyes and stretched lazily on the soft bed. He hated being woken up in this way.

Unconsciously, he reached for the sheet, intending to drag it over his head and go back to sleep. But his questing fingers found only his nightclothes. The cover was now on the floor.

For a moment, a fragment of the dream he had been immersed in, lingered in his mind, and there was a vague memory of something significant that had happened once. But then like an ephemeral puff of smoke, it vanished without a trace.

"EEEEKKBBRR," his Owner called once again, hopping up and down on his thin scaly legs whilst flapping his wings furiously. This wing beating business and the flurry of dust it kicked up, always caused San to cough. Belatedly, he tried to cover his mouth but the tickle was already there in the back of his throat and his body launched itself into full scale paroxysms of coughing.

Unfortunately, this agitated his Owner even more, who then accelerated the hopping and wing flapping, causing San to cough even longer and harder.

"Stop flapping around," the boy managed to gasp out. "It just makes you look like a huge chicken, you know. It's not exactly a threatening look, if that's what you were aiming for."

OwnSan's bald head was almost scraping the wooden ceiling and was causing San to nod *his* head up and down very quickly, just to keep him in sight. Put together with the coughing, this resulted in him feeling quite sick, his head movements were so jerky and rapid. Instead, he swallowed back any further coughs and tried to keep his head still and only move his eyes, keeping them fixed on his Owner.

This wasn't any better or easier and made him wonder if his eyes might roll themselves right out of his head. San sniggered at the idea of his eyes rolling around on the floor, following OwnSan wherever he went, following him up and down, round and round and round, rolling and rolling.

"Now that might just give *you* a bit of a shock," he stated, knowing full well he wouldn't be understood anyway.

Sensing that his Pet was not paying attention, the Eyon took a huge breath, causing his feathered chest to expand, and prepared to shriek again. It was doubtful that OwnSan realised San found it all highly amusing – Eyons were not known for their sense of humour, but still, it didn't pay to be openly laughing.

The Eyon's chest puffed out to its full extent, displaying his colours of muted green and grey, interspersed with swirls of gold.

Colourful and beautiful as OwnSan was, San couldn't help but be reminded of the chicken dinner he had had he previous evening. This made him snigger even more as the ludicrous image of OwnSan perched on a giant plate appeared in his mind.

Groaning now with suppressed mirth, he shook his head in an attempt to rid himself of such thoughts. Clearly, the Eyon was in a hurry this morning.

"EEEEKKBBRR!" he squawked impatiently once more, his scaly throat clicking and screeching out the strange mixture of sounds even more than normal and turning it almost into a reproach, rather than just San's Eyon name.

The boy swung his legs to the floor. "Ok, ok, I get the message, Clickclickclicky," he said jokingly, using the nearest attempt he could make, to match the sound of his Owner's Eyon name, CLCLCLEE.

This had a strange effect upon OwnSan, who now stood, head cocked to one side, as if waiting for San to say something else in his strange sounding version of Eyon, which didn't quite manage to hit the right notes.

"So what do you expect? I'm Human. And if you care to remember, I once tried so hard to match your shrieks, that my lips dried up and cracked." San touched his lips at the memory, his hand unconsciously trailing down to rest on his throat, which had also suffered badly in the attempt, becoming raw and strained.

OwnSan remained rooted to the spot, listening intently and regarding San with eyes very wide, as if he had never really seen him before. As if he was looking at him for the very first time.

"You know I was actually worried that my tongue might be permanently stuck to the roof of my mouth, after that."

"Yyymklllllljjjhhdiiieeerroooo," shrilled the Eyon, either in response to what he assumed San was saying, or regarding something completely different, there was no way of knowing.

"I haven't a clue what you are on about but look I'm getting up, ok?" he shuffled himself to the edge of the bed, preparing to shift his weight onto his legs but in no real hurry to do so.

"Yyymklllllljjjhhdiiieeerroooo."

"Yes, yes OwnSan, I'm getting up," he groaned, as he stood, stretched, pulled off his nightclothes and discarded them in a heap on the floor. He would tidy the room and remake the bed later. Or maybe he wouldn't. Did it really matter, anyway? He'd only be getting back into it later, messing it up once more.

Seemingly happy that his Pet was now responding appropriately, and recognising the human version of his name in San's sentence, OwnSan stopped flapping his wings and jumping around. "Kkkkbrr," he called to San's retreating back, ruffling his feathers happily this time.

Unpuffed up, the gold feathers looked less majestic than before. San wasn't sure if the colour had really changed, or if it was some kind of illusion. And whether it was done deliberately to get attention, or just happened naturally and without any effort.

OwnSan waddled into the other room, leaving him alone to ponder that thought. Taking full advantage of the solitude, San headed for the washroom, deciding a little impromptu experiment was called for. He took the largest breath his chest could hold and shook himself all over. Cheeks puffed out with the held-in breath, he regarded himself in the mirror. He looked rather ridiculous but basically no different to how he had before.

He could just make out a high-pitched whine and series of clicks, coming from the other room. It sounded vaguely like "Kkkkbrr."

"Hmm and Kkkkbrr to you too," he mumbled to his reflection, "whatever that means." Like all Pets, he was happy to respond to the few phrases he recognised and if the truth were told, ignore those phrases which he vaguely understood but didn't *want* to obey. He figured that being dumb was pitiful, but *acting* dumb when it suited you, well that was nothing short of genius!

Opening the Clean Zone cubicle doors, he stepped inside and waited for them to fully close behind him, before choosing the first selection from the programme panel in front of him. He pushed the button and sighed as the perfect mixture of warm water and steam washed away the last remnants of sleep.

Mischievously, he leapt up and down under the water spray, flapping his arms and nodding his head in an imitation of OwnSan. "Kkkkbrr," he told himself.

Eventually the water ceased its flow but just as it was replaced by a current of warm air, thick with a scented moisturising fluid, the washroom door opened and OwnSan entered the room.

It was an unprecedented situation and unfortunately for the Eyon, too good an opportunity to miss. Body and hair still soaking wet from his shower, San ignored the drying cycle and instead, wrenched open the cubicle doors and launched himself out of it, in one quick movement.

OwnSan, was clearly taken off guard. Then suddenly as he realised his Pet's intentions, his face morphed into a mask of horror and he shrank backwards and away from San, as if trying to press himself through the wood of the closed door.

Dripping puddles onto the wooden floor where he stood, directly in front of his Owner, San clenched all his muscles tight into him, before he shook himself vigorously, jettisoning water in every direction, with OwnSan somehow becoming the unwilling recipient of most of it.

"UUUHHHHHGGGTTTT," he shrieked, holding his wings out to the side and looking aghast down the length of his body. With an urgency that rather startled San, the Eyon began to brush away the droplets of moisture, shaking himself and fluffing his feathers at the same time.

"Oh ok. Um, sorry," San apologised, watching the commotion he had caused. "I guess it wasn't as funny as I thought it would be."

Mostly the Eyon looked the same as ever, except for around his chest, which had taken the brunt of the splash. Here the Eyon's body looked deflated, strangely pushed in. Probably it was just that the wet feathers now clung to his skin, instead of puffing out but the sight of it make San feel a little sick. It looked indented, like a cavity. Like a wound.

San swallowed the lump which had arisen in his throat. The feeling of uneasiness, of a wrongness here, which sometimes was so strong, it woke him in the middle of the night, resurfaced. Not for the first time, he wondered what would happen if he left his Owner. Assuming of course, it was even possible to leave.

Still rubbing at his feathers to help dry them, OwnSan turned abruptly from San and hurried back through the door. All at once San felt miserable. He had upset his Owner with his stupid prank. How much worse would they both feel, if he abandoned the Eyon who cared so much for him?

Unwittingly, his eyes sought out their reflection in the mirror. He supposed he didn't really look any different to how he normally did. His skin was the same shade it always was, a sort of burnished olive. And his nose and mouth were as distinctively wide as before. His eyes were still brown, his hair still dark blonde and he still had a smattering of freckles that could just be seen on his nose - but he was starting to *feel* different.

Whatever it was that was causing this change of feeling was not apparent from the outside. But that didn't mean it wasn't there. And it wasn't all the time either. It was just that sometimes...sometimes he had this feeling that things should be different to what they were.

He shook his head to clear it and hurried back to the bedroom. Now was not the time to be dilly dallying with idle fancies.

"I'm out now and getting ready" he called, his tone trite and apologetic, trying to make it up to OwnSan for spraying him.

Turning his back on the rumpled bed and abandoned nightclothes – what he couldn't see, he didn't need to fix – he selected a stripy red top and grey trousers from his wardrobe. Pulling them on quickly, he took a moment to run his fingers through his hair in a vague attempt to smooth it into some form of style.

But on the very brink of leaving the room, he stopped and instead returned to the wardrobe. Squatting down, he reached into the furthest left hand corner, fumbled around for a moment, then when his fingers found what they sought, he grasped it and pulled it out into the light.

Light bounced off the small metal object as he turned it his fingers. Examined so many times, over so many years, its image was imprinted in his mind, the weight and feel of it stored in his memory. Yet it still held some magical power over him, so that he became transfixed at the sight of it.

The size of a small flat pebble, it was almost circular. He lightly ran his finger over its one smooth curved edge and one roughly hewn one. It still looked as if a part, almost half, had been roughly hacked off and no attempt had been made to smooth this newly made edge. There was also a small hole in the top, through which, a worn old strip of leather had been fed. Too small for him now that he was fourteen, it had once been a necklet.

He remembered wearing it when he was younger. Wearing it every day, until one day the leather was suddenly too tight, too small for his neck. He had removed it then and placed it for safekeeping in the wardrobe. But out of sight, had not meant out of mind. Not for him, anyway.

No other Pets had anything like it and everyone who saw it remarked upon it. But no one could explain it. Nor did they seem particularly bothered by that fact. Only San did. Only *he* felt that there was some truth there, waiting to be found and that maybe the truth resided as much in the missing part, as in the part that he had in his keeping.

Something occurred to him. If there was one person who might possibly understand the significance of it, it was probably the one person San had never spoken to… yet, anyway.

Closing the wardrobe door without replacing the necklet, he instead wound the leather strap round and round his upper arm, till it was tight enough to tie and not slip down. Then he carefully folded the short sleeve of his top over it, so that it was hidden from view, whilst the lower part of his arm remained visible. He didn't know why he was being careful to keep it hidden, it just seemed important and he went with his gut feeling.

That done, he hurried through the wooden doorway, the metal cool against the side of his arm, where it lay.

"I'm on my way," he called, finding that the occasional progress report halted any potential wing flapping flurries. The floorboards felt warm against his bare feet and he was suddenly struck by the beauty of his home, here in Low Forrest.

The harsh sunlight, which pierced the window in its strong and direct glare, was now mellowed and softened in the burnished reflections of the polished wooden walls. The knots and imperfections of the wood resembling tiny worlds of intricacies, too complex to be fully understood.

In passing, he glanced through the window to find the view as breathtakingly beautiful as ever. An amazing variety of trees stood like proud sentinels around a spectacular natural lake. Trees stretched on into infinity in every direction – luscious light-green foliage appearing to vie with emerald and jade for the eye's attention. Yet the trees also seemed to be collaborating with one another, joining forces in an attempt to outdo the drama of the brilliant blue sky reflected in the shimmering perfection of the silvery lake.

This scene, with its myriad colours and composition was so intense and so contrastingly stunning, it almost made San's eyes hurt. Each tree was unique, either in size or shape or shade to its neighbour, just as the houses lodged within the heart of the tree, sitting snug amongst its highest branches were different. There were large tree houses and small ones, round ones and rectangular ones and even some which didn't fit any one particular shape but instead were a weird blend of curves and angles.

Similarly the colours of the houses were all different. No, actually he thought, that's not true. The colour was all the same – green – it was the sheer variety of shades of green which made them seem so dramatically different. Yet what struck San at that precise moment, was how each tree house conformed to and in fact complimented, the size and shape of the tree it was lodged in. It was almost as if each house had merged and blended with the branches to become a living part of its tree.

The day was warm but a slight breeze rippled its way across the surface of the lake and was answered in the shimmering of the leaves on the trees. To San it almost looked as if the trees were waving to one another, calling "How are you this fine morning?"

A vague memory tiptoed once again through his mind but like a fleeting shadow on a wall, it evaded his grasp and was gone. All he was left with, was that feeling of wrongness, that somehow things were not as they should be.

Shaking his head as if awed by the wonderous sight before him, he approached OwnSan who was already plugged in to his machine and oblivious to everything around him.

Striding towards the kitchen, he spoke to his Owner as if the Eyon were actually interested and listening, it helped him feel less alone, less abandoned.

"Ah what wonders I will create for us this morning, my Owner, I will surely surpass myself!" His sarcasm went unnoticed as usual.

He was relieved to see that the wet feathers had dried out and looked completely normal once more. The butterflies which had been fluttering in his stomach ever since the prank, now seemed to dissolve and disappear and were instead replaced with hunger pangs.

Working swiftly if not particularly skilfully in the kitchen, he cooked up what he hoped was an appetising breakfast. He filled two plates from the steaming pans in front of him, and carrying them back into the other room, placed one in his own place and the other ceremoniously in front of OwnSan.

"You will see that we're trying out a new recipe today – congealed scrambled egg *with* shell, on a bed of cremated bacon. I'll excuse you if you don't applaud me for my inventiveness." He softened the jest with a wide grin. Life was just too boring if you couldn't stick your tongue out at it every now and again.

Belying its looks, this time the food actually tasted ok and if you could tune out all the slurps, grunts and general noise which came out of the Eyon's full to overflowing mouth, it was a rather pleasant meal. San chattered on between mouthfuls of food.

"I slept quite well, thanks for asking. And no, I wasn't too hot or too cold but I could have done with another couple of hours. Oh and it would have been nice to have awoken to birdsong, rather than Eyon screech! "

It was a one-sided conversation, more of a monologue really but he preferred that to the alternative – the empty silence, where his inner-most thoughts grew in significance and importance, until they were all consuming.

OwnSan sat erect beside San, symbols and figures scrolling rapidly across the screen in front of him, whilst he shovelled food into his mouth with one taloned wing tip. The information moved so quickly, each line seeming to blur into the next, that there appeared to be no definition of meaning. A single talon from OwnSan's other wing tip extended into the input terminal of this electronic box, serving to connect him directly to the machine.

There was a thin keening noise, only interrupted by occasional soft bleeps, coming from somewhere in the room. Even after all these years of living together, San was never sure if it was the machine which emitted the noise, or if it came more directly from his Owner.

He had once spent an entire afternoon trying to ascertain the source of the noise, completely without success. Frustrating as it had been, he had learned something that day – if you were going to spend time and effort doing something, you may as well make sure it was something worth doing. He intended to stick to that philosophy.

# Chapter 2.

"Breakfast won't be long, I promise," Loni called, stirring the mushrooms in the hot oil, trying to be careful not to splash her favourite red top.

"RRDDTT," replied Little, then looking at Loni's uncomprehending face, "RRDDTT" he said again, this time jabbing a talon in the vague direction of her midriff.

This time, her gaze followed the general direction of his pointing wing, to find a spattering of oil soaking into her previously only unstained item of clothing and therefore, her very best top. "Oh well, at least now it'll match everything else I wear," she sighed then smiled impishly at Little.

"EEESSS," he responded in an attempt to agree with whatever it was that she had said. "EEESSS," he whined again, to give the statement some emphasis and profundity. This time the word did sound slightly more like "yes" to Loni's ears and less like the normal screeches of his speech patterns. He had obviously been practising and she was impressed.

The day had started like all the other days. She had awoken at roughly the same time she always woke at and had got washed and dressed, the same as she always did. She had untangled her long dark-blonde hair as usual, by dragging a brush through it. A boy had once suggested her hair was a dirty-blonde colour – needless to say, after the withering glare she gave him, he never suggested it again. And she had prepared herself for the coming day.

She had chosen clothes that she thought complemented her skin tone, and which were both clean and grease free – no mean feat. She had pulled them on quickly, not bothering if they sat right or whether or not they were rumpled here or there.

"They're on, they're clean and they are nice colours – that's enough isn't it?" she had justified it to her reflection in the mirror.

Sometimes she wondered why she looked so different from everyone else. Her skin was darker and tanned more easily and although many other Pets had the same hair shade as her, or brown eyes, her combination of features made her stand out as one of a kind.

It wasn't a *bad* kind of difference, she supposed. In themselves, her features weren't that spectacular but when put together, they made up a very pleasant face. But it was a face remarkably unlike the other girls in High Woods, who tended to have petite features set in pale or rosy skin. Instead of a cute pointy nose, the bridge of *her* nose was wide, as was her mouth, with full pink lips which were invariably pulled back in a smile whenever Little was around. Which of course, was all the time.

She had cooked them a fabulous breakfast this morning – fried mushrooms and tomatoes on a bed of crispy toast, just as Little liked it. But no eggs. Ever.

She hadn't been able to cook eggs that since the day Little hatched. It was silly really. She knew that cooking eggs were not the same as Eyon's eggs but the thought of it just made her stomach heave in somersaults, so she had given up trying. And anyway she doubted that either Little or OwnLoni had actually noticed.

Little loved her cooking. Well actually, Little loved everything about Loni, from the smell of her hair to the funniness of her toes. She deliberately wiggled her bare toes on the floor and watched his face as he began to squawk in uncontrollable glee.

"HHHEEEEEEHHHHHEEEEE!" he screeched, pointing one taloned wing at them and holding his considerable stomach with the other. "HHHEEEEEEEEEEHHEEEEEE."

It wasn't the same as a Human giggle but was just as contagious and Loni found herself laughing along and doing a little dance on the kitchen floor. She pirouetted, and pranced and leaped and tip-toed, all the while humming a tune she made up, all for Little's benefit.

"I can twirl, I can whirl, but I can't sit, 'cos my pants don't fit!" she sang, in between bouts of her own giggling. Little was completely bent over now in gales of laughter, his breath rasping in to his body through snorts and other strange sounds of uncontrollable mirth. She stopped messing around to let him recover.

In truth, Loni wasn't sure *why* he found her toes so hilarious, unless of course it was because he didn't have any. But that didn't really make much sense, she mused, because it wasn't as if the sight of his scaly talons sent her into fits of laughter. Still, the fact that he loved her remained true and she was glad because she loved him twice as much.

"You know you can laugh at my toes as much as you like, feather ball, but I remember when you were just a big egg," she admonished him jokingly. She could only vaguely remember the time before he hatched, about eleven years ago. OwnLoni had seemed to spend such an eternity checking the egg and turning it and clucking and screeching over it, that Loni had begun to wonder if perhaps something was wrong.

"And then you hatched – a perfectly beautiful bundle of pink and green feathers and little bald head. And straight away, I knew that I would only ever call you Little, even though I was three and you were already bigger than me." It was a story that she had told and retold him, never really sure how much of it he understood. Yet, each time he stood listening attentively as if hearing the words for the first time and understanding every syllable.

Of course Little was not his Eyon name and considering his already large size, it wasn't even appropriate - and yet somehow it was the most appropriate name in the world. Loni realised that by his immediate adoration of her and everything she did, he had become her friend and her playmate but more than anything else, he had become her responsibility. He was her little "Little" and always would be.

"Ok, then Little, grub's up," she announced piling three plates high with the sizzling food. Little, full of excitement as ever, at the prospect of freshly cooked food, began to hop up and down whilst simultaneously rubbing his stomach and squeaking, "EEESSS, EEESSS, EEESSS."

"Honestly, Little, you'd think you have been starved," she replied, correctly interpreting all the stomach rubbing and excitement as his way of announcing that he was very hungry.

"Goodness knows where you put all the food you eat. One day I expect you will just explode and there'll be bits of you all over the place and I guess I'll be the one who has to stick you all back together again," she teased in mock horror.

Little, completely oblivious to what Loni's strange words actually meant, reacted instead to her tone of voice and replied "EEESSS," with some considerable mock solemnity of his own.

"Come on then you big ravenous Eyon, help me carry these to the table," she laughed, thrusting one of the plates in his direction and watching as he tried to curl his talons around the plate, in a vague imitation of how she used her fingers to hold it. It wasn't as firm a grasp as hers but it was enough for the short distance from kitchen to table. And he liked to help her, liked to feel like her, as though they were not two different species after all.

He grinned, his face all pink and shiny and happy. Given their strange feathered bodies, Eyons had remarkably Human faces and features. Loni thought that this was particularly true of Little, who had the most startling vivid blue eyes she had ever seen.

Together they carried the three plates to the dining table. Loni put her own plate down at her usual place, next to where Little was sitting. He watched intently, whilst she carried out her usual ritual of taking her knife and fork into her hands and cutting up the food on the third plate into easily digestible chunks.

"No, Little, you've got the knife in the wrong hand again," Loni admonished gently, prising the cutlery out of his clumsily grasping talons and replacing them the correct way around. "Ok, now hold down the toast with your fork before cutting with the knife," she demonstrated again for his benefit. "Yes that's it, you've got it now," she encouraged.

She watched his efforts a moment longer, before reaching across the table to deposit the third plate, with the cut up food, in front of her Owner. As usual, OwnLoni had already connected to her machine and was oblivious to their presence.

Not for the first time, Loni wondered if OwnLoni would even notice if she got no breakfast, or if the breakfast was a disgusting dish of lukewarm sludge. For that matter, would she notice if Loni delivered it to her whilst standing on her head, wearing her socks as gloves and her pants as a hat and singing "Zipedeydoodah, zipededay". Probably not, she guessed, but it would definitely tickle Little, she chuckled to herself, conjuring up the image in her head.

"Oh well back to reality," she shrugged, quickly noting which wing her Owner was using to interface with her machine, before carefully wrapping OwnLoni's other taloned wingtip around the handle of a spoon. But just before she let go, Loni gave the wing a little squeeze. Not enough to hurt either of them; perhaps not even enough to be noticed by OwnLoni but enough to allow Loni to feel she had communicated her presence and with it, her love, to her Owner.

As usual the Eyon gave no acknowledgement, other than immediately beginning to eat quickly, if not particularly enthusiastically. This caused her wing to be rapidly moved up and down, back and forth, from the plate to her mouth. Full spoon, empty spoon, full spoon, empty spoon, full, empty, full, empty.

The visual illusion this created, was both strange and fascinating. Black and white feathers in almost stripe design, moving against the still background, of a black and white striped feathered body, did something to the watcher's eyes. Loni thought of it as 'eye ping pong'.

Without conscious effort and in fact beyond her control, her eyes were always drawn to the kind of spiral that was produced by the movement, the black and white seeming to merge into one colour. Only the smattering of purple on the feathers seemed to prevent her from being pulled into a catatonic state, where she existed slumped in a corner, mesmerised by the swirls.

She shook her head in an attempt to clear her vision. It was not a good idea and made the spirals even worse. She shut her eyes whilst the room stopped spinning and turned her head away before reopening her eyes. And then something curious happened. Just in the split second that it took to shut her eyes and reopen them, she saw something. Something recognisable from the screen but not *on* the screen.

Instead, the image seemed to be printed on the insides of her eyelids as if projected there by the screen itself. Like a wet hand pressed against a window, the image held for only a moment in time before obscuring into blurriness again. But for that moment it was there. The pupils in her eyes contracting and dilating in reaction to the contrast of bright screen, followed by inner darkness, seemed almost palpable in her head. But her mind latched onto the image anyway and processed it.

What she had seen was a tiny picture, no, not a picture, a *list* of pictures, one below the other, each with several lines of squiggles alongside them, and adjoining little boxes. In some cases the boxes were empty and in others, strange symbols filled them. She recognised the pictures, images of a variety of foodstuffs but not the significance behind them. Turning her head back to Ownloni and the screen she looked for the image again.

But just as it is impossible to distinguish individual drops of rain in a thunderstorm, so it was futile to try to isolate any one image from the rapidly scrolling screen. Whatever she had seen was gone, or rather, as she suspected, *her ability to see it* was gone. Whether that was one and the same thing was irrelevant because it sure amounted to the same thing.

She turned her attention back to Little. "What would happen to either of us without the other?" she mused. It wasn't that OwnLoni was a *bad* Owner to Loni or egg-mother to Little – she was just a *typical* one. Most Pets didn't really mind and in truth she hadn't either – that was until Little hatched and came into her life.

"From the very first moment I saw you, I knew that everything would be forever changed. I was so excited when a tiny crack in your egg widened and a baby Eyon popped out." It made her smile just to remember it.

"You blinked your huge blue eyes, and I loved you straight away," she told him. His pupils had still been dilated from the darkness inside the egg and her heart had melted. Straight away she had grasped his soft wings in her chubby little three-year-old hands and led him over to OwnLoni, who of course hadn't noticed her new hatchling.

'Come see your mummy,' she had said to this strange new and wonderful creature, her voice quivering with excitement. 'I am Loni. I am your friend. I am going to look after you,' she had promised solemnly. She had meant it too. And in the intervening years she had kept her word and she always would.

"We played 'hide and go seek' among the bedcovers and 'who can bounce the highest' on the beds the day you hatched, Little." Loni smiled ruefully. "Luckily we were both smaller then, or we would have brained ourselves on the low ceiling." Her gaze shifted up to regard the ceiling now, as her mind remembered.

Once OwnLoni had noticed her hatchling, she had disconnected from her machine and hurriedly checked the new arrival over, all the while watched over anxiously by Loni, who already felt responsible for this big friendly bundle of feathers. Satisfied that all was well, OwnLoni had patted them both on the head, before pointing a talon at Little, as Loni had already nicknamed him, and wailing out some indecipherable noise which turned out to be his Eyon name.

Funny how that now seemed to have happened so long ago, yet simultaneously felt like it had just happened yesterday. She glanced at the fourteen triangular symbols on her left forearm.

"I suppose that when I was born, it was the cause of some excitement. At least I hope it was."

She had been unintentionally speaking aloud and didn't expect an answer but got one anyway.

"ESSSSSS, ESSSSS," pronounced Little solemnly, making her smile in the process. It was just a pity that

Humans never got to know and remember their birth parents.

"But I know what it would feel like to give up someone I love." She turned to him, needing to feel he understood what she was saying. "My heart would surely snap in two if ever I lost you. But they gave me away without even asking my opinion, without giving me a chance to say what I wanted."

And she already knew the established answer to this, because she had heard it voiced so many times by older Pets, to younger Pets. They had done it because they had to. Because at the age of two, she would not have chosen to be taken away, even if it *was* for her benefit.

She understood and accepted all of that. "What I can't understand, can't accept is how Human parents sever the tie so completely. So *finally*." Her voice had become softer and more thoughtful till it had an almost dreamy quality to it. Her head told her they had to but her heart told a different story. So softly that only her own heart heard her words, she murmured, "I could never do that."

Loni suddenly became aware of a screechy chattering beside her that brought her right back to the present place and time. "Mmmiillluuyyttrrr," Little shrilled at her brightly, drying to dispel the dark mood that he had sensed but not understood.

"Ok, I see that you have already fetched the ball." She planted a false smile on her face, which naturally morphed into a real one, as soon as she raised her eyes to meet his. Then slung the bag with the ball in it, carelessly over her shoulder.

"Ok, Ok, let's go," she agreed, quietly relieved to have been interrupted on her painful thoughts. Quickly gathering up the empty, yet still incredibly messy plates, she carried them through to the kitchen and deposited them in the sink. "Out of sight, out of mind," she stated emphatically, knowing that she would have to wash them up sooner or later.

But something struck her about the phrase. Perhaps that was exactly how she had been viewed by her birthing parents, already forgotten a moment after being handed over. She would probably never know. And anyway, she had her family now, didn't she? She had Little!

"Ready?" she asked, taking up her position behind him and wrapping her arms snugly around his scrawny neck.

As if she weighed no more than one of his own feathers, Little bounded over to the outside door with Loni still firmly attached to his back. Flapping his wings dramatically, he launched them both out of the doorway. Loni held her breath in excitement as for the *first time ever*, Little managed to climb even higher in the sky, soaring above the tree-tops for a few snatched seconds before losing height again.

It had only really been a momentary vision but she felt as if the scene was immediately etched in her mind in fine detail. For the first time, she had seen why "High Woods" was so called. The Woods part was of course obvious, there were trees everywhere you looked and in every direction. But she had not realised that such a wide and beautiful landscape existed beyond the high trees – lush green grasslands rolling on seemingly into infinity, dotted here and there with patches of wildflowers in a riot of colours. It was a scene almost *too perfect* to be natural, as if its very perfection made it seem contrived.

Having tasted momentary success, Little seemed undaunted by his inability to continue to fly as high as he wanted and strained to climb high once again. A passing bird seemed both startled and amused by this clumsy attempt at graceful flying. In a seemingly mocking display, the bird flitted around them, flying above, then below, then beside them. But as with all previous attempts, Little was unable to maintain altitude and the bird, bored by its too-easy victory, continued on its way. Little and Loni flew several circuits around the neighbouring trees before alighting to the ground.

It was another thing they shared, this love of flight and the freedom it gave them. But from what she had seen, she figured Eyons weren't meant for flight – or rather not *real* flight. They were fine at hopping about from one place to another, or flying from the ground to the tree houses, or vice versa, from home to ground. But she had never witnessed them climbing or swooping and soaring on the currents of the winds, majestically gliding at will as birds do. She wasn't sure why this was so. Perhaps the weight of their big bodies dragged them down too quickly.

Indeed past experience had taught Loni that flying high and big bodies weren't exactly a good match. Several of Little's previous attempts to fly above the trees had ended disastrously. There had been the time when somehow Loni had become entangled with him and they had landed in a painfully crumpled heap on the ground.

Or the time when he had flown too close to neighbouring trees and they had crashed headfirst into the branches and got lodged there, upside down and with flailing arms, wings and legs. OR the worst possible occasion, when somehow and to her everlasting amazement, he just plain *FORGOT* to fly – literally forgot to open his wings and flap them. This had resulted in an immediate and rather painful plummet back to earth. But at least he had never forgotten again – or at least hadn't forgotten again *yet*.

And yet, this time he *had* managed to soar, even if it was only briefly.

"Surely if you managed it once, you can do it again," reflected Loni. Unable to communicate fully with him, somehow she knew that he was thinking this too, just from the look of proud amazement on his face. Full of wonder at their accomplishment, they proceeded to play even more energetically than usual.

"That's cheating you know," she teased as he hopped high into the air, just managing to swipe the ball with the very tip of his wing and send it crashing back to her. Laughing, she smashed her bat fiercely into the ball, sending it flying back to him. Her aim was good and the ball soared past him, just beyond his reach.

"PPRREEOO," he shrilled in mock annoyance.

"I know, I know. I won *again* and it's just not fair to you, little Little, is it?" she responded. "But then again, you *cheat* – and yet you still don't win! Never mind, I still love you. Now what shall we play next?"

# *Chapter 3.*

It hadn't taken San long to clear up after breakfast. He had thought about just stacking the dishes and leaving the washing of them for another time but decided he might as well just get on with it. Because whilst he worked, he could plan how he would approach the man and the subject of the necklet. What he would say and what he would ask.

A shiver of anticipation ran down him. Perhaps this man would shed new light on the situation. Perhaps after talking to him, San would feel appeased, relieved and there would be no more thoughts of running away. Because that would surely be the best situation all round, wouldn't it?

Just as he finished putting away the last dish, OwnSan appeared at his side. "Oh well that's just typical isn't it?" he joked. "You only come to offer help when I'm done. Where were you ten minutes ago, huh, when I was facing a mountain of dirty crockery?" But of course he knew exactly where OwnSan had been – connected up to his machine.

But it seemed that the Eyon had a specific purpose in mind. Hooking his talons lightly over San's arm, he used his free wing tip to trace over the symbols on the boy's forearm.

A single talon outstretched, the others all curled back into his wingtip, OwnSan glided over the first nine symbols, only to stop directly over the tenth.

"Yes, I am fourteen years old now OwnSan. What is your point? Clearly there is one," San said wearily. But instead of even attempting verbal communication, the Eyon simple took him by the arm and led him over to the broom cupboard.

San felt a guilty flush seep over his features. "I didn't mean to break the handle, you know, it was an accident. And I only put the bits in there till I could figure out how to fix it." His words would all sound gibberish to his Owner but San felt obliged to say them anyway. To have stood silently, would have seemed as if it had been done deliberately rather than accidentally.

The offending article, which had previously been attached to a drawer in the kitchen, lay exactly where he had left it, on the floor of the cupboard.

Ignoring the handle as if it were of no consequence, OwnSan reached into the recess and withdrew a strange shaped tool along with a piece of wood San didn't remember seeing in there before.

"Hey, where did those come from and what are they for?" he followed OwnSan as he shut the cupboard door and strode towards the external door of the house. OwnSan pulled open the front door and stood waiting on the small landing platform. San stood where he was.

"Eeeekkbrr," the Eyon called, waiting for San to come forward. San hesitated. It was a long drop to ground level and he normally only ventured beyond the door, whilst firmly seated on OwnSan's back and ready for flight.

Placing the wood and the tool on the narrow platform, OwnSan stepped back into the room. Wing tip extended once more, he pointed first at San's triangular time markers, then at the platform.

"Yes, yes, I get the idea. I'm old enough to do some other task now. But we are way up high here, you know!" Then again, the Eyon would never put him at any risk, not deliberately anyway. It was just the fact that there was a real possibility that the danger of San falling from a great height, hadn't actually entered the Eyon's brain.

Slowly he edged out onto the platform. Thankfully his fears were unfounded, as the Eyon placed his large body between San and the edge of the platform. Turing him round to face the front of the house, it was clear at once what was wrong.

The wooden canopy, which sheltered the platform from the elements, had come loose and a large piece of wood hung down limply. "Oh wow, I hadn't even noticed that. Ok, so what do I do?" he shrugged his shoulders slightly and held his hands out in front of him to indicate he was at a loss.

In response, the Eyon dumped the wood right in to his outstretched hands. Reaching up, OwnSan pulled away the old wood. Now it was brought to his attention, San could see it was rotten and warped. Realising what to do, he held the new piece in place and looked to OwnSan for further instruction.

"What now?" he asked, hoping that it wouldn't take too long as the wood was heavier than it looked and his arms were already feeling the strain. OwnSan lifted the machine and switched it on with a flick of his talons. A slight gurgling sound was emitted and there was a strange smell too. He lifted it to one side of the board that San held and all at once there was a difference in the weight of the wood against San's arms.

Having done one side, the Eyon stopped and offered the machine to San. "Ok, my turn. Can I just let it go now? Will it stay up?" Gingerly he let go of the board and although one side was still loose, whatever the machine had done to the other side, was holding it firmly in place.

"Like this? Is this ok?" He moved the machine over the wood as OwnSan had already demonstrated. There was a small vibration which travelled the length of his arm but other than that the tool was not difficult to use. "What about the edges? Do I go all over them to fix it securely?" He made a circular motion with the tool to indicate his questions. OwnSan copied the movement.

"Ok, here goes then." Slowly he moved the tool across every edge, watching as it seemed to meld the new wood into the old, so that the joins were invisible and watertight. Once he was finished it was simple to locate the off switch and turn the device off and admire his handiwork.

"Hey, it looks ok, doesn't it?" He smiled, genuinely pleased at his efforts. Raising both hands high, OwnSan first waggled his talons down to waist height, then with talons flat and outstretched, swept his wingtips outwards and away across his body.

"So when it rains, it will just run off the wood again, I get it!" San nodded his understanding. "Hey, I've got an idea." He dashed back inside and recovered the broken handle. "Can I use this to attach it back on?" he looked down at the melding tool and indicated the kitchen with a nod of his head in that direction.

"Fhhhhggggcvg," agreed OwnSan, seeming to grasp San's idea.

"Ok." San shot into the kitchen, relieved that the repair task was so easily solved. Two minutes later he had completed the task, put the equipment away and was ready to go for the morning activity. Eagerly he hopped onto OwnSan's back and held on tight as the Eyon launched himself off the landing platform and into mid-air.

San thought that most of his friends wouldn't be there yet and perhaps wouldn't arrive for another half an hour or so, but for once that didn't matter at all. This time San sought someone else entirely, his eyes feverishly scanning the ground for any sightings of this man.

"Well more fool them, if they want to spend so long clearing up," he said into the feathers on OwnSan's neck, attempting to cover his interest in who was around, for some reason. But the one person he wanted to speak to, was already there.

Jed lazed under a tree, stretched out and seemingly disinterested in what was going on around him. Which, to be fair, wasn't really a lot anyway. Some boys played ball nearby and a group of women seemed to be chatting about something which was funny, he could hear their laughter as he passed overhead.

Hoping that OwnSan would stop nearby, San was disappointed to realise that they were headed for the far side of the lake, the furthest point from where Jed lounged. San's heart sank. It wouldn't be impossible to talk to Jed, it was just going to be more difficult.

Finally OwnSan touched down. There were a group of children playing nearby who San knew well, although they would not be his first choice of people to spend time with. But he needed to appear casual, and dashing off to speak to someone on the other side of the lake was anything but casual. So whilst his mind whirred on how to get near Jed in a non-obvious manner, San strolled towards the little group.

"Jon, Jon, where have your wings gone?" taunted one of the girls as the others sniggered cruelly at the boy who stood amongst them sporting the most ridiculous multicoloured top and trousers. Although rather wicked, San had to admit it was also rather witty, as Jon did indeed now resemble OwnJon. He stifled a snigger and looked back at OwnSan who was now plugged into his portable machine and in a world of his own.

"It seems to have slipped your attention that OwnAmy has dressed you in that bizarre pink and yellow dress, which reaches all the way to your toes and makes you look like a baby Eyon," San remarked out of some sense of loyalty to Jon, who had always been the closest thing to a best friend he had. Besides he was just grateful that OwnSan never interfered with his choice of clothing, like some Owners did with their Pets.

"Never mind about the lack of wings Jon, just come over here and I'll shave your hair off, then you and your Owner will really match," one of the older Pets, who really aught to have known better, had called from one of the various crowds dotted around. San couldn't tell exactly who had spoken, or even from which of the ten or so groups nearby.

For his part, Jon didn't appear to be bothered by all the taunting and instead lifted his shoulders high and stuck his head forward, pulling his arms to his side. "Just call me OwnJon from now on," he rallied back at them, flapping his arms in a rather effective imitation. San guffawed at the sight but couldn't stop himself from commenting, "well rather you, than me!"

Without appearing to be doing so, San watched as more and more Pets arrived and were deposited by their Owners. Slowly, he moved from Jon and Amy's crowd, towards a different group of Pets, strolling over and immersing himself in the conversation, before nonchalantly claiming to have to speak to someone in the next group about something. Then, making vague excuses, he moved on to the next and the next.

But there were at least two hundred such groups between where he now stood and where he had last seen Jed. And even if he managed to make his way through and across all of them without being noticed, by the time he got to Jed, there was the risk that he would be gone already.

There had to be another way.

And there was.

He would have to swim across. He would just have to make it look casual and unplanned. Which in a way it was, because if he had planned to go swimming, he would not have bothered having a shower earlier on. What a waste of time that had proved to be.

Pleased with how casual he had managed to make it seem, he was finally at the edge of the lake, where several other swimmers had already taken to the water. He dropped his clothes in a pile. No point in folding them as that would have been too out of character, he thought.

The shallow water was warm and inviting from the heat of the sun. But the further he swam into the centre of the pool, the deeper the water became and the colder it got. He had considered swimming around the edge of the lake, sticking to the shallow parts but apart from the extra time this would take, he also worried that it would look planned, as if he had some destination already in mind. Which of course, he had.

So instead, he swam for a little while, then turned onto his back and tried to make it look as if he was lazily drifting, rather than heading directly for the other side. But the coldness of the water was beginning to take its toll on him. The cold began to seep right into the marrow of his bones and after only a short time, he no longer knew where his legs ended and the water began.

He began to suspect that a little while longer spent in such cold conditions and he would actually stop caring about his legs and everything else. No-one knew how deep the lake was in the centre and no swimmer had ever managed to dive to the bottom. And suddenly the pull from that unknown depth seemed almost too strong to resist.

Thoughts of the necklet and the mysteries it contained made his heart hammer in his chest and his breath catch in his throat. Put together with the numbness in his limbs, it was making progress both slow and dangerous. So to distract himself, San thought instead about the lake itself.

It was easy to imagine that there was a whole different world down there. That the lake hid some great city of mystery, that secretly rose majestically up in the moonlight every night, whilst Eyons and Humans slept peacefully in their beds. Perhaps there would be wild parties and the inhabitants of this watery place would dance on the water and sing with wet warbled voices.

Floating still, he used his hands, hidden under the water to try to steer and propel himself further along. He wondered what the inhabitants of such a watery city would look like. Would they have gills like fish or some strange way of breathing never encountered before?

As his mind latched on to the idea, his imagination took flight and he began to picture the strange looking creatures he had created. Some would have scales like fish, their bodies glistening dark grey as they silently swam through the deep water hunting for food. Their teeth would be razor sharp – all the better to bite you with, their eyes merciless…

Suddenly his heart lurched with terror, as he felt a cold scaly hand wrap itself around his ankle, ready to drag him down to its watery lair where it would no doubt swallow him whole before spitting out the bones!

Frantically he kicked and struggled against the imprisoning monster's grip, his heart and mind competing to be racing the fastest. It was to no avail, the monster held him tight in its grasp and he could not escape. He was doomed. Unwilling to go down without a fight, he struggled for freedom, even as his head sank below the surface of the water.

Holding his breath, he opened his eyes underwater to confront his assailant. If he had to die, he at least wanted to uncover the mystery of the creature that was to be his downfall. It was, he thought, to be his final act of bravery…but his attacker was gone. Even under water he felt his eyes widen…his could only mean one thing…he creature was invisible! Things were even worse than he had imagined!

Doomed now, San sank lower, resigned to his horrible fate, yet still managing to mull over in his mind, the terrible irony of it all. He had only swam this far, to get to the one person who might help him understand things, who might make him change his mind about leaving OwnSan and now he would be leaving him anyway – by drowning.

And then another hand had grasped him, this time by the arm, and now he was being tugged in a different direction. 'Just my luck,' he thought, 'now there are two of them and they're fighting over me. They'll rip me in half with their teeth, before battling over my poor bloody remains...my entrails spilling into the water, my blood turning it into a crimson pool...'

His lungs were on fire, fully extended in his chest, straining to hold on to the air inside them. No longer able to hold on, he released his final breath into the unforgiving water. His body began to shut down. There was a strange ringing sound in his ears but it didn't worry him, it didn't last for long enough to do so. His mind became cloudy and vague, as he began to lose consciousness. His vision darkened.

So it was rather a shock when he was unceremoniously hauled OUT of the water rather than down to its mysterious depths. "Stand back, give the boy some air, some space to breathe," called a deep gravely voice.

Strange how the voice seemed to be far, far away and yet right next to him at the same time, thought San hazily. His lungs, almost empty of air, were instead now bubbling full of murky water.

'Their underwater city is like home, just a bit darker...' was his final thought before WHUMPH something heavy landed on his chest and WHUMPH... there it was again. Spluttering, coughing and spewing out the inhaled water, San was helped to sit up. The heavy hands which had previously been pounding on his chest, now thumped across his back, helping his lungs to expel the last of the liquid.

Streams of dirty water gushed out of both nostrils and his open mouth simultaneously. Even more awful, was the very thin but very long piece of pond weed which suddenly appeared, having obviously been either up his nose or down his throat. Nearly drowning was definitely not a glamorous look, he thought groggily.

"Thought we'd lost you there," said the gruff-voiced man, from somewhere behind him, continuing to pound on San's now aching back. Still coughing violently but desperate for the man to stop pounding on him, San gestured that he would be ok now.

"Where is it? Where's the monster that attacked me? What have you done with it?" he croaked, his throat raw after all the coughing, eyes darting nervously around.

All he could see were lots of Humans and Eyons, including OwnSan who was hopping anxiously from one leg to another, screeching "EEEEKKBBRR, EEEEKKBBRR!" whilst doing some sort of worried wringing of his wings – there was no captured monster anywhere in sight.

"Here's your monster," the gruff voice replied, as San raised his eyes to see who it belonged to. Jed stood grinning in front of him, pulling a section of vine from the mass of foliage which had somehow tangled around San's arms and legs. At once everything became clear. There was no monster, only in San's imagination. Relieved, yet also strangely slightly disappointed, San took some time to examine his surroundings.

He was close to the water's edge, at more or less the midway from where he had started and where he had planned to go. "I noticed you drowning," somehow Jed managed to make the remark almost flippant, "and thought I'd better save you before your Owner laid a big egg in fear!" he joked. He flopped down beside San.

San stole a worried glance in OwnSan's direction, who seemed reassured enough to have calmed down and plugged back into his machine. Everyone else was similarly unconcerned about the silly boy in their midst and had resumed their original conversations and activities.

Their worlds had gone back to normal and they didn't give another thought to the bedraggled boy and now equally bedraggled man, who sat side by side.

"You are quite old, at least forty," blurted San. He hadn't meant to say it out loud, it had just come out. He glanced at the clusters of triangles on the man's outstretched arm and thought he had better try to remedy his comment, which might otherwise be taken as an insult.

"But you're still fit and strong...unlike many others of your advanced age." Having done so well with the first part of the sentence, he figured he kinda blew it again with that last remark. "Sorry it seems the nearly drowning has affected my brain," he smiled limply in apology to his hero.

"Not your brain that's got the problem I think, - it's your mouth!" the man smiled, revealing a good sense of humour. He had a certain look to him, small in stature with a lean wiriness to his frame. His face was strong with a firm jaw line and a mouth which looked as if it would brook no arguments. Deep set eyes, that seemed to take everything in to be considered fully, sat beneath dark eyebrows currently raised in amusement. San had seen him around but had never spoken to him.

"I was coming to see you...swimming I mean. I wanted to talk to you." And he had wanted to talk to him because of what he had heard about Jed, what others had said.

In fact, now San came to think of it, he wondered why he had never spoken to this man directly. Why had he never asked, if all the things other people had said that *he* had said, were true...or even if he *had* actually said all those things...

Because, what he *had* said, well that was just crazy wasn't it?

More than ever, San felt compelled to find out the truth or at least what this man thought was the truth.

# *Chapter 4.*

Loni sometimes wondered if all the exercise that Pets were encouraged to do, was as much to keep them socialised as to keep them healthy.

As if on cue to demonstrate the point, one of the girls, roughly her own age, bounded up to her. Bright yellow top and lime green trousers were topped with the perkiest, blondest, swingiest, ponytail Loni had ever seen. The girl seemed to bounce rather than step, bound rather than walk.

"Hi Loni," the girl smiled at her, a 200 watt smile in a 40 watt brain. Loni mentally scolded herself for that unkind thought – but there again it *was* true! "Hi, OwnLoni's Hatchling," Mandy added turning the smile on Little, unknowingly rankling Loni in the process.

Loni couldn't count how many times she had told the girl his name was 'Little' but poor Mandy just couldn't grasp the complex idea that he already had a name apparently.

"I know your Owner has a hatchling called 'OwnMandy's Hatchling' and that Penny has 'OwnPenny's Hatchling' and that every other hatchling is called after its Owner, till it gets a Pet of it's own," it was almost painful, this repeated attempt to get through to the girl, "but Little's name, is Little, remember? Because he's not like every other hatchling." She felt herself emphasize that last bit, hoping that it would be the last time she had to remind the stupid girl.

She could feel Little sniggering beside her, feathered shoulders shrugging rapidly up and down. He had definitely got the general gist of the conversation and fully caught the animosity radiating from Loni.

'Traitor' thought Loni 'lets see how funny you think it is when OwnLoni tries to connect you to one of the machines. Who'll be laughing then?'

Except that she wouldn't be laughing at all and neither would he. It was a thought which had only recently occurred to her. But once it had, the idea refused to go away. Instead it had taken firm root in her mind and germinated. Sometimes she woke, sweaty and twisted in rumpled sheets in the middle of the night, with remnants of a nightmare in her head. Nightmares of the day when Little would be taken from her.

Ok – physically he would still be there – but once he had been connected to the machines perhaps he would change, perhaps he would 'switch off' from *her*. There was no way of knowing. And Loni didn't know what they could do to prevent it from happening.

Her thoughts were interrupted by a kind of chirping noise. She realised it was coming from Mandy who was apparently still talking at her. Loni had missed whatever had been said but she figured that was no loss anyway.

"Yes, Amanda," she responded smiling. It was a fake smile and hurt her face but she held it and was rewarded when Mandy bristled. Apparently she considered herself more of a Mandy than an Amanda.

The girl stood still, apparently waiting for something, one foot firmly on the ground, the other poised with only the toes on the ground, so that her one hip stuck out at an angle. It was a cute look, Loni had to admit, but not one that she would have posed herself.

Loni was tempted to say, 'can I help you?' but that would have come across as rude, so instead she looked back at Mandy and waited. Without the smallest shred of embarrassment Mandy took her cue.

"I was wondering if me and Lizzie could use your ball?" Again the 200 watt smile. "Ours is stuck in the tree!" she finished brightly, either indifferent to any offence she had caused or oblivious to it. Loni didn't know which and by now didn't really care either.

The cheek of it! Loni's face flamed red in temper at the implied insult. So they wanted to use her and Little's ball! Not ask them to play, just use their ball. She was about to give them a piece of her mind when a strange rustling sound distracted her.

Little had followed the direction of Mandy's pointing arm. He had flown up to the trapped ball and even now was freeing it from the thick branches where it had lodged. Unrestrained, the ball fell down from the tree and landed at Loni's feet.

She wondered how Mandy would react if she gave it a swift kick and send it flying back up into the tree it had been lodged in. She was sorely tempted. The *only* thing which stopped her was the thought of the look that would be in Little's eyes. He would find it funny but he would also think it was wrong and his eyes would mirror his disappointment in her. And that was a look she never wanted to see.

Mandy bent to pick it up. "Hey, thanks, OwnLoni's Hatchling," she trilled, before bouncing off to play once more, no longer a care in her head.

Little fluttered back down to Loni. He had what could only be described as a rueful look on his face.

"Oh, Little, you're just too nice, sometimes! But you make me a better person just by knowing you." She hugged him tightly. Taller than her by at least a head, it meant that her face was buried in his feathery chest. She resisted the temptation to sneeze all over him, as his feathers tickled the tip of her nose.

"UUUCCkkkkLL," he responded in Eyon, his face brightening at the implied compliment.

"Come on then, let's play goals." She mimed kicking the ball at something then scoring, jumping up and down, hands raised in the air in triumph till he got the idea. In response he imitated her, except that rather than merely lifting his wings, he flapped them, giving himself mini lifts in the air.

"Ha ha, clever clogs, very funny! You know you can't do that! That would be cheating!" Eyes twinkling, she smiled indulgently at him, her baby Eyon.

"Where do you want as your goal?" she asked. Little indicated the nearest narrow tree trunk. He liked to make it as difficult as possible for her to score a goal. "Ok then, my goal is that one" she pointed to an equally narrow one. She waited for him to nod his head in understanding.

"Let the match commence," she bellowed as she sneakily took control of the ball and kicked it towards his goal. It was a good kick but fell short of the tree by a good distance. Little threw himself into her path and there was a minor tussle over who was going to reach the ball first. Of course a bit of rough and tough wasn't exactly in the game rules but it added to Little's enjoyment of the game. Loni didn't mind it either.

Arm pushing wing, leg pushing leg, they shoved and pulled and pushed each other out of the way. But even in sporting battles they were gentle with one another. Giggling, Loni wrapped one of her legs around both of Little's, grappling him to the dry, dusty ground.

"Ok, get out of *that* one, you big feathery Eyon," she teased.

A cloud of dust, disturbed from the ground, floated up and covered them both. Coughing and sputtering they were forced to abandon the holds they had on one another and get back on their feet. This time Little was first to reach the ball.

With a mighty kick, he sent it spinning towards Loni's goal. She held her breath. She couldn't outrun the ball and couldn't catch it either. All she could do was watch. The ball, still on course for her goal, suddenly veered *off* course. It had hit a tuft of grass and been diverted from its intended target. A sudden collective "OH!" alerted Loni to the fact that they had spectators.

"He nearly had you there Loni!" a voice called from the side. Loni didn't even look over before she responded.

"Nearly isn't enough, I'm afraid!" Her tone of voice was light and bubbly, her former good humour having been restored.

She hadn't even had to look up to see who the voice belonged to. She had instantly recognised it as Isaac.

Without looking, she also knew how he would be watching, sitting cross legged, his own ball, if he had one with him today, resting in the space created by his knees. His hands would be drumming on the ball as he watched her and Little play, his head inclined towards some other boy, with whom he had been playing. She knew all this without looking, because that's just how it always was and always would be.

She ran for the ball. So did Little. She got there first by virtue of being both faster and closer.

"AND LONI GAINS CONTROL OF THE BALL. WHAT WILL SHE DO WITH IT?" The mock commentary, conducted in a voice of high excitement came from Isaac of course. She swept past Little, deftly avoiding his foot stuck out in her path.

"AND NOW WE SEE A GOOD TRY FOR A TACKLE FROM THE EYON, BUT NO THE GIRL LONI HAS AVOIDED IT AND...OH NO!"

The assembled crowd of Pets went wild. It was a cacophony of sound. There were boos, cheers, laughter and cries of dismay as Little hovered into the air, hopped over Loni and seized control of the ball once more.

It was a cheating move for two reasons. Firstly he could fly somewhere faster than she could run and secondly she couldn't fly at all! But Loni was used to Little's cheating and was ready for him. Just as he prepared to lift himself into the air once more, ball neatly balanced on his feet, Loni threw herself at him.

Managing to hurtle herself, just as he took flight, left her grappling around his ankles. The girl-sized attachment to his legs, pulled him off balance and they both fell in the dust, Loni still holding on to him. The crowd gasped transfixed as the ball rolled towards Little's goal post.

"WILL IT, WON'T IT? WHO KNOWS..." The ball seemed to be moving in slow motion. It rolled and rolled with nothing and no one to stop it. Little and Loni lay on the ground transfixed and watched its progress.

"OH! AND IT'S *YES*! IT'S A *GOAL*!" shouted lsaac. Loni helped Little to his feet before jumping jubilantly up and down, arms in the air.

Playing his assigned role of 'disappointed in defeat', Little hung his head. But Loni just caught the crinkling at his eyes and the slight upturn of his mouth before his face was hidden from view. And she knew that the heaving of his shoulders indicated humour rather than dejection. Under the pretext of celebrating the goal, she took a sneaky look around.

Not one single other Pet played a game elsewhere. All games of ball, or those involving ropes or other toys had ended. All the little huddles of chattering adult Pets had been broken up. Instead, *every single Pet,* whether male or female, young or old, had settled down to watch her and Little play ball.

They had stopped their own activities but had no intention of joining in with her game. They were merely content to watch. It was always this way when she and Little played football. No other Pets could have elicited such an audience.

Of course both of them played dirty, after all that was half the fun of the game wasn't it, and sometimes they made up the rules as they went along. All the other Pets played very niccly with each other, never breaking the rules, never being sneaky. But Loni suspected that it wasn't this deviation from the straight and narrow which captivated their attention.

It was something about the sight of the Eyon running around and being fully immersed in a Human activity. And she couldn't blame them for their curiosity. Dotted around, like toadstools in a field, the other baby Eyons stood sentinel and unmoving behind their adults.

"They are nothing more and nothing less than Owners-in-training." Loni wasn't even aware that she had spoken aloud, her voice hushed, yet filled with a burgeoning sense of wrongness.

With no Pets of their own yet, the hatchlings had no real interaction with even the Pets who shared their household. They neither expressed any interest in them, nor generated any interest from them. Only Little was different.

Plugged into small portable devices, similar to those which were used in the houses, the adults were oblivious to everything around them. Loni wondered how the hatchlings learned what to do. There never seemed to be any instruction going on. Instead they seemed to watch and wait. Then one day, they turned up with their own machines and that was that.

In some cases the Eyons stood fairly close together. Stood within a wingspan of one another, if only they had cared enough to stretch them out. She wondered what would happen if she deliberately crashed full force into one of them. Would it send him or her toppling into another and another and another, until they all lay prostrate on the ground, still plugged in, still oblivious?

"COME ON LONI, WAKE UP!"

The shout had the desired effect and she raced after Little. But it was too late. While she had stood lost in thought, he had collected the ball. He aimed, and shot. Straight into her goal. Wings raised, he pirouetted and waggled his not inconsiderable bottom in her direction.

"That's a new one!" she called to him, amused by his antics.

From there on in, she played like a thing possessed. She cut him up, he cut her up. She managed to kick the ball out from under his feet, he simply *threw* the ball at least once, then had the sheer audacity to try to deny it! The crowd thought that was hilarious and even she was laughing. Once he even feigned a bad fall and just lay there on the ground, whilst she rushed over to him in alarm. Then, as she knelt down to him, he leapt up, got the ball and scored again.

Finally, the score a tense 12-12, the game was called to a halt by the sound of Loni's name being called.

"GGNNNCCCHHHBBBB!" then, more softly when she saw she had Loni's attention, "Ggnncchhbb," OwnLoni squawked hoarsely. The screen of the portable machine she held in her talons was dark, its power switched off. Playtime was clearly over.

Without their game to watch, the audience broke up and resumed their own pastimes. Backs turned to her, they simply wandered off. No comments were made, no goodbyes called, no 'see-you-later' offered. The game was over and therefore her relevance to them was finished.

The illusion of being an integral part of the society of Pets was shattered. Loni was no more one of them, than was Little. She didn't truly fit in. She knew it and they knew it too. Shrugging her shoulders at Little who actually looked more crest-fallen than she felt, she tried to indicate that it didn't matter. And actually, as long as she had him, it didn't.

But she had also noticed something else, something she had probably *seen* before but never really *looked* at. She saw the gentle touches that Pets gave their Owners as they passed them in the field, the subtle caresses of fingers over wings and backs, the little glances to make sure that the Owners were alright.

And she *noticed* something else too! She noticed that whilst the Owners attention never once deviated from their machines, each touch caused a subtle shifting in their posture. It was almost as if that small contact meant the same thing to both owner and owned, assuring each of the other's love. It was as though each gesture had penetrated beyond the Eyons' unblinking exteriors and directly touched their hearts within.

# *Chapter 5.*

"Look San, I don't KNOW the truth any more than you do – but I do know what I've heard and what I've felt," said Jed passionately. "This idea that being a Pet is for our own good, just doesn't feel right to me."

"No, it doesn't feel right to me either," San admitted. It hurt him to do so. He loved OwnSan. But there was something so wrong about the situation. Yet he could not identify what that was.

"I admit there are some mutually beneficial things about the Eyons having us as Pets and us having them as Owners. But sometimes I think we resemble servants more than Pets. Although well loved and well treated ones, I grant you."

They had moved slightly, to sit in the shade of a large tree. An hour had passed since San's near-drowning episode and their clothes had dried in the warmth of the sun. Only the wrinkling of the material and a murky smell which lingered on them, gave any indication of what had happened earlier. Eyons worked diligently on their mobile machines whilst their  Pets frolicked in the water or played games or just chatted.

"Surely we were meant for more than this…" Jed gestured wildly around them, "…this existence." His voice remained quiet but lost none of its intensity. "Why has nature given us a brain if we are not to think, but merely intended to thoughtlessly while away our time? Why were we given arms and legs if not to use them in some meaningful and industrious way?" He held his arms up, fingers clutching at nothing, before dropping them to his lap as if in demonstration.

"Why do we have hearts that are capable of feeling joy and sorrow, yet live our lives lovelessly? Other than a love for a species which is not our own?" He turned the weight of his full stare on San. "When was the last time you felt really happy? Not just fed and watered and exercised like a good little Pet. But actually happy?"

He waited a moment for San's response and when none was forthcoming he continued desperately on. "Can this REALLY be all there is?" His voice trailed off at the end, as if he was beaten by his own suggestion of meaninglessness.

San hesitated momentarily. They had been talking in such depth that his head was so full of thoughts, images and opinions that he wasn't even sure where to start anymore. But one thing was for certain – nothing he said to Jed would be ridiculed. Whatever he said, would be considered seriously. Somehow, the very weight of consideration, that Jed would give to anything San said, put a terrible responsibility on him. He wasn't quite sure how it could be, but he felt that what he was about to say, would have implications not only for himself but for Jed too. That possibly what they were about to discuss, would one day shake the very foundations of life as they knew it.

"I've been having this dream...except I'm not really sure that it is a dream." San faltered, unsure of what he was about to say. "What I mean is...it's like some weird combination of dream, nightmare and memory, except I don't know which bit is which," he continued, his voice slow and tremulous.

It was easy to recall the dream and explain what took place during it. Conveying the emotions that coursed through him, whilst he was in the grip of the dream, was much more difficult.

"I think the woman is the key to it somehow. I don't know her and I've never seen her before, except in the dream and yet I do somehow know her. Its almost like somewhere inside I recognise her and a part of me doesn't want to know whatever it is she's trying to tell me."

He paused for breath. Jed waited, sensing that San needed space and time to gather his thoughts before continnig.

"And then there is this." Reaching under his sleeve, where the necklet still lay concealed, San untied it and passed it to Jed. Only at the very last moment as he passed it over, his slight hesitation betrayed how important and significant he thought the object was.

Placing the metal part in his left palm, Jed used the fingers of his right hand to trace over the carving that embellished the object. Head lowered to examine the necklet more closely, his expression was hidden in profile from San. It was only as Jed raised his eyes once more to meet San's own, that San saw how they shone with excitement.

"I have heard others talk of this necklet. Heard them mention it in passing as if it is only slightly less interesting than a new recipe for chicken stew." His voice was incredulous. "And I had hoped that one day you would show it to me."

"Yes I know. No one else has one. No one has ever seen anything like it. Yet that doesn't even *bother* them. This is why I was swimming out to you, to show you this and ask your opinion." Suddenly he felt shy, embarrassed that he had admitted to putting so much store in another's opinion.

Jed seemed not to notice. His gaze had returned to the necklet and he held it aloft by its leather cord and watched as it twirled in the air, shimmering as it caught the light.

"It appears to be two halves of a body, an upper half and a lower half. But the positioning is strange." Carved so that they were opposite but facing into one another, the head faced the feet and legs, which were upside down.

"There's something about it that I can't explain but which makes me sure that it's meant to represent two bodies and not just one cut in half." Jed pondered for a moment before continuing, "yet the entire thing has been cut in half, separated for some unknown reason."

"And someone, somewhere, put this on me before I was rehomed as a Pet." San's voice was eager. Jed, in voicing his thoughts was serving to affirm the ideas San already held.

"So the big question, is not so much what it is, as *why* it is the way it is," Jed supplied.

"And of course, who has the remaining piece?" finished San. That was the particular question which had been burning in his brain. "Does that make any sense at all?" he searched Jed's face for an answer.

"More to the point, after everything that we've discussed does it truthfully *not* make sense to you? Do you honestly not recognise the woman in your dream, not realise her significance to you?" prompted Jed in response. San stared blankly back at him.

"Well, I guess not!" laughed Jed. "Look, we all have to come from somewhere, don't we...Humans, Eyons, it doesn't really matter what we are, we all have to come from some other being, some other person. Do you not think that this woman could be your birth mother? And that for some reason *she* put the necklet on you," prompted Jed.

A light breeze suddenly seemed to spring up from nowhere, playfully blowing strands of still damp hair around San's face.

"My birth mother,"whispered San almost to himself, unconsciously smoothing down his unruly locks. Funny how such a little phrase could echo so resoundingly around and around his head, he thought. Like a spiral twisting in the breeze, he suddenly found himself considering both the necklet and the dream from new perspectives, new angles and patterns making themselves suddenly blindingly obvious to him, before being obscured again in the next turn of the wind.

How had he even managed to *not* realise this before? Why had it taken a near drowning to make things clear? For just a split second as realisation dawned, the playful breeze seemed to transform into a harsh wind, sending icy shivers down the length of his spine.

Involuntarily San's body shook in a huge shiver. "Yes, that makes sense. But *how can I* remember her? It can't be a memory, can it? Can you remember that far back Jed? Back to before you were two?"

"No, in truth I can't. I *am* a lot older than you but that's not the reason why. Like everyone else I would have thought it was impossible but yet it seems the most likely explanation."

He shuffled uncomfortably before continuing, almost reluctantly, "unless the dream is just something your mind has conjured up...perhaps to explain the necklet? What worries me the most though, is how you've described her behaviour. I mean it's not a happy dream is it...you're not happy having it and she's certainly not happy in it. Have you thought about that?" His face looked suddenly old and drawn. "The feel of violence in the dream...could it be that you remember some of the wars that rage across the Human villages?"

San didn't have an answer. It wasn't something that he had been able to pass off as meaningless, even to himself. It was even less possible to do so with Jed. He felt as old and tired as Jed looked. He wished he was like other Pets – oblivious to everything that didn't fit into their perfect little worlds – and content to do so. But he wasn't.

"Look San, I'd be the first to admit that my Owner has always treated me well...but...I just can't believe that we were meant to live like this." Jed's tone suddenly changed, as a rather blandly coloured Eyon ambled towards them, shrugging his wings in a restless fashion.

His tone shifted from one of ardent curiosity and ferventness to one which was falsely jovial and light. San instinctively knew that for some reason Jed did not want his Owner to be aware of the seriousness of their conversation. It was the words which were being said, not the tone in which they were issued which was important. And Jed had known that San would recognise that.

"Perhaps you just have a better memory than most, or even a more vivid imagination. Or perhaps *you* will be the one to find the answers." His voice was still light and mild but he could not mask the flash of fire that came from his soul and showed so clearly in his eyes. Jed stood up as his Owner approached, indicating that playtime was over.

"I hope that we get a chance to talk again soon. You've given me a lot to think about," San called to Jed's retreating back as he was whisked briskly away by OwnJed. He had taken his cue from Jed and his voice was light and without any intensity.

His arms enfolding the neck of his Owner, ready to be flown back to his home, Jed's face was in partial shadow making him once more a man of mystery as he turned for the final time to his new friend.

"If you don't look for answers for yourself, then do it for me – do it for all of us *PETS*. Had San imagined it or had that last word been spoken contemptuously? The chill wind blew the last of the warmth of the sun from his body and the sky seemed to darken instantaneously. Filled with an ominous sense of foreboding San studied OwnSan who stood nearby. Plugged into his machine he stood still and silent and oblivious to San and everything else around him.

There was no denying that he loved OwnSan and that the love was returned. Even so, his home was a prison and OwnSan his jailor. San knew in his heart what must be done. He had no choice. He had to leave, had to find the truth.

What revelations lay ahead and how would that knowledge change him? How could he leave OwnSan and what would become of either of them? He realised that what he was suddenly contemplating was unheard of and it struck fear deep into his heart, not only for himself but also for his Owner.

Would OwnSan grieve for him? Would he miss San? Would he search for him, terrified for his safety? Or would he continue on with life, living as he did now...choosing another Pet to replace San. "No, he wouldn't do that," San assured himself, "he wouldn't just *replace* me!"

These were all valid considerations yet they were not enough to justify inaction. He was compelled to seek answers to a myriad of questions, all jostling for attention in his brain.

Funny, he thought, if he had known how monumentally important the day would become, how life-changing an event it would be, he would have spent longer in preparing a feast of a breakfast. And he would have left the washing up undone.

He smiled. Let the adventure commence.

# *Chapter 6.*

L oni was restless. She had been in bed for ages and ages *and ages* and now she just couldn't sleep. The bedclothes were a knotted, tangled mess around her and with every passing minute she seemed more awake and less likely to *ever* sleep again. She had been dreaming, or rather having a nightmare and it was this which had woken her. She had flailed about in the bed, turning this way and that, arms outside the bedclothes, then inside, then out again. She had curled her legs up to her tummy, straightened them out, curled them up once more, then flipped over to lie on her other side, repeating the process all over again.

It wasn't that she wasn't comfortable. She was. Neither was she too hot nor too cold. It was something else entirely. Something wasn't right. But what was it? Her heart was pounding and her throat was dry – yet she was sure she wasn't ill. It was a different sort of pounding... more nervous than any sickness and she suspected her throat was only dry because she was breathing so rapidly and so heavily.

Unnecessarily careful not to wake Little, who was still softly snoring in his bed, just opposite her, she pulled her legs free of the covers and stood up. Past experience had proved him to be a deep sleeper, but there again that was normally true of her too. Yet here she was, wide awake. Perhaps he was only sleeping lightly too tonight, she wondered.

"Little are you awake?" she called softly on the off-chance that he was. There was no response.

It was the little cardboard box which was on her mind and which worried her so much. The box which had suddenly appeared without her even *noticing*, but which now sat, seemingly full of its own importance, on the worktable next to OwnLoni's machine. It had been a nightmare about it, sitting there unopened and so carefully inconspicuous which had disturbed her sleep. The *little cardboard box,* which she somehow knew contained all her worst dreads and fears.

Without even realising that she had moved, she now stood in front of the terrifying box. Hands shaking, she reached out and very carefully and quietly, she teased one flap away from the other and the same again with the remaining two folds. Silently bending the folds back as far as they would go, the full horror of the contents was unleashed.

The force of the discovery was almost physical, so sharply did she feel it and she rocked back on her heels, one hand gripping the table for support, the other clamped fast to her mouth. Yet she could not prevent a thin reedy whisper from escaping her over and over again.

"No, I can't let it happen. I won't let them take him from me ...I can't let it happen ...I won't...."

But if they stayed, that was exactly what would happen. One day Little would just be hooked right up to this, his very own portable machine, new and shiny and fresh out of its cardboard box. And he would be given his own house. His own Pet.

Not even taking the time to close the flaps again, she raced, heart thumping, back to the bedroom. Even as fast as she moved, she did so quietly, worried that the frantic pounding of her blood through her veins was enough to wake the household. Her legs could not carry her fast enough to catch up with her brain, which was racing ahead to the horrors of a life empty of her Little.

Hurriedly she dressed, throwing on her clothes with abandon, uncaring as to which top matched which other item, such was the urgency she felt. Whilst the conscious, rational part of her brain tried to consider her actions and perhaps even stop them, another part of her brain was urging her on, compelling her to move and move both silently and quickly. She was leaving. And she was doing it right now!

She didn't know *where* she was going ...hadn't even known that she *was going* until now. The rational part of her brain was no longer in control. Yet she realised that her mind was not full of urgent, unanswerable questions. Instead, she felt strangely calm and almost serene. But there were preparations she would need to make.

She considered waking Little but clumsy by nature and befuddled by sleep, he would slow her down. "Better to organise this by myself," she thought.

Grabbing the cloth bag she usually stored all their play things in, she tiptoed out of the bedroom and into the kitchen. Silently transferring all the toys onto the kitchen floor, in a neat pile, she refilled the bag with food for the journey. She cut thick slices of ham and tore chunks of bread from a large loaf. She then put these together in a large container and placed it carefully in the bag.

A chunk of cheese found half mouldering at the back of the cupboard would also be useful. Taking a sharp knife, Loni carefully trimmed off all the blue mouldy bits before placing it in the tub at the bottom of the bag.

She scanned the rest of the contents of the cupboard. Most of the food was in tins which would be too heavy to carry, or glass bottles and jars which would be too heavy *and* too liable to brake, so she would just have to leave them. It wasn't a lot of food to take, but it would have to do.

Besides, she didn't want to leave OwnLoni with an empty cupboard. Who knew how long it would take the Eyon to go to the store house for more supplies without Loni's prompting? Considerate in spite of her fear, she carefully placed the used knife in the sink out of the way.

Just as she was about to close the cupboard door, she noticed something right at the back, hidden away behind stacks of tins and jars. Crackers. A whole packet of unopened crackers!

She scanned the cupboard again, in case there was anything else worthwhile lurking, hidden in there. But this time she found nothing.

She was ready. Only one thing bothered her. How to leave a message behind. How could she show that they would all be together again one day? Because they would. She was sure of it. This was just a temporary measure.

Maybe if they stayed away for a while…just long enough to make a protest…The root of an idea began to take hold in her brain and it felt so right she didn't even question it. OwnLoni thought the time was now right for Little to be connected, thus the appearance of the box. So what would happen if he was gone for a while? Would it somehow be too late to connect him up, when they returned?

Loni didn't blame her Owner. "It's the Eyon way after all," she argued with herself. "But I can't, I *won't* allow it." Another thought struck her. Was it the Eyon way? Were there other forests of Eyons, just as there were villages of Humans. And if there were other Eyon places, did they all hook up to machines? Or was it just here, just in her forest?

Perhaps life elsewhere was very different indeed. Perhaps elsewhere Eyons lived side by side with their Pets, if they had any, because of course it was always possible that they didn't. Perhaps elsewhere Owners andPets shared a common language and communicated freely, engaging together in everyday activities. Perhaps elsewhere she and Little would just fit in as the norm.

Her mind was bursting with the possibilities.

Reaching back into the cupboard she seized a jar of half empty chocolate spread and moved silently to the work area. She grabbed a sheet of paper from OwnLoni's machine and dipped a finger into the dark gooey chocolaty mess.

At the very top of the paper, she hastily drew a rendition of herself and Little flying high above a series of mountains and lakes, smiling and looking excited. She added the moon and the stars and an owl watching them – in her mind this seemed to show that although what they were doing was unheard of, it was not a foolish thing.

At the bottom of the page she scibbled a drawing of them together and happy but at an unknown location. She deliberately made this vague with trees partially obscuring their bodies.

Then she linked the two pictures with an arrow going from one to the other, forming a complete circle. Loni hoped that this managed to show that when the adventure was over, they would be returning home.

Finally, at the centre of the picture, right in the middle of the circle, she drew a large pair of pursed lips – a kiss from her to OwnLoni. Then with much trepidation, she went to wake Little up.

Putting her index finger to her lips in a sign to be quiet, Loni gently shook him. This appeared to have no effect as he seemed completely oblivious to her presence and instead began to snore even more loudly.

Undeterred, she began to shake him more vigorously, to no avail. Yet again she shook him, this time more vigorously still, until eventually he was rocking back and forth in his bed so much and so quickly, he appeared to be attempting some form of strangely horizontal dance.

Loni stifled a giggle as she tried a different tack. This time she tried to pull the covers off his sleeping body. But each time she pulled them down, he merely dragged them back up again, still swaying to the new rhythm in his sleep.

Finally, in desperation, she stood back for a second to gauge it just right. Then, as he swayed to the left, balancing precariously on the edge of his bed, she gave just a *tiny* tilt to that side, just enough to give his body the momentum it need to tip him right over the edge and onto the floor.

WHUMPH – the whole house shook and for a moment she feared that they had woken OwnLoni, who slept in the next room. From racing about, Loni's heart now suddenly decelerated so rapidly she feared it would stop altogether as she held her breath and listened for the sound of her Owner's high-pitched wheezes.

Minutes seemed to pass into eternity before she heard a vague "EEEEEEEEEEEEEOOOOOOOOOOOOHHH HHHHHHH," and knew that OwnLoni remained deep in sleep. Little meanwhile, stood patiently waiting for her to let him know what was happening, rubbing his eyes with his wing.

This was no mean feat when your wings end in several sharp pointy talons, any one of which could easily poke your eye out. When he had first hatched she had been both terrified and horrified every time he had done this, but by now she had kind of got used to the idea, and could even think of it as a bad-taste joke "skewered eyeball for tea, anyone?"

Taking him by the wing, she led him to the work room and showed him the box and its contents. Eyes wide and full of horror that she was certain were reflected in her own, he shook his head in denial.

"I know, I know and I feel the same Little. We can only stop this if we leave. But it's a choice I can't make for you." She hesitated, her voice soft and she hoped comforting. "But if you stay, I will still have to leave. I couldn't stand to have you taken from me every day of my life and be forced to watch it happen."

A thick tear rolled down one of her cheeks but she bit back the others. He had to make the right decision for him, by himself. She managed a thin smile.

"I'll always love you, wherever I am and however far apart we are. And I'll always remember how we are..." her voice caught and broke and she took a second to compose herself before amending, "remember how we were..."

"OOOOOOO!" Little cried, his eyes suddenly seeming impossibly big for their sockets, his mouth still holding the shape of the sound even as his voice faded away.

"GGOOO EEE IIIITTHH," he semi-whispered at her urgently, grasping both of her arms in his wings so that she got the full sense of seriousness he intended.

"Are you sure you want to come with me? Please think about it... I'll always love you whether you come or not... and also you should know, it could be dangerous... we might find a Human village, be caught up in their wars," she stopped, unable to continue. Her voice was tight with emotion and streams of tears were already coursing down her checks. But with the thoughts of Human villages came the thoughts again, unbidden, of her birth parents and she wondered how much of this decision to go was also driven by the need to find out about herself, her origins.

She could also tell him that there was a possibility that other Eyons did not spend their lives hooked up to machines. But she remained quiet. To have said that, would have influenced his choice too much and may also have given him false hope. She held her breath, desperate for him to make the choice, yet simultaneously terrified it would be different to what she hoped.

"GGOOO EEE IIIITTHH," he assured her. Wiping the tears from her face, she disentangled herself and reached past the hateful box to pick up the chocolate-spread marked paper. Unwilling for a moment to let him fully commit to the idea without as much discussion as possible, she made one last attempt.

"I hope we only have to be gone a short time. Just long enough for OwnLoni to realise that you are not like the other Eyons. Just a little bit of time to let us get the idea of connecting you up, out of her head. Do you understand, Little?"

"ESSSSSS." He nodded emphatically. He understood they were leaving and why - but the rest of it? Loni wasn't so sure. But it didn't matter anyway, she would protect him at all costs. Stomach still tight with apprehension, she passed the smeared message to Little who sniffed it and raised it to his mouth...

Just as it was about to disappear down his throat, Loni realised his intention. "No, no," she hissed quietly at him "you've not to EAT it, you've *to read* it!" She mimed holding the paper close to her face and dramatically moved her head in the direction of the arrows, signalling her interest in the drawings.

A look of comprehension suddenly passed onto his features and he examined the paper closely before replacing it on the table. He seemed to grasp the ideas that she had put down and turned to her his kind face worried. Then grasping Loni's right hand in his right wing, he placed his left wingtip flat in the centre of the circle where Loni had already drawn her lips. Motioning with her hand, he traced the edge of his wing onto the paper. Instinctively Loni knew what she was to do.

She fetched the jar and removed the lid once more. Taking another fingerful of spread, she used it to outline the shape of his wing-tip on the paper – this was *his* goodbye. The moment was forever ruined however, when he then insisted on licking the remaining chocolate off her finger. 'Eyons just don't have a sense of occasion', thought Loni.

Together they peeked through the doorway of OwnLoni's bedroom and each said their own, silent goodbye. Loni moved away whilst Little peeked in at his egg-mother. She wanted to give him some privacy. What she was doing was hard enough for her – she figured it had to be almost impossible *for him* to leave. That he was unhesitatingly willing to do so, only showed how much he loved Loni. It was no more or less than she loved him right back.

Hand in wing, they walked to the door. The night air was cooler than expected and seemed to carry a strangely exotic scent. Pulling the straps of the food bag high onto her shoulder, Loni clasped her arms around Little's neck and prepared for flight. She felt his chest expand as he took a huge breath and then they were off, whooshing into the inky-black sky as if they had every right in the world to be there.

# *Chapter 7.*

'Funny how even familiar things look different at night,' thought San. The moon looked somehow brighter and closer. It seemed to shimmer in the night air, as if held aloft by some gossamer thread that was both too fine and too magical to be seen. And it appeared to be lit by the velvety blackness around it, rather than lending *its* light to the night. Perhaps if he just reached far enough, he might actually be able, not just to touch it, but to pluck it right out of the sky and use it as his own personal path finder!

He had been travelling for some hours and had just about got used to the initially terrifying sounds he had heard. After all, once your heart has been quaking with fear for quite a while, at all the strange 'ccrraaasss' and 'rivvettsss', that can be heard all around and you *haven't* yet had your head bitten off and chewed and thrown into the nearest bush, you kind of began to accept it.

Of course he still didn't know where, or even *what* all the sounds came from. He didn't know if they came from a veritable army of strange creatures. Or, and perhaps somehow more scarily, if they came from a single source. One single, solitary, ferocious animal, which was walking alongside him but shrouded in the night! Drinking in his scent as its stomach rumbled, demanding attention.

Because *that* was what he hadn't managed to come to accept yet, the way the darkness seemed to fold around him, immediately cloaking from view the path he had taken. Luckily he knew this area well. This was where the lake was and he was able to skirt around it quite easily. As long as the ground was good and firm ahead, when he moved on to unknown territory, he'd be fine.

He reached his arms out into the darkness, stretching them as far in front of him as he could, before circling them out to his sides. In every direction he could *just about* make out his fingertips. But the image was vague and sort of grainy, as if the night was made up of grains of sand that overlaid everything and obscured it from view. So it *was* actually possible that a monster walked parallel to him but hidden in the blackness.

Just as he had that thought, the very tips of his fingers seemed to touch someone – something obscured and hidden by the night. He snapped his fingers tight into his palms and wrenched his arms rapidly back to his sides. Had his fingertips been a breath away from plunging into an open mouth with razor sharp teeth? Or the fur of a creature with suckers on its back which would attach itself to him and feed him, little by little, into its six hungry mouths? Had he alerted some creature to his presence, that had previously been oblivious to him?

Without conscious effort his legs stopped moving and his breath stayed unexpelled in his throat. Had the creature also stopped, listening for him? For a brief moment he saw in his mind, images of himself panicked and drowning in the lake, convinced he was about to be eaten alive. Was he being similarly silly now?

But wouldn't that be typical, if because of an earlier mistake, he ignored all the warnings of imminent danger and *practically threw* himself into the jaws of a boy-eating, bone-crunching monster? At least there would be no evidence of what happened to him, of how stupid he had been!

He stood, breath held for an age, before it came again, "Riivvett".

Then from the other side of him and even louder, "RIIVVETT, RIIVVETT." And all at once the sound seemed to surround him, "RIIVVETT, RIIVVETT, RIIVVETT, RIIVVETT." BUT NOTHING HAPPENED TO HIM! He wasn't mauled, eaten or even licked, tasted and spat out as vile. Absolutely nothing happened.

Perhaps the creature didn't fancy a boy for dinner! Perhaps it had tried one previously and found their meat too tough, too stringy? Or maybe, just maybe, there was never a monster there in the first place. Either way, since he obviously wasn't going to be consumed as dinner for something, he let out his breath and resumed walking.

He realised that with every step he took, he was moving further away from all that he had known. Even on the verge of leaving, he had failed to recognise how much he had just taken for granted, how much he didn't know about the world outside of his own forest. He hadn't even been sure of which direction to start walking in!

Trying to think about it logically hadn't helped either, as it was based on nothing. He'd never heard anyone mention the location of *any* Human villages and even if they had, there would be no way of knowing if it was the particular village he sought. So he picked a direction at random and just kept moving.

It had occurred to him that on waking and discovering he was gone, OwnSan would be worried. But it wasn't as if he could leave his Owner a message in any way. And even if he could, what would it be?

How could he explain that much as he loved his Owner, there were too many mysteries presented in his dreams for him to ignore. That there was a desire to see a Human village with his own eyes. That he needed to understand why Pets were bred and given to Owners. That he had to find out what the necklet meant and why he had been given it.

Locked into these thoughts he didn't immediately detect the presence of another, walking beside him, matching him stride for stride. Until suddenly it was there, an overbearing sensation of being watched which made the hairs on the back of his neck stand up in a rush of fear.

The voice, when it came, was like nothing he had ever heard before. "Wherere arrre yoou going?" It was almost as if the speaker's voice was rusty from lack of use. There was a hoarseness to it, which was overlaid with a thickness on the consonants and a sharpness on the vowel sounds. Yet there was no denying it was understandable. It was also terrifying, issued as it was from an unknown source.

San froze in fear. He *knew* his fingertips had touched something back there, he just knew it. And this person had been following him all this time. But who was it? For a moment a clear image of Jed filled his mind, before being rapidly dismissed. The voice wasn't Jed's ...it wasn't anyone he knew, he was sure of that.

And clearly this stranger meant him no harm or he would have acted before now. So there was nothing to fear. In theory. Yet he remained afraid. He resumed walking, although with a wider gait than before, flexing his muscles and readying them to run if need be.

"Who are *you*?" He decided to ask some questions of his own before he answered any, but was dismayed to hear the thin wobble in his voice, which did little to convey the image of bravado that he had hoped for. "Are you from one of the Human villages?" And if he was, what did that mean? Why had he not already attacked?

"Likke yoou, I too amm a Travelller," came the answer from the darkness. And now it seemed the person was so close, San could feel the stranger's breath caress the air right in front of his face.

What did that mean exactly, 'traveller'? He decided to dismiss the comment for now until he knew more about the situation.

"My name is San" he volunteered. He figured it wasn't giving much away but would reassure his follower he felt safe and secure. Even though he didn't feel at all that way. But he did not want to appear weak, vulnerable.

"I wass...aamm...callled RRiiiaaaannn." Again there was that weird mix of sharp and thick sounds and a hesitancy, as if he had not been used to having a name at all. San tried to gauge the age of the man who accompanied him from the voice alone. It was not an easy task but he figured the speaker was around eighteen to twenty triangles…much older than himself but much younger than Jed.

With every three steps he took, the last three faded into the pitch blackness around him and it was hard to concentrate and make sure that he didn't just walk around in a huge circle, whilst also thinking about who walked beside him.

He had taken a wide path around the lake, fearful of repeating the near-drowning incident of the earlier day. After all, if he had left secretly in the middle of the night, only to drown in the very same place that he had *nearly* drowned in so recently, not only would he be dead, but he'd look really dumb too.

His active imagination immediately set the scene in his head. His body would be found floating face down in the water and all his friends, including Jed and their Owners, would gather there together with OwnSan. They would stand there, sadly shaking their heads and saying "Poor San, he was just too stupid to live. He didn't learn from the first time he nearly drowned and had to go and do it for real. Poor, poor stupid San." Even in the darkness, San's face burned with embarrassment at the imagined humiliation of it all.

"Huungry?" The voice interrupted him once more. Not a statement as he initially thought, but a question, he realised, as he found that something was being offered to him across the darkness. Reaching blindly to where he thought the stranger's hand would be, his own hand encountered a thick wedge of meat, a slice of bread seemingly wrapped around it.

"No sooo fresshhh buu yoou caann eeet et," proclaimed his companion and followed this with such noisy eating sounds that he was clearly following his own advice.

San brought the food to his nose. There was a rather ripe scent to it, almost as if the food was on the verge of turning rotten. Then again, he was hungry and had no other means of sustenance. He took a huge breath of air, gulped it into his lungs, then stuffed as much of the food into his mouth as he could fit, chewed and swallowed before his nasal senses caught up with what he was doing.

He thought about all the delicacies he had left behind. Thick slices of meat and thickly buttered bread, sharp pickled onions and jaw-clenching gherkins, sticky jam on crisp toast and saliva-inducing chocolates and sweets. He unconsciously licked his lips at the imagined melange of delightful flavours, but the only taste on his tongue remained the cloying taste of the rank meat mixed with the heavy dank essence of the night, cool and slightly damp.

He hadn't needed to think of food before he left. Stomach full of supper, he had gone to bed fully intending to feign sleep. He had waited a long time for OwnSan to disconnect from his machine and there were several blank periods, where he suspected he may have dosed off. Fortunately or unfortunately, depending on how you looked at it, the recurring dream had woken him up.

"Wherere arrre yoou going?" Even repeated, the question startled him all over again. He had almost forgotten that he was not alone, he was so caught up in remembering.

"I don't know." The truth sounded so lame – almost as though he were trying to hide his real intentions. He thought he had better clarify it. "I mean, I know where I want to go, but I don't know where it is or whether I am going in the right direction." He wondered if that sounded like gobbledy-gook or conversely whether it revealed too much.

Nervously he carried on. "I don't know what lies ahead of here – or to either side for that matter – but I'm looking for a Human village." He was aware that there was a risk involved in telling this man his intentions but he did it anyway.

"Have you come across any?" he enquired hopefully.

"Huuummmannn villlagggesss, I avvoyyyddd."

"Yes, the wars, I know it might be dangerous…" he was cut off, prevented from saying any more by the man's abrupt interjection.

"Therrr arrr nnnnooo warrsss!"

"You mean the wars have stopped? There's no more fighting?" San was both relieved and excited. "They must have stopped only recently then, as we have not long had some new Pets in our forest." It was a statement rather than a queation.

"Jjuussttt nnno warrsss. Didd theyyy sstopppp? Werrr they nevvverr therrr? I ddo nnott nno."

San was perplexed and for a moment didn't know how to continue the conversation. He thought about asking what the man meant by suggesting that the wars had never happened at all but it was probably only that he meant he had never seen any. Everyone knew that the reason Humans gave their children to the Eyons to be raised as Pets, was to let them have a better life. A life away from the squalor and the violence of the Human wars.

Then the natural rejoinder occurred to him. "What about you, where are you going and where have you come from?" And then almost as an afterthought he added, "and are there others? Other Humans travelling around, looking for something?" It was certainly a thought which had not occurred to him before.

The pause was so long that for a while San wasn't sure if his companion just wasn't going to answer him or whether he was now alone once more, the man having stopped walking some time ago. And then the silence was broken.

"Wheerr haave I commmm frommm? A goood queshtion and I wisshh I could ansswer yoou ..." and then almost too quiet to hear, San *thought* he heard "I wisshhh I knew myselll," but perhaps that was his imagination.

"My path is unclearr and uncertin." The voice was somehow beyond sad, as if the man was without any hope in his life and mired in misery.

San didn't know what to answer to that, so he said nothing and waited instead. "Tell mee instead about yoouur liffee Sann, so that I willl undersstand whyy yoou arre here. Forr I hhave seeenn, nnno othersss travelling, neitherrr Huumann nnorr Eyon. Onnly yoo. Aand mee."

San didn't know whether he was disappointed or pleased. In a way it was nice to know that he was different, braver than others. Yet it was equally disappointing to know that no one else, other than this stranger, would be able to fully understand his need to leave – apart of course from Jed – and even he hadn't had the courage to do more than think about it.

"I keep having this dream," San said into the darkness. Rian said nothing, he merely waited for San to continue in his own time. They walked in silence for a while whilst San thought of how best to explain it.

"In the dream, I get the feeling that the woman, who is about to tell me something very important. She opens her mouth wide…much wider than anyone ever really could…and instead of words, what comes out is this stream of paper. And then her head starts to spin round and round, increasingly faster and faster." He took a breath, aware that his heart was hammering in his chest at the vivid memory of it, recounting it here, in the dark.

"The paper flies from her mouth in streams, the printing on it getting bigger and bigger as it spills onto the floor, piling up in untidy heaps. And all the while she woman screeches this awful noise." He turned to where he thought the man walked in the darkness, wishing he could see him, wishing it was not dark.

"Her head's then spinning so fast that I can't even see her eyes or mouth anymore, it's like all her features have blurred into a horror mask with a gory, contorted hole in the centre. Then there are these harsh clashing colours and angles and the dream is gone." Relieved to have come to the end of recounting the dream, he now carried on in a lighter tone than before.

"I suppose the effect is frightening, yet it never really scares me. I feel confused and  bewildered even, but never scared. But I've often wondered if I am *supposed* to be scared. I mean I wonder if my mind just conjured the entire thing up to deliberately scare me, though I don't know why."

Rian listened intently, never giving an answer, an opinion but the very air seemed more heavy with the intensity of his listening.

San explained how in the middle of the dream, he felt himself straining to read the printed symbols, turning the bundled paper round and round, trying to find the right way up. But that try as he might, he was never able to decipher any meaning from them. Yet he couldn't stop trying.

"Sometimes when I wake, I wonder if I would be able to read them if I were standing upside down on my head, with the paper held behind my left shoulder and looking at its reflection in a mirror. And when the dream comes again, I try, I really try to do that, but…" he shrugged.

"So that's why I had to leave." He chose not to mention the necklet which still lay under his top. He figured there was only so much information his companion could take in at a time. The story of the necklet could wait. "My friend thinks the woman in the dream is my birth mother and that it means something real."

Still Rian said nothing and San felt obliged to fill the silence. Somehow afraid to say more than he already had, he changed the subject.

"Now there will be no trips on OwnSan's back to the store house for anything I need. I'll just have to find whatever I can." He hoped that Rian realised that he had said this for his benefit, that he did not intend to be a burden on the older man.

"There aarre thingss morr immportant than a foooll stomik," responded Rian slowly. If he had noticed the abrupt change of conversation, he chose not to bring attention to it.

San thought the comment was true and untrue at the same time. When you were really hungry there was nothing *more* important than the emptiness in your belly.

But he had to concede that Rian had a point and he was glad of the diversion.

San laughed, thinking about how much prompting it sometimes took to get OwnSan to take him to fetch more food. "I guess OwnSan would have agreed with that, it sure did take a *lot* of effort, sometimes up to three attempts to get him to take me to the store hut."

San, ever the optimist, *always* gave OwnSan the benefit of the doubt and started subtly, by shaking the big Eyon's wing and pointing towards the kitchen.

Only when that failed to elicit a response, did he move to the next stage, of grasping the wing more furiously in one hand, whilst using the other hand to jab the air pointedly in the direction of the kitchen, then rubbing in circular motions across his stomach. When that tactic too failed, as it often did, he resorted to dashing into the kitchen and throwing open the door to the cold box. That done, he would then rush back to OwnSan and throw himself down prostrate at his feet.

From his vantage point at his machine, OwnSan could clearly see the empty cold box and the poor starving Human at his feet and would usually take action. Subtlety was lost on Eyons, San had long ago realised. Yet on at least two occasions, even this extreme pantomime had failed to get OwnSan's attention.

"Once, in desperation, I had to resort to thrashing about on the floor as if I was having some kind of starving reaction." He hoped that had not been an accurate prediction of how he would eventually become – writhing about in agony as his empty stomach tied itself in ever tightening knots, his internal organs withering and atrophying away.

"Usually the 'dead San on the floor' thing did the trick and he'd take me to the store house straight away," he finished. Both were quiet for a moment, walking with their own thoughts and memories running through their heads. Something occurred to San.

"Did you ever wonder where all that stuff comes from? You know the food and the clothes and everything else? It's always just *there*." The question was only met with silence. Either the stranger didn't know or just didn't care.

The store house was the largest, widest and tallest building in the circle. Everything you could ever need was in there somewhere, including racks and racks of folded clothes.

Having no need for clothing themselves, Eyons were indifferent to the concept of clothes cut to flatter the human form and instead settled on utilitarian considerations of widths and lengths. All heights and widths were catered for, from small to large, fat to thin, short to tall, young to old. It wouldn't matter if you were a tiny, skinny, fifty year old Pet, or a tall, horrendously fat eight year old Pet – there would be clothing there to fit.

Although perhaps if you *were* a horrendously fat Pet, you wouldn't be able to be flown there to collect it – but that was a different matter altogether. But without exception, the clothes were so plainly cut and fixed together, that they gave a kind of 'one size fits all' effect.

Yet the colours on offer…well that was truly staggering. The range and depth of the colours meant that even choosing a white top was something of a decisive event, with the choice of white, nearly white, off white, nearly off white, apple white, peach white and lilac white!

"OwnSan always let me choose my own clothes. But what about you, *your* Owner?" San felt that having given so much information about his own life he was at least entitled to some explanations in return.

"I haave no Ownner," came the response.

San didn't understand. "Do you mean your Owner was old? Did he die?" He stopped, waiting for the answer and when none was forthcoming he continued on, "Didn't you get taken on by another Owner then, a younger one who didn't have a Pet yet?"

San stood waiting for the answer. The unseen man also stood silently, having stopped when San did. San knew he hadn't walked away, he could just make out the quiet sounds of his breathing.

The air had a coolness to it, San hadn't noticed before and he couldn't prevent himself from shivering. His legs were sore and tired and he had travelled so far he was bone weary. His body cried out for rest.

"I will leeeve yoou now Saan. Yoour paath goess onn aandd, iff yoo carry strayytt onn yoo will surely finnd somm Huumann villages. Altho I doo nnott nno iff they arrr the ones yoo seeek." He carried on, unwilling to let San but in. "Mmy paath endss heer."

San wasn't sure if this was really true or whether something he had said had made Rian want to part company with him.

"Why Rian? Why does your path end here? Why not come with me?" asked San, now shivering violently. He sank down onto the bare earth and huddled his body into himself for warmth.

"I caannnott." Yet despite his words he did not move away. "Yoou aarre coldd aand neeed to resst. I will makke yoou a ffire before I go."

Was it San's imagination or was there a reluctant note there? And what was it Rian was reluctant to do? To go? To stay? Or to make the fire?

There was a sound of breaking twigs and rustling leaves and then suddenly there was warmth and light. San pulled his tired body closer to the warmth of the flames but as soon as the first flames had taken told, Rian had moved back, away from the illuminating fire and into the obscuring darkness. San could just make out his pale face.

Rian looked more or less as San had imagined him to be. He had a youthful face with pleasant features but it was his hair which caught San's attention. It was long and unkempt as if he was long past caring how he looked. Bits of twig and other debris lodged in it as if they had taken up permanent residence. Which, under the circumstances, perhaps they had!

And even as San watched, Rian stepped further and further back into the darkness until he had almost faded from sight. With a single bound San was up and racing to where he thought Rian would be. If for no other reason than to hear a Human voice, San didn't want him to go.

Arms outstretched into the darkness, San ran towards the sound of retreating footsteps. And smashed into a large feathered body!

The air was whooshed right out of him and he was knocked onto the ground by the force of the contact. He sat there dazed and uncomprehending. Rian was an Eyon! But how could that be – he could talk and be understood – and he had hair, lots of it – Eyons didn't *have* hair. But he had feathers too!

Mind in turmoil he grasped the proffered hand and let himself be helped to his feet. Then his mind registered what had just happened. "You have hands!" was all he was able to blurt out, the enormity of it all rendering him almost speechless.

Rian sighed deeply "I wannted to avooid thisss. Itt iss my ownn fowlt. I shood havve left yoou alonne." The strange voice was cracked with raw emotion. "I thoughtt I could help yoo, butt I caann nottt even hellpp myselff!"

Treading a tightrope of sentiments, aware that one misstep could send either or both of them into the lonely chasm on both sides, San knew he had to consider his next words carefully. Fear and wonder, curiosity and dread all flitted through his mind. So many questions to be asked. Yet he knew that the answers to the questions were less important than helping the creature before him, which stood still shrouded in the night.

"Come back to the fire with me, at least for a little while. Have a rest. You can still go afterwards if you like. But please sit with me a while and tell me what you know. Please." San tried hard to keep his tone balanced and unwhining.

Rian said nothing but let San take him by the hand and lead him over to the campfire. The bright orange glow from the flickering high flames did nothing to hide his appearance and everything to reveal it. And the full absurdity that was Rian was laid bare before San and he felt something in his heart wither, as he looked at the half Human, half Eyon who stood before him, head bowed piteously.

# *Chapter 8.*

L oni and Little had travelled as far as they could that first night. Which hadn't actually been that far, Loni had to admit, due to *her* inability to fly and *Little's* inability to walk fast, before settling down to rest until the light of day.

She had tried to make as comfortable a bed as possible for them, but the hard ground was no real substitute for the comfort of the beds they had left. She wished she'd had the foresight to bring a blanket. It wasn't particularly cold and she didn't need it for herself but she could have used it for Little. His feathers kept him warm and snug but underneath all that colourful fluff she knew he was just a bag of frail bones.

If only she had brought a blanket she could have folded it up under him, cushioning him. At the very least, they could have huddled together under it and been lulled into a feeling of security.

Loni suspected that Little was far more tired than he was letting on and possibly a little afraid too. Holding his wing in her hand as they had walked in the dark, she had tried to reassure him about the strange noises they had been hearing. "Don't worry Little. I don't know what's making those noises but whatever it is, it won't hurt us and anyway I'll always keep you safe."

She had used her gentlest and most sincere voice to try to convey the meaning, in a way he would understand. She gave his wing a firm stroke, "you know underneath this girlie exterior lies a body that's strong and a heart that loves you. We'll be ok. Ok?"

Her raised intonation at the end had clearly suggested a question to him and she was gratified to hear his response, a clear "ESSS" if a bit shakily spoken. His eyes had seemed larger than usual too, the whites shining out into the darkness.

They hadn't been able to go much further before tiredness had overtaken the young Eyon. He had slowed right down and appeared to be walking with his eyes almost closed. Loni knew they had to rest before either he tripped and hurt himself, or just fell down in exhaustion.

Like others of his kind, Little could sleep in an upright position, sort of huddled over his own feet but he never did. Instead he preferred to sleep the Human way, lying flat and if possible, cuddled into Loni.

Normally this wasn't a problem, but here, without the cushioning effect of a soft bed, Loni was worried. Oh, Eyons looked big and tough and the adults were strong enough to fly with a fully grown Pet clinging to their backs. But therein lay the crux of the matter. Their bodies were strong, yet the bones that held the muscles were delicate and thin. You only had to see a wet Eyon once, to realise they were all feathers and hot air. Perhaps they *had* to be like that to be able to fly.

"Come on Little, lets sleep till we feel less tired" she suggested, pulling him down beside her in the dark. "Nooo, nooo sleepee. Ittle nooo sleeepee," he asserted, vigorously shaking his head back and forth. But she knew it was a fib, told for her benefit.

"Yes, Little, we need to sleep. I need to sleep and so do you." She was firm and unrelenting.

"OKKK Loneee. Luvv oooo," he cooed, lying in the darkness cuddled into her. "I know Little. I love you too." She was struck by the thought that he had never said her Human name before, as well as how beautiful it sounded the way he pronounced it.

But it seemed there was more on his mind, and tired as he was, he wanted to talk. "Luvv ooo Loneee." He was so tired his usual screechy tone was replaced by a slurring sound, making him strangely more understandable than normal. "I know Little. I love you too," she repeated.

Little struggled to sit up a bit, determined not to fall asleep before he was finished. "NOOOO WAAN LONEEEE GOOO WAAYYY!"

"You don't want me to go away? You want us to go back?" Having understood the words, she was now struggling with their interpretation.

"NOOOO WAAN LONEEEE GOOO WAAYYY WIII NOOO IIITTTLL." His voice was firm, assured.

"I won't go away *without* you Little." She told him.

Yet for a moment she had thought about it. But only because she thought perhaps he would be happy connected to the machine and she couldn't have witnessed that. She wondered now why she had had such little faith in him.

And maybe that was how her parents had felt, how all the Human parents felt when they gave up their children. They thought the children would be happy – and safe. But being forced to witness it was another matter entirely.

"Come on, we need to sleep now..." She broke off feigning a yawn which then turned into a real one. Little shut his eyes and curled back into her side, all care forgotten. She hoped. But just as she had that thought he startled her by speaking again.

"LONEEE GOOO WAAYYY... LEEEEVVVV OWWWNNNNLONNEE." It wasn't an accusation, merely a statement. And it was true, she had left OwnLoni behind. He had kept his eyes closed as he said it and they remained so now, as if he could not bear to meet her gaze.

"Yes, that's true Little and I know it's hard for you. It's hard for me too! But we will go back as soon as we can. I promise you. And I'll *never* leave you. Never!" she promised.

It was only the faintest muffled snuffling sounds that indicated he was crying. Unable to offer any more assurances than she already had, she instead curled her body into the warmth of his and placing her arms around him, waited for his quiet sobs to subside.

"Maybe not all Eyons hook up to machines Little. Maybe there are places where they just live like you and me. And maybe if we can find one of those places, we can show them back home, show OwnLoni that it doesn't have to be like that." There were a lot of maybes in there and she hoped she wasn't building their hopes up only for them to be dashed down...but they needed hope to go on.

It seemed to take a very long time before he stopped crying, each sob seeming to hack a tiny piece from her heart, till it felt like it was in complete tatters and could never function again.

But eventually, the tears dried up and his body relaxed into hers. Loni deliberately slowed and deepened her breathing in imitation of sleep, hoping that Little would be lulled to sleep.

She had only needed to pretend to be asleep for a few minutes before he drifted off, he was so tired. And it wasn't that she was any *less* tired than him. It was just that she wanted some free time to think. Time to contemplate what they were doing, why they were doing it and what they should do next. *Without* having to guard her expressions or tone of voice from him.

Keeping him unafraid and unworried was only part of her responsibility to look after him. And it was a relief that she could be free of that while he slept. So for just a little while, she vowed to try to use this time constructively, to think things through, so that she had a clear plan by the time she drifted off to sleep.

So she lay in the darkness and as she was soothed by the regular if somewhat noisy snoring that issued from Little, she thought about what she had left behind.

Her home in High Woods was all she had ever known, all that she could remember. Their particular tree house was beautiful, but actually no better or worse than any of the other tree houses. It was well constructed and had everything a Pet and two Eyons could need. High Woods was a beautiful place, but probably no more beautiful than any other woods.

What had made the place special, was the people there. No, that wasn't right, she thought suddenly. What had made the place special was the *Eyons* there – *her* Eyons, OwnLoni and Little. Yet, even OwnLoni was not completely included in their special relationship. *Her* love for *them* was no more nor no less that what any Owner felt for its hatchling and its Pet.

The flip side of this now struck her with such clarity she heard her own breath hiss in her throat. Just as she had no Human friends, Little had no Eyon friends. He had found everything he needed in her company, just as she had in his.

Loni thought back to the time before Little's hatching. There was a vague memory trying hard to surface. It was like a knot in a chain. The harder you pulled, the tighter the knot became, until suddenly it was so tight the metal warped and one link joined to the other becoming inseparable…

Her eyes began to close as her body demanded the rest it needed so much. But her questioning mind refused to be silent and carried the thought into her sleep.

Links joined together, pulling so tight that they are inseparable. Like clasped hands, holding tight, holding tight, resisting all effort to pull them apart. Then the chain is broken and they are apart. Her hand is searching, searching for that missing link but it is gone. There is much screaming and wailing and it is only when she needs to draw a breath that she realises the screaming is coming from her.

The thing she was trying to hold on to is gone, all gone and nothing will ever be the same. There are no clear images, instead everything is a kaleidoscope of colours. Then the dream shifts as dreams do. Now she can see herself clearly and a part of her brain wonders how this can be so. If this is a memory, then surely she should remember it as she actually saw it, looking through her own eyes and not as if she is seeing herself through someone else's eyes.

Yet, there she is, just as if she is not herself, but is instead watching herself! She understands that this is part of the process of dreams, even memory based ones, but remains unnerved by it.

She is young in the dream. Instinctively she knows how old she is, without even trying to focus on the triangular age markings on her arm. She is three years old. And Little is hatching. Dream Loni is so excited, her face is all lit up and glowing and she is hopping up and down. Now there is a crack in the shell and Loni is fit to burst with excitement.

In her sleep, Loni's brow wrinkled in concentration. There was some other emotion Dream Loni was feeling but she couldn't quite grasp it, couldn't quite understand it, no matter how hard she tried.

No-one heard the words that issued forth from the dreaming girl, as she lay there curled next to her only friend, the baby Eyon. "Now I'll have my other half back," she muttered time and time again. Instead, the light breeze carried the words away and buried them underneath last season's leaves.

# *Chapter 9.*

"What *are* you?" As soon as the words were out of his mouth, San regretted them.

Head still bowed, the pitiful creature hugged his all too Human arms even closer around his very Eyon torso, as if to comfort himself. He reeled visibly at San's unsubtle comment, as if the very words themselves had the power to wound him. Pain lanced through San's heart that he had been so inconsiderate, so insensitive and he would have gladly bitten back the words if only he could have done so.

"I no nott whatt I aamm." Rian stood, head still bowed, the picture of abject misery. "I aamm Eyyon borrnn, fromm my ownn egg-motherr. Neitherr Huumann nor Eyyon – I amm both anndd neither." Each word was spoken in misery and yet not contemptuously, not spat out but rather droned out, as if it were not the first time the words had been voiced.

San interjected. He knew the story without ever having been told it. He understood Humankind and the nature of Eyons too.

"And they laughed at you didn't they? The Pets? They laughed and made fun of you! The Eyon who would never be able to fly, the Human with an Eyon body."

San could picture it all so clearly. Could picture too, how the solitary Eyons would react, how they would keep their distance even more than normal, from something they could not relate to – *someone* they could not relate to.

"I couldnn't fly, I couldnn't connectt to the machinesss. I wassn't wortthy. Yett I was toleratedd." Rian's head seemed to have sunk even lower onto his chest. "Butt when the time camme to havve my ownn housse and Pett I couldnn't."

"I didnn't wantt all tthe pitying loooks frromm the Petss anymore, all the whispered commentss I could underssstand. Sso I lefftt."

Rian slumped to the ground as if the effort of relating his tale had stolen the last of his energy. With legs which suddenly seemed to have lost their solidity, San carefully lowered himself to the ground as though he were a very old and very frail man. He felt very weak.

It was all just too much to take in at once. Yet after a moment, he became aware of the leather strap bound around his upper arm, keeping the necklet close and hidden from view. He too had kept a secret from this new companion, hadn't he?

He reached under his sleeve once more, and untied the strap as he had so recently done with Jed. Palming the necklet before it had time to fall to the ground, he held it out for Rian to take. Gently, as if he was afraid that San would recoil in horror from his touch, Rian accepted it from him.

"Whatt isss thisss?"

"I don't know. I was kind of hoping that you would."

"Tell mmee whatt yoo do knoww off itt." Rian held the necklet in his palm, fingers closed over and around it as if he was absorbing energy or heat or something from it.

"You can't see in this light, but it has something carved onto it. It looks like the top half of one body and the bottom section of another. I think my mother might have given me it."

"Yesss maybee. Thatt may welll bee sso." He paused for a moment. "I haav neverr seeenn anythingg like thiss butt itt musstt meen somthingg."

"Yes, I think so too. So I need to find my mother and find out why I have this. And why I am so different." In a strange way he felt guilty about suggesting that he was different to other Humans. It almost felt as if he were just acting sorry for himself with no good cause, unlike Rian who clearly was so different from others of his kind. If Rian could even be said to have a kind, he was so utterly unique.

In a quiet hesitant voice, Rian offered his own tale.

"I wass hatchedd thiss waay...came rite owtt off my eggg with fingerss and toess...and feathersss. Myy eggg motherr didn't really care...butt herr Pett lafffedd and laffedd..." Rian broke off in pain at the memory.

San was tempted to reach out to him, to offer some consolation but he didn't want Rian to think he pitied him. So he stayed quiet and let Rian continue in his own time.

"Her Pett wass a girll, a womann really, cruel and nassty. Shhee prettendedd to bee myy frendd. Andd shhee toldd mee too pluukk the feathersss owt." Rian's voice had grown thick with remembered pain. Tears coursed down San's face as he visualised the young Rian plucking out his feathers in desperation to fit in.

"Therree wass blooodd everywherre...andd painn. I pluukkdd them all owt...andd shhee just laffed and laffed."

San waited for him to continue in the ensuing silence, wishing that he had the woman in front of him right now. He had never hated anyone he hadn't ever met before but somehow it did not seem inappropriate.

"Andd all the Pettss laffedd wenn they ssaw mee. The Eyonn with no feathersss, justt arms and toes." His despair was palpable.

Like being dealt physical blow, San felt himself sway, as Rian uttered the words.

"And your feathers, they grew back didn't they?" He asked, already knowing the answer. There was a lump in his throat that was hard to get the words past.

"Yesss thay grew bakk ...butt the name callingg andd the jokes didntt endd. Aandd what made itt worsss wass that I couldd understand them. I neww what they wwerr sayying."

San was sickened by the account of the torture which must have filled Rian's every waking moment. He tried to reassure him. "Not all Humans are like that Rian. In fact most probably aren't ..." He didn't know how to continue. What could he say...that Rian had just been unlucky? That was just too much of an understatement. So he said nothing.

"I could havv left yoo beforr yoo…beforr yoo saw meee for what I amm. I could havv told myself that itt was better for yoo, betterr for mee." Rian seemed to be struggling to put his thoughts into words. "Butt now I cann see that yoo arr diffferentt too other Pettss. Sso I willl hellp yoo findd whatt yoo arr looking forr. I knoww howw itt feeells too bee diffferentt." He paused a moment and San stayed quiet, not trusting himself to be able to speak if he opened his mouth.

"I know that therr arr Huumann villages farr behind uss back the way wee havv come. Butt thatt wwould mmean turninngg backkk anddd I don't thinkk thatt iss a verry goood idea.

Farr to the sside off uss lie Eyon forests…but ahead iss unknown. Yett I feeell that it iss therr thatt yoo will findd the answers yoo seeekk. Anndd I willl help yoou," he reiterated.

San felt the pinprick of tears start at the corners of his eyes. Rian had been so mocked, so derided and reviled all his life. He had been treated as an abomination, an abhorrence against nature and yet he was still so willing to help a virtual stranger, to put San's needs before his own considerations.

"No, I can't let you do that." Close to tears San's voice had lost all sense of conviction. "The Pets in my home all talk of the wars. Of course no one has seen them exactly but the say that they are terrible, that the villages of Humans are dirty and war-torn, that Humans are vicious without Eyons." San felt repulsion at the idea that Humans could treat each other so badly.

"Vishuss Huumans, I havv already hadd experience off," Rian added wryly, "though I havv seen no warrsss, although in my village too they talk off such thinggss.

Aandd I willl help yoo." It was a statement, not a suggestion. San was deeply touched at the generousity of spirit his companion showed. He wondered if the situation were reversed, if he could have been as brave, as self-sacrificing, as willing to endanger himself to help another.

And there was something else too...something which could not be seen with the eye, only felt with the heart, a pure clear light emanating from deep within, unsullied by petty considerations of appearance.

Grey feathers undistinguished by any bright bold colours were further dulled by grime and debris, yet an inner radiance shone out of his eyes, as if this mortal body were but a good disguise for some kind of other being – one which was too good for this earthly plane. Almost transcendental, Rian was beautiful.

And the more San looked at him, the more this inner beauty seemed to transform his unusual exterior so that what had before jarred the eye, now caught it with such exquisite grace.

"Don't you know what you *really* look like?" asked San wonderingly. It was only when Rian seemed to hunch down even further into himself, hiding his face in his hands, that San realised his mistake.

"I mean ...don't you see how *beautiful* you are? Don't you see that once the initial surprise of seeing you is over, that somehow you look *right*. Because you do, and that's the weirdest thing...you actually look as though you were meant to be how you are."

Rian was silent, so San continued, the words now bubbling out of him with no prior consideration – they were just the truth and didn't need to be held back or analysed.

"Rian, there is a light which shines from you. I don't know how or even why…but its there and anyone who doesn't see it …well *they* are the unworthy ones," San finished. There was no more to say for he had spoken the truth. Every word had come straight from his heart.

Matted hair obscuring his face, San couldn't tell if his words had comforted Rian at all. It was only when the young Eyon raised his face to the firelight that San saw the effect his speech had had. Before him was a countenance which shone with goodness, as if it were imbued with the whole world's share of kindness and decency.

"Sann, my friendd – may I call yoou thaat, it iss a termm I haave never beeen able to usse before – yoou are a goood persson andd I amm gladdened to haave mett yoou."

"Lett uss sitt awhile annd bee warmed by the fire. Anndd thenn wee will continuu our jounrney. Butt whenn wee findd the Huummans, andd whenn yoo arr safe thenn our pathss must part. Yoou have lightened my haart but the world iss yett a crool place and I will nott willingly hinder yoou by stayying with yoo."

"Of course you may call me friend and I hope that I may call you the same Rian. I will sit quietly and if it helps you to talk about yourself, then you have a willing listener. But if you do not wish to relive those times, then I understand." He paused, not really wanting to say the next part, but knowing that he must, that it was only fair.

"And I understand that you may feel you need to leave me there, but maybe it won't be like that. Maybe you will find a place where you feel you belong, where things are right for you." San was quite amazed at how tactful he had managed to sound. In truth, he wasn't sure if this could really happen but they both needed some hope.

They sat in silence for a moment or two before Rian seemed to relax. Holding his hands out to the warmth of the flames, he fixed his gaze on their flickering light and talked, his voice full of emotion.

After a while they spoke of other things and found a gentle companionship in discussing the merits of tree house life. It seemed that the everyday aspects of their lives were filled with the same mundane realities.

"And what are those machines anyway?" San asked finally.

"Thaat I do nooo," laughed Rian. "Theyy are worrkkk. Theyy arrr the thinnngss that arrr needed."

"The things that are needed?" echoed San.

"Yessss, the fooodss thaat arrr neeeded by the Ownersss aand the Petss aand requestss forr otherr thingsss thaat arr needed," explained Rian.

"Other things that are needed…" mused San. He was aware that he was repeating what Rian said but he couldn't seem to stop himself.

"But where do all those things come from?" he asked.

"Thaat I dooo not no."

"Do you know anything else about the machines?" asked San, genuinely curious now.

"Yessss. The machinnnesss tell who isss doing whattt and wherrr."

"Who is doing what and where…like the Pets in my home?" San was so surprised at this his whole body turning towards Rian in the asking of the question.

"Nooo, nottt the Pettsss, the Ownersss…and other plasess."

Other places? What other places? San was dumbfounded and it took him a moment to respond.

"What other places?" he asked, his voice unintentionally sharp.

Rian gave no answer this time, merely shook his head to indicate he knew no more.

They sat in silence for a while.

"I'm able to walk again now, if you are?" San deliberately chose not to refer to Rian's previous assertion that their paths would eventually diverge.

"Yesss I amm ready tooo."

San didn't think he was mistaken when he heard the touch of relief in Rian's voice. Each of them, for their own reasons perhaps, needed each other.

Together they kicked the dying embers of the flames and extinguished its heat and light. Without the revealing flicker of the firelight it would have been easy for San to believe that he was just talking to another Human. Easy to forget that here was something, *someone* so unique, that he might for once get some insight into all the mysteries which confounded him.

But there was much that Rian did not know. He didn't know why the Eyons were so solitary. He didn't know why they chose to fill their time with work. And most of all he didn't know where he could fit in.

After a while they became too tired to talk and walked awhile in silence, continuing to push on into the treacly blackness. Fragments of his conversation with Rian, echoed around in San's head. There was just the smallest glimmer of a memory lurking there right at the back of his mind.

The fingers of his right hand flexed unnoticed as he chased the flicker of memory around his head before managing to corner it. Mentally he grasped it and shook it out flat and open in his mind, like a rug on the ground.

"We get trained, don't we?" he asked suddenly. Sensing Rian's confusion he tried to elaborate. "When I was younger and OwnSan cooked with me watching him, he wasn't just cooking to feed me was he? He was teaching me how to cook!" he heard his own voice rise an octave in surprise.

"He was training me!" he exclaimed. "He was, wasn't he?" It was suddenly important to him to seek his new friend's opinion.

"Yesss training forr wenn yooo didd itt alone," agreed Rian.

"And the Eyons who flew into the store house with huge packs on their backs, then emerged a little later without those same packs... they were restocking with fresh supplies." No longer needing Rian to confirm it, San's mind roared with connections.

Caught up in this reverie, he didn't see the bush directly ahead of him until he had slammed his whole body into the thick of it. One branch smacked him squarely in the face whilst another did the same with his legs. Startled out of his inner thoughts, too fast to take stock of the situation, his first impulse was to fight. He grappled with the branches, twisting them backwards and forwards and kicking, before his brain registered that there was no real resistance, only that of the foliage itself.

Simultaneously amused and disgusted at himself for his ability to be terrified and captured by a bush, he let go of the branches and sidestepped away, brushing any stray leaves from his clothing. Rian waited patiently to one side, not laughing not making fun of him in any way.

And it was this quiet empathy which made him realise just how deeply hurt the young Eyon had been, by the cruel taunts and remarks. A strange and previously unconsidered thought struck him. Perhaps being human and having humanity were not necessarily the same thing. Perhaps humanity was not an integral part of human nature, nor indeed the sole prerogative of humans.

Now that he remembered so clearly, he wondered how he had ever forgotten so much. There were so many memories. OwnSan gently tucking him into bed at night, his talons trying to pull the covers over San without ripping the fabric to shreds. Being pushed into the cleaning cubicle while OwnSan stood outside it, his wing extended in through the slightly open doors, to press the controls.

"I laughed and laughed as his wing got soaked," he remembered. But he had been surprised at how delicate and thin the bones beneath had been, when they could be made out against the wet feathers. Then as the drying cycle had begun, he had watched fascinated as the feathers dried and puffed up to their usual magnificent plumage.

The recent image of the wet feathers on OwnSan's chest came to the forefront of his mind once more, that sickening hollow and shame flooded over him once more.

He shoved the image to the back of his mind. What was done was done. But he would make sure it was never done again.

"When did I take over looking after him and me?" He couldn't be sure but was fairly certain he must have been about six at the time.

Looking at the evidence it would have been easy to conclude that Eyons had Pets solely to train them as servants, but in his heart San knew that was not true. There was a bond of love there and it flowed as strongly and surely in one direction as it did in the other. How awful it was to think that Rian had never experienced anything like that in his life.

Yet San had left all that behind. He had had to. Perhaps one love, regardless of its strength, could just not make up for other things which were missing, for swome other kind of love that he could not even define yet.

Tiredly, they trudged on, sometimes talking, sometimes silent. For some reason he couldn't explain, San was determined to just keep putting one aching foot in front of the other, until daylight appeared or until he became too exhausted and had to stop to rest. Or until his feet actually fell off the ends of his legs or just plain disintegrated, which he was beginning to believe was entirely possible.

Only after a while, did he realise that he was no longer lifting his feet cleanly from the ground but was instead using a shuffling movement to keep going forward. By now the first signs of dawn were appearing, a thin light trying to edge away the darkness.

They halted for a moment to assess the unfamiliar surroundings.

Funny how the bush looming right in front of them suddenly seemed larger, and look, it got larger again. And Rian too, standing next to him, just an arm span away, suddenly seemed to be growing taller and taller.

His tired mind, starved of sleep was desperately trying to tell him something but for the life of him he didn't know what it was. There was just this miniscule little voice, whispering right at the back of his skull and so he tried to concentrate, even as he watched fascinated as the bush got even bigger till it was looming right over him. Then suddenly the voice in his head found a way to shout, to really, really shout, "sinking …I'm in sinking sand."

His brain suddenly seemed unusually capable of running two separate but simultaneous trains of thought with one marvelling over the absurdity of thinking that both the bush and Rian were growing and the other frantically panicking and planning an escape route. Aware of the two inner conversations, San wisely chose to consciously ignore one and focus on the other.

"Grraabbbb the bushhh!" cried Rian.

San reached out and managed to grasp a part of the looming bush, just as the mud now encasing his legs up to and including his knees, gave forth a horrible sucking sound.

"Hollldddd onnn."

"I'm holding on! Hurry!" implored San, feeling the bush start to give in to the strain. In the few seconds that it took Rian to skirt around the edge of the mud, to the other side of the bush, San was sucked even deeper into the bog. He had a feeling that once it reached his waist, there would be no getting back out.

" Jussstttt hollldddd onnn."

Rian thrust his body into the midst of the shrub, using his weight to hold the roots down, to prevent them from being dislodged, whilst San grappled with the other side. The bush bent further sideways, straining at the enclosing earth, but held its ground. Hand over hand, San used its leverage to claw his way out of the bog until he was lying full length beside it on the ground.

Day had dawned during the long moments of his struggle and the perspiration of fear and effort beaded both his and Rian's faces. San was further dishevelled by being caked in thick, smelly, sticky mud. Aware of what a close call he had just had, he was for a moment, speechless.

"Itt sseemsss thattt yooo arr nott safe alonnn Saann. I will havv to watch ovverr yoo all the time." They were true words but spoken with a soft smile.

"Thank you Rian." San wasn't sure if he was thanking him for saving him, or for the offer of accompanying him for as long as he needed him to. In truth, he thought it was both. And as he turned his head in the blossoming daylight, to find swamp surrounding him in every direction, he was more than a little relieved at Rian's offer.

Patches of dark glistening mud seemed to undulate in the early morning sun for as far as the eye could see, alternating with clumps of bushes and scrub, to make a truly unlovely landscape. He compared this sight to the memory of his beautiful home in Low Forest. The two places were worlds apart.

He was exhausted physically and mentally. He could go no further. But neither would he be able to sleep. The rumbling in his stomach had worsened and now threatened to overwhelm him.

"I'm hungry. Do you have any food left?" he asked hopefully.

"No, there isss nothinn lefftt. Stayy heerrr I willl search for foooddd." Rian's tone made it clear he thought San would only land himself in more trouble. San had to concede that maybe he had a point!

He watched as Rian carefully negotiated his way through the bog until he was no longer in sight. But it's awful hard to sit still and wait when your stomach is crawling with hunger and finally he was forced to do a little searching of his own.

Having demanded food for so long and being consequently ignored, the rumbling in his stomach had increased to volcanic proportions and with every step he took it lurched with painful spasms. But it was not just food his body craved. It was water too. His heart sank at the thought.

Exhausted, he lifted his head once more to survey the terrain. Rian was still nowhere in sight, nor was there any evidence of food anywhere. Neither would there be any clean water to be had here, not in this swamp. But perhaps the water at the edge of the swampy patches would be ok to drink. He would have to take a look.

Unable to lift his feet off the ground anymore, racked with fatigue as he was, he shuffled over to the nearest bog. His mind was trying to shout loud in his head but only the tinniest internal voice could be heard. This little inner voice was worried. He could hear the anxiety in it but for a moment he was confused about the need for it.

"Don't go too close. Stay away from the edge. Don't lean over the swamp. Don't…" the voice trailed off as his conscious mind took over.

The liquid in the bog was *something*, but that something definitely wasn't drinking water, that was for sure. The bogs hadn't just been appearing to undulate in the sunshine, they actually *were* undulating. Tiny bubbles floated on the surface of the mud, as little insects hovered above, occasionally dipping into the bubbles to deposit something.

His exhausted mind looked in awe at the little creatures. He had never seen anything like them before, or if he had, then he had never really *noticed* them. Their tiny wings were iridescent in the morning sun, seeming to shiver with an ever-changing array of colours as they hovered. They appeared to be almost completely still, just sort of hanging in the air. But if you looked closely enough you could see the furious beating of their wings. All that effort just to stay still.

The world really was a wondrous place and he had never seen that before. How many wonders would he miss if he just lay there and died, he mused. His head almost hurting with the effort, he wondered just how long it would take him to die if he didn't *try* to drink the murky liquid. Then in a moment of blinding clarity, he realised what the tiny insects were doing at the swamp. He wondered how many insect eggs were contained in just one of those bubbles. Millions probably!

But however many or few, he knew it would be too many for him and he would either be very ill for a very long time, or if he was lucky he might just die outright. Suddenly the absurdity of the situation struck him and he tried to laugh.

"Die if you drink the stuff, die if you don't!" But the laugh caught in his parched throat and resulted in a wheezy rasp.

He sank to his knees in despair, his body sliding down in defeat. All hope was lost. He had no idea where Rian was or even where the bush was that he was supposed to have stayed by. He had been foolish to have wandered off again, so it was really no surprise to find himself in this predicament.

His eyes took in the scene around him, to immortalise his final resting place but something wasn't quite right. There was something red filling his vision, not the brown and grey of the bogs and scrub surrounding them. And there was something blue too.

His mind frantically tried to assimilate what it was seeing with what it knew already. The sky. The sky was the blue thing. Somehow he had turned his body as he had slumped to the ground. And the blue he could see was the sky. But what was the red thing? He squinted his eyes, trying to focus them.

It was not a red thing. It was *many* red things. Berries. Hundreds and thousands of bright, red, shiny berries bursting from the branches of a large shrub. Just waiting there to be eaten, they were his for the taking.

"Food… FOOD." He wasn't even aware that he had spoken, so narrow was his focus. Energy renewed by this promise of immediate gratification, he managed to pull himself back into a sitting position. From there he stood, oblivious to the aches and pains in his limbs and how his muscles screamed for rest.

"Rian, Rian. I've found us food." But there was no response. Either Rain was too far away to hear or his shout had not been as loud as he intended. He would try again in a moment, he vowed.

Bunch after bunch of wild red berries he plucked, stuffing them into his mouth with abandon, uncaring of his filthy hands. The juice ran down his chin and at first pooled in the neckline of his top, before eventually soaking into it. Red berry juice merged with red top. Only the wetness and stiffening of the material betrayed the truth of his desperate gorging. It was not something he was overly concerned about, especially in comparison to his mud encrusted trousers.

The berries were a strange and unfamiliar taste but not entirely unpleasant. They were a peculiar combination of sweet and sour but with a rather bitter aftertaste. But the aftertaste didn't worry him too much, for as soon as one bunch was devoured, he moved on to the next. The bitterness was thus disguised by the next mouthful of fruit.

Finally, appetite sated, he stopped. His stomach was still cramping but he was fairly sure the pain would stop soon. Perhaps, more importantly, the juice had given his body its much needed liquid. Now what it demanded was rest. As the berry bush had already fulfilled one of his needs, he figured it would perhaps be good luck to use it for this need too.

Wearily he crawled under the thick branches for whatever protection they offered and curled himself into a ball. Mercifully, sleep claimed him immediately and he was oblivious to the discomfort of his wet and dirty clothing. His breathing became deeper and more regulated as his sleeping body took in lungfuls of the scent of warm damp earth. He slept as all around him the world came back to life.

# *Chapter 10.*

Now the sun was high in the sky and the day looked to be already established, as stretching and yawning, Loni and Little awoke and rose from their makeshift beds. The long grass was flattened where they had lain but not with a true impression of their individual body shapes.

Instead, they appeared to have rolled around in their sleep, distorting the image so that it looked as if two horrendously misshapen monsters had suddenly fallen down to slumber peacefully together in the grass.

Drawing herself up to her full fourteen year old height, Loni winced for two reasons. Firstly and most importantly, every joint, sinew and muscle in her body throbbed and as if that wasn't punishment enough, secondly she realised in her haste and single-mindedness to leave, she had pulled on a pale lemon short sleeved top and a pink skirt. Not only were these a ridiculous combination in their own right, but she had managed to outdo herself by wearing one white sock and one pink sock. She would certainly not go unnoticed by anyone they happened to meet!

Little was also standing now and looking at the flattened grass "OOOEEEEE HHHEEEHHHEEE," he giggled.

"I know, it looks as though a big fat monster lay there, instead of just a girl and a baby Eyon," she agreed.

Little wasn't happy with the reference to a baby apparently as he looked her right in the eye and stated, "FFFFGGGGGGGGYYYYRRR."

Loni didn't have a clue what this meant but she was able to interpret it anyway, due to the hurt look Little was exhibiting and the fact that he was almost standing on the tips of his feet-talons, trying to make himself as tall as possible.

"I didn't mean, like a *baby*, I mean a real baby, all newly hatched and everything. I just meant a young Eyon, not fully grown," she hastily backtracked.

"OKKK Lonee," Little seemed to concede the point and let her off the hook. Loni let her indrawn breath out. She had learned early on not to upset Little. Wonderful as he was, he was a terrible sulk when really upset and would go in a huff forever if necessary, dragging himself around and looking miserable.

Legs aching from the punishment of the long walk she had already dealt them, Loni knew that any pains she and Little already had, were probably about to get much worse before they got any better. All she could see was grass.

"Grass, grass, grass and even more grass," she muttered to herself. In every direction. Long, long grass which rose to her hips and made walking hard work, as it involved more of a sort of high kicking swishing gait to wade through it, than a normal stride.

Glancing at Little, she was surprised to see how unperturbed he seemed by their predicament. Then again, maybe with his strange sort of rolling hip gait, this sort of terrain actually suited him better. Of course he also had the option of flying. But she didn't. And it wasn't fair to expect him to fly carrying her for any length of distance.

Trampling down the remaining high grass between the two flattened areas, she turned the site into a makeshift picnic area.

"It's not ideal but it's soft enough at least." She divided the food carefully. She had to make sure they ate enough to keep their strength up but not enough to make them feel too full to move quickly. More importantly, she had to ensure that there was enough food left, to see them through the rest of the day and possibly the next day as well. After that...who knew?

"Well at least there's one good thing about eating on the run," she said wryly, "no dishes to be washed afterwards!" Little chuckled, willing as ever to join in on the joke. If Loni thought it was amusing, then so did he!

They ate in silence, each pondering their own thoughts. Loni was dismayed at how little food they had left. Very soon, they'd have none at all. It was her problem and therefore up to her to solve it. Whatever food they had left she would give to him. But what happened when there was none left. What did they do then? Return home? No, not an option, or at least not an option *yet*, not till some time had passed anyway.

"We *have* to find another Eyon forest, we have to see if there are differences there. Then when we have done that, when we have proved that you don't need to be hooked up, then we can concentrate on finding our way back home." She stated it matter-of-factly, as if it was already a known fact that Eyons lived different lifestyles elsewhere, refusing to give in to the fear which gripped her heart. She had to be strong, for both of them.

And she couldn't let considerations of how they were ever going to *find* the way back, when the time came, sway them from their purpose. They had left to avoid Little being hooked up, to show that they would not accept that. And they wouldn't. Ever.

"Essss Lonnee. Nootherrr forressstttt," he agreed as if it was just something they did every day. Find another forest, get the Eyons there to communicate with the Eyons back home, find the way home and live there happily ever after.

So why if it was so simple, was there a gnawing churning feeling in the pit of Loni's fairly empty stomach? Unable to face her fears head-on, she changed the subject, as much to distract herself as to distract Little.

"Did you enjoy that, Little?" she asked smiling and already knowing what the answer would be.

"GOOOODDD OOOOODDD!" he responded, smacking his lips together for emphasis. All food tasted good to him!

Breakfast over, they resumed their walk. At least the long grass made it easy to see the path they had taken so far. It was trampled in their wake and looking back Loni was relieved to see that they seemed to have followed an almost perfectly straight line since they had entered the meadow.

"Look we're going straight on. That ought to mean that we'll not go round and round in endless circles. And eventually we will come out to what lies beyond here," she informed him. "What do you think we'll find Little?"

"OOODDD, OOODDD, OOODDD!" he replied, his eyes crinkling at the sides so that she wasn't sure if he was making his own joke or whether he really did think they'd find piles of food at the edge of the grassland.

"Well, at least we're heading somewhere, not wasting our energy chasing our tails, or at least your tiny pink and green tail feathers."

For hours and hours they walked, sometimes side by side, sometimes one after the other, when the grass became too thick and hard going, taking turns to lead. It was more logical that Little go in the lead. He was both wider and taller than Loni and could therefore make a good clear path for her to follow. But this didn't seem right.

It occurred to Loni that the most danger lay in the unknown, so most of the time she took the lead and kept Little safe behind her. She had no idea if the wars waged by the Humans were contained within the villages themselves, or whether they spilled out into surrounding areas. So it paid to be careful. She also needed to keep a lookout for any Eyon places.

"Do you think that Owners and Pets always live in tree houses?" she asked Little, who seemed surprised at the question.

"Wwaatt?" he responded.

"Do you think that Owners and Pets always live in tree houses?" she repeated, unsure as to whether he didn't understand the question or what she meant by it.

"Doooh ohhh," was the unexciting response, which caused them both to lapse into silence for a while, frustrated at their inability to communicate more clearly.

Using her arms as much as her legs, Loni pushed and stomped her way through the field, making the path as wide as possible for him.

"Are you ok, Little?" she asked periodically, just to make sure he still was.

"ESSSSSSSSSSS, OKK," was his constant response although it sometimes varied from loud and exuberant to quiet and reflective.

In a strange way, it was one of the most exasperating and yet exhilarating experiences Loni realised she would ever have. Always close from the very first moment, this experience was drawing her even *closer* to Little, making them more fully aware of each other's intentions, even if language sometimes got in the way.

Occasionally they rested. Little tried hard not to show it, but Loni always knew when he needed to rest. First of all he began to slow down, then his eyelids began to droop and his voice to slur. Finally as he became too tired to continue, his already hip-swishing gait became more erratic and he stumbled rather than walked.

What concerned her, was that his need for a rest was becoming more and more frequent and the periods between rests were shortening. How much longer could he kekp this up? On the other hand, surely the sooner they got out of the long grass the better, the more likely they were to find food. Yet again, if he needed to rest, should she be pushing him to go on? Her mind was in turmoil.

Then suddenly, for no real reason that she could see, they began to communicate better that they ever had before. She wondered why this should be so. Was it just that now words and the communication that went with them, had a greater importance? Or was it that they were more in tune with one another? Or just that here, they had time to listen properly with no distractions and no beeping machines in the background? Just time, space and the soothing rhythm of walking together?

She decided to test her theory out. "All those times when we played games, why do you think no-one joined in?" she enquired.

"ESSS AAMESSS!" he gasped excitedly.

Belatedly she realised he hadn't caught the full meaning of her question. She tried again. "No, not *now,* not games *now*! I said why do you think no-one joined in? When we played games I mean?"

"TOOOOO OOOOODDDDDDD."

Loni couldn't help but let loose a huge chuckle. "OF COURSE! You're absolutely right, we just played too good for anyone else!"

And she noticed something else. Little was getting closer to an approximation of human speech. Not all the time, or even with any level of consistency, but sometimes, just *sometimes* he said something that sounded more than just vaguely human. A word here, a syllable there or even just something about the intonation but there was something, definitely something.

The village came into view by surprise and they had already taken a final step out of the meadow before they even realised it, so deep were they in exchanging information.

Roofs, their thatches shinning golden under the midday sun, were nestled on top of solid timber framed huts. The huts were huddled close together in a seemly random formation. And yet something about them suggested that it wasn't random at all. An amazed glance passed between Little and Loni. Never before had either of them seen, or heard of such a thing.

Tree houses, devoid of their trees and instead plonked squarely on the bare ground! And so close together! Didn't the Eyons who lived there need their privacy as much as those who lived in "High Woods"?

Unable to accept what her eyes were telling her brain, Loni stood transfixed to the spot, clutching Little's wing to prevent him blundering onwards. This was a new and unexpected development and they had to think carefully how to proceed…

And then fate stepped in, in the form of a gaggle of young children, who suddenly spilled forth from one of the houses, screaming in mock terror and oblivious to the strangers in their midst.

Time seemed to suddenly stand still. Then, as if in slow motion, the children turned. All together in formation, much as a flock of birds would, they altered direction and immediately everything changed once more.

Startled by the appearance of the strangers, the children in the lead came to an abrupt halt, causing the children in the middle and back of the crowd to slam into the ones at the front, quite *unlike* the grace and symmetry of birds.

It was anyone's guess who looked the most amazed – the gaggle of dishevelled, raggedy, barefoot children, or the equally dishevelled but finely, if rather bizarrely, clothed Human and her Eyon companion.

Held in a timeless bubble, both groups were frozen, immobile, each drinking in the differences in the others' appearances. It was probably the sudden cessation of noise which alerted the others to the fact that something had happened.

Her skirt covered in what appeared to be flour, a woman emerged from the closest hut, wiping her hands on a towel and with a look of vague rapprochement on her face. It was only when she saw the halted bunch of children, still rooted to the spot and following their gaze, saw what had rooted them there, that she screamed.

And Loni instinctively knew and recognised the scream. It was a full out and out terror scream of the sort that cannot be mistaken.

And Loni's response? Well in the face of all that terror and unpredictability she let her own vocal chords have their way …and she returned the scream.

# Chapter 11.

Someone was washing San's face with a rough hot towel, that had a strange off- putting odour to it and a coarseness that tickled the skin it touched. He tried to swipe it away but only succeeded in having the palms of his hands washed too. Whoever it was, was certainly persistent.

It had to be OwnSan, even though he had never used this tactic to wake San before. Eyes kept tightly shut he could almost believe that he was at home in bed and everything *he thought* had happened the previous night had all been just a dream. Except that his bed felt harder than usual and the air didn't smell like home. So if he wasn't at home and it wasn't OwnSan washing him, then..?

Eyelids wrenched open to their widest possible dimensions, he stared at the strangest creature he had ever seen. Rows of sharp pointed gleaming white teeth were visible from the creature's open mouth, which seemed to be laughing at him. He wasn't sure if this was a good or bad sign. A large lolling tongue drooped from one corner of the mouth, glossy with thick saliva. And even as he watched, the giant mouth came closer once more and the tongue descended to his face, wiping its icky foul smelling drool all the way up from his chin, to the tip of his nose.

Without even consciously realising what he was doing, San sat bolt upright and scooted away from the thing, wiping his face roughly with his arm as he did so. But rather than follow him, the thing chose to sit down on its hind legs - he could see that it had no arms or wings, only four identical length legs- and wait, keeping its eyes riveted on him. From this further perspective, he could view the whole of the creature, not just its mouth. And it *was* the weirdest thing he had ever seen.

Dark brown hair covered the whole of its body, thick and dense but short and coarse and *different* to Human hair. There were no feathers, wings, arms or fingers, but there were claws, although these were not sharp and fiercesome but small and blunt looking instead.

Four legs connected to a short stumpy body, which had at one end a hairy tail that moved from side to side continuously, and at the other, a head with strange features. Two ears, two eyes and a nose, that looked as though someone had got hold of it and used it to stretch the face out to make a whole new different shape.

It didn't appear to be particularly vicious but he wasn't going to take any chances. Pulling himself up to his full height, he found he towered above the creature, which was a good start. Baring his teeth in what he hoped was a terrifying display, he waved his arms at the creature which now stood staring at him with rapt attention.

"Shoo. Shoo. SHOO!" he cried, each one louder and fiercer than the last.

All the vigorous movements made him even more queasy and suddenly his sick stomach presented his tongue with a mouthful of thick putrid bile. His cheeks bulged with the effort of containing it and his eyes bulged in sympathy. Sweat beaded his brow and he was both hot and cold simultaneously. His brain didn't seem to know whether it should be trying to swallow it back down or spitting it out. And all the while the strange thing looked on, unmoving apart from its long tail which continued to swish backwards and forwards and the panting sound that issued from its still open mouth.

"Shoo." There was less conviction in the cry this time, as a more urgent need came calling upon his poor wracked body. Alone with the strange thing, scared and in the middle of a horrid swampy bog, having eaten poisonous fruit, San could see no point in holding on.

Cold, clammy hands pulling at his clothing, fingers frantically fumbling with buttons, he ripped his trousers and pants off together, and let them fall unheeded at his feet. Then, having enough presence of mind to move slightly away, he emptied his bowels and his stomach in simultaneous actions, his body jerking first one way and then the other.

On and on it went. Even after the time when San though he must surely be empty, it went on. And on. And the thing stayed with him, refusing to leave.

"Are you enjoying watching me like this?" he moaned at the animal, embarrassed and humiliated that *anyone* should see him thus incapacitated, even if it was just some weird creature. The thing made no sound, just continued to regard him with its big eyes and sharp teeth.

"Well I guess I'm safe from you. If you were going to eat me you would have done it by now."

The creature gave a low whining sound. San wasn't sure if that was an agreement with what he had said, or a disagreement.

"Course I don't reckon I taste very good at the moment." And maybe that was the point, maybe the thing was waiting till he was well, before devouring him. He knew he should be worried but he had no energy left for that somehow, he was too busy dealing with the aches of his wracked body.

After what appeared to be a very long time, the pain began to subside but it was replaced by something equally horrendous. A fever had him in its grip and now it began to squeeze tighter. Beads of perspiration popped out all over his body and he became slick with greasy sweat. His teeth which somehow felt soft in his mouth, began to chatter with cold and his body was shaken by violent shivering.

Eyelids beginning to close automatically, his vision was reduced in stages, as the blinds to his eyes were lowered, without his permission. Just at the last possible moment before he became unconscious, the tiny little voice in his head spoke up again. Luckily it warned him to fall only onto his right side, away from the mess he had emitted. He didn't even feel the creature settle itself by his side, curling itself into him and whimpering lowly.

Nor was he aware of Rian finding him much later, after searching for some time. He was not aware of the fresh water his friend trickled into the side of his mouth as he lay unconscious on the ground, or of being moved away from the mess. Nor was he aware of the fear Rian had felt when he saw San guarded by the strange creature and the bravery he had shown in approaching anyway. None of this concerned him.

He was hot but he was cold. Or more accurately the skin that covered his body was hot, but inside it, there was only cold. No, not skin. He didn't have any of that. It was something that *looked* like skin, that *felt* like skin, that even *acted* like skin. But it *wasn't* skin.

"Fightt the feever Saan. I willl sstaayy byy yoor side buutt yoo musstt fight itt!" Rian continued to cool San's face with splashes of clean water and drip it into his partially open mouth.

"Keeep drinkkinnn iff yooo caann," Rian urged, watching San's throat as it struggled to swallow the small amount of liquid there.

"WOOF WOOF," the strange creature seemed to agree, trying to lick Rian now as he bent over San.

"Stopp thaatt!" Rian admonished but there was no anger in his voice and the creature disregarded it anyway, returning its attention back to San.

San was only very vaguely aware of this noise and it had no relevance to him. He was made of some kind of metal. Silver and shiny and glinting in the sun. But he wasn't working right. His core temperature was too low for correct operational purposes. He would have to raise it somehow.

"Too cold..." He hissed through clenched teeth.

Just as he reached that conclusion, his delirium changed focus as his fevered mind tried to expel the poison from his body and fight the invading bacteria.

Now he was a boy again, not a metal thing but a *very* young boy. And he was on the back of a large Eyon. An Eyon who wasn't OwnSan. And there was something different about this particular Eyon, something around the eyes. Almost as if this one had a more gritty determination about its tasks than OwnSan, a steelier core.

"You're not OwnSan," he mumbled.

"Noo, I amm Riiaannn, remember?" soothed the Eyon, mistaking San's comment as being about him.

And then in San's memory, he and the Eyon were flying high in the sky. San reached up to the sky with both arms, trying to touch the sun. Instead, his flailing arms caught the hair of the strange creature around the neck and dragged it down towards him again, from where it had arisen.

Rian cast a worried eye at the sick boy with a tight hold on the unknown creature but to his relief the animal did not look in the least vicious anymore. It merely resumed its former licking of the boy's face.

"Saaannn caann yooo heeer meee?"

There was no response, or rather, no rational one.

The delirious San tried to shout a warning to the hallucination San, the one that he could see clearly but only in his head.

"Hold on, hold on tight!" The boy gripped the animals' hair roughly now and jerked it to the side. The thing whined but otherwise gave no reaction, seeming to understand the hurt had not been intentional.

"Yoo arrr safe noww!" rasped Rian, wondering what was going on inside San's head.

Lost in his hallucination, San tried to warn the young 'dream San'. "If you let go you will fall. You must hold on with both hands," he called. His voice sounded loud in his head but what issued from his mouth was a thin reedy whisper.

"Yoo arrr safe noww!" Other than repeating himself, Rian didn't know how else to help. So he said it again, just for good measure and just in case some of it was getting through to San's fevered brain.

"Yoo arrr safe noww!"

But the boy's perspective had shifted and he was now looking down on the Eyon and the young San from above.

"How is that possible?" his delirious mind scrabbled for an answer. "I must be able to fly." Of course he could, it was the only logical answer.

The boy didn't need to hold on with his arms around the Eyon's neck. He was strapped in to some kind of harness, which held him securely in place. And now he could see better what the real situation was. The child *hadn't* been reaching up in delight and amazement to the sky. No, he had been reaching back. Back to the place he had been taken from.

San's arms dropped sharply from the creature he had been clinging to. To Rian's surprise the thing seemed disappointed at this and sidled even closer to San, as though trying to get him to re-establish the hold.

Still oblivious to the real world, San was struck by a certainty that cut through his delirium, as only truth can do.

There were tears tracking down the child's face and his little body was wracked by spasms of grief. Lying there curled up on his side, his mouth opened and a thin stream of watery vomit projected itself from his stomach onto the hard baked earth.

He was trying to think this thought through, when another spasm wracked his body. This time his stomach emitted such thick and putrid vomit, that he could feel it coming all the way up. It clogged in his throat and filled his nostrils with a vile stench. He couldn't swallow it, he couldn't breathe. He couldn't even think anymore. He was too overwhelmed.

His body made one furious and desperate attempt to rid itself of the poison it had consumed. Vomit poured from his nostrils and mouth simultaneously, as his stomach finally emptied itself.

His temperature dropped degree by degree, the sweat on his skin cooling him down, until once again it was within the normal range. Unconscious from the effort of saving itself, his body and mind closed down for much needed repair.

The day progressed, the sun making its usual arc high in the sky, the little insects continuing to increase their numbers by laying eggs and the eggs continued to hatch into new insects. All were oblivious to the strange trio in their midst - the Eyon who cradled the head of a sick boy in his lap, and the dog who curled so snugly into the side of them.

But the unusual scents that pooled around him *had* caught their attention. Many of their species had flocked to these new and warmly viscous fluids to lay *their* eggs and now these too were undulating with aerated bubbles.

# *Chapter 12.*

Loni and the strange woman's screams seemed to gather momentum from each other, the two voices appearing to fight for supremacy of pitch and terror. There was another sound mixed in there too, a sort of high pitched whine, shrill and rasping at the same time. Loni realised that Little was screaming, in reaction to her terror. It wasn't the same as the sound she was making but it was a scream nonetheless. She turned to him, the rational part of her brain intending to stop his screaming, allay his fear. But she couldn't stop her own.

The face she turned to him therefore, was the very epitome of a mask of fear, eyes wide and face white. One look at her and he actually screamed louder than before, his own eyes growing wider and wilder. That hadn't worked, so instead, she turned away from him and towards the woman.

Their eyes locked on each other, neither Loni nor the woman seemed to pause for breath. Instead, they seemed to be drawing it into flared nostrils and back out of their wide open mouths, in a never-ending shriek. Perhaps this would have continued on endlessly, if Little hadn't had to pause for breath.

This cessation of noise on *his* part, seemed to bring about an effect in the other two. Still screaming, Loni instinctively pulled Little behind her as if to shield him, even as the woman herded all the children back into the hut, finally wrenching her eyes from them in order to slam shut the heavy door.

Her scream lessening to a wail before finally subsiding, Loni heard the sounds of a latch slamming on the door and something heavy being dragged across the floor.

Out of the corner of her eye she was aware of other figures, adults and children rushing, or being pushed and pulled into other huts. She hadn't noticed them before, so focused had she been on the woman. But there had obviously been others. Lots of them by the look of it. Yet suddenly they were alone, everyone else was gone.

Astounded and mystified as to the woman's reaction, Loni turned in a full circle before finally facing Little again.

"What just happened?" she asked, knowing full well that he didn't understand either but feeling compelled to ask anyway.

'DOH OHH LONEE.'

No, neither did she.

"They can't have thought we are savage Humans from a Human village, because you are an Eyon!" she rationalised.

Huts encircled where she now stood. They weren't houses in the same way as her tree house had been. Here, the dwellings were round, with little pointed roofs. But it wasn't just that.

Somehow these huts seemed *lesser* than her home had been. It was a funny word to use and she wasn't entirely sure herself, what she meant by it. But it fit somehow. They were definitely *lesser*. Up close the wood seemed rough hewn with bits sticking out all over the place. There must have been gaps too when it had been built and some of these seemed to have been filled in with something other than wood. Something hard and greyish coloured. She had no idea what it was.

There were no gaps in the wooden walls of her home. Her walls were smooth and shiny with each piece of wood sitting snug against its neighbour. How different it was here. And the roofs too were different. They seemed to be made of bits of twig and straw strung together. Not quite haphazard, but not too carefully placed either, they looked randomly and quickly bound and roped into place. And most strangely of all, there were no windows to be seen in any of the huts.

"Well we were looking for a place where Eyons and Pets lived a different type of life and I think we may have found it!"

Little remained silent as Loni stepped towards the hut the woman had gone in with the children. Aware that what she was about to do would disconcert these people further, if any could see her, but unable to stop herself, she reached one hand out and placed it on the wooden door.

All around her in every hut she could hear raised terrified voices and bolts being drawn across sturdy doors. There was not a single person left in sight. Fires had been left untended, chores had been abandoned and games had been forgotten.

One arm hanging limply at her side, she used the raised arm to knock lightly on the door of the hut.

"Hello?" she called. Her voice sounded strange and tentative even to her and she glanced back at Little who had remained a few steps away, watching intently.

Quiet as it had been, her call seemed to cut through all the noise coming from the huts. The air became deathly silent and still. Not a single solitary sound could be heard. One heart beat passed into two, then four, before there came a muffled but recognisable sound. What could only be a baby's cry pierced the air and was followed by a low tremulous crooning.

Loni's brain instinctively recognised that this childish wailing was different to any she had heard before...younger and more infantile. This crying came from a child much younger than any she had ever seen. It came from a baby. And babies were *never* Pets.

And her heart recognised something too. It recognised that the sound of cooing appeasement being issued to the baby, came from a human mouth, not an Eyon one. There was something so right about the sound. Not the crooning itself, that was just a song sung low and quiet. No it was the combination of the two things, the baby's cry and the answering lullaby.

Unable to look away from the door, she was forced to back up to return to where Little still stood, head cocked to one side.

"You heard it too didn't you? It was a baby, wasn't it? A real baby!"

"BAAABBBEEEEE," he mimicked. He had heard it too, but she wasn't convinced he understood the significance.

"Maybe this is a 'rehoming' village." Her tone was at first flat. This wasn't what she had been seeking at all. They would not find any answers to Little's machine dilemma here! Then as the significance of what her mouth had uttered, reached her brain, something else occurred to her.

"Maybe this is the rehoming village where *I* came from!" Her heart actually missed a beat at the thought. But alongside that interesting idea, came another one, equally as compelling but more immediately relevant.

"If this is…a village of Humans, I mean, then we are in danger!"

"Aangeeeerrr?" His raised intonation at the end served to indicate that he didn't understand.

"Danger, trouble…um," she tried to think of how to explain. "Bad for us!" she ended lamely. Little blinked his big eyes at her, his gaze not wavering from her face.

"They have wars all the time. The villages of Humans are always fighting with each other. All the Pets know that. That's why they give their children away to be Pets. To keep them safe." She wondered fleetingly why she was having to explain this to Little, why he wasn't already aware of this. But this was not the time to question him.

She cast her gaze around. There certainly didn't seem to be any fighting going on at the moment, nor did it look as though there had been any recently. Then again, what would she know.

"I'll explain later. Come on!" Dazed, she stumbled forward into the clearing at the heart of the little village, pulling Little with her. In one spot, a pile of clothes lay abandoned, either waiting to be cleaned or mended, Loni wasn't sure which. She felt a hundred eyes upon her as bending down she grasped one of the items to examine it better.

Picking it up, she realised it was a pair of roughly sewn trousers, the material equally course and rough. She had never felt anything quite like it.

"Look, trousers!" She surprised herself with how she sounded. Like she was amazed they would wear trousers! She chided herself for her foolishness.

What was strange though, was that all the garments were the same material and colour, a sort of bland beige. Ok, not identical colour, but not far off either. It was more like they had all started the same colour and some had been washed more than others. Or, the thought suddenly struck her, that in fact they were colour*less*, that the clothes were just the actual colour of the fibres used to make them.

But at least it fit with what she knew about Human villages, that life there was hard and full of squalor and deprivation. Then again, nothing here *looked* that squalid and deprived.

"Well at least they wash their clothes!" she said quietly.

Carefully she placed the trousers back on top of the pile. She still felt watched, although she knew that was unlikely. With no windows, the people in the huts would have only been able to peer out at her from the unfilled cracks. But the sensation persisted. Like pinpricks across her body her nerve endings were almost electrified. She could feel every fibre of the clothing which touched her skin, every hair follicle and every particle of dust which alighted on her. Her skin crawled with the weight of observation she was under.

It was Little who discovered the source. From her peripheral vision she saw him raise one wing and point, a hushed, "waaasssss thaaaaa?" issuing from between fear frozen lips. Very slowly and carefully she turned to where he indicated.

A pack of ferocious creatures regarded them from the other side of the clearing, long mouths left slackly open to display two rows of sharp pointed teeth. They had a confident arrogance about them, as though they knew that their own fierceness made them immune to fear. Camouflaged by the colour of their thick dark fur as they lay unmoving on the ground, it was no wonder they had not been seen.

"Don't look at them," she hissed at Little, slowly lowering his arm back to his side. "They haven't come over and they probably won't, if we just ignore them." She tried to sound as if she knew what she was talking about.

"Itttllll noooo loooooo," he affirmed, in what was his quietest whisper. Following her own advice, Loni averted her gaze.

Chickens wandered aimlessly across their path. "At least *they're* not frightened of us," she whispered. She had never seen these animals before either. Or more accurately, had never seen them *alive*, with feathers and walking around, but they were easily recognisable from the raw ingredients she used to make dinner at least once a week.

"I've never seen a live chicken before," she said wonderingly. Then as the thought took a deeper hold in her brain she said it again, this time directed at Little.

"I've never seen a live chicken before Little. I didn't even know what one looked like. How is that possible?" she nodded to the hens to emphasize her question, afraid that pointing might somehow excite the strange pack which watched her, and send them charging over.

"Dohh Ohh," intoned Little, who seemed similarly confounded by the differences between this place and their home. Loni wasn't sure if this was the "Don't know" in direct answer to her question, or if it was the "don't know" standard response, when Little had failed to grasp her meaning.

Either way, unperturbed about that, when everything else was so strange, she carried on.

"And I never knew that they would look so much like you. I mean their head and faces are different…" she looked at Little's oddly human face then back at the hens, "but their *bodies*, well they're almost the same, although of course Eyons are much bigger and more brightly coloured."

In response, Little forgot about their current danger and flapped his wings, pulling his head backwards and forwards in a very good impression of the hens. The hens did not look very impressed, although they seemed to have ceased their clucking, as if they too were waiting to see what would happen. A bolt of fear shot through Loni's heart but the creatures with the teeth did not move in the slightest and she ceased worrying just long enough to giggle, in spite of herself. But all that was just avoiding the real issue here.

These people were clearly petrified of her and Little, but why? Little for his part, didn't look so much scared, as he did hurt by the Pets' reactions to him. His big eyes seemed even larger than usual in his sorrowful Eyon face and Loni's heart bled for him. How could she try to make him comprehend something even she didn't understand?

There was only one way to find out what was going on, but it would have to be done with tact and diplomacy, something she generally wasn't very good at.

"Maybe its YOU they're scared of Little. I know its stupid but I can't think of anything else."

His eyes revealed how hurt he was by this thought but she continued anyway. "Could you just go and sit back there, at the edge of the long grass. Just for a bit, till I can get this sorted out," she pleaded, aware that none of what she had said had turned out to be either tactful *or* diplomatic.

"OHHH OKKKK LONEE." In his upset at being effectively abandoned, Little had gone back to full Eyon volume. Loni grimaced and dared a look behind her shoulders to the pack of strange things. Sure enough their attention had now gone up a notch. Mouths now closed, their long pointed ears stood erect on their heads and Loni had the distinct impression that the fur around their necks and backs also stood on end.

"I don't know what that means but I don't think it's good," she said to Little indicating the creatures with a jerk of her thumb.

"Okkkkk Lonee, Ittl gooo, Ittll sorrrrreeeee Loneee," he said dejectedly.

"It's ok Little, don't worry. Just go quietly, ok?" she tried to smile reassuringly. Thankfully he shuffled off to do as she had asked. She gave him a moment to settle himself, then for his benefit and to make sure he wasn't worried about her safety, she fixed one of her brightest smiles onto her face. It was difficult to do and she felt as if her face would crack with the effort, but she kept smiling anyway.

Taking a deep breath, she once again approached the hut the woman with the children had retreated into. Holding her breath to bolster her courage, she knocked on the door, but more firmly than before. She was aiming for an assertive but friendly knock. She didn't want to come across as either aggressive, or conversely timid, to *either* the people *or* the animal things. But it was hard to strike the right balance when facing a closed door with who knew what behind it and a pack of watching wild things at your back.

"Em hello. My name is Loni, and my Owner is Little... or at least that's what I call him. I'm sorry if we startled you, but we mean you no harm. Will you please talk to me? I am alone now, Little has gone back to the edge of the long grass. We have travelled so long and so far and..." here she faltered, running out of words. What was she going to tell them anyway? She didn't even know herself what her plan was, so how could she explain it to them.

There was no answer from the hut. So she tried again.

"I don't know why you are so afraid, I have not come from another Human village. I mean you no harm." Still silence.

"I only want to talk to you and perhaps ask if you have some spare food...we've been travelling for such a long time and I'm sure Little is hungry, even though he's so lovely he wouldn't want me to know that he's not getting enough food."

She paused again and when she was still only met with silence, she felt obliged to fill it with the sound of her own voice.

"He wouldn't want to worry me, but I know he's probably starving by now…" she trailed off, finally out of things to say.

Then she had an idea. "If you tell me which house is your store house, I will fetch some food for myself. You needn't worry that we will be a burden to you, that is not our intention."

This elicited no response either. She couldn't just go barging around. She would have to wait it out. One thing was for sure though – these Humans were even *less friendly* towards her and Little, than the ones back home were!

The door remained firmly closed and the pack animals seemed to have lost interest in her now, laying their heads back on the ground, their ears once more flat against their skulls. Glancing at Little and motioning for him to stay where he was, Loni sat down directly outside the hut and prepared to wait. Surely someone had to come out at some time?

It seemed to take a very long time but finally there was a voice from the hut. Probably the woman she had already seen, thought Loni.

"It is too early for you to have come again. What do you want? Where are the other monsters? Why are they hiding this time and why are you with them?" The woman's voice was sharp with fear but there was another quality there too. Loni thought that it might be defiance.

"I don't know what you mean. What monsters? And no-one is hiding. There's only me and Little!" she replied, raising her voice slightly to make sure it carried through the wooden door and into the hut.

"And I've never been here before!" she added, belatedly realising what the woman had first said.

There was no answer and since she could think of nothing else to say that would improve the situation, Loni sat quietly. She tried not to fidget just in case someone *was* watching her, but the ground was hard and her bones were already sore. So she sat as still as she could with the minimum of fidgeting. Her patience was rewarded.

There was a teeth clenching screech of metal on metal, as the bolts were cautiously drawn back. The door was opened just the merest fraction, to enable the woman to slip out, before someone else slammed the bolt back into place. The gap had been so narrow and the hut so dark, that Loni had no idea who had slid the bolt closed again.

For a moment the two females looked at each other, both obviously surprised at the other's appearance. The woman's clothes were rough and had a home-made look to them, the same as the others Loni had examined in the abandoned pile. Colourless, voluminous skirt matched with colourless voluminous top, they were held up and cinched in at the waist by a broad leather belt, giving at least some definition to her body.

The fit was reasonable in some places and rather loose in others. Clearly aesthetics had been compromised for the functionality of the garments. Even the belt, plain and unembellished, seemed to have been produced to fulfil a purpose rather than for mere decoration. They were a world away from Loni's own clothes, which were softer and more colourful.

Actually, in truth everything about the woman and her home looked alien and unfamiliar to Loni, from the little huts on the ground instead of in the trees, to the apparent absence of Eyons for all these Pets.

But it was what the woman did next that was the most worrying and unexpected thing.

"CAIN, VIXEN, ALL guard!" The command was more than enough to get the animals' attention. Thrusting her arm in the direction of Little, both the creatures and Loni were in no doubt of her intentions.

Loni's heart leapt with terror and for a moment her tongue felt as though it was stuck to the roof of her mouth in fear.

"NO! NO! PLEASE DON'T HURT HIM!" Meant as a shout, she feared her words would be less effective carried on the croak that they were issued on. But fear had stolen her breath it seemed.

Yet it was enough even so. The woman turned her head to look appraisingly as Loni before further instructing the creatures which had stopped in their tracks at the sound of Loni's voice. Midway between the woman and herself and Little in the background, they stood riveted to the spot, ears held high and alert, awaiting further instruction.

"Please, please don't hurt him." This time it was a plea for mercy.

"VIXEN, CAIN guard but not harm!" The woman modified the command.

Loni managed to take her eyes off the creatures long enough to shoot a look to Little. 'Be still,' her look said, 'be still and give them no cause to harm you.' She thought it with her heart as much as her head and hoped that somehow he would realise what he should do.

Even from here she could make out the whites of his eyes as he looked at the two creatures who now watched him so avidly. One to either side of him, they stood erect and proud, every muscle and sinew in their body tense and ready. Little was terrified. So was Loni. And it was down to her to get them out of this situation.

Loni swallowed down the sudden lump in her throat. She was going to need all her courage here and there was no time for fear or trepidation.

Having secured Little to her satisfaction, the woman now turned to Loni. She thought about standing up, but intuition told her to remain seated. If she stood up the woman might bolt again. And if the woman bolted, surely Little would be attacked? She wasn't concerned about her own danger, only Little.

For a moment the woman stood towering over her. Then with a quick glance around, presumably to assure herself that everyone else was safe and out of sight, she sat down. Her eyes had darted to the long grass as if she expected hordes of Lonis and Littles to appear on the horizon. When that didn't happen, she glanced quickly once more at Loni before checking that Little was still well guarded by her animals.

For a moment Loni had thought that she might abandon the whole thing, as she had paused mid-fold on her way to the ground. But after that initial hesitancy, she continued. Although she was careful to place her body in a position where she could keep a watchful eye on Little, who remained unmoving where he stood.

And as the woman settled herself, from the corner of her eye, Lani noticed, first one, then two, then finally all of the remaining pack creatures take more interest. They drew themselves up to stand, one by one, then as a pack, approached where Loni and the woman sat.

# *Chapter 13.*

At some point whilst San was unconscious his fever had abated and he had passed into a more normal slumber. His body, sick, weak and hungry, had demanded the rest that it needed to recuperate. And while he was unconscious the animal thing hadn't attacked or eaten him. Nor had it deserted him. Instead it lay curled around him, its head resting on its forepaws, its eyes closed as if in sleep.

He looked at it close up. He had a sneaky suspicion that it wasn't as asleep as it appeared and that thought was confirmed when he caught it peeping at him from the corner of one eye, the other remaining closed. Eye to eye they gauged each other and like the slow start of a pendulum, the creature's tail began to swish the bare earth in an increasing arc, until its full potential was realised.

"I guess me shouting *shoo* didn't scare you then, huh?" After the events of the previous day, San wouldn't have at all been surprised if the thing had answered him in a way he understood. So he was rather disappointed when the creature's only response was a deep, "WOOF."

But under the circumstances a woof was preferable to silence, even if the loudness of it at such close proximity did rather startle him.

There was a strange laugh then which brought his head up sharply and fixed his attention to one side of him. Rian stood there, nibbling on red berry after red berry, bunches of them held in his hands.

"No! No, you mustn't eat those, they're poisonous!" In his anxiety he tried to rise to his feet but found his weakened limbs would not immediately respond.

"Poissonnooosss too yooo buut nott tooo meee!" explained Rian, popping another nonchalantly into his mouth.

"Oh!" was all San could think of to say at this explanation.

"Yooo haavvv beeen verry sikkk. Hoow doo yoo feelll nooow?" asked Rian, his voice reflecting his concern.

"Ok." He though for a moment, "or at least I think so!"

Hesitating for only a second, San reached out his hand and stroked the head of the creature. The hair felt silken and not at all as he had expected. And it seemed to be a pleasurable experience for both of them, the creature nuzzling his hand with its nose when he stopped, as if it was trying to get him to do it again.

"Itt seems to likkkk thaaatt," observed Rian.

"Do you have a name?" San enquired, wondering if the creature could say anything other than woof.

"WOOF," the thing responded.

San tried again. "Do you live here?"

"WOOF."

"Are there others like you?"

"WOOF."

"Can you say anything else, other than WOOF."

"WOOF WOOF!"

"HA HA very funny!"

"WOOF WOOF WOOF!" Tongue lolling out of its mouth again, San wondered how he had ever thought the creature was vicious, it just looked as if it was enjoying a joke at his expense. Even Rian was laughing now.

"Ok I get the joke. You can stop now."

"WOOF WOOF WOOF!"

"So I guess it's down to me to name you then."

"WOOF WOOF WOOF."

"Well I'm not gonna call you WOOF, if that's what you're thinking. I think there's enough of that going on already."

"Woof!" The creature moved with him as he sat up, pulling on his abandoned mud encrusted pants and trousers and started to take stock of his surroundings.

San turned to Rian. "Well he wouldn't shoo when I told him to, so I guess that's it. He's now named 'Shoo'." He turned to the creature. "Ok? Shoo, you understand?"

"WOOF WOOF."

"NO not Woof. *Shoo*," and he was laughing at his own joke now, along with Rian.

Although he had a foul, sour taste in his mouth and a disgusting scent in his nostrils, San was surprised to find that he was pretty much ok.

"Well maybe not ok," he admitted ruefully to Rian and Shoo, but better than he would have thought. His head was splitting with pain but for some strange reason his stomach no longer hurt and he didn't seem hungry or thirsty. Perhaps somehow, his body had managed to retain just enough sustenance to keep it going.

"Or perhaps after everything that has happened, my stomach has decided that it's safer to be empty, than full of poison." Shoo was either mulling that idea over or completely uncomprehending. Either way he was silent. But Rian agreed with him.

"Yesss itt iss bessstttt too lett yoor bodyy staayy emptiii forr aa wwhile."

Wary of where he placed his hands as there were undulating pools of bodily fluids all around him now, San managed to pull himself upright. His legs were shaky but they would carry him he decided.

"Arr yoo well ennuuufff too mooov onnn?" enquired Rian. "There's no choice. We have to get out of here." San bent down to stroke Shoo's soft hair. "But as for you, well you are free to stay or come with us."

Yet he stood still, unwilling to make the first move lest the thing took him at his word and abandoned them. But he needn't have worried, for after a moment Shoo stood up and led the way forward with a loud "WOOF WOOF," looking back to make sure that they were both following.

Luckily, during the night and early morning they had come further through the swamp than they had realised. In fact, although not completely out of the other end, they could just about make out where the bogs were and where in the distance, the ground looked firm and solid. And Shoo seemed to know exactly where they should walk and where to avoid.

So they walked, sometimes side by side where the terrain would allow and sometimes single file where necessary. And sometimes just for a change they ran. San didn't really have the energy to move any faster than a walk, but there was something about running with Rian and Shoo by his side, that elevated his spirits and made it worth the extra effort.

Keeping to a straight path was impossible, as they had to avoid all the swampy patches, but they tried as best they could to stay on a vaguely straight course. And they talked.

"Wennn yooo werr sikk…yoo talked abowt yooor Ownerr." Rian's voice was hesitant as if he wasn't sure he should broach the subject.

"Did I?" San thought back. Yes, he remembered there had been something about OwnSan. What had it been?

"Oh yes. I think I was remembering when I was given up by my birth parents."

"Yooo caann remember thaat?" Rian's voice was incredulous.

"Yes, a little bit but there was more than that too."

He remembered how the focus had shifted and he could see himself in another situation. He hadn't appeared to be much older than he had in the previous part of the visions, but he was certainly happier.

"Then I saw me shrieking with excitement, as I sat on OwnSan's back and he twirled me round and round."

He stole at look at Rian, who had grown suddenly quiet.

The memory replayed itself in his head. Faster and faster they had spun, till all the forest was a blur of green. Finally the Eyon had stopped and encouraged the young San to slide off his back. OwnSan had looked happy and relaxed as did the young version of himself. Even captured in his memory, San was amazed to see such an unusual expression on his Owner's face.

"It was different for you wasn't it? Life, I mean."

"Yessss. Nott a Pettt, nott ann Owner. I amm nothingg."

"No Rian you are *not* nothing. You are *very much* something."

San reached out, grasping Rian's arm firmly in his hand, forcing the Eyon to make eye contact with him.

"You are my friend." San stated emphatically.

"Woof!"

"Yes, he's your friend too, Shoo!" laughed San and was gratified to find Rian joining right in.

"You must have seen many things on your travels." San deliberately did not lift his voice at the end, did not turn the remark into a question. If Rian wanted to talk about it, that was fine but if he did not, well that was fine too.

"Nott reelly. I travelled att nightt mostly aandd sleptt inn the day so thatt I woodd nott bee seen."

"Yes, I suppose that makes sense." San thought about something that Rian had said before that intrigued him.

"You said before that you had not seen any signs of wars… but you had seen Human villages?"

"Yesss. I passed them att night."

"Are they very different there?" He knew it was a stupid question to ask. How could Rian even tell, in the dark and with everyone asleep whether it was different from the way Pets lived.

Rain thought for a moment, considering the question.

"Therr iss a diffferrentt feel to a Huuman village too aan Eyon one. A diffferrent kind of quiet."

San mulled that over for a while before asking Rian to explain further. But Rian was unable to. It was just a feeling he had.

Eventually, after what seemed like an entire lifetime, they reached the end of the swamp. The sun, which had been high in the sky for many hours, had grown tired and had begun to hide itself from view behind convenient clouds, as if weary of their lack of progress. And the air too began to smell different, fresh and fruity.

"Have you ever seen trees like those ahead before?" enquired San as they approached.

"Noo."

"Woof."

"Nor has Shoo," joked San

Not particularly tall but densely branched, the trees stood close together in a clump. Branch arms entwined, finger-tips touching, they looked like a group of very old friends having a good gossip. San's eyes widened, as taking several steps towards them, he began to make out the significant colours in their midst, the oranges and yellows and greens and reds.

A slight breeze tilted the nearest branches in his direction. One of the limbs, ever so slightly longer than the others, wagged up and down in the wind. It was an accusatory finger pointing at him, whilst the rest of the trees shook with laughter.

'Look at the silly human,' it seemed to say, 'he thought apples and oranges and pears came from the ground! Thought you dug them up! As if such sweet things could be found hidden in the murky earth!'

Of course he realised the trees weren't *actually* mocking him. That was only his imagination. But it was strange how embarrassed by his own naivety he was, even though there was only Rian and Shoo there to witness it.

Closer and closer they drew to the trees.

"I can almost taste those fruits!" he said excitedly to Rian, his mouth filled with saliva at the prospect of such juicy fare. His stomach, quiet for so long, began a slow, low rumbling, half in anticipation, half in warning.

"Wee will neeedd to bee carefulll," urged Rian. But San refused to have his enthusiasm dampened.

"But this is *safe* fruit, I'm sure of it. It's not as if they are things I've never eaten before," he replied. Even if he had incorrectly guessed their origins. And neither apples, oranges nor pears had ever made him violently ill. Shoo rolled his big brown eyes up at him as if he couldn't trust San's judgement and said nothing, instead looking to Rian as if even *he* knew the voice of reason when he heard it.

"Traitor!" muttered San under his breath but they all knew he didn't mean it.

Belatedly San realised that where there was food, there was also the possibility of houses.

"There could be Eyons here!" He wasn't concerned for himself but for Shoo and Rian. And he was afraid of losing his chance of finding out what his dreams and the necklet meant. To have come so far, only to be thwarted from achieving his ultimate goal would be unbearable.

Caught up in that idea, he stopped dead in his tracks, one foot still hanging in mid-air. When he placed it back on the ground, he did so unthinkingly, put it too close to the other, lost his balance and almost keeled right over. Only Rian grabbing him had prevented his fall. He deliberately refused to look at his friend for fear that he would be laughing.

Instead he looked at Shoo who looked back at him, a strange expression of disbelief on his canine features.

"Oh well, don't you take that lofty expression with me, it's easy for you to balance - you've got *four* legs."

"WOOF WOOF!"

"And the same to you fur-face!" but he was laughing all the same. And when he looked at Rian there was no derision there on his countenance. Instead there was only a gentle smile.

"No, therr arr no houses heer."

The trees were too small, their tops too close to the ground and too close together. There simply wasn't enough height to build a house within these branches.

"But we could have just blundered right into the middle of something. We should have been more careful. We must think in future."

It was only after the words were out of his mouth that he realised how easy and right it had felt to be saying *we* instead of *I*, how much better it had made him feel.

"Does it look safe to you Rian?"

"Yesss!"

"Ok, then, shall we?" Grinning and with unspoken mutual consent they threw caution to the wind and *ran* towards the trees, Shoo bounding along beside them.

Standing underneath the spreading branches, the trees weren't quite as small as they had looked from a distance, nor were the fruits. Oranges as big as his two hands balled together, jostled one another for space along the tree limbs. Apples as shiny as OwnSan's machine glistened invitingly and pears hung heavy and enticingly from other branches, other trees.

What a feast they were about to have! San reached up to the nearest branch but it was just beyond his reach. A different tactic was obviously required. He threw himself into the air, leaping up and down, trying to snare either a fruit or a whole actual branch that he could hold down. This was unsuccessful too.

"What if you lift Shoo up and he can pull the branch down to us?" He asked Rian. It sounded like a good plan. Rian could not fly nor could he lift San up in his arms, as he would be too heavy for him. But coming up only as high as his knees, Shoo was neither too big, nor too heavy to be lifted above Rian's head.

Arms fully extended Rian thrust the creature at the fruit, whilst San shouted, "pick it, pick the fruit Shoo!" But Shoo just swished his tail even faster and pedalled his legs in the empty air.

It was no good. Perhaps having four legs was a disadvantage after all. San realised *he* would have to climb the tree. Rian's fluffy feathery body would never manage the task, so it naturally fell to San. In a way he was relieved that this was a task only he could do. It sort of redeemed himself in his own eyes for all the foolishness of his recent exploits. It was surely just a question of technique, wasn't it?

"I've never climbed a tree before," he informed Rian and Shoo, now safely back on the ground. "Then again I'd never climbed *down* a tree before I did it."

"WOOF WOOF."

"Taakk yooorrr ttime aandd ggo sloww," advised Rian.

"Yes, you're both right. There is a first time for everything." He wondered if he had to ascend the tree as he had *de*scended the other one, but in reverse, as it were. It seemed like a good idea.

He positioned himself at the base of the tree trunk, legs wrapped around the trunk, arms encircling it. The bark was rough against his face so he held his head away slightly.

Grasping the trunk with his thighs, he pushed himself a few inches higher, using his hands to pull himself up. It was hard work but the rewards were going to be worth it. He wasn't even concerned when a particularly rough patch of tree snagged his trousers, causing a few threads to tear and a small hole appear near the knee. Things had already been far worse, after all.

Hand over hand he shinnied up the trunk, before edging out onto the thickest branch laden with fruit. Legs dangling in the air, he settled himself comfortably on the branch and plucked the juiciest pear he could see. Unmindful of the juice which splattered out as he bit into it, he munched his way through half of what the branch had to offer, carefully tossing the remaining half down to Shoo and Rian, who both ate as if hungry but without much obvious enjoyment.

Then he moved onto the next branch and the next, working his way through its produce. It seemed that Shoo would eat the pears and some of the apples but not the oranges, which didn't interest him in the least. Rian was less fussy, not seeming to have a preference at all, just eating whatever was thrown to him.

After a while San got bored with the tastes and textures. Pear after pear, apple after apple and orange after orange he ate, dropping the cores and the peel on the ground when he was done with them. He tried to pretend that they were other things instead of what they actually were.

"Gonna have roast chicken with sausages and mashed potatoes now, followed by a huge lump of chocolate," he held aloft a pear and an apple. All of these and more were possible to imagine to some extent whilst munching on apples and pears. But oranges could only *be* oranges, their juice and flesh was too strong to be mistaken for or disguised as anything else. Perhaps that was what Shoo objected to, he wondered.

Off the ground he had a better vantage point to see in all directions, though the thick foliage of the trees did partially obscure the view. He was surprised to see how remarkably delineated the landscape was. Back the way he had come, the swamp could be seen in the distance as a large greyish brown area, but where it stopped, it finished in an almost straight line. It was almost as if someone or something had drawn an invisible line across the grass. *All* of the swamp was one side, not the tiniest mud patch sullied the other side!

On both sides of the swamp the ground lay even and flat, as it did directly opposite the swamp. "It's just typical that I didn't manage to go around the swamp, instead of through it!"

"Itt woood haav certinlyy beenn lesss interestinn too haav gonn rownd itt!" agreed Rian, mouth still full of apple.

"Then again if we hadn't have gone through it we wouldn't have met you, would we shoo?"

"WOOF WOOF!"

"Yes, that's right! Just think of all the interesting banter we would have missed out on! Just doesn't bear thinking about does it?"

"WOOF WOOF"

The pile of discarded fruit cores and peel got higher and higher, reaching a little mini-mountain before it toppled over and spilled its contents across the ground.

"*How* did you leave? I don't mean why, I *know* why…but how?" San didn't want to upset Rian but his curiosity *was* piqued. Rian seemed to consider the question a moment, continuing to chew on his apple before swallowing the last bite and tossing the core onto the discarded pile.

"I jusstt walkedd awayy."

San said nothing and Shoo refrained from barking so that the moment took on a magical quality, as if the very air was holding itself still, waiting for Rian to continue in his own time.

"Theyy werr jusst sstandinn therr…aandd no-one wass lookinn att mee…aandd thenn I realissed thaatt they *never noticed* me anymorr…nott evenn to make funn ovv…itt wass like I jusstt stoppedd *beingg* altogether…" Rian trailed off.

"So you just walked away from them." It wasn't a question. If anything, San meant it as an affirmation that he understood how Rian must have felt.

"Yess I walkedd awayy. Aandd whenn I gott too the edge ov the clearinn I looked back…buut they hadn'tt moovedd, hadn't noticedd I hadd gone."

There was a deep silence as they both thought about what had been said. A thought went through San's head but he did not have the insensitivity to voice it. So he was surprised when Rian spoke it himself.

"Aandd whatt iff they hadd noticedd? Whatt iff theyy hadd called too mee? Couldd I havv stayed therr miserabll forr the rest ov my life? Couldd I?"

San wasn't sure if it was a rhetorical question or not but either way he could give no answer. Because it was exactly what he wondered about his own leaving of OwnSan. Instead he chose to bring the attention back to their present circumstances.

"I'm stuffed. I can't eat any more, not even if my life depends on it. But I don't want to just leave it all either."

"Wee cannnott stayy heer butt wee musstt take ssuumm with uss."

With no bag to carry the fruit in, they would have to improvise. They couldn't carry much loose in their arms, or for very far, so they had to think of something else. Then San had an idea. He couldn't use his top because the sun would burn his exposed back and shoulders… but he *could* use his trousers.

Taking a pair of trousers off whilst straddling a branch is not an easy or particularly elegant thing to do, but somehow he managed it. He tied the very bottom of the legs together and was pleased with the result - a large, if strangely-shaped sack.

"Pikk the oranges firsstt. The pearrss arr too sofftt too ggo at the bottomm!" instructed Rian, watching San place the fruit carefully at the way down to the bottom of the legs. There was no point in taking more than either of them could comfortably carry, so when he reached that point he simply used the trouser belt as a drawstring, tightening it as much as possible and gently lowered it into Rian's outstretched arms.

Legs bare and unprotected, he decided it was safer to hop down from the tree than risk climbing down. He just had to avoid landing on either Rian or Shoo or all the discarded bits of fruit. He wished he'd had the foresight to throw the cores further away. Aw well, hindsight!

# Chapter 14.

Loni stared at the creatures. Long hairy bodies held aloft by four vertical legs, one at each corner and heads which sat along the same plane as the body, rather than directly on top of it, they were strange looking things. With long pointed faces topped by triangular flapped ears, and forward facing eyes, Loni had never seen anything like them before. She held her breath as the creatures continued to approach.

"The dogs will not harm you."

Loni hadn't realised that her fear had been so obvious but it wasn't just herself she was worried about. Little also stood still guarded by two of these creatures, too far away for her liking. She wished now that she had kept him at her side. At least then if the 'dogs' as they seemed to be called, had attacked, she could have thrown herself between them and Little, giving him hopefully, just enough time to escape.

"It's not me I'm worried about!"

"Settle, Sham, settle Bachus. All SIT!"

The woman looked at her strangely but spoke with a calm conviction Loni prayed was justified. Yet she ignored the implied concern over Little and if anything, seemed dismissive of Loni's fears.

"The dogs will do only as they are told. And they have only been told to *guard*."

There was no hesitancy in the words and yet Loni had the distinct impression that the woman meant that *for now,* he was safe. There was no assurance there for the future. None given and certainly none taken.

Tails softly wagging, the dogs did as they were bid, curling themselves around each other for comfort. The woman had said the names of two of the animals but there were at least five or six surrounding them. Loni didn't dare try to count them for fear of catching their eyes and starting something off.

She was disconcerted that they were only an arms reach away from her but consoled herself with the thought that they were under the woman's control. She hoped that was enough and that she never had occasion to find out.

The woman's sleeves were rolled up to the tops of her arms and her hands were still covered in flour from the baking she had been doing, before all this had erupted.

Her limbs were strong and muscular looking, yet she was quite petite, probably barely taller than a few of the thirteen year old Pets Loni knew back home. And her body was that of a fairly young woman. But there was something about her, some unusual air of authority which made her seem much, much older than she really was.

It was something about the way she carried herself. There was a sense of readiness there, as if she was more prepared for battle than she was for flight. This was an alien concept for Loni, something she had never encountered before. Yet some part of her, deep inside, instinctively recognised it, some primal instinct. And perhaps that was exactly how all the people were here, how they *had* to be, fighting with other villages all the time.

There was a wariness to the woman that was just overlaid by weariness, a resignation that wasn't complete and possibly never would be. Loni suspected that the weariness would be shrugged off like an unwanted blanket whenever the woman felt that action was required. What terrible knowledge must be contained inside this young woman to make her like this, wondered Loni.

The woman was visibly shaking and Loni was astounded to notice little beads of sweat standing out just above her upper lip, which quivered, keeping time with the trembling of her mouth. Closer to finding the truth than she had ever been, Loni's stomach began to clench, keeping its own rhythm with her heart. She could feel a pulse throbbing deep in her stomach and across her body her nerve endings began to tingle.

"Settle, Sham, settle Bachus, settle all," repeated the woman even though none of the dogs had moved a muscle as far as Loni could tell. She wondered if the woman was just concerned that the animals would react to her own evident fear. She hoped Little was staying calm  but didn't dare look over, lest it started a chain of events she couldn't control.

She concentrated instead on the tingling sensation she was feeling. At first it wasn't unpleasant but it soon became so. From a mild tingling, it increased, so that it felt as though a thousand little ants were rampaging across her body. Repulsed, she felt the hairs on her arms stand up on end and had to fight hard to keep her face passive, calm but attentive. She couldn't put this woman off talking to her. Not at any cost. And especially not because she just had the heebie-jeebies!

Without understanding what these people feared, Loni realised she could easily upset the situation again. The silence was heavy with anticipation on both sides and she wasn't sure how long she could actually sit there in silence. Or how long she could keep Little from trying to come over. She could feel his gaze burning into her as she studiously avoided looking at him.

There was a sort of snuffling sound as one of the dogs rearranged himself and the rest of the pack shuffled slightly to accommodate him. Loni seized the chance, while their attention was thus diverted to shoot Little a warning glance. 'Stay where you are for now. It won't be for long, promise!' she thought at him.

Finally the silence was broken. The woman's voice, spoken at such close proximity after so long a silence, sounded loud and made Loni jump. She could have kicked herself as she realised that her fright had made her miss the first part of what had been said!

"... why are you here? Why are you helping the monsters with their harvest of our children? Why are you betraying your own kind? Who *are* you?"

The woman's voice was a mixture of fear and confusion. But the predominant emotion was clearly hatred and her eyes burned into Loni's.

"This is different from all the other times in the past. Why? What has changed?" she cried desperately. Beads of perspiration ran freely down her face and her eyes were welling with suppressed tears.

Loni's face must have shown her own bewilderment as she managed to mutter, "I don't know what you're talking about. Honestly I don't."

Her voice cracked with emotion as her mind began to process what the woman had said. What could she have meant by saying the children had been "harvested"? Why were these people so terrified of Little when they already knew he wasn't another warring Human? And what was she supposed to say and do in this situation?

For a moment she wished she and Little had never left home. There was danger here, both immediate and future. More danger than she had even thought there might be.

"Monsters..?" she asked, her voice sounding strange and timid, its normal tone altered by having to squeeze itself out of a throat that was tight with fear. She could only assume that the woman had meant Little. Or if not Little himself, then Eyons. But the Eyons were not monsters... Ok, granted they had a rather strange appearance but 'monsters' was taking it too far. Unless that wasn't what she meant.

"MONSTERS!" There was no mistaking the emphatic tone used, nor the outstretched arm pointing in Little's direction.

One of the dogs, Loni didn't know or care which, raised its head at the tone and regarded its mistress with a readiness Loni didn't like the look of.

Perhaps there were some things that were better left unsaid and unknown but it was too late now. Loni knew in her heart that she'd gone past the point of no return. She knew that what she was about to discover would alter her perception of her whole world forever but that like the river that flows inexorably onwards, she had no choice.

Yet for all of Loni's fear she could not stop herself from challenging the woman's remark. "Eyons are *not* monsters..." She had been about to remind the woman that they loved and provided well for the Pets, taking them in and sheltering them from the wars of Humans, but she got no further before she was interrupted.

"Child, I know very well what they are, and they are *monsters*. Monsters of the vilest kind."

Loni didn't care for the derogatory way the woman had called her a child. Yes, she was a child, but it didn't make her a simpleton! She drew in a large breath ready to dispute the issue for as long as it took but before she got the chance, the woman continued.

"Have they held you prisoner for so long that you think like them now? Have they poisoned your mind with their evil thoughts and doings?"

Lost for words, Loni shook her head 'no'. None of it was true. But if she just denied it all, would the woman believe her? Somehow she didn't think so.

"I don't understand what you are talking about. But if you let me, I will try to explain who we are and why we are here." Loni held her breath. What would happen to her and Little if she wasn't allowed to explain?

"So explain then."

Loni got the strong impression that it wasn't really permission to make an explanation, that she had been given. It was more of a veiled threat.

Afraid to point to Little, in case he took it as an invitation to join them, she kept her hands firmly at her sides and tried to keep her head from nodding in his direction. She could feel his eyes intently watching her for some signal that he could return. But she didn't dare let him yet.

"We, my Owner, Little and I, have come from far away," she stopped. "Well, actually he's not really my Owner, his egg-mother is, but you know what I mean…" she trailed off. Did this woman know what she meant? Possibly not! She would have to be really careful with what she said and not make any assumptions. She tried again.

"I live far away with Little, the Eyon over there," her fingers twitched as she suppressed her natural desire to point, "and my Owner the Eyon OwnLoni." She stopped as she saw the woman's eyes widen involuntarily at this information.

She tried to remember at what point the woman had been surprised. Was it the living far-away part? No, she didn't think so. It was something to do with her comment about living with Little. Something in Loni's mind opened up then and she remembered how her listener's eyes had stretched *even wider* at this reference. But it had been the word 'Owner' which had caused the initial reaction.

But for the life of her, she couldn't figure out what was wrong, or so amazing with what she had said. It was only the truth.

A little voice spoke quietly in Loni's head. It was so calm and so quiet that Loni could have missed it…except that she couldn't.

"No, it's not *the truth*. It's *my* truth. But it's not *hers*. Her truth is something else." It was such a tiny voice, yet it cut through all her thoughts like a hot knife through butter. And it had much the same result. Loni's mind was figuratively divided between what she knew and what she was about to discover.

The woman waited for her to continue.

"I was…*we* were happy there," she corrected herself quickly, but before she could continue, she heard the hiss of indrawn breath from her attentive listener. Something she had said had further shocked this woman and once more the dogs were interested in her, watching her carefully. She waited for a response but other than the woman's eyes becoming more guarded and narrower, there was none. She decided to continue. There was really no alternative.

"But there was something missing and I  still don't know what. And then it was time for Little to be connected up…and so we left." It was a bit of a simplified explanation but under the circumstances perhaps it was better to be succinct.

"You left? You escaped you mean?" clarified the woman.

"No, we just left. We had to, it was either that, or I would have lost Little. He would have become like all the other Owners."

Again there was no response so she continued, trying to put her feelings into words.  Suddenly it struck her that this was not dissimilar to the "conversations" she had with Little. Both she and the woman spoke the same language but their experiences and perception were so different that it rendered the language opaque. Implied meanings and observations did not have the transparency they should have had.

She couldn't take anything for granted. The little voice spoke up again. 'Be careful,' it warned. Then for added emphasis, as if she really needed it, it was repeated in a more tense tone.

'Be careful and THINK before saying.'

Both she and Little could be in real danger here.

Suddenly the sensation of crawling ants was back. Except this time they were joined by snakes which slithered around in the pit of her stomach and coiled tensely there.

# *Chapter 15.*

San's trousers as a sack idea worked quite well but it was heavy to carry, even though they took turns with it and sometimes even carried it between them for short periods.

Now it was San's turn again. He tried slinging it over one shoulder but it bumped against his back with every step he took. That was bad enough, but soon it felt as if his shoulder joint would surely tear loose from its socket if he carried on. He tried the other shoulder. Bumping bit aside, that was fine. For a while. Until *that shoulder* began to throb and ache.

He passed it to Rian but when his turn came round again, his shoulders were still sore from the previous occasion. So he tried clutching it to his chest and wrapping both arms around it but that meant he couldn't see where he was going and he was sure that would end in disaster!

It also resulted in a rather ungainly sort of waddling walk, which when put together with the fact that he was no longer wearing his trousers, made him look rather ridiculous. It didn't matter that there was no one else around apart from Rian and Shoo to witness it! So he settled in the end for holding the sack one handed at his side, transferring it from hand to hand and thus side to side every few hundred steps or so.

This made progress slow but short of eating all the fruit at once, he wasn't sure what they could do about it. Anyway, it was somehow becoming more bearable. Perhaps his muscles were strengthening or lengthening or doing whatever it was that muscles did. He didn't really care as long as the pain lessened. Perhaps his muscles weren't doing anything. Perhaps his brain had just got used to the idea and stopped registered the pain. He wondered if that were at all possible.

"Could you have taken a Pet of your own?" San had been mulling this idea over for some time before asking it.

"I don'tt know. Itt iss nott the saamme forr mee as other Eyonss."

"You mean they wouldn't have let you?" He wasn't sure who 'they' were but it seemed a valid question.

"No. I meann how could I take a Pett whenn I don'tt work like other Ownerss aandd I speek like a Huumann?"

"Mmm. I see what you mean." And then something so simple and obvious occurred to him, he wondered why it hadn't occurred before.

"But if you can understand Eyon *and* Human speak then couldn't *that* have been your job?"

Rian regarded him blankly, forcing San to elaborate further.

"I mean you could have explained to the Pets what their Owners were saying, what they wanted. Couldn't you?"

"Yess buutt all the true Eyonss waant, iss too work and everyone already knows thaatt."

He had San there. It was true and there was no getting away from it. They carried on in silence for a while then, still taking turns with carrying the fruit.

Finally San's stomach began to rumble again. Soon it was so loud that Shoo began to bark in response to it, as if in conversation.

"Rumble."

"Woof."

"Rumble, RUMBLE."

"Woof, WOOF."

He wasn't sure if Shoo thought he was deliberately making the noise or whether the creature was being funny. But soon it started to get on his nerves and he told Shoo off.

"RUMBLE."

"WOOF."

"STOP IT SHOO!"

"RUMBLE, RUMBLE!"

"WOOF, WOOF!"

"I SAID, STOP IT SHOO!" San bellowed with Rian joining in.

Shoo suddenly quietened and seemed to slink down lower to the ground. For a moment San worried that they had scared the creature, till with the furthest part of his peripheral vision he saw the still swishing tail.

Choosing to ignore San's stomach, they carried on walking for some time, needing to feel they had covered some distance before allowing themselves to rest.

"Besides we might as well keep going whilst we can. If we stop now there's nothing to look at and nowhere to rest comfortably."

The ground was firm but pretty unremarkable terrain. The fruit trees were long gone and when he looked back, San couldn't even make them out as tiny mounds in the far distance.

There was nothing to be seen behind them. Only the faint dusty trail which marked their progress through it. There were no trees, hardly any grass and nothing to remark over. Nor was there anything different to be seen to either side. Or ahead. Just land rolling out flat in every direction.

Finally San stopped. "Come on, we all need a break."

"WOOF, Woof." No disagreement there.

A combination of monotony, sore muscles and hunger had forced a rest. Sitting down on the bare earth without his trousers wasn't the most pleasant of experiences. However, due to recent circumstances, nor was it the most unpleasant he had suffered. But it didn't make him want to linger.

"There's not much point in tipping all the fruit out onto the dirty ground, just so we can have a selection, is there?" he asked, passing one of the fruits from the top to Rian and placing another on the ground in front of Shoo.

"No. Aandd thosse will go off first anyway."

He wasn't sure if that was actually going to prove to be an issue – the fruit going rotten before they ate it but it was certainly wise to bear it in mind. Of course that also implied that it could be a very long time before they found any other source of food. That was perhaps a more likely problem, he thought, looking at all the nothingness around him.

"Nothingness," he mused, "is a funny word. Is it even a word at all?"

"I don'tt know," rasped Rian, whilst Shoo gave his usual, customary bark.

"Oh how would you know? One Eyon and one strange unidentified thing!" But his tone was light and teasing as it can only be with someone who actually cares about those who he is teasing.

"Woof is the only thing you can say!"

He wasn't sure if it was a word, but it certainly fit the description of this place. It was full of nothingness. He sniggered to himself, liking the sound of the word he had made. He wondered how he could fit it in to everyday conversations back home, assuming he ever got back home that was.

Munching on a pear he thought about an imagined conversation with one of the boys back home.

"Perhaps I'll brush my hair differently and when he asks me what I've changed, to look so different, I'll say 'Nothingness'."

San could only laugh when Shoo and Rian both simultaneously regarded him with looks that said 'what really?' Shoo's comical look further embellished by pear juice dribbling out of the corners of his mouth. San had to admit the look was apt.

"Ok, that was stupid, the real answer would be 'I brushed it like this' or possibly 'nothing, really' but it definitely wouldn't be 'nothingness'. You're right, I know." In fact he couldn't think of a single situation where he could use the word ever again. Except here. Here, the word just fit.

Meal over, they resumed walking. Initially, although somewhat lighter, the bag seemed just as heavy as before, but once more they got used to it. A breeze started up. Actually San wasn't sure if it really *started* up or whether they had just walked into the area where it had already been blowing.

"Do you think that if we walk back a few steps there will still be a wind? Or now it has us in its grasp, will it just surround us and follow us back, so that it will seem to be blowing everywhere?"

"Woof woof!"

"Yes, I agree," nodded San solemnly.

"I'mm beginningg too think the other Eyonss werr wise nott too engage in such fasinatingg converssaationn."

And San was amazed and gratified by the light mockery shown in the tone. Perhaps he had been right after all. Perhaps there was more than one reason for his search for answers. Perhaps Rian was meant to be with him – and Shoo of course. Perhaps they had been meant to find each other.

Then he noticed the change in the air. There was some different quality to it, a tang on his tongue and lips that he couldn't quite identify. A salty, almost gritty feeling to it, which washed over his face with the blowing wind.

Ahead too, the landscape had changed. Instead of the land rolling ahead of them as it had done for so long now, it appeared to have come to an end, as if they had reached the end of the world and would soon fall off.

True, the tufty grass and earth still unfolded into a rolling plain with every step they took, but there, not so far in the distance it seemed to stop. Just stop and vanish into thin air.

And then suddenly San discovered the cause of the mystery. He turned to Rian to find that he too was astounded by the sight, and had already hurried slightly ahead.

His pace and heart simultaneously quickening, with his free hand, he grabbed Shoo by the scruff of his neck and held on tight. Bent over like this, one hand now dragging the trousers, the other still securing Shoo tight to his side, he approached the end of the land and stood in amazement at the panoramic view he was presented with.

The trouser bag fell unheeded to his side, but none of the fruit spilled out. Instead the fruit held the trousers in an almost vertical position so that it looked like half a person still wore them. It was a weird looking thing and strangely reminiscent of the engraving on the necket. San would have laughed at the sight, if his attention had not been directed elsewhere.

The land ahead was sheered off and fell steeply in the most rugged of cliffs. He stood on the precipice, where one more step would surely catapult him and Shoo to an early death. For a moment he swayed precariously as his balance was affected by the view, before he heeded Rian's hissed, "LYE DOWWNN!" and dropped to his knees for safety, now clutching at Shoo with both hands.

This was a scene such as he had never before witnessed and his eyes drank it in, even as his mind refused to register it. Veritable flocks of brightly–coloured Eyons crisscrossed the sky, just below where he and Rian lay side by side, with Shoo pulled in between them. Some with Pets riding on their backs, others flying solo, but all of them weaving in and out of each others' flight paths without incident.

Never before had San seen so many Eyons all in one place, never had he witnessed such dexterity of flight as he was now seeing, such skill and obvious coordination. Shoo cowered into him, quivering and terrified, burying his face in the folds of San's top. He wanted to stroke the creature, to reassure him but to do so he would have had to remove his hands from the scruff of Shoo's neck and something warned him not to do so.

So instead, he intensified his grip and bent his body around the creature to shield it from view. His eyes lighted on one particular Eyon, a largish orange and greeny-blue one which seemed even more graceful than the others and followed its progress across the sky.

This particular one was flying solo and seemed to be in no real hurry to reach its destination, as it swooped and turned and spiralled its way through, around and between the paths of its fellow creatures. Then just as San wondered if it would come crashing into the face of the rock almost directly beneath where he crouched, it disappeared.

He and Rian exchanged looks in silence, over the top of Shoo's head.

There was no squawking in fear and terror, no flurry of broken orange feathers floating upwards and no muffled thump of feathery body hitting rock. There was nothing. Not a thing. 'Nothingness' the voice inside San's head whispered, its tone full of wonder.

He shuffled awkwardly over to the very edge of the land and looked down the long drop of the cliff face, to the sandy stretch of beach far, far below.

What he saw filled him with awe and amazement. What he had expected to see was the sad and broken body of the brightly acrobatic Eyon, lying on the sand far below him. Instead, what he actually saw were *holes* in the Cliffside. No, not *holes*, his frantically working mind tried to clarify for him, not holes at all. What he was looking at were caves. Homes for these Eyons. And there were *hundreds* of them.

He was just about to describe it to Rian when it happened.

It was the slightest change in the quality of the air, the slightest puff of unnatural wind that gave it away. That, and the tiniest sound of wings flapping, *almost silently*…just not quite. A split second of recognition of what the sound and feel of the air suggested, passed through San's head but it was too late to avoid his fate.

Sharp talons pierced his top and underpants, as the Eyon hovering above, took hold of him with a swoop and a screeched "WWWWUUUUUBBBBBRRRRR."

"RIAN! RIAN!" Arms wrapped around Shoo, he could do nothing to prevent himself from being lifted. As if in slow motion he saw his friend *spring* from the ground where he had lain, only a split second ago and launch himself at the back of the large Eyon.

Seemingly unaware or perhaps just uncaring of the strange Eyon now on its back, his captor merely stretched her wings wider and prepared for flight.

"Hold on, hold on tight," San shouted to Rian aware that Rian was simultaneously shouting the same back to him.

"Holldd onn tight." And something about that phrase echoed once more in the back of San's head, before he pushed it out to focus on the immediate peril.

Swooping high once more, the Eyon held him firmly in its grasp and Rian safely on its back. Then, continuing to shriek loudly, it flew with great speed towards one of the caves in the cliff, San still immobilised in its hold just as the terrified Shoo was held in his.

His trousers lay where they had fallen, a strangely fitting memorial to the adventurous boy that he had been.

# *Chapter 16.*

The woman held her gaze with Loni, eye to eye, heart to heart and soul to soul. They had sat in silence for some time, both thinking about Loni being "happy" in her home. After the words were out of her mouth it struck Loni that she had never really thought about whether her home had made her happy or not before. It was a complicated train of thought to pursue, mixed in with all the emotions that it was.

Thinking back she knew that mostly she had been happy, sometimes more than others. Until of course she had found the machine ready and waiting for Little...then she had been *terrified*.

There was also the feeling of something being missing, that she sometimes had, but it was separate from, and different, to what she felt about home. Home was home and always would be.

The woman was also contemplating the implications of what Loni had said, but Loni was fairly certain she was viewing the comments from a far different perspective. She would no doubt make her own judgements.

For a good length of time Loni had avoided looking at Little. She didn't dare take her eyes off the woman beside her, lest the situation change and also because she was worried that Little would see through her false expression. Her face ached with trying to keep a bland expression fixed in place and she was beginning to feel her muscles tightening up. If she stayed like this much longer she would surely turn to stone!

Her patience was rewarded once more. Slowly, colour seeped back into the woman's face and her features softened. Loni guessed that with her sharp blue eyes and golden blonde hair, she would be beautiful when she was relaxed and happy. But it was the sharp intelligence that shone from the woman's eyes that held Loni's own eyes captive.

After a brief hesitation, she reached across and took Loni's hand in her own, giving it a reassuring and encouraging squeeze. "I believe you. Or at least I believe that *you believe* you are telling me the truth. There is no guile in you child."

Was that an improvement? That at least the woman realised she was not lying even if it meant she thought Loni was actually too stupid to know the truth?

"Tell me what has brought you here and I will try to answer all of your questions as best I can, if you will try to answer mine as honestly as you can," she continued, seemingly unaware that her words could have caused offence. Her voice was soft now, all traces of fear and threats gone. Her hands were rough but they held Loni's own gently but firmly.

Loni's breath came out in a great big "whoosh" of suppressed air. Her heart was still beating fast but more with excitement now than apprehension. Released from the woman's stare, her gaze travelled down to their joined hands. Veins stood out, raised and clearly defined on the back of the woman's hands. They were like the hands of a much older Pet.

"I would like nothing better than to do that but please first tell me what I may call you," responded Loni, her mind frantically trying to organise her thoughts into some coherent kind of explanation.

"I am known as Sophia, First Woman of The People. What are you known by child?" At Loni's uncomprehending look, she explained further. "I am the Leader of my people."

Loni understood now. "I am Loni. And the Eyon I am travelling with is Little. Please may I call him over, he'll be terribly hurt if I don't?" She knew that she risked upsetting the situation again but she couldn't just leave Little there forever. And anyway hadn't Sophia said that she trusted her now? This would be proof of that trust.

A flicker of doubt crossed Sophia's face but her eyes remained locked on Loni and she had obviously decided that there *was* something she could trust there, so she nodded her agreement.

But then Sophia surprised her. Just as Loni considered how best to invite Little over – whether it was best to go fetch him, call to him or gesture – Sophia took the initiative.

"Stay. Quiet and calm and STAY," she said, turning directly to face the dogs, then more forcefully, her eyes sought out the two largest in the pack. "Bachus, Sham STAY!" she commanded. Loni watched fascinated, as the pack leaders lowered their heads once more, the others following suit.

Then Sophia turned her attention towards the dogs which still guarded Little. "VIXEN, CANE, RELEASE!" she called. As soon as the words were spoken, the dogs abruptly changed their demeanor. Ears and hackles lowered they ambled back over towards Sophia and the rest of their pack.

Still holding tight to Loni with one hand, Sophia used the other to beckon to Little. Arm outstretched, she curled her hand and forearm back into her shoulder a couple of times, in a 'come here' gesture.

Little didn't need to be asked twice. Loni grimaced as he leapt up and started to half fly, half waddle over. 'Subtle as ever,' she thought. Her hand, the one being held by Sophia, was grasped more firmly and she felt more than saw, the involuntary tremor that ran through the woman as she watched him approach. Sophia was still plainly terrified yet she kept her nerve. Filled with admiration and respect, Loni hoped that she too would be as brave, in a similar situation.

Slowing down as he got closer, Little took in the quiet dogs and the joined hands and was smart enough to realise that a tentative bond was forming here. Unsure what to do next, he waited for Loni to pat the ground next to her, before he took up the indicated position.

To her credit, Sophia didn't even flinch when he wrapped his wing around Loni's free arm. But she kept her own free arm folded into her lap. Clearly she had gone as far as she was prepared to go in the trusting stakes at this time. Loni's admiration remained undiminished however.

"This is Little. He's about eleven now ..." Loni was interrupted by Little's raspy confirmation of the facts.

"ESSSSS, ESSSS," he screeched excitedly.

And then two things happened simultaneously.

"He can TALK..." Sophia blurted out, just as there was an explosion of barking as the largest of the dogs reacted to Little's screech. The dog stood, hackles raised on the nape of his neck and bared his teeth. Loni felt Little's talons dig into her arm as he tried to control his obvious fear.

"QUIET, CANE. SIT!" commanded his mistress. Immediately, if rather reluctantly, the dog obeyed.

Loni wasn't sure if Sophia's comment was meant as a question or an exclamation but she figured it was a little of both. She was going to have to do some explaining before she could really tell their story.

"Yes, he can talk. But it's not quite the same as us, Humans, I mean. He can't make all the right sounds, but sometimes it's very close. And he tries hard. Very hard. I've never heard of any Eyons who could talk before and I guess you haven't either. But Little's different." She paused, thinking how best to try to explain.

"I don't know *why* he's different," thinking about her friend made her smile and a little of the old Loni resurfaced. She giggled, momentarily forgetting about their strange situation. "Do *you* know why you're different Little?" she asked him directly.

"ESSS," came the almost immediate response. Loni had expected this, so she continued unabashed, "go on then, tell *us* why you're so different!"

This was met with only silence but Loni didn't mind, because it illustrated her point perfectly. "You see, he's different, or together *we're* different but he doesn't 'get' everything I say. Although he gets the essence of most of it. I reckon the other Eyons just aren't interested." She stopped, waiting for Sophia to ask any questions before she continued.

"Do you mean he can say things other than 'yes'?" Sophia paused as the thought turned around in her head. "And does that mean you can speak his language …what do you call it 'Ayon'?"

"Eyon," corrected Loni and

"EEEEYYYYOOOONNNN," shrilled Little almost simultaneously. Loni giggled again at the startled look which momentarily clouded the woman's face.

"No, before you ask, he won't have understood all of that. He's just reacting to the word 'Eyon' that's all. And in answer to your question I can understand some of his sounds for things but I can't copy them."

"Eyon. So that is what they call themselves. So many hundreds of years, so much hatred and fear – and we never even had a name for them." Sophia was talking out loud but something about the way she did it, made it seem like she was talking to herself. Her gaze had shifted from Loni and seemed to be almost turned inward. Her eyes had lost their focus and her mouth had gone slightly slack.

"We call them 'The Monsters'." Again she seemed to be saying this to herself rather than to give the information to these visitors. "Never have I heard anyone refer to them as anything else, nor even question that. And I have never given thought to what they may call themselves. Yet we call ourselves 'The People'. We have a name for ourselves…why should they not have one for themselves?" she stopped.

Unsure as to whether she was expected to answer or not, Loni said limply, "I don't know." Little took this as his cue for a response and added, "Dohh Ohhhhh," with an extra long final sound for added emphasis.

Loni shot him a warning glance. Now that he had joined them and was sitting wing in hand with her, she had a sneaky suspicion that he no longer recognised the gravity of the situation.

This was confirmed when he began to tickle the inside of her palm with his scratchy talons, expecting her to shriek and giggle. Instead Loni carefully pulled away slightly from him. Luckily Sophia was too wrapped up in her own thoughts to notice.

Fazed by this unusual turn of events, Little searched Loni's face for what he had done wrong. But a small shake of the head and a reinsertion of her hand into his wing tip, soon reassured him that he was loved still but also that he must behave.

But Little's playfulness had not gone entirely unnoticed. One of the dogs, a smaller, younger one that she hadn't noticed before, had got to its feet. Taking a few small strides, it was suddenly at Little's side. With no noise to precede its attack, it launched itself at him, grabbing a mouth full of feathers and wresting them from side to side.

Little, shocked and in pain, let rent a huge howl and began flapping his wings. Suddenly everything seemed to happen at once. Loni sat shocked and unable to move as Sophia merely leant forwards and gave the dog a firm slap on the rear.

"Bad puppy Blissen," she turned apologetically to Little "Sorry he's a bit playful sometimes!" Chastened, the dog stood immobile, still attached to Little, whilst

Sophia picked it up and inserted her hand into its mouth to dislodge Little's feathers.

Loni shook her head dramatically at Little. 'Don't make any fuss,' it implied, 'we are so close to learning something.' But his dramatic miming of looking at his rumpled feathers and then the puppy, then the feathers again, told her that she would have a job to console him later.

Sophia, caught up in her own thoughts, hadn't noticed this exchange.

"Perhaps we never gave them a real name because to do so would have made them more real in our lives. More *present*. Thinking of them as *monsters* we could bury what atrocities they do to us, bury it deep in our minds and …just accept it. Accept it, the way the wind blows the long grass and the rain lashes the ground. Accept it and carry on with our lives."

Sophia turned to look directly at Little. "That time has now come to an end. Now we must know the truth. The sun has brought you to us. I pray that the tale you will tell will harness the sun in the sky and keep us from rain."

A shiver was sent coursing down the length of Loni's spine, in spite of the warmth from the sun. Somehow she suspected that whatever tale Sophia had to tell, it was not going to harness *her* sun in the sky and keep her and Little from the fiercely pounding rain.

# Chapter 17.

Shoo wasn't heavy but even so, San was terrified that the burden would become unbearable or that the little creature would wriggle out of his grasp, or that his fingers would just slip from Shoo's thick hair or...or anything that might happen.

He felt as if he had been holding his breath forever. He was frightened to exhale, frightened that at the speed they were travelling, if he let his breath out, he would never be able to draw another one in. He worried that the air would just rush past his mouth, as he tried desperately to suck it inside.

Then he would surely begin to thrash about in paroxysms of suffocation, at which point the Eyon currently holding him so tight, may get a scare and release him from its grasp. Then he and Shoo would plummet like rocks towards the sea below. Or maybe their fall would be broken...by several of the very treacherously sharp jutting cliffs. He wasn't sure which would be worse.

They could die a *thousand* deaths in the time it took to reach the rocks, limbs flailing mid air before finally finding purchase around the jagged shards which impaled them. Embracing the rocks in a death-hug, they would be found gorily dead, as the sea washed carelessly over their battered and broken bodies.

But the sea in its vastness and magnificence commanded his attention and he couldn't maintain his fantasy for long. Never before seen but immediately recognised, he knew at once he was looking at the sea. He had heard tales of one great water, so unhindered by land and so infinite, that it filled your vision for as far as could be seen. A water that was not calm and serene but instead was *alive*.

*No one* back home had seen it. But the stories had been passed down through generations of Pets. Other tales had been told too. Tales of high mountains and of lands where the winter cold bit deeper and for longer, than it did in Low Forest. He had always thought that was exactly what they were, tales, told to amuse, to entertain. Now he saw them for something else entirely. They were the truth.

For what seemed like a zillion years, but was probably only a minute or two, the Eyon flew on, to some unknown destination. Far, far below, the sea swirled and crashed in an almost mocking way, as if it were trying to reach out to San and Shoo and bring about their demise.

High and low they were swooped, under flying Eyons and over others and several terrifying times, through narrow gaps *between* them. Each time he shut his eyes tight and prepared to crash into their feathery bodies.

For all of this time, not a peep emerged from Shoo, not a single solitary woof. Just a strange whimpering sound, interspersed with huge wracking shivers. And each time they emerged unscathed at the other side.

Just as he finally got used to the terror, they approached the cliff face at such a great speed he was petrified once more. They were being taken into one of the caves, of which there were hundreds of identical entrances.

San shut his eyes tight. It didn't matter to him which cave they went in and quite frankly he didn't think he could stand the suspense of whether he, Shoo, Rian and the unknown Eyon could all fit through the little doorway simultaneously. Or whether they would just jam there before slowly sliding down the cliff to the waiting angry sea.

It was the smell and the sudden darkness behind his closed eyelids which told him that they had made it safely. That and the fact that he was released and unceremoniously dumped on something soft.

He dared to open his eyes. He was sitting, Shoo now on his lap, on an unmade bed, one made for Human proportions. Rian must have already slid from the Eyon's back, for he was now standing opposite San, next to what appeared to be a small wardrobe.

In spite of himself, San felt himself sink into the softness. It seemed so long since he had sat in some comfort, that part of him just wished he could lie down and go to sleep right then and then.

But apart from anything else, it would have proved impossible as Shoo was intent on pummelling his small body into San's stomach. He seemed to be trying to crawl underneath San's skin, pushing himself so close, San couldn't tell where he ended and Shoo began. But Shoo wasn't the only one who was surprised at this strange turn of events.

Their captor was standing opposite Rian, to the other side of San, forming a perfect triangle of participants in this drama, watching and waiting. Yet the Eyon seemed less surprised at San, than she did at Shoo and Rian. Eyes wide, she extended one taloned hand in Shoo's direction, only to snatch it back at the sound of the low growl which seemed to issue from deep inside the back of his throat.

"XXXWWWWTTTTTGGGG," the Eyon shrieked in seeming retaliation, its mouth making the widest 'o' possible.

"Iiiiihhhhhmmmfffssss. Ttttfffffllllllsssggg," rasped Rian in response.

At once, all heads swivelled in Rian's direction. The sound had not been exactly the same as that produced by the other Eyon but it was close enough.

The full Eyon turned to look at Rian. By the movement of its head, San could actually follow its gaze as it took in the Eyon body, topped with the Human arms and full head of Human hair.

"What's going on Rian?" hissed San in a whisper that turned out to be louder than he had intended.

"I haavvv tolldd herr that Shhooo isss *yooor* PETT…" he was interrupted by the Eyon before he could finish.

"CCCCCDDDDGGGGGRRREEEHHHHFFFTTT TKKKKJJJUUBBBTTTFFFRRDDDDMMMNNNSS SS." The screeches were so loud and echoed so much in the cave, that San couldn't tell if they were one word or lots of words all strung together.

Shoo gave a low growl once more. San gave him what he hoped was a reassuring pat on the head and hissed, "stop it Shoo. Friend." Then looking directly at the Eyon, very slowly, as if it could understand him, he stated, "he doesn't mean it, he's just scared, is all."

"Hjjjkkdkdijjjjjlliimmmmssjshhhdbbhjsnjdjnnnnnnnmfjj uuudnhswwwaaa," said Rian in response to what the other Eyon had said. Then he inclined his head slightly towards San, whilst still keeping his eyes firmly fixed on the Adult Eyon. "Shee saayss shee'ss neverrr seeenn anything like mee beforrr."

"Like you haven't heard *that* before!" said San, then immediately regretted it. "Sorry, I didn't mean that the way it came out," he faltered.

"I knoww. I haavv tolldd herr yooo arrr my Pett and she seesmss too havv accepted thatt."

San smiled at the new Eyon, hoping to smooth relations along a little. But as soon as he caught her gaze, she gestured to the wardrobe in a 'well go and have a look' sort of movement, vaguely waving her wing in that direction. Rian watched quietly, without speaking.

Timidly and rather reluctantly, San stood up and deposited Shoo on the bed. Shoo stayed where he was put and showed little inclination to move. The creature was still shaking but no longer making any noise to go with it. Satisfied he would wait quietly, San approached the wardrobe. The catch was stiff and he had to pull on it for a few moments but once the door finally sprang open, he understood everything.

The air inside the wardrobe was stale and musty. He turned his head aside, drew in a sharp breath of relatively good air and held it while he investigated the contents. It was full of clothes. Elasticated skirts and tops with easy to do up buttons for old arthritic hands. Flat, comfortable shoes and an assortment of very large and very strange items of underwear.

"These are the clothes of an old lady, an old Pet," he informed Rian who couldn't see the contents from where he stood. Putting two and two together – the unmade bed, the stale clothes and the absence of said Pet, San figured the old lady had died. He didn't know what to say but figured that he had to say something.

He turned to the Eyon, "I'm so sorry. You must have loved her very much."

He didn't really expect a response but he got one anyway. "LLLLPPPPPRRRROOOO."

"It's just our luck to be spotted by an Eyon who's still mourning its dead Pet and looking for a replacement!" he sighed heavily.

The Eyon stood, head still cocked to one side, watching and waiting for his reaction. Her feathers were beautiful, almost iridescent. A sort of shiny silver, with gold and blue shot through, so that they seemed to almost shimmer. It was the shimmer which gave away her sex. Usually, but not always, he had found, the female plumage was more shiny than the male's and sometimes their faces were a little softer too. But this one was particularly beautiful, with long dark eyelashes. Or at least she was to him. Who knew how Eyons measured beauty, or if they measured it at all. He made a mental note to ask Rian about that someday.

"In the meantime I guess we'd better deal with the situation here." He had spoken as much to himself as to the others present. Yet all appeared to be listening intently, focused on him and waiting. As if she knew and understood what he had said, the Eyon took a step towards Rian.

Wingtips extended, she grasped both his Human styled arms in her talons and lifted them gently away from his body. Head held first to one side, then the other, she examined him fully, taking particular note it appeared, of his fingers and ragged fingernails. Replacing his arms to his sides, she then turned her attention to his hair.

Using the talons of both wings once more, she lifted the curtain of dirty matted hair and examined it closely. For a moment San wondered if she was going to pull her talons through it like a comb but instead she replaced it carefully on Rian's shoulders. Whatever it was she was thinking, she kept it to herself.

Unable to stop himself, San's attention was caught by something in the wardrobe. Using the very tips of his fingers, he held aloft a particularly gigantic pair of pink underpants.

"WOW these are BIG underpants! I recon you and me could fit in these together if we tried Shoo!"

Was it his imagination or did Shoo look at him disparagingly then?

"Maybe if I held them above my head and jumped from the cliff doorway, the wind would catch in them and let us drift gently to the beach below. What do you think?" he joked.

"One thing is certain though, there's no way I'll be wearing those. I would literally die first," he vowed.

"Perrhappss thaatt iss whaatt happpennedd too the lasstt Pett," replied Rian, amused at his own idea.

"Perhaps, presented with these atrocious pants, she just lost the will to live. Just lay down on the bed and gave up breathing." San carried on the idea. He wouldn't have been surprised. It would certainly be his reaction if made to wear them!

"VVVNNNBBBBRRR," clicked the Eyon, pointing to herself, her large brown eyes still watching him intently.

"Thaatts herr name," explained Rian, somewhat unnecessarily.

"San," replied San, pointing to himself, figuring there was no reason not to give his real name.

"WOOF WOOF," Shoo supplied, apparently not wanting to be left out.

"Yeah and that's Shoo. We called him that because he wouldn't go away…" He trailed off not sure what else to say. Should he introduce Rian, or let him do that himself?

"ZZZZAAAAA," the Eyon tried to copy the sound she had heard. It was close but not quite right. Too high pitched and whiney at the start before turning into a deeper rasp. But it still made the hairs on the back of San's neck stand straight up. Apart from Rian, who didn't really count, he had never heard an Eyon get a word so close to sounding right.

Then again, he had never really heard an Eyon *try* to get a word right. He wondered if it was the Eyon, or the situation it had found itself in that was different.

Could it be that having 'found' them as it were, the Eyon had realised they already had names. Rather than having to rename them herself, she had decided to find out their existing names.

Once more, all eyes turned to Rian.

"Rrrrriiiiiiaaaaannnnnnnn," he supplied.

"KKKLKKHVGGHHJUGHJITTTTSSSXX.
RRRREEEWWWJJJJTTTTFFF
OOOOOPPPPYYYYHHHZZZXXZZ."

"Shee wants too know how I cann talk too yooo."
Rian informed San before screeching out his response.
"GGGGFFFSSWEEE      IIIIHHHGGTTYYDDSS
UUYYTRRPPQQWW KKKLIIIUUYP."

Then for San's benefit he interpreted, "I'vvv sedd I
donntt knoww. I waass hatched thiss way."

Apparently accepting this information, the Eyon
turned her attention to Shoo.

"SSHHOOO," she intoned, hairless head cocked to
one side and talons pointing at the unusual creature she
had found herself faced with.

"You've got it. And I will call you Vinnbr, ok?" asked
San. It was as close as he could make to the sound she
had made.

"VVVNNNBBBBRRR," she repeated. He wasn't
sure if it was an affirmation that she understood or rather
the reverse, that what he had said sounded so different to
her ears, she repeated her name for his benefit.

There was nothing else he could call her really. She
already thought that Rian was his Owner, which of
course raised the problem of whether or not she would
be expecting him to call Rian "OwnSan".

He couldn't do that, not even to cover their story. For
a start, there already *was* an OwnSan and *he* had been left
far behind in their forest home. And whilst San was not
physically with him, the link remained forged in his head
and his heart and his soul. One Owner, one Pet – it was a
bond which he could not break.

Yet another, equally insistent part of him refused to
allow him to think anymore in terms of being actually

'owned'. He had come so far, done so much and experience had made him so changed from the boy he had been back home. How could he ever go back to being just another Pet again?

"We are going to have to make the best of things till our chance to escape arrives," he told Shoo and Rian, aware that only Rian actually understood him.

Meanwhile he still had to deal with the clothing issue. He carefully folded the pants and replaced them in the wardrobe. Then flashing what he hoped was a winning smile, he shut the wardrobe door.

Big mistake!

"LLLLPPPPRRRROOOO. LLLLPPPPRRRROOOO."

The door was wrenched firmly open again in Vinnbr's taloned grasp, as she used her other wing tip to propel him closer to the displayed clothes. San's smile quickly turned to a grimace of horror.

"Yoo arr goingg too haavv to pick something…yoo arr too dirtty!" explained Rian with a grimace intended for San's benefit alone.

The assembled clothes were awful, there was no other word for it. Flicking through garment after garment on the rail was no help either. As soon as his eyes dismissed one horrendous dress and his hands consigned it to the 'rejected' side of the rail, he was presented with an even more horrific one. And all the while Vinnbr stood behind him making her wishes clear.

"LLLLPPPPRRRROOOO!"

"OK, OK I'm looking."

"WOOF WOOF." Shoo hated to be left out of a conversation.

Exasperated, San turned to Shoo.

"And you had better shut up, or she'll have you wearing something too!"

As if he had understood every word, Shoo gave out a quiet whimper and settled himself more comfortably on the bed, head flat between his front legs and feigned sleep.

"Oh great Shoo, thanks for the support!" San muttered. In truth he was relieved the little creature had calmed down. He had been worried about the Eyon's likely reaction if Shoo had growled again.

In desperation, having reached the end of the rail with no reasonable dress to be found, he had to backtrack and find the *least* horrendous one. It was a close contest. Was it to be the bright yellow polka dot one? At least it was a cheerful colour. Or the pale peach one? *Peach !!* He wavered, undecided.

"Yoo hadd betterr hurryy upp," advised Rian who had now settled himself comfortably on the bed and was now regarding the scene being played out before him with some amusement.

San's mind went in one direction, then the other, before coming back again. Peach, yellow, peach, yellow, pe…Then the choice was taken away from him.

Losing patience with him, Vinnbr reached past him, her talons grasping the closest item.

"LLLLPPPPPRRRROOOO."

She pulled a huge putrid green dress off a hanger and thrust it at him. San was mortified.

"Shoulda chosen quicker!" he scolded himself. Now he knew he had no choice. When it came to the crunch, you didn't argue with an angry Eyon.

Besides if he did *this* without too much dispute, she may let him off with putting on any other items of clothing. After all, there was always the underwear still there, *still available*. Maybe if he didn't push the Eyon too far, it would work out to his advantage. And the giant underpants would remain where they were, folded up ready and waiting to be worn by the next unfortunate Pet.

"LLLLPPPPRRRROOOO!"

"Look, I'm putting it on!"

Rian watched the exchange without interrupting. There was nothing he could add anyway, it was fairly obvious what was happening.

Reluctantly, San slipped the dress over his head. It really was huge. The neckline gaped over his small shoulders and the sleeves, which were probably supposed to reach the wearer's elbow, reached all the way to his wrists. Thankfully the hem just reached the floor rather than sitting puddled on it. It would have been just too much bad luck to have had to pick it up every time he moved.

"Verryy fetchingg," rasped Rain who had the good grace to look abashed at the icy glare San directed at him.

It was a tough compromise to pacify her, yet try to maintain his own dignity and somehow he thought she had come out the better of the two of them. He could feel Shoo's eyes boring into his back but when he looked at the bed, Shoo was doing a good imitation of being fast asleep.

At least Vinnbr seemed satisfied with the idea of him wearing the dress over his own underpants and top. Whilst this did nothing to help the aesthetics of the overall look, he was relieved, because it spared him the horror of the dress resting fully on his bare skin. He just hoped the previous occupant hadn't actually died whilst wearing it. Now that would be too gruesome!

Satisfied with the result, Vinnbr stepped back to allow him to close the wardrobe. She stood a little off to one side and his gaze was drawn past and beyond her, to where a tunnel he hadn't noticed before, stretched out. It wasn't quite in line with the entrance to the cave but still seemed to burrow deeper into the cliffside than he would have thought possible.

Following his gaze, Vinnbr turned and moved towards the tunnel. San and Rian followed, curious as to where it led, Shoo now trotting obediently at their heels.

"So much for being fast sleep," whispered San at him. For a moment he could almost have sworn that Shoo grinned mischievously back at him.

The rough rock walls were jagged and sharp and had a chipped look to them, almost as if they had had bits removed from them, chunk by chunk, till the tunnel was hollowed out enough to allow passage through.

"How was this done?" he wondered aloud.

"I donntt knoww. I haavv never seen anythingg like it," responded Rian, running his hands over the rough walls.

It didn't look natural but San wasn't aware of how else it could have occurred. It wasn't as if the Eyons could have clawed out a passageway, regardless of how sharp their talons were. Surely nothing could break up solid rock?

And it was strangely illuminated. He couldn't see the source of the light but he realised it was coming from whatever was ahead. The light shone around Vinnbr, finding little chinks between her and the rock as she moved, so that the amount of illumination constantly changed.

The Eyon almost completely blocked the narrow passage but there was plenty space for San, Rian and Shoo. San couldn't *quite* fully extend his arms out in the tunnel but they were at least more than half stretched before he could feel the rough stone between his fingertips. Thankfully, the ground was much smoother, with just the occasional small bump or dent in it.

Then Vinnbr stepped aside and San, Rian and Shoo emerged from the other end of the tunnel into a blaze of light.

# *Chapter 18.*

L oni now knew that *her* tale would have to be told first. And knew that she would have to tell it well, to redeem Little in this woman's eyes. If Eyons were really seen as such monsters here, for whatever reason and whether justified or not, then she could not but fear for Little's safety. Perhaps it would be best therefore to tell the story to everyone, straight away.

"Will you ask your people to join us now Sophia? You know you can trust us and they have nothing to fear."

Sophia nodded her agreement. "This is a tale all should hear." She raised her voice. "My People, you have nothing to fear from this child and her Monster," she cast an apologetic look at both Loni and Little and whispered, "sorry but it's our word for you, until we know everything". Then louder, back to the villagers, "come out when you are ready and have no fear."

One by one, the huts opened and people emerged, some old and some young but all without exception white faced and large eyed. Soon a larger circle was formed around the original one, and another behind that, as the people who came out of the huts encircled their trusted chief and these very strange strangers.

What struck Loni as they appeared, was how much they all resembled one another. She couldn't really put her finger on it, but there was a definite uniformity of look. And it wasn't just the roughly made clothes. It was something about the people themselves, the blend of hair, skin and eye colours. And even within this uniformity, there were those who resembled one another so much, that it had to be more than mere coincidence.

As her people began to appear, Sophia had taken charge of the situation. "We shall resume our talks, as soon as all who are prepared to hear, are ready. This child speaks the truth. It is a truth which may gladden our hearts or may crush them. But hear it we must."

Then her tone changed to a much sterner one and Loni saw why she was the leader here.

"No harm will be given to these …" she had been about to say 'people', but couldn't bring herself to use the term, as it was one Human and one Eyon she was referring to, so quickly had to find another word "… visitors. This is the word of your Leader. And *all* will obey it."

Finally, it seemed that the entire village was assembled. Loni looked around in amazement, at the sheer volume of people. There were at least two hundred there, ranging in age from little children to very old men and women. And although they were sitting in circles, with Loni's circle the innermost one, something about the way they sat, seemed to suggest they were in little clusters, strung out into an overall circle formation.

Loni wasn't sure where to begin but luckily Sophia spoke up first.

"The child has a given name of Loni and her Monster is her *companion*," she stated the final word carefully, keeping her tone flat and unambiguous, as if oblivious to the gasps of amazement from the assembled villagers.

"His name is Little and he can understand some of what we say." Loni wasn't sure if there was a warning implied in that last bit but she made no comment either way.

"We call them Monsters but his kind are really called Eyons," Sophia continued, presumably so that they would better understand Loni's expalations.

Loni noticed that she still pronounced the word slightly wrong more like 'Eeoon' rather than the correct 'E Y O N' with every sound given the same emphasis. But that wasn't important.

Sophia turned to her. "Carry on now, please," she requested. So, taking a deep breath, Loni explained as best she could, who she was and how she came to be sitting on the ground there.

"... and so when I found the machine, I knew that we had to leave. Only for a while, only long enough for them to see that Little isn't *like* the other Eyons." She paused for a moment, seeing the looks that this idea elicited pass through the crowd. How it made each of the Humans look to another to gauge their reaction.

Sometimes the conversation was solely between her and Sophia for long stretches, sometimes Little tried to join in, with Loni interpreting for him and sometimes there was a babble of voices, as the villagers all chipped in with questions or little bits of information.

Shrugging free of both Little's and Sophia's hold, Loni turned her right arm over to show the triangular marks on her arm. "I noticed you don't have these. Or at least I couldn't see any on you. Do you know what they are?" she waited for a response.

Sophia traced her finger tips over the marks on Loni's proffered arm.

"The skin is smooth, yet the lines seem set into your skin and darker than the rest of the skin. How is this done? Is it painful?" she drew her hand away as the thought occurred to her. "Does it hurt you if I touch it?" Her expression was full of concern.

Loni smiled. "No, it doesn't hurt. And it didn't hurt to have it done. And every year I get another triangle. That's how all the Owners and the other Pets know how old you are, by these markings." She stopped again as she realised why Sophia's eyes had widened with surprise once more.

"Pets! You are *Pets*?" Sophia's disgust was more than apparent.

"Oh yes 'Pets'! That's what we call ourselves. Well it is, and it isn't...it's kinda complicated I guess," she fumbled in her head for the right way to explain it.

"We're Humans...but we're Pets too. We go where we are taken and do as we are told," she corrected herself when she saw Sophia's stricken expression. "I mean...nice things. Things like swimming or playing or...or anything." Her mind was strangely blank, she suddenly couldn't think of a single fun thing she normally did.

"But you are *Pets?*" Sophia could not keep the note of disbelief from her voice. Loni could not understand why this was so.

"But you know that already. You give up your children to the Eyons to have a better life than you can give them, away from the..." she had been about to say 'squalor' but managed to stop herself in time. "Away from the fighting and the danger. So the children get a safe home and the Eyons get a Pet." She stated it for the fact that it was, Little nodding beside her.

"We *give up* our children...to be *Pets!*" Sophia's tone was incredulous and there seemed to be unease in the crowd. Suddenly it appeared as if the throng was leaning in further towards Loni and Little, straining to be closer, to listen more intently.

Loni completely misinterpreted the significance of this new development and continued on oblivious to the reaction of the people surrounding her.

"Yes. But is it any different from those creatures you keep, the ..." Loni struggled to remember the right word, "the dogs? You said they help you with hunting ...but that's not the only reason you keep them. You keep them because you like them. They are *your* Pets."

There was a hiss of indrawn breath from the assembled crowd and Loni knew she was right. It was a turned around way of thinking but it was right nonetheless and no-one could deny its truth, even if it would take some getting used to.

"Yes, you are of course right. *They* are *our* Pets. The difference is, that they are free to come and go at will. Can the same be said of you?" Sophia asked, her tone flat, her eyes asserting that she already knew the answer.

Aware that Sophia said it neither to anger, nor to be contentious, Loni stated the plain unembellished truth. "No, Sophia, we are not." She hesitated a moment, unsure how to carry on. She decided to go back to her original point and leave this other difficult concept till later.

"Anyway, the triangles are done with a machine that lets out a thin stream of red light. It tickles more than anything else. New Pets don't have them of course, so they have to get them as soon as they are re-homed."

"Re-homed from here!" Sophia stated it as if it was an entirely new concept to her and Loni wondered why this was. There was a deathly silence from the villagers. All the peripheral conversations had ended. All the whispered 'did you hear that' and 'imagine that' comments had died – there was no other word for it. Once more every single person sat silently, struck dumb by the recent revelations.

"Or if not from here, then from somewhere else just like here!" Sophia's voice was strangely quiet.

Loni was surprised at that comment. Of course there were other villages. Who did these people wage war with then, if not with other villages. She looked at Little for confirmation.

"ESSSS," he nodded in agreement.

Whilst Loni told them how she cared for and was cared for *by* her Owner, she sensed a growing resentment. The air seemed to shimmer before her with repressed anger, which emanated from the villagers at her declaration, that generally speaking, Human Pets were happy with their Owners and that the Eyons cared well for their Pets.

She found herself shuffling uncomfortably on the ground as she made this statement, not because it was *untrue*, which it wasn't, but because in a strange way it made her feel like the traitor Sophia had previously claimed her to be. It was such an alien concept to the people here, who lived out their lives independent and separate from, but in apparent fear of the Eyons. Although she still didn't know why that was.

Loni saw the villagers drink in her every word, as they listened to her side of the story, their bodies hunched forward in rapt attention. Occasionally someone would adjust themselves slightly but only momentarily and quietly, so focused were they on the information she was providing.

A small child had climbed onto Sophia's lap as Loni talked. Sophia absently stroked the little girl's hair as she listened, her fingers automatically smoothing out the tangles. A part of Loni's brain began to wonder what it would have been like, to have had a real mother to look after her. The little girl certainly seemed to be responding to it, as she leaned further back into Sophia's lap and stopped wriggling around.

She was cute, with huge brown eyes set in a chubby little face and looked to be a little bit younger than any child Loni had seen before. Her frank stare mirrored those of the people around her. But what was interesting, Loni noticed, was the absence of fear in the child's face, that was so apparent in the older children and adults. Thumb stuck firmly in her mouth, she gazed at Little with awe and fascination but absolutely no fear. Loni knew there was a significance to this, but she didn't know what it was.

And so the sun continued its progress through the sky as the three female Humans and the one male Eyon sat in a circle, surrounded by other wider circles of villagers and talked as best they could.

# *Chapter 19.*

S an blinked at the sight. Overhead lights shone down on a gleaming kitchen. Set into the very rock of the cave, the bulbs were hidden so far within the stone, that they appeared to be tiny stars in a black sky. Looking up, you could forget that you were in a cave, the impression was so good.

"Do all the caves have lighting like this, do you think?" he wondered aloud.

"Probabblyy," replied Rian, his attention also captivated by the shimmering lights.

It was beautiful – there was no other word for it and it was of course necessary to have lights. But done this way? So artistically? And then an idea came to him. It was a feeling that had started in his chest and moved to his head. A tightness that quickened his breathing and seemed to grip his lungs with cold hands, began to ease, as he looked upwards into the false night sky.

"AH! Perhaps it is necessary, to create an illusion of space and freedom, this far into the cave," he mused, answering his own question. Perhaps anyone having to spend all their cooking and cleaning hours in here, would begin to feel trapped, cornered, and generally short of breath.

"I think yoo mayy be rightt!"

San's eyes followed the lights to their end destination where they shone down onto flat stone work surfaces and moulded cupboards. He had never seen a kitchen quite like it. He couldn't stop himself from reaching forward and running his hands down the smooth wooden cupboard doors.

"LLLLPPPPRRRROOOO," Vinnbr urged.

San recognised the same sequence of sounds that she had made before.

"Shee wanttss yoo too try itt," confirmed Rian.

This was a shade of wood he had never seen before, light and almost without colour. Whether it was natural or had been modified in some way he couldn't tell. But it was perfect here. It alleviated the darkness and brought a feeling of warmth to the otherwise cold stone kitchen.

Inside, the cupboards were the same shape and functional design as back home, except that they were moulded from the actual rock. He closed the door softly on the assembled crockery and turned to examine the oven and hob.

"Is it the same as your kitchen back home?" he enquired, aware that he couldn't take anything for granted.

"Nott reallyy. Somme bitss arr andd somme arr differrenntt."

The oven appeared to be fairly similar to the one he had operated but it too was set into the stone walls. The hob, or what he assumed to *be* the hob, was completely strange to him.

On OwnSan's, he used four rings which individually could be turned on to heat up. These stood separate to and proud of the flat plate, into which they were set. But here, what he assumed to be the hob, looked instead like a sheet of black glass set on top of the stone. He held his hands above it for a moment, just in case it was on. It didn't appear to be hot. Wonderingly, he ran his fingers over the surface.

"Beee carefulll!" warned Rian.

"LLLLPPPPRRRROOOO."

Smooth, so smooth, with four little semi-circles painted on it. Was that to indicate where the pots should be placed? Nor were there any dials to operate it. Instead it appeared to be controlled by buttons. Full of curiosity he pushed one of them. It had a tiny diagram above it which seemed to show to which semi-circle it belonged.

Finger still depressed into the button he thought to look at Vinnbr for approval. Seeming to understand his surprise and need to explore, she caught his gaze and nodded assent.

"LLLLPPPPRRRROOOO."

A tiny click happened underneath his fingertip then another and another. There were obviously different degrees of heat which could be applied through this device, in the same way as the control knob he was used to.

He watched, fascinated as the correct semi-circle at first glowed a dull red before quickly escalating to a red-hot haze of colour. He could feel the intensity of the heat on his skin and quickly turned the appliance off before moving away.

"Wow that heated up faster than the one back home!"

It was the familiar mixed with the unfamiliar of this kitchen, which made it so strange. Somehow it would have been less disconcerting if the whole thing had been different to what he was used to. But it wasn't.

"Clothes washing machine, almost identical to the one back home," he ticked off a list of familiar things, "and a sink." Curved out smooth and shiny and dark from the rock walls, it was worlds away from the only other sink he had used, a huge silver metal thing.

Kitchen utensils were stored neatly inside a drawer, made of same light wood, and food was stored in the cold store.

"All normal things." But there was a stone table where the legs actually rose still attached from the stone floor, and two stone chairs. Not normal. Thankfully he realised that the chairs were not still attached to the floor… the messy way he ate, it would put the clothes washing machine to a lot more use, if he couldn't pull the chair under the table. Not that he intended to stay. He just had to look as though he did.

Rian interrupted his thoughts. "I haavv never herdd ovv anywherr like thiss. Haavv yoo Saann?" he asked.

"No," shaking his head at the strangeness of it all.

"LLLLPPPPPRRRROOOO. LLLLPPPPPRRRROOOO."

"Looks like we are on the move again."

Taking the initiative, San left the kitchen behind and re-entered the stone passageway. This time the light was much brighter as he was in the lead, with Rian and Shoo following close behind and then Vinnbr. The passage way itself was not lit, so relied on light filtering in both sides, from the kitchen at one end and the living area at the other. Without Vinnbr's large body to block it out, there was enough light to see easily and he didn't need to put his arms out to steady himself.

He was aware of the Eyon following closely in his tracks. She seemed to be prepared to let them explore without interference, just urging them on. Emerging from the passageway back to the room which led in from the Cliffside, he scanned the area for another doorway. There had to be a bathroom somewhere.

He had been so focused on the human bed and wardrobe that he hadn't taken much else in. Now he noticed other things. The big Eyon bed. The work area, exactly as expected, held the same type of machine that OwnSan connected to and scrolled the same indecipherable symbols across its screen.

This was set into the gloomiest corner of the room. Except that it wasn't a corner at all. Approaching it, he realised he had found the entrance to two other areas. He moved around the machine until he stood directly in front of the first one. He could make out the hole cut in the rock to serve as a doorway, but nothing else. Unlike the kitchen, this area was not illuminated.

Suddenly wary, he turned to Vinnbr. Was it safe to just step into the darkness beyond? "Am I to go in there? Is it safe?" he asked her although he knew that Rian would have to translate.

"YYYTTTREEFGHVFFDDD HHYYYYBBBBVGTHDFFRT," asked Rian in Eyon.

"HHHGGGGRRREEEEE," came the response, waving them away into the darkness.

"Shee hass said whatt liess beyond butt I will lett yoo discoverr for yoorself," smiled Rian, implying that whatever it was, wasn't bad.

Fairly sure that the Eyon wished him no harm, San picked Shoo up before he took a tentative step forward, then another and walked through the doorway into the new dark room.

As soon as his feet hit the ground, he heard a faint "SWISH" coming from behind him and lights blazed on. Squinting in the dazzling light, so unexpected after the darkness, he spun round in reaction to the noise, turning his back on the room and all that it contained. He felt Shoo's little body give a sudden jolt and the little creature began to whimper in fear.

# *Chapter 20.*

Finally Loni's tale was told. Her mouth was dry and her throat filled with apprehension as she prepared to take her turn to listen. Her mind was in turmoil, trying to reconcile what she knew, with what she was now seeing reflected in the faces of the people here, as they tried to absorb all the information she had given them. Looks of disbelief had been replaced by something else. Some other emotion that Loni was not familiar with.

But then with every word that Sophia spoke, a clarity began to form in Loni's mind. Gesturing every now and then to her people for both support and confirmation, Sophia described how they lived under constant threat of the next Eyon raid. The *next* time that the monsters would break down their doors in the middle of the night. The *next* time that their hearts would be broken and their children stolen from them. The *next* time that their children would be harvested for the monsters' feasting. Because that was exactly what they presumed to be happening...that their children were being taken away to be roasted and eaten.

Loni's eyes got wider and wider as she listened and Little sat straight and tense at her side.

Sophia's story began long, long ago, many generations before anyone assembled there in the circle was born, but the tale was as terrifying, as it was old.

It had been the dead of night. A night with a full clear moon in the sky when they had come for the very first time. Winged monsters, they had descended from the sky with evil in their hearts.

Deathly silent, they had approached with stealth and attacked with speed. Surprised from their slumber, the villagers had at first been merely bewildered, such was their naivety. But as their eyes adjusted to the gloom in their huts and they became aware of the strange creatures in their midst, their bewilderment turned to fear and then terror.

"The monsters had seized every young child from the clutches of its parents, holding the child aloft and shrieking to one another in triumph as they did so. They were everywhere and all at once, too big, too strong, too prepared. And the villagers were just as equally unprepared." Sophia's voice shook, tremors coursing down her body as she spoke.

"How could they have known? They were peaceful farmers and gatherers of food. They had no knowledge or experience of battle, nor had they ever thought they would need any. They had no weapons. But they did have farm tools. Wickedly sharp scythes and pick axes for breaking the ground and cutting the harvest. That same night, under the cold gaze of the full moon, those sharp tools were used in a new and novel way."

Loni gulped as her imagination brought the story to life in her head.

Sophia continued. "Tools lying abandoned were hastily grasped and wielded. Blades were used to hack at the intruders and picks were embedded in feathery bodies. In retaliation, sharp claws were used to rip the villagers apart. There was no discrimination in the killing…women and old men, older children and young adults. All who fought back were slaughtered. The bloodshed was atrocious and many lives were lost, both Human and Eyon. Only those who wielded no weapon had been spared."

But the monsters had been victorious. They had taken every child under the age of two and shrieking loudly, had carried them off, never to be seen again. The sound of the Eyon cries had seemed to be an affront to the cool night air, a mocking crow of victory over the desperate villagers.

Defeated, the decimated villagers had watched their children being carried away and had no other recourse than to hold their arms to the sky and beg their return. But it was to no avail. Nor had that been the end of it.

Instead, the surviving Eyons had returned the following night with reinforcements. This time the villagers were also better prepared. Even so, they were both outnumbered and out manoeuvred. And this time the monsters took all of the children.

"The people knew it was a warning. They knew the older children had only been taken to illustrate the point that they *could* be taken. Twice the People had fought back. And twice they had lost."

Sophia continued as Loni and Little sat mesmerised by such distressing information.

"So the People learned a lesson. They searched for their children but found nothing. They buried their dead with honour and respect and then quietly got on with their lives again. Wives remarried, babies were born. But the people were changed. Hearts so broken cannot fully heal and lives so shattered cannot ever fully recover." Sophia took a gulp of air as she gazed around her people as she told the sad tale, *their* sad tale.

"They lived in constant fear of the monsters' return; constant vigilance and they hardened their hearts in readiness. And when the Monsters returned, as the people always knew they would, they were resigned to their fate."

Loni thought she knew what was coming and she wanted to stop Sophia talking, stop these words which impaled her heart. Yet they *were* only words and these people had lived through far, far worse. It would do them all a great dishonour if she were not brave enough to even hear their tale. So she bit her tongue and let her ears remain open.

"Years had passed since the first attack but it had not been forgotten. But instead of fighting back, this time the villagers suffered their young children to be taken. Just let them be taken, with a last kiss and a prayer. And in doing so, their older children had been spared.

They had learned to sacrifice some, so that others would be free. They had learned to live with the pain and suffering in their hearts and to cry silently at night in their beds."

But of course in its own way, this merely perpetuated the situation. Because the Eyons only ever took small children, the older children were left to grow and breed and produce an ever ready crop of young Humans for subsequent raids. The story reflected the history of these people - unrelenting and unforgiving.

"As time went on, the raids became more specific and the Eyons selected only the children who had seen their first cycle of seasons but not yet their second.

And now here you are, to tell us of how the children, *our children*," for a moment her voice cracked, "believe that we *gave them up voluntarily*. That they are brainwashed, with tales of how we wage war with other villages and are no more than blood-thirsty savages! And you tell us that our children are *Pets* for these liars and thieves?" Her tone had risen as she continued, anger sharpening her words to daggers.

Little slumped dejected beside Loni. She had attempted to communicate everything to him, by way of gesture and rough pictures drawn in the dirt at their feet and he had seemed to get the thread of it. Only vaguely was she aware of the low keening noise he was now emitting in his misery.

As hard as it was for Loni to face the horrible truth, of how she herself must have been snatched from a loving mother, it was equally hard for the villagers to accept the truth of their children's existance. All around, she could hear voices repeating the same thing, over and over and over.

"They are alive," they said, "*alive! ALIVE!*"

And what other implications did this have? Did it mean that she herself had been born and raised in this village until being snatched before her second birthdate? Was her birth mother here?

The villagers had progressively shuffled forward as they strove to make their own voices heard in the excited babble and Loni feared Little was feeling oppressed by the sheer volume of Humankind he was surrounded by. He would surely be terrified that he was about to face the consequences of the villagers' loathing.

But looking around, she was surprised and relieved to realise that he was in no danger. Angry and filled with hatred for the unknown Eyons as they were, Loni had expected the villagers to be a threat to Little. But they seemed to have accepted his innocence. Unanimously, they were hurt and bewildered, but not one single face displayed the disfiguring emotions of hatred and revenge. It was a side of Human nature she had never seen before, a willingness to look beyond the superficial.

She turned her gaze to Little. The keening noise which came from him was louder now, as he rocked back and forth where he sat, clutching his wings into himself. Thick heavy tears streaming unchecked down his chubby cheeks, it wasn't clear whether he was crying in sympathy for the villagers and their lost children, or in disgust and loathing for his own species. In a way it didn't matter whether it was one or the other, or even both, it was all such a mess and so soul-destroying.

For a moment Loni stared stupidly at the thick pile of coloured feathers that lay around her feet. Where had they come from? And then the answer was blindingly obvious.

Sharp talons digging unheeded into his own soft body, Little clutched at bunches of his feathers and tore them from his body. A wet ripping sound accompanied every tug and Little's blood flowed freely from newly bald and abraded skin.

Strangely it was Sophia who stopped him, as Loni looked on in shock and horror.

"No, you must not blame yourself. You are as innocent as the children who have been taken and we cast no blame on you." Her voice was soft and firm at the same time.

Little looked at Sophia.

"I nott no beforr…nott no," he whispered so softly that Loni almost didn't hear. He turned to her, his expression heartbreaking for her to see.

"I nott no, Lonnneee."

"I know you didn't Little. I didn't either," she comforted him.

Now all the explanations had been provided by Sophia and Loni, all that was left, was to listen to the individual tales. Tales told by the mothers and the fathers and the siblings of the lost children and to hold hands, and wings too, and cry over them.

Loni lost count of the number of times she was asked if she could recall seeing this baby, or that child, with the bright red hair so distinctive, or the little scar on her top lip that she got when learning to walk, or a little boy with a sharp nose or full mouth or so on. And on and on.

All she could do was say no, she was sorry but she couldn't identify them, she couldn't help them. Yet in her head she wondered what she could do if she *had* recognised a description. How could these people be reconciled with children who were content to be Pets? Would forcibly dragging Pets away from the Owners they loved, not just be perpetuating the misery? Was there an answer to this predicament? If there was, she couldn't see it.

# Chapter 21.

San's pupils contracted automatically, adjusting to the sudden glare of light. In front of him was a stone door, completely blocking the entrance he had taken to this room.

Panicked, he pushed against the door with all his might.

"Come on, come on," he groaned, somewhat encumbered by still holding Shoo. The door was solid and would not shift.

"Maybe if I put you down …" but as soon as he said it he realised he would not do that, in case they became separated.

"Rian, Rian!" he called frantically, But the stone walls and door  seemed to almost absorb the sound and probably served to keep it from escaping the confines of where he stood.

They were trapped! How long would it be before the air became thick, the oxygen used up? How long would it be before they began to suffocate in this tomb? Already the air felt thicker and he had to concentrate on dragging it down into his lungs. And then he thought to turn around.

His eyes were assaulted by the torturous instruments of none other than a toilet and Clean Zone cubicle. He was in a washroom! Not a tomb for capturing unsuspecting Pets, after all!

Still carrying Shoo, he walked to the far end of the smallish room to investigate. The toilet and cubicle were similar enough to what he was used to, with only slight differences. The walls and floor were bare rock as he had come to expect and now that he was being more sensible, he could even see the rails on the floor the sliding door had moved along.

But there was no handle or lever on the door. He had no idea what had caused it to shut or more importantly, how he was to get it back open.

"Any ideas, fur face?" he asked Shoo, ruffling the small creature's hair to help calm him. He was rewarded by a wet slimy tongue lick across the face.

"That sorta gratitude, I can live without," he said ruefully, wiping away the slobber with his free hand.

He felt the rough wall on one side of the door. Perhaps there was a hidden button there, he couldn't immediately see. But all that met his searching fingers was the cool stone. Planning to go to the other wall next to search, he took one step forward across the middle of the room...and the door slid open, making the same 'SWISH' as before.

And stayed open.

This time he looked downwards. There just by his foot, was a button set into the stone. One foot planted firmly on the ground, he used the other to lightly press on the button. The door closed, the door opened, closed, opened, closed, opened. But the lights stayed on.

"Well look at that Shoo! Did you ever see such a thing!" he said amazed.

Mystified as to what he was up to, Vinnbr and Rian stood just outside the doorway watching him.

"Guess I'm the weirdest Human she's met," he grinned at them both. "Does *she* know that other homes are different to this?" he asked Rian.

"I could askk butt thaatt mayy brrringg otherr quesstionnss thaat wee mayy nott waanntt tooo answerrr."

"Yes you are right!"

San stepped out of the room and towards Rian and Vinnbr. Immediately the lights clicked off. Somehow the room knew he had left it. He swivelled his head around rapidly, trying to see what had caused this. But there was nothing to be seen. Turning back to Vinnbr, he saw her still watching him, her head cocked to one side again. Then she did something really unexpected.

Grasping his arm with one of her wing ends, careful not to dig her wickedly sharp talons into him or Shoo, she pulled him towards her. It was so quick that neither he nor Rian had time to react. Then propelling him round, turned him to face the stone doorway again.

Theatrically placing her foot on the inset button on this side of the door, she lifted him high in the air, as the door swooshed open once more. His first thought as he was hoisted unceremoniously towards the ceiling, was that she was finally bored with him. She was going to dash his brains out against the hard rock and use his blood as paint for her bedroom! Shoo must have thought the same because he began to bark loudly.

"WOOF, WOOF, WOOF, WOOF!"

He wriggled around in San's arms so much, San nearly dropped him on Vinnbr's head.

"TTYYYYFFFFRRR!" the Eyon screeched in seeming response.

But dashing out his brains wasn't her intention at all! Up close he could see two little nodule things set into the stone ceiling. They were not part of the natural cave. He reached out his hand to touch them.

As his hand passed over them, the lights in the bathroom came on! Another wave of his hand over them, turned the lights off. These were the things that had sensed him going in and out of the room. Needing the lights on or off.

Satisfied that he understood, Vinnbr now carried him and Shoo aloft to the other dark recess, with Rian following on behind. Depressing the floor button and carrying him past the sensor, she finally set him down in the other illuminated room. The door and lights worked exactly the same here, but it was not a room *he* would be using.

This was the *Eyon* toilet area and contained the usual large toilet and washbasin, made to Eyon proportions. To be honest if he tried to use the toilet, he'd probably fall down it and be flushed right away!

"Well Shoo, guess you're gonna have to use one of these bathrooms 'cos the option of going outside, isn't an option at all!" He informed the creature.

"If I were you, I'd choose the Human one over the Eyon one any day," he joked.

But that give him another idea.

"Rian come here a moment," he called.

He waited till Rian shuffled past Vinnbr before putting Shoo down on the floor and grasping Rian's arm led him over to the large mirror set above the washbasin.

He turned Rian to face the mirror.

"Open your mouth as wide as you can and say aaaaa," he instructed.

"AAAAAHHHHHHHH!" Rian obliged.

And there it was. The inside of his own throat and Rian's, bare and exposed, both with a thick dangly bit hanging down in the middle. It looked like a big pink worm, all yucky and raw looking. Rian's was bigger and slightly flatter than San's but they were similar.

"Theyy aarrr diffferrentt."

"Yes they are a *bit* different but also quite similar. That's why you can talk like me *and* like the other Eyons. If only we could get her to open her mouth we could see how different you are."

He turned again to face his friend.

"You could ask her," but a thought occurred to him, "but perhaps you don't actually want to know?"

Rian's eyes seemed to cloud over as if the prospect of finding out *how and why* he was different was painful to him.

Not looking at either San or Vinnbr, but instead at his reflection in the mirror he called to Vinnbr.

"UUUULLLOOOOPPPPSSAAARRRHHUUFFF CCCVVCCCN."

There was something there at the very back of his throat which San hadn't seen when Rian was using his Human speech.

It looked almost like a little bit of thread, no, more like a strand of spaghetti that curled up on itself at certain sounds. San opened his own mouth again just to be sure.

But no, he only had the one dangly bit right there at the back, not the spaghetti thing too.

And then Vinnbr appeared behind him.

She opened her mouth wide.

And Rian opened his.

And since everyone else was doing it, San joined in.

"AAAAAHHHHH!" screeched Rian.

"AAAAAHHHHH!" simultaneously screeched Vinnbr.

"AAAAA!" screeched San.

"WOOF! WOOF! WOOF!" barked Shoo from the doorway.

And San could see, clear as anything, the spaghetti thing at the back of Vinnbr's throat. It was longer than Rian's but curled up just the same. But there was no wormy pink thing in her throat, just the spaghetti thing.

"Did you see the difference?" he asked Rian.

"YESSS!" Rian seemed surprised that there had been such an obvious difference.

"Maybe its not the dangly things which control the sounds we make...but they are different...and I guess where there is one difference there are bound to be others!"

Experiment over, Vinnbr seemed to lose interest immediately. Leading the way out of the room, she settled herself by her machine as soon as the door had swished shut behind them. Plugging one of her talons in, she connected up and turned her full attention to the scrolling screen.

San, Rian and Shoo were as good as alone again. But this seemed to be a new concept to Shoo. The little creature approached Vinnbr cautiously, sniffing the ground around the Eyon's feet. Head outstretched and body somehow kept as much at a distance as was possible, he seemed to be expecting the unexpected at any moment.

"Don't worry Shoo. She's past noticing us now. I could probably rearrange all the furniture around her and she wouldn't even notice."

The thought occurred to him that he could probably run around naked shrieking, or conversely put on every strange item in the wardrobe and jump up and down in front of her and she wouldn't even bat an eyelid.

That part of life here was obviously no different. He had a thought.

"Rian can you watch her on her machine for a little while and tell if it is different to what Eyons do at your home?"

He wasn't sure if that was significant, but it certainly wouldn't do any harm to find out.

"YEESSS!" Rian agreed, taking up a place behind where Vinnbr sat.

San's stomach grumbled loudly, reminding him that none of them had eaten properly in some time. He re-entered the midnight kitchen with Shoo close behind.

'Stars' glinting down on him, he took time selecting the ingredients for a meal.

"May as well look for the things I like best and cook what I want. How do you fancy breaded chicken, on a bed of spaghetti, with anchovies on the side?"

Then he thought of Rian and Vinnbr's open mouths and suddenly the spaghetti didn't seem so appealing after all!

Excited by his tone of voice, Shoo gave out a little yip of pleasure.

"She won't notice what food I make anyway, so lets have what we fancy, what do you say, Shoo?"

"WOOF WOOF!" tongue lolling out again, Shoo seemed to be in full agreement.

"Once, just for a laugh, I gave OwnSan a plate of shredded toilet paper - unused of course - and a side order of soap," he informed Shoo. San had thought OwnSan would find it at least *amusing,* even if he didn't find it as downright hilarious as San himself did. But when, still attached to his machine, OwnSan had lifted a spoon full of the stuff, ready to just shovel it into his mouth, San had been horrified. Quickly he had jumped in and whisked the spoon from OwnSan's grasp. He had rapidly replaced the jokey plate, with the plate of real food and OwnSan hadn't even noticed!

That was part of the trouble with Eyons – life was safe and comfortable – but also more than a little boring. And they didn't *get* jokes - not even practical ones!

The contents of the kitchen cupboards were similarly boring. Either the last Pet had had a very bland taste in food, or Vinnbr had been cooking for herself for quite a while. Disappointingly, there were none of his favourite foods. Instead of the hoped for food, there were unopened tins of bread and packets of dry crackers.

The cold store was similarly disappointing. No breaded chicken at all! Instead there were chunks of ham and some other pale meat which looked a bit like chicken but wasn't. San took out the container with the strange meat in it and sniffed suspiciously at it. It smelled ok and didn't *look* off but he had no idea what it was.

Carefully, he sliced a little bit off one end of the joint. It had quite a hard, dry texture and seemed firmer than chicken. Popping the piece in his mouth, he chewed vigorously. Whatever it was, it was tasty!

"Well it's not like we've got much choice." He tossed a bit of the meat to Shoo, who seemed to catch it and devour it in one swoop.

Dejected that he wasn't going to be able to tantalise his taste buds with any delectable morsels, San made sandwiches with as much care and attention as he could.

He opened the tin of bread and separated the slices. Then, mixing mustard with mayonnaise, he spread it thickly on every slice. For good measure he added a little extra mustard to the slices of bread intended for Vinnbr. Once the sandwiches were fully assembled he made up some drinks. Tea for her, since she had some unopened bottles in the cold store, coffee for himself and Rian and water for Shoo, who had wrinkled his nose in distaste at the scents of both tea and coffee.

A glass of tea in one hand and a platter of sandwiches in the other, he carried them through to the living area and placed them on the desk in front of Vinnbr. He wasn't sure if she saw him or merely saw the food appear in front of her but her free hand reached out and lifted a sandwich.

She took a bite. There wasn't even a squawk but San could tell the mustard had kicked in, by the huge gulping sound that followed and by how quickly she reached for the tea.

She must have drained half the glass before she lifted another sandwich to her mouth.

He caught Rian's gaze.

"Well, now she knows how I felt when she picked me up in those big claws of hers," he said by way of explanation, sniggering quietly.

Fetching Shoo's food and drink from the kitchen, he placed them on the floor by the bed. But even before the dishes were put down, Shoo had his face buried in them, clearing the plates before San had time to fetch Rian's.

Re-entering the room with his own and Rian's food and drinks on a tray, he waited for Rian to settle himself on the bed, before he too sat down. From this position they could watch this new Eyon and eat at the same time.

"Well, is it the same?" he asked.

"Yesss. Aa little differrennt maybee buutt mosttllyy the same."

A thought struck San. It suddenly occurred to him that Rian was starting to sound clearer, more understandable to him. He wondered if this was just that he was becoming used to him, or if Rian was actually improving, maybe due to constant practise.

Having waited for San to speak but getting no response, Rian continued anyway.

"Shee iss ssendingg aandd rreceivving infforrmaishon. Whatt iss neededd here and whenn itt iss neededd by."

Still chewing his food, he stood up and moved around to stand in front of the machine. The Eyon seemed completely unaware of his presence, her attention was so riveted.

He noticed that if he looked closely, he could see the screen reflected in her eyes. Looking like this, the symbols seemed to be embedded in her eyes rather than reflected onto the surface of them. It was too creepy for him to watch for long.

Vinnbr just sat there unmoving once her food had been eaten and Shoo was once more asleep on the bed. This time it was for real. Legs pedalling empty air and mouth issuing the softest of whimpers, San wondered if he was dreaming about being carried into the cave. But nightmare or dream, San decided to let the animal sleep. Who knew what lay ahead and how much chance of rest any of them would get.

He was anxious to leave this place and be on his journey again but the only way out, was the way they had come in. He made his way over to the entrance to the cave, stopping short of the actual doorway, fearful of becoming dizzy and falling out.

As he had before, on the cliff top, he dropped to his knees and crawled to the edge.

The doorway was astounding. There was no lip or edge, it was literally a hole in the cave. Shimmying himself down to ground level, he dangled his head out of the cave and drew in a large breath of the salty air.

# *Chapter 22.*

It was the hardest day Loni had ever had to live through and nothing that had ever come before, had in any way prepared her for it.

She hadn't been especially active but every bone in her body ached. But it ached with more than mere physical strain. It ached with a despondency so deep, that it made her weary. Her head hung low. She couldn't even find the strength to hold it up, or the will to search for that strength. It was as if all the fight had left her body. And yet it wasn't.

Somewhere in the deepest, darkest core of her, a hurt smouldered. She hurt for these people who had lost loved ones so cruelly. And she hurt too for her beloved Eyons, who were so despised by these people.

She hurt at the thought the Owners could be so cruel, so uncaring and so selfish in their needs. She hurt because they had lied and cheated and made a mockery of the genuine affection and high esteem they were held in by their Pets.

An affection believed to be grounded in gratitude, it was in reality grounded on lies. Lies that the children had been gratefully handed over for the assurance of a better life. Lies that Human villages were war-torn and war-ravaged. And the worst lie of all. That the Human nature was so damaged, so degenerate, that they could not help themselves from waging war.

And she hurt for herself, because somewhere, somehow, she fit into this crazy puzzle. But more than any of that – more even than all of that put together, she hurt for Little. She hurt because he did.

She watched as he sat quiet and huddled, as Sophia bathed his self-inflicted wounds and tied a thin bandage around the worst of them.

"That should hopefully keep any infection out," she said, finally twining the ends of the last one around each other to secure them in place.

Loni had wanted to do this task for Little but he had shrunk from her touch, as if ashamed of the love they felt for one another. It had pierced Loni to the core but she realised that for now he needed to grieve.

"But I don't understand. WHY can't we just go there, just take our children back?" asked one of the men in the outer circle. He had a large red face which was currently full of anger and confusion.

Sophia sighed. "We have been over and over this now Steven. I know you have lost three of your children to the Eyons, but…" Sophia held her hands up to the sky in an attempt to show that all of this was beyond her control.

"We have to accept that that they are no longer our children!"

There was a general intake of breath from the crowd. The idea had previously been skirted around but never so fully expressed.

"They will ALWAYS be our children," shouted Steven.

"Yes, in *our hearts* they will. But *their* hearts belong to the Eyons now."

There was a deathly silence from the crowd.

"To take them away from the Eyons they love…well that would be as bad if not worse for them, than when they were first removed from us!" And she was right of course.

"But we have only this child's word for that!" continued Steven, undeterred.

"Yes, but she is pure of heart and of word. And you can all see that." Sophia gestured to Little then. "And here is the rest of your proof, that what she says is true, should you still need more proof."

Two hundred pairs of eyes regarded Little and his suffering, two hundred hearts cried out in empathy. Loni brushed away the tears that would not stop flowing from her eyes.

"And even if we did. How could we identify our children? How could we tell a fourteen year old that we recognise him from when he was just two years old?" Still silence from the crowd but Sophia continued, needing them to see the sense in what she said.

"We have a choice. We can leave the past where it is and let it remain the past, so that we can concentrate on making a new future," she looked around the assembled crowd as she spoke, trying to make eye contact with each and every person in turn.

"Or we can bring the past *into* the future and ruin every life, past, present *and* future! You know in your hearts what must be, must be."

Like a balloon, blown up for too long, the latex expanding and expanding, becoming thinner and thinner, Loni felt the situation could explode at any moment. And it wasn't herself she was worried about. It was Little. Lovely Little who would never do any harm to anyone or anything.

"The Humans are loved, I assure you. And they are happy. I think Sophia is right, you must accept they are gone." Loni paused and took a deep breath because what she was about to say required a courage she did not feel she possessed.

"But you must *not* let any more children be taken. It must *stop now*. I give you my word that all I have said is true and that I will do all I can to help you." She glanced at Little and caught the intent look he gave her. "*We* will do all we can to help you," she amended.

Finally no one had any more to say and one by one, just as they had appeared, the villagers left the circle and resumed their chores.

They left quietly, in the same manner as they had arrived but it was a subtly different quietness. Before, there had been much fear and tension. Now fear had been overtaken by a deep sadness that was tempered by a grudging reverence.

It was almost as if they were a little in awe of her, thought Loni. She wasn't entirely sure why this should be so. Was it because she had learned to live happily, with creatures they viewed as monsters? Or did they see in her, the glimmer of a hope that things would be different from this day onwards?

Almost without exception, each adult who had left the circle had shown some mark of respect towards both Sophia and Loni …but also towards Little. There had been a small wave, a raised hand or a nod in their direction to indicate respect. In acceptance of the facts, they had found an inner peace which had eluded them for so long.

Soon they sat alone as they had at the very beginning, what seemed like a million years before. Just Loni, Little and Sophia.

The pressure from the people who had so recently encircled them had forced them tighter together in their circle. Loni noticed that sitting cross-legged the same as before, Sophia's knee was just touching the side of Little's leg. And yet Sophia hadn't recoiled from this. Whether or not she still hated the Eyons, at least where this particular one was concerned, she was forgiving.

"The day has grown late and night will be upon us soon. We must find you somewhere to sleep for tonight. Other long term arrangements can be made in the morning." Sophia rose and shook the dust from her clothes. Her face was closed and Loni could not read what was going on in her head.

"Thank you Sophia. We will be glad of a safe sleep tonight. But tomorrow we must leave. We left home to change our future, to prevent Little from being made to be like every other Eyon back there." Loni paused momentarily as her thoughts came together in her head.

"Now I can see how it is not just *our* future and way of life that we need to change, it is everyones." The enormity of the task facing her was daunting but she would not let it overwhelm her into inactivity. "Whether or not we can change things, we at least have to try." At her side Little was nodding his agreement.

"Yes, I understand. And perhaps that is for the best. My people are quiet now, thinking about all that you have said. But later..." her eyes momentarily clouded over, "later, when it has all sunk in, I fear that there are those who will cause trouble."

Startled, Loni responded rapidly to the implied suggestion of violence. "Sophia you *must* not let that happen. The Eyons," she corrected herself, "*my* Eyons are not vicious. They are not warriors or fighters. And the Pets are happy. Please Sophia you must give me time to sort this out. Just some time I beg of you. We will change things, I promise." Even as the words were out of her mouth, Loni wondered how she could possibly keep this promise.

"Child, I was right about you. You are strong and you are true. But my people have lost so much for so long..."

Loni didn't dare let Sophia finish so she interrupted.

"You are their Leader Sophia. You can convince them to wait, to give me time."

"Time is a luxury many do not have Loni. But I give you my word that no-one will leave this village before thirty suns have crossed the sky. After that, I make no promises. Even though nothing can be gained from snatching the children back, there are some who will still want to try." She smiled wanly, "I'm sorry but thirty suns time, is all I can give you."

Sophia held her gaze, her eyes worried. "Are you sure you want to leave here? We will take you in and provide for both of you, as our own. I give you my word. You are but a child, with only a young Eyon as travelling companion...I would prefer that you stay. Things may be strange for a while but no harm will come to either of you. My people have seen for themselves Little's complete innocence."

There was a part of her which was sorely tempted, yet Loni knew that her heart had no choice but to refuse the invitation. "I may only be a child but Little and I have a *purpose* and it is not one which can be readily abandoned. I believe that it has chosen us, to fulfil it, as much as we have chosen it."

Unsmiling, she took Sophia's hand once more in her own and squeezed it. "Thirty suns in the sky and not a day less! Promise…" Loni had been about to say more, but she was interrupted by the sudden arrival of a villager she hadn't seen before.

From his expression of horror as his eyes swept across herself and Little, Loni guessed that he hadn't been a part of the assembled circles. For some reason he had stayed away. What could have been more pressing to him, that he had not come with the others, to question these strange visitors? Perhaps she was about to find out, thought Loni, her curiosity kicking in.

His face was flushed and sweaty but it was Sophia who was his main point of interest and after the initial wide-eyed gaze, he seemed to dismiss Loni and Little as of no consequence to him.

"Sophia, please come quickly. It is Louisa! It is coming and something's not right!" Placing his hand on her arm he began to pull her back in the direction he had come from.

Without removing his arm, Sophia let herself be led to one of the huts on the outskirts of the village. But just before she disappeared inside she called to Little and Loni.

"Come and see for yourself what it is to be Human." Her tone of voice was heavy, almost challenging. Despite her weariness, Loni was intrigued. They had learned so much. Was it possible that there was more yet to learn here? She had always prided herself that she was prepared to meet any challenge but was this a step too far?

Loni and Little looked at each other. Should they follow as Sophia suggested?

"Well we either follow her I guess, or we sit here on our own. What do you think?" she asked the perplexed Eyon. It was only fair that he made the decision really. He was very much the outsider here, even more than her, and she didn't want to force him into any situations where he would be uneasy.

"OOOOLLLOOO," intoned Little, pointing his talon in the direction Sophia had taken just in case Loni didn't get his meaning. The other wing he wrapped around her, as they followed the path Sophia had taken.

Everyone they passed made way for them. No one stopped and asked where they were going. Instead the villagers continued with their chores. But as Loni and Little approached, they moved to one side, out of their path.

Gaze averted, each man and woman concentrated on his or her task. But it was the subtle way that the spaces were closed up again, after they passed through them, people side-stepping back to their original places that gave it away.

No one wanted to be too near to Little.

No one wanted to risk the chance of accidentally brushing up against him, or touching him in any way. Respect, it seemed, could only go so far. A stabbing pain bit deep into Loni's heart and tears stung at the corners of her eyes. Leaning in closer to Little as they walked, she held him tight but careful of his sore spots, where he had plucked his feathers. No one would hurt her Little …not without killing her first anyway.

From the outside the hut looked the same as all the others. It had the same windowless walls and heavy door and was roughly the same size and shape. But the noises coming out of it certainly didn't sound Human. Strangely none of the villagers seemed surprised by the noises, although she thought that they seemed to be deliberately avoiding looking at where the counds came from.

Unsure of what to expect, Loni sheltered Little with her body as best she could, as they tried to slip unnoticed through the doorway. But there was a step leading up to the hut, which they hadn't seen or expected.

Loni's foot caught on it and she stumbled inside. It was only the fact that she was holding on to Little that kept her upright.

Unused to the idea of *stepping up* into a home, Little then stumbled, just as Loni had before him. She felt his big Eyon body ricochet against her back and had to tense her own muscles to prevent them both falling.

It wasn't spacious inside. There was a little open area in the middle of the hut which looked as if it was used as a fire. Twigs and dried leaves were piled into a mound and surrounded by a circle of stones.

'Surely this would create a lot of smoke in the room', thought Loni. Then she looked up at the roof. There at the very top, in the centre of the roof, was a small hole which presumably let the smoke out and fresh air in.

It was the loudest "AAARRGH!" she had ever heard, that drew her attention away from the ceiling. There, on the other side of the hut from where she now stood, was a woman lying on a low bed. She tried to draw Little's attention to the woman but when she looked at him, she saw that he had immediately noticed the woman, unlike her.

As soon as she *did* notice her, Loni wondered how she could have missed her in the first place. There was nothing much else in the hut. Just the fire area, the bed and a few piles of clothing and meagre possessions.

The woman was drenched in sweat and looked as if she was working hard at something. But Loni had no idea what it was. A thin blanket covered her but there was no mistaking the huge belly which was concealed under it. She was clearly grossly misshapen. Perhaps that was the cause of her pain.

Loni wondered why Sophia didn't just give the woman some 'Pain Remover'. True it was a vile tasting liquid and she seriously doubted that it would straighten and slim the woman's contorted body but it would certainly take the pain away. Once, Loni had used it when she accidentally fell out of the tree house. She had just swigged a mouthful straight out of its blue bottle as soon as OwnLoni had discovered her gone and flown her back up.

It hadn't healed the cuts and grazes but it *had* taken all the sting and hurt out of them. Of course she could have used the "Heal Up" liquid in the red bottle for the cuts but that was even more vile tasting than "Pain Remover". So she hadn't bothered. Her arm didn't hurt anymore and it would heal in its own time, she had figured.

Loni was surprised though that the woman had such a huge stomach, as her face and upper body seemed slim and fit. Watching closely, although not understanding anything that she saw, she witnessed the man squeeze the prostrate woman's hands in his and place a wet cloth across her forehead.

"One sun down and another up, Louisa has been pushing. And still it is not come!" The man seemed to be exploding each word out of his body as if ridding himself of them would improve the situation.

"AAARRGH!" the woman repeated, her face screwed up in agony and her jaw clenched. Loni noticed a throbbing pulse at the woman's temple and another at the junction between jaw and neck. The pain was very obviously severe. No wonder the other villagers hadn't wanted to come in! Perhaps it was even something contagious!

Bending down to the woman's level, Sophia took a moment to sweep the sweat darkened hair away from the strickened woman's face.

The woman didn't even glance up at Sophia, or seem to notice Loni and Little, still standing in the doorway. Loni wondered what her reaction would be if she noticed Little. Would her screams get even louder and more hysterical? Was that even possible?

"Oh Louisa, I feared for this. Don't give up. Keep fighting, keep pushing. The People *need* you Louisa. You cannot give up. I beg you." Sophia's voice was loud and strong and could be heard over the woman's heavy breathing.

Mystified still, Loni watched her then turn to the man and say in a much quieter voice, "time is short now and we must help her. You must be strong for her, Alzakery. You must be strong for them *both*. Do you understand me?"

Loni thought she saw something flash in Sophia's eyes but she still didn't know what to make of it. The man nodded silently, his eyes brimming with unreleased tears. She wondered who the other person Sophia mentioned was. Who was it that the man had to be strong for? And more to the point, why?

Suddenly she noticed that the blanket seemed to be pulsating and rippling. And the more it pulsated, the louder and longer and harder the woman screamed. It was as if her huge stomach had a life of its own, thought Loni. It was as if it was trying to devour her. She clutched Little's wing now more for her own support than to comfort him.

Terrified yet also fascinated by this grotesque scenario, she stepped forward. Her body seemed to have a will of its own and she could not prevent herself from daring to go closer. Her heart was thudding so much in her chest, that she was sure that it could almost be heard above the woman's screams.

Sophia moved too now, and Loni wondered if she was equally fascinated and repelled at the same time. Sophia knelt down at the foot of the woman, gently peeling the covering away from her body.

# *Chapter 23.*

The drop from the cave, to the sandy beach below was terrifying but as long as San only dangled his head in mid-air, he was sure he'd be fine. His centre of gravity was well inside, he just had to make sure it stayed that way.

They were trapped. No other way out of the cave than this and no way to exit safely from here, other than on Vinnbr's back. So whilst she was otherwise engaged, it made sense to try to find out as much information as possible about life here. Then he could make a plan.

He felt Rian approach behind him but keep his distance, away from the entrance and out of sight of anything beyond it.

"Whaatt arr yoo doing?"

"Wait and see!" he replied.

"Hello." he called. His voice echoed back to him, bouncing off the cliff face opposite, before ricocheting like a bullet and veering off to impact on all the other sides. The echo changed his call into 'helloo..lloo..lloo..lloo' getting a little quieter each time until the sound faded altogether.

"Bee carrefulll," urged Rian, taking a step further back.

There was nothing and no one around, either Eyon or Human. It struck San as a little strange, that the sky which had previously been so full of Eyons, was now so dramatically empty. Was it coincidence or was it something to do with his arrival?

That was one of the things he had never understood about Eyons – how solitary they chose to be. They did sometimes speak to each other but it always seemed to be functional, befitting some practical purpose, rather than conversational. Just as Rian and Vinnbr's had been.

It was the way they stood when they talked that gave it away. Bodies held rigid, they would shrill and burr at each other loudly. Even if two Eyons reached out to one another, whilst the physical gap between them would not be too wide to be breached by their outstretched wings, something *else was*, some other kind of gap. Some other indefinable quality that kept them apart.

"Perhaps the Humans here are the same as the Eyons - solitary." If that was the case, he'd have to think up a different plan of action to the one he was currently formulating.

"I donntt knoww."

Or perhaps he just hadn't been loud enough to be heard from inside the caves. He'd have to try a bit more loudly next time.

He wondered what would happen if he said a longer sentence. Would each word echo independently of the others, or would it be only the last word which would reverberate on and on? He thought he'd give it a try and find out. He took a deep breath and prepared to boom his voice out to its full vocal capacity.

"Hello all you other Pets. Where are you?"

He could hear the first word he spoke echoing back and forth, even as he shouted the next and the next and the next. It was a weird effect and he wondered if what he had said could even be made out, between all the echoes. Or would it just sound like one big noise?

He waited for a response, craning his neck out further over the drop. But not far enough that anyone would even get a hint of the awful green dress he was wearing. He didn't want to risk being ridiculed.

"Whatt cann yoo seee?" enquired Rian.

"Nothing yet really, only the other caves."

There were holes to either side of him, above and below. But not close enough to touch, even if he could manage to stretch his fingertips out safely. Still nothing happened.

He would try saying one word at a time to counteract the echo.

"Hello." He paused, waiting for the echo to die before continuing. "Anyone...at...home?"

It struck him as a kind of stupid thing to shout but then again what would be a smart thing to say? Surely the smart thing would be whatever got the desired response, he reasoned.

Even shouted, at full volume, he had managed to keep his voice light and carefree. He really didn't know what to expect but he figured he'd get a better response that way than if he frightened them all to death.

Would a hundred Pets stick their heads out of doorways and demand to know who he was and what he was doing? Would no one take any notice of him? Or perhaps, most worrying of all and also perhaps the most likely to occur, maybe all the other Owners would hear him and come flocking to the doorway screeching and demanding answers he could not give. And then horror of horrors, Vinnbr would punish him by making him wear THE UNDERPANTS!!!

Of course on second thoughts, probably most of the Owners were already hooked up to their machines and oblivious to everything around them, just as Vinnbr was. So maybe he should try again.

"If you can hear me, come to the doorway of your cave. Don't be afraid!" he called loudly, remembering to space each word out to avoid a jumbled echoey mess.

Suddenly there was a huge response. He couldn't tell if it was because he had shouted louder this time, or whether it was because he had assured them there was nothing to be afraid of. Or was it because they were all too stupid to figure out for themselves where the noise was coming from and what they should do about it? Either way, the result was the same. Heads poked out of hundreds of cave mouths, above, below, beside and even across from him.

"There are hundreds of them!" he informed Rian.

It was a strange scene. Disembodied heads hung in mid-air but not all were angled the same way. Some seemed higher up their doorway than others; some were right way up, others upside down.

From the look of it, some must have been lying almost flat on the ground as he was, whilst others were kneeling or even standing. They were either mad, brave, or holding onto something for safety and he reckoned it was the latter, or at least he hoped it was.

There were big heads, small heads, young heads and old ones. There were even fat and thin heads. For a few minutes the strangeness of the scene distracted him from his original purpose. He wondered briefly if he were to see their headless bodies, as it were, if he could correctly match body to head.

"Do you think a fat, round head would go with a fat, round body and an elongated, thin head go with a tall, thin body?" he asked Rian but got no response.

He racked his brains thinking about all the Pets he knew.

"Have you ever seen anyone who had a fat head and a thin body or conversely, a thin head and a fat body?"

"I donn'tt thinkkk so!" Rian sounded neither interested nor disinterested.

"A girl I know, Victoria, has really long, thin arms and legs…they are like bits of twig someone has stuck to her body for a laugh…and the roundest fatest face."

He had never said it out loud, but San had often thought that she looked as though someone had stretched her body, much like an elastic band, whilst holding her head in its original shape.

And then on letting her body go, had found that *unlike* an elastic band, her body *hadn't* snapped back to its original shape. Instead it had just stayed stretched thin and taut…with a little round head on top.

Coming out of this reverie, he realised that all eyes were upon him. Either they had all managed to figure out in which direction the shout had come, - and he thought that was unlikely, due to all the echoing - or they knew there was a stranger in their midst and they knew *exactly* which one of them it was. Perhaps they weren't all so dumb after all!

The echoes had finally died and had been replaced by an eerie silence. Now that he had their undivided attention, he didn't know what to say. His tongue felt thick in his mouth and he was strangely nervous. His heart was thudding against his ribs and he wasn't sure if it was in fear, excitement, anticipation, or some combination of all three.

He needed to clear his throat before he spoke but daren't do it here, as it would echo back and forth and make him look and feel foolish. He ducked his head rapidly back inside the mouth of the cave, coughed loudly, quickly told Rian what was happening and then, throat clear, stuck his head back out.

He wondered if his momentary absence would cost him his audience but he needn't have feared. All the heads, and presumably the bodies too, were exactly where and as he had left them. Or at least that's how it looked. If indeed some of them had adjusted their positions, well he certainly couldn't tell. They had waited patiently for his return, all heads and eyes riveted to his cave, waiting for him to reappear.

"My name is San and I have come from far away." He paused as before between each word, to make sure they could be made out from all the echoing going on.

It was only as he finished, that it occurred to him that they might not understand anything he said. And not just because of the echoing either! What if here they spoke they same as the Eyons, in shrills and burrs? Or perhaps they had their own, completely different and separate language? How would he be able to communicate with them then?

There was a moment of silence and suddenly the day seemed to darken, the light fading ever so slightly. Like a switch flicking, the sudden loss of brightness, even though it was only slight seemed to be a catalyst.

The silence was shattered by a hundred voices all talking at once. From every direction, across, to either side, above and below him, voices called to him, straining to be heard. It was an absolute rabble and he couldn't make out a single word that was being said, or even if any, or all of it, was being spoken in his language. Each person seemed to be trying to shout louder than the one next to them and the resultant noise was echoing around the cliffs and building into a deafening crescendo.

# *Chapter 24.*

L oni watched as the blanket was pulled away and in an
instant all became clear. All her misconceptions were
washed away on a tidal wave of comprehension.
Protruding out from beneath the blood drenched skirt
Louisa wore, was the curve of a small head, its fine baby
down plastered slick to its skull.

And not the tiniest piece of shell in sight. Either the
baby had cracked out of its shell inside the mother, or it
had never had one in the first place. Somehow the
second explanation seemed the most likely.

The potential for new life had never been this real
before to Loni. Even Little's egg cracking, was nothing
compared to this. She had never seen or even *heard* of
anyone witnessing such an experience. Hadn't even
*thought* before, whether or not Humans cracked out of an
egg the same way as Eyons.

Nor did she have any way of knowing if this was a
particularly exceptional arrival of a baby or an

unexceptional one! All she knew was what she saw; the agony; the blood …and the miracle of a new life.

"Louisa is giving birth. Her body has been a home for this child for many months and now the pains ripping through her, are serving to force its delivery into the world." Sophia seemed unaware that she had once more turned Loni's world upside down. That once more, all she had previously thought to be true, to have believed in, was proving false.

Her breath caught in her throat and she heard or felt - she wasn't sure which, her attention was so focused on the woman - Little make a strange sound of astonishment as he too realised what was happening in front of their eyes. Her mind reeled.

A baby, a live baby, not encased in a shell, but instead grown completely inside of another person, was about to emerge. To be born. It was at once a wonderful and terrifying sight.

Still kneeling, Sophia placed one hand on the baby's head.

"It is presenting too twisted and it is too late to try to turn it. We will have to get it out quick – for both their sakes."She turned to Loni, who was still standing staring, open mouthed.

"Louisa is our birthing nurse, the one who helps with all the babies being born. But she cannot help now, with her own. *You* will help me Loni, will you not?" she asked, her tone turning the question into a statement.

Loni got the impression that Sophia didn't really expect an answer but she couldn't stop herself. "Me! Me, help? But I don't know anything about having babies…there *must* be someone else!" She was almost wailing herself now. And then she felt a gentle pressure on her back. Little was pushing her ever so gently towards Sophia. He wanted her to help.

"There is no one brave and strong who is not related to her here," Sophia paused before continuing, seeing that Loni still did not understand. "What we will have to do will be difficult enough for us...but *impossible* for any who love her...and there are *many* who do," she smiled sadly down at Louisa before turning the full force of her attention back to Loni.

Suddenly the villagers' diligence at their tasks, their averted gazes and seeming unconcern about the noises emanating from the hut, all made sense. It was a sham. They were terrified about what was happing to Louisa but could do nothing about it.

Loni shot Little a petrified glance. What if she did something wrong? What if she actually made the situation worse somehow? What if...?

Little caught her gaze and held it for a moment. His eyes were steady and fixed firmly on her face. 'You *have* to help,' his eyes said to her and even though his mouth remained firmly closed, she heard his voice in her head. Little wanted her to help. Little thought she *could* help. Sophia and the woman Louisa needed her. What was there really to be unsure about?

"You are but a child, I know. But your wisdom and your strength are beyond your years. You are strong and brave Loni. Will you help me? Please!" Sophia implored.

Loni understood the significance of what was being asked of her and she nodded her assent, "tell me what to do!" She had no sleeves to roll up and wished suddenly that she had. Somehow the idea of rolling them up before she began seemed appropriate.

"We need clean hands. Wash them here and make sure you clean them well." Sophia had moved over to a basin of warm water at the back of the hut and was now drying her hands thoroughly on a clean towel. She watched Loni lather, then rinse her hands and passed her the towel to dry off.

Reluctant to assume her duties in this task, Loni considered folding the towel neatly and placing it next to the washbowl. But that would be cowardly, procrastinating just to delay helping. And Loni was not a coward. She moved over to join Sophia at Louisa's side.

"Help me pull her into a sitting position. Here, like this!" Sophia placed the crook of both arms under one of Louisa's armpits and waited till Loni did the same on the other side.

Louisa was a dead weight but together and with additional help from Alzakery, they managed to manoeuvre her into a more upright position. Her eyes flickered open and closed continuously but Loni didn't think she was even aware of their presence. She seemed to be in some altered state, where only she existed, alone with her pain.

Sophia turned to Little. "I'm sorry but you cannot be here, if she were to see you..." she didn't need to carry on, Little had already backed up towards the doorway, out of Louisa's line of sight.

Loni hoped he wasn't offended but was fairly sure that under the circumstances he wouldn't be.

"Sophia..." Louisa croaked, brushing Alzakery's hand away from her forehead, where he was still trying to cool her brow. "I think the child is dead or very weak. There is no push from him now, only from me."

Another intense contraction gripped her.

"Sophi…" Eyes still closed, her face contorted in agony. Every sinew and vein in her neck stood out, as she struggled to finish saying the name. The last syllable was screamed out and became an elongated, "AAAARR!"

Loni's nerves felt as if they had been scraped bare by a sharp knife. Louisa's scream echoed on in her head.

"Give her the 'Pain Remover'! Give her it now!" shrieked Loni in response.

"Whatever that is, we don't have it!" hissed Sophia. "Keep calm and help her. That's what we need to do. That's all we can do."

A lightening bolt of fear shot through Loni's heart. If Sophia had never heard of 'Pain Remover' then this woman would have to suffer. It was barbaric and didn't bear thinking about.

Another scream issued forth from Louisa and Loni felt like joining in. But instead, she placed her palms where Sophia told her and moved them as she was instructed. Her hands, still small and childlike worked on manipulating the baby around the right way. She couldn't get it all the way round, without harming it, or Louisa, or possibly both of them, but it certainly began to look less twisted.

Her hands and wrists were slick with the sticky blood flowing freely from Louisa and she was glad of the clean rag passed to her from Sophia. She wiped the blood away and was dismayed at how red the rag looked afterwards. So much blood. Surely losing this amount of blood was not normal? The situation was bad and there was a horrible suspicion in Loni's mind that it wasn't going to get any better, either.

Looking up momentarily from her task, she was relieved to find that Little had found a role to play in the proceedings and seemed to be collecting the used and dirty rags for disposal and issuing fresh ones from the doorway.

"So many children have been helped into the world by you, Louisa. So many women comforted. What a sad twist of fate that your own labour is so hard, the pain so unforgiving," Sophia muttered, her voice catching on every word. Loni only just heard the words, so quietly were they spoken. She got the impression that Sophia was talking to herself more than Louisa.

Alzakery remained at Louisa's head, comforting her and speaking softly. He continued to wipe the woman's face, keeping it cool and washing away the sweat. Loni wasn't sure if this was doing much good, as Louisa was still not fully conscious but she figured they each had their own role to play and that role was his.

The baby's head felt tiny and strangely soft under her hands but also rather cold. Instinctively she knew that wasn't a good sign. A bit more of it protruded now but not enough to see its features. The thought occurred to her that for the first time she would see a new born baby. Not only that, but she would see it with its mother and father.

The thought had come unbidden into her mind 'mother and father' but she did not question it, as it so clearly was correct. These people were *together* in the truest sense of the word. Man and woman, mother and father. And their child. They were a family.

Would the baby look like one or other of its parents, or like a mishmash of both of their features? A deep shiver of anticipation ran down Loni's spine.

But another thought snaked into her brain then. How long would they have this child before it was snatched from them? How long would it be before they could safely love it, safely call it theirs? Perhaps in helping to bring the child into the world, she would have a responsibility to help protect it and keep it safe. Perhaps life was not just luck or chance, perhaps it was destiny? And maybe this was another part of her destiny.

After a while they got into a strange kind of rhythm. Louisa screamed and pushed, as her abdomen rippled with a fresh contraction, and Sophia and Loni, massaged the emerging infant out of her inch by inch.

"Ok, the head is out. Now come the shoulders. Stay strong Louisa," urged Sophia.

The shoulders did follow but it wasn't an easy process. Both shoulders emerged at the same time, prompting fresh screams from the expectant mother.

Sophia had instructed Loni to try to manipulate the baby so that one shoulder came out before the other, as was the usual way, apparently. Loni had tried desperately but the baby was jammed into its position and could not be moved without harm.

Liquid ran down her face and involuntarily she tasted it, as it trickled into the corners of her mouth. Sweat mixed with tears. Her brain was fully occupied with what she was having to do but her heart was heavy with foreboding.

Clutching the infant by its shoulders, Sophia gave one final tug and managed to pull it free from Louisa's body. There was a horrible wet sucking noise as the child emerged on a river of blood and mucous. Loni's stomach flipped over in a sickening somersault at the combined sight and sound.

Gaining control of herself again, she looked over to Sophia, who now cradled the baby in her arms. It was *so tiny*. But that wasn't what seemed to concern Sophia. The child was completely still and a strange blue pallor suffused its skin.

Long seconds passed, as Sophia and Loni stared at each other over the body of the small unbreathing infant. Then in an unspoken agreement, they turned their attention to the little body, and away from its mother.

Deftly, Sophia used a clean sharp knife to cut a cord which seemed to anchor the child to Louisa. She tied a knot in it, fingers working quickly and precisely. Loni briefly wondered what would happen to both the protruding piece of cord from the baby and the length that was still attached its mother.

Kneeling together, they laid the baby on a pile of unused rags. Instructed by Sophia, Loni used the same massaging technique on the child that she had been using to assist its delivery, whilst Sophia gently blew the first breath of air into its lungs.

Its downy hair was still stuck to its scalp by its mother's blood and its skin was pallid and mottled, yet it was the most beautiful thing Loni had ever seen. Perfect little fingers and toes just where they should be, the nails so tiny and amazingly formed. Every limb correctly aligned and proportioned, every feature even and symmetrical. A perfect baby in every way…except alive.

On and on they kept trying to revive the infant. Minutes passed and Sophia still blew into its lungs and Loni still massaged its chest. There was no time to talk, to explain, but Loni realised that time was of the essence here. However long it took, she would keep trying until Sophia told her to stop and she didn't think that would happen for a very long time.

Slowly colour seeped back into the child and it gave a muffled cry. Loni's heart leapt with joy. Yet she could not look around. *Would* not turn her gaze on the child's mother, who now lay so quietly, so deathly quiet, all energy spent.

In their haste to revive the baby, they had turned their backs on Louisa and Loni was now afraid to look around.

Instead she looked at Sophia, and saw in that gaze the mirror of her own fears and hesitancy.

"You have done well, Loni of the Eyons. But I'm afraid we are not done yet. Come, let us show Louisa her child." Sophia struggled to her feet, still holding the baby.

But they were too late, as deep in her heart Loni had known they would be. Louisa's eyes were staring into eternity now, cold and empty and devoid of all life. Loni hoped that *somehow* she had held on just long enough to know that her child was safe and well. Somehow it was important that Louisa had known that. Loni could only hope that she had.

Alzakery, seemingly unaware that Louisa was gone and could no longer hear him, was babbling away to her.

"We will call the child Callum if he is a boy, just as you wanted or Ellie if…" He stopped to look up at Sophia, as she presented him with his child.

"She is gone, Alzakery, gone now. No more pain, no more suffering. But she gave you one last gift," she held the child out to him, "she gave you your son."

Clutching his son to his breast, Alzakery rent the night air with his screams and the villagers listening and waiting in their huts, once more bowed their head in sorrow and unending despair.

# Chapter 25.

"STOP. ONE AT A TIME," San bellowed at them. But even to his own ears, his raised voice was lost among the racket that was being made.

What could he do to make them quieten down? And then he had an idea. He pulled his head back inside the cave mouth and kept it there. There was a sudden cessation of noise. Surprised by his disappearance everyone had stopped shouting.

"Whaat arr theyy saying?" enquired Rian, eager for news.

"I can't tell right now, they're all talking at once!"

As soon as there was silence, he protruded his head once more. Big mistake! His head reappeared and they were off again, the noise only slightly less than before. Once more, he ducked his head back into the cave. Once more, the shouting stopped. This time he counted to five before he stuck his head back out.

Like pulling the trigger of a gun, the moment his head was out, there was a chain reaction and the shouting

re-commenced. But he was sure that this time it was ever
so *slightly* quieter. He ducked his head back in, counted to
ten and looked back out. He was starting to feel a bit like
the turtles he sometimes saw at the edge of the lake,
scrawny necks being pulled into their shells at the first
signs of danger. But there was definitely less noise now.

Having found a working strategy, he was compelled
to carry it on until he got the desired effect. Back and
forth his head went, just like the turtles'. And each time
the noise when he reappeared, got less and less. By the
time he had counted to twenty three before looking out
again, the excited babble had stopped entirely.

Rian sat down by San's feet, holding them in place
and preventing San from falling out of the cave if he
became too over-excited or animated.

They were waiting for him to say something.
Incapable of organising themselves, he figured he would
have to do it for them. He couldn't point, as he risked
falling to his death if he lost his balance and Rian lost a
grip on his feet, so instead he nodded his head in the
general direction of the opposite cliffs.

"You will have to take turns in talking." He made sure
to pause so that he would be understood. "Say one word
at a time and speak loudly, so that everyone can hear and
understand. If you want to talk, nod your head and I will
give you a turn."

Most of the heads began vigorously nodding up and
down but some were still. Either they had no questions,
or were confident that they were the same questions
which would be asked by someone else. He picked a
bobbing head at random.

"The boy with the red hair. You go first," he
commanded. In a strange way, he felt very powerful.

Perhaps this was how Eyons felt, making all the decisions. "I could get used to this feeling very easily," he murmured to himself. Then to Rian he explained, "sorry but you are gonna just have to hear my side of the conversation now. I'll explain the rest of what is said, later to you."

"Thaat iss fine Saan."

"Where have you come from? Is it far? How did you get here…"

The red-haired boy's excitement got the better of him and the rest of his words came out too quickly to be heard clearly. The resultant echo was too jumbled up for San to make any of the words out, so he said nothing and let the boy try again. There was no point in shouting back, not only would it take too long but as the boy was still talking, San would effectively be shouting over him.

'Red hair' was probably about the same age as San but the eager softness of the boy's features made him seem younger and helplessly naïve.

"Where…have …you…come…from?" he bellowed across the void. It was a simple enough question but San wasn't sure how to answer it. He was a stranger in their midst but he couldn't tell his whole story, spacing out every word, it would take too long. And he needed the right information from them. But to get that, he would need them to be on his side.

And then of course there was Rian. There was no way he would be telling anyone about him. He would not use Rian's tale to captivate and astound *or* to pull new friends to him.

He couldn't give only half an answer. Hehad to respond in a way that answered the question, without provoking too many others. Then when they were at ease with him, he would slot his own questions in.

"Far away in a forest," he called, counting to five between each word. There was a sudden babble of noise in response, as a couple of others and the red-haired boy all shouted something at the same time. Clearly the other Pets felt the boy had had his turn. San would go with the majority ruling. He indicated with his head again.

"You next, the man with the blonde hair," he called to one head which stuck out very high from its doorway. This man appeared to be standing up and San's stomach did somersaults at the mere thought. He hoped he was holding tight to something!

"Are...there...Owners...where...you...come...from? " blonde  man bellowed.

San thought this was a stupid question. Of course there were Owners, there were always Owners weren't there? Unless of course they thought he was from one of the Human villages! And that immediately answered one of his unasked questions. They knew that there were Human villages somewhere. Did they know where though? He thought how he could answer the question briefly.

"Yes. We live in the trees there." This time he only counted to four between each word. It seemed to be long enough to let the echoes die out.

The questions which followed were predictable and didn't tax San's brain to respond to.

"How far away did you live?"

San didn't know but assuming he had travelled in a straight line then it couldn't have been too far away, so he replied, "not far." They were satisfied with that but then wanted to know more about his life and the other Pets there.

"What are tree houses like?"

"They are made from wood and very warm."

"Do you have toilets?" asked a young girl who obviously thought that it was possible *not* to have a toilet.

"Yes but smaller than here!"

"Do you look after your Owner?"

It was the first reference made to OwnSan and San hesitated, worried that it would lead to others.

"Yes," he responded, deciding to keep it succinct and straight to the point.

"Did your Owner bring you here?"

"No."

"Where is your Owner?"

"Back home."

It was the truth and unavoidable. He decided to forestall any questions by asking some of his own now that he had their full attention and their trust.

"Do you get taken places to play?" he asked, directing the question to a boy who looked to be a few triangles older than himself.

"Yes, most days we get taken to the beach. But sometimes we go to the factory."

San's ears picked up at the sound of the unknown word. The beach was a dead end, braced on three sides as it was by the very rock they lived in. But the factory, whatever that was, could be a possibility.

"What is a factory?" San asked in what he hoped was a casual tone.

"I don't know really – a place we go."

Not the best answer. San tried to approach from a different angle.

"You get flown to the factory, I guess?" That had to be true, didn't it?

"Yes, of course!" The boy's tone indicated that he was bored with this line of questioning and eager to be having his own answered. So for a while San suppressed his agenda and answered more questions, waiting for the opportunity to insert his own once more.

Many were about where he had been and what he had found there. And they were especially interested to learn about Shoo.

"Were you scared?"

"I was the first time I saw him but not anymore."

"Can I pat him if I meet him?" enquired the little girl who had been curious about the toilets.

"I'm sure he won't mind."

It was hard work, shouting back and forth but at least he got some information, in return for the information he gave out. It seemed that life here was the same as in Low Forest. Only the scenery was different. And just like back home, *no one* had *ever* left their Owner and gone off on their own. Except for him. And whilst they knew there were Human villages somewhere, no one had seen them and no one had any idea where they could be.

Eventually the sun began to descend and the air grew cooler. There were less heads protruding now. Either most of the Pets had had their curiosity satisfied, or their Owners had called them.

Having got as much information as he could from them, San said goodnight to the few remaining faces and turtled his own head back in for the final time. Brushing the dust off his clothing from where he had lain on the floor, he gave an account of the other sides of the various conversations, aware that Rian had already heard his side.

"They seemed friendly enough and happy enough but…" he couldn't finish the thought.

"Buutt theyy arr jusstt Pettss. Aanndd yoo arr nott jusstt aa Pett anymorre," Rian finished for him knowingly.

"No, I'm not just a Pet. And now I have an idea of how we can get out of here. But I am going to need your help."

"Of course, Sann. I will always help yoo."

"Good, come on then. We're leaving tomorrow, so tonight lets rest and feast. And I will think through the plan more carefully." San smiled at his friend.

Coming back into the living area, neither of them were in the least surprised to find Vinnbr still attached to her machine and Shoo still fast asleep on the bed.

San's stomach was rumbling once more and he really couldn't face the idea of sandwiches again. But there was nothing else to have. This time, Rian helped him in the kitchen and San was forced to play things straight. Bread, butter, mayonnaise and meat - no mustard.

As expected, Vinnbr ate the food without either reaction or attention to it. And Shoo managed to rouse himself, yawning and tail wagging, just long enough to eat the new meal, even licking his plate clean of crumbs.

San removed the awful dress and hung it back on its hanger in the wardrobe, first making sure the necklet remained firmly straped on his arm and well hidden under his top. Then he sank down onto what was going to have to be his bed for the night, to eat his sandwich.

He chewed each bite methodically as he watched Rian tear into his with wild abandon. There was no need to make conversation. It was a relaxed silence but there was one thing he needed to say.

"I'm so glad I met you Rian." He smiled.

"I aamm tooo Saann."

Then, without a bed of his own and unwilling to take Vinnbr's without her permission, Rian hunkered down on his feet as only Eyons could and closed his eyes.

Sitting there quiet and still, with Shoo curled snugly into his side, San thought of all that he had done and learned. He had come so far …and yet nothing was really all that different here. Perhaps nothing was different anywhere. Perhaps he had made a mistake in leaving his home and OwnSan behind him. But the necklet, tight on his arm, reminded him that he did have a purpose.

Pondering these thoughts, his eyes grew heavy. His empty plate slipped unnoticed to the floor, as his body gave in to its need for sleep.

Stomach fed, his body curled itself into a ball on the soft bed, with Shoo in the centre of it, head curled onto tail. He didn't even stir, as unfamiliar talons patted his head softly and dragged the heavy blanket up to cover them.

# *Chapter 26.*

The air inside the hut seemed thick and stale. Loni tried desperately to draw it into her lungs but it seemed to clog sickeningly on the back of her throat. A low wheezing issued from her mouth. She could hear it clearly and she knew it was of her making – yet she seemed to have no control over it. She gulped at the treacly air but it refused to budge.

Behind her lay Louisa – dead – with so much to live for. And beside her, kneeled Alzakery – alive – but with nothing to live *for*.

The irony was inescapable. In gaining a son, he had lost his wife. In gaining a son, he had condemned himself to live in fear and expectation of the next raid, where the only person he had left to love, would be snatched from him.

Loni sank to the ground, her knees giving way to exhaustion and despair. Her head hung low once more. It seemed to be too heavy for her neck muscles to support and her long thick hair curtained her face. Her throat felt tight and she wanted to cry. Actually, she wanted to scream and shriek and rage at the world. But the hot releasing tears would not come.

Perhaps she would have felt a bit better if they had. But the tears were not hers to shed. They were by rights Alzakery's tears and to have denied him the full right to his grief, would have been too cruel, too brutal. And she would not do that. So she swallowed her tears.

A feathery touch caressed her arm and helped her to her feet. Little's face was wet with his own tears and he seemed suddenly much older than his eleven years. As if viewing the scene from far away, Loni watched as he helped Sophia straighten Louisa's body out and cover it with the blanket once more.

She noticed how respectfully and carefully he placed her limbs. He copied Sophia's movements as he straightened the woman's legs and collected the used rags. But when Sophia placed Louisa's right arm flat on top of the blanket, he did not copy her with the other arm. Instead he chose to angle Louisa's left arm so that it seemed to reach for her husband and son at her side.

Something inside of Loni broke. She suspected it was her heart but the pain wasn't localised enough to tell. It radiated out from somewhere near her heart but encompassed her whole body.

She felt rather than heard a sob escape her and tightened her arms in toward herself, all the better to keep her emotions under control. That it should be Little of all people, and more so because he wasn't even a *person*, rather than in spite of that fact, who made this gesture on Louisa's behalf, just broke Loni's heart.

All at once the air seemed no longer thick. Now it felt too thin, with a nauseating odour to it. Loni's stomach began to churn and her head began to spin. She staggered outside, tripping once more on the step on the way out, as she had on the way into the hut and leaned against the outside wall for support. The air outside had grown much cooler than the air inside the hut and her body grew goose pimples. But she didn't notice.

Alzakery's wails filled her every sense. She could smell and taste his sorrow. It was bitter copper served on a ferrous plate and the serving was too huge. She gulped at the cool air but her body was now in complete revolt. Pain suffused her stomach and she doubled over as a thin stream of vomit forced its way out of her body and onto the ground at her feet.

She hadn't been aware of Little or Sophia's exit from the hut, they were just suddenly there beside her. She hoped they hadn't seen her being sick. For some reason she was ashamed of herself, almost as if it were a sign of weakness on her part. She needn't have worried. If either of them *had* seen they made no reference to it.

"Thank you Loni for all your help but the time has come to let Louisa's kin take care of her. We did all we could and now it is their turn to prepare her for the next stage, her journey onwards from this life."

She wasn't startled and she didn't jump when Sophia spoke. It was as if her body was too numb to feel anything anymore, just too drained of emotion.

She felt Sophia's hand gentle on her elbow, leading her away from the hut, as two weeping older women entered it. Even tearstained and with eyes swollen and bloodshot, there was no mistaking the familial connection between the women and Louisa. Loni wasn't sure if it was the shape of their features or the general look of them, but there was undeniably something, even in the dim light of the moon.

"Louisa's mother and aunt will clean her and prepare her for burial. May the sun shine on her and keep her from rain." Sophia sighed wearily. "Now let us get you and Little a bed for the night."

Loni noticed vaguely how Little's name had been used. Not 'the monster' or even 'your Eyon' but 'Little'. Was that what it was all about, she wondered? Had fate decreed that Louisa should die, so that Sophia and her people would be indebted to Little, and thus indirectly the Eyons, for trying to help? Had destiny taken one woman's life, so that others would see the *humanity* in one who clearly wasn't human at all? Or was it all just random? Was there even such a thing as fate?

Loni stumbled over the uneven ground and would have fallen if not for the arms linked around her waist which served to keep her upright. Little at one side of her and Sophia on the other, they half carried, half dragged her over to the hut Sophia had earlier barricaded herself into. It seemed like a lifetime has passed since then.

"You may share my hut. I am alone since..." she faltered and Loni was unsure whether it was something she could not bring herself to say, or whether it was merely through tiredness.

During that minute of hesitation Loni could have asked the question, but her tongue would not form the words. In truth she thought maybe it was better left unsaid. How many more revelations could she take on this one day?

Sophia continued, "I live alone." This time there was no sense of an unfinished meaning. Loni detected a faint sound of relief in her tone, that her hesitation had not been picked over.

"So there is plenty room in here. Please take my bed for tonight and I will share with one of the other women."

Sophia disappeared so rapidly they didn't have time to object, even if they had had the energy to do so. Loni didn't feel bad about taking over Sophia's hut for the night. She thought that Sophia would be glad to take solace in the company of one of her closest people. And she and Little needed some alone time too, after the trauma of recent events.

Like Louisa's hut, this one contained only a bed, a fire area and a few bundled possessions. Laid flat on the ground, the bed looked comfortable if rather basic. But was still a better option than sleeping on the bare ground as they had done previously.

Silently they sat down side by side on the bed, each deep in their own thoughts. Loni wasn't sure quite how long they sat there, unmoving, untalking, but it must have been a while. She heard a quiet knock on the door and watched as it was eased open before she could respond.

Sophia stood in the doorway with two steaming plates of food.

"It is late and we have missed supper but the People have put food aside for us. I know you may not feel like eating, as indeed I feel the same. But life goes on and although we can no longer help Louisa, there are many others who still need us."

Loni couldn't be absolutely certain but she thought that Sophia had inclined her head ever so slightly towards

Little as she said this. And it was true. He *did* need her. So reluctantly and without any appetite, Loni ate.

She didn't recognise the food but she was neither intrigued by what it was, nor worried about it. She just shovelled it into her mouth, chewed and swallowed, before picking up another mouthful. And then when she had cleared her plate, she undressed, climbed into bed and she slept. Because she had to and because it was what her body demanded.

Comforted by Little's presence, her body twisted towards his, in their shared bed and her hand grasped his wing and held on tight. But even as she slept, her mind ticked over all the newly apparent injustices in the world. A world which had once been so seemingly familiar to her and was now so obviously alien.

And she dreamed. Twisted nightmares, memories mixed with rich imaginings of all the horrors she had heard and witnessed, filled her head and lanced daggers through her heart. She tossed and turned and fought with the bedcovers. It was a long hard night and her body blanketed itself in sweat.

The moon, high in the sky, cast a dim glow over the huts in the village. It lengthened them out in their own shadows, till they looked like nightmarish freaky shapes, filled with unnameable horrors. Which indeed perhaps they were.

A thin keening still rent the night air interrupted by harmonies of harsh sobbing. An owl bore witness to the frailties of the human heart and quietly 'twit-twooed' in seeming empathy.

And as for Little? Well the young Eyon's dreams were filled with a burgeoning horror at the actions of his own kind and a blossoming feeling of kindredship with these strangely fragile and breakable humans. His mind worried over what his heart felt. But his heart was resolute in its unshakeable beliefs.

And so the young Human and the young Eyon slept fitfully together, bound ever closer in the silken gossamer threads of the heart and wrapped in the bond of love they shared. Only the dazzling of the morning sun would force them into awakening, to face the challenges of the new day.

# *Chapter 27.*

San had to admit it felt good to be clean again. But not at the cost of his liberty. Perhaps there were some things which exacted *too high* a price.

Shoo however, didn't seem to be enjoying the experience at all. Barking excitedly when San had taken him into the Clean Zone, the barks had soon turned to whines as the jets of warm water began.

"Shush Shoo. I may not have told you this before. But the truth is you stink."

"WOOF, Woof, hmm, hmm, hmm," Shoo's noises got softer but no less insistent.

"I know you're not enjoying it. But trust me, we both need this!"

San was surprised to realise that Shoo's fur was not actually as dark as he had thought, nor was he as plump and healthy looking.

"You were just covered in mud and dirt weren't you, poor thing?" San rubbed the creature's fur to help the cleaning process along. The water going down the drain was almost black.

Reluctant to leave the soothing effect of the hot steam and water and determined to get them both squeaky clean, he took a longer clean than usual. It was only when the skin on his fingers and toes started to pucker and the water finally ran clear, that with regret, he finally raised his arms to begin the drying cycle.

Hot air streaming in jets into the cubicle had a strange and unwelcome effect on Shoo who shook himself so vigorously that San was splattered with water all over again.

"WOOF WOOF!"

"Yea, thanks SHOO!"

Clean, dry and dressed in only his own pants and top, with a now clean and fluffy Shoo at his side, San headed for the larger Eyon toilet area.

Rian was still there, washing his face and hair in the large sink. San had tried to convince him it would be a much easier task in the clean zone cubicle but Rian would have none of it.

"Told you, you should have gone in the cubicle!" he stated, watching Rian trying to rinse the soap out of his very long hair.

"Aanndd I tolldd yoo thaatt Eyons doo nott haavv showwerrs!" was the exasperated response.

"Yes, well you'd have probably got stuck in there anyway, you huge clump of feathers!" he joked.

"Clummpp ovv feathersss aamm I? Lettss see iff yoo still thinnkk thaatt the nexxt time yoo wantt too dangle frromm a cave!" But he was smiling as he said it.

San left him to it for a moment and headed off to the kitchen. Third or fourth time round, he was still fazed by the twinkling stars effect. If he were to carve out some holes in the ceilings of his tree house, would he be able to insert lights into them, he wondered, or would the effect be different there?

Pulling open the cutlery drawer, he was relieved to find exactly what he needed - a sharp pair of scissors. He headed back to the bathroom and Rian.

"Pull your talons through your hair to comb it and follow me," he instructed, leading the way back to the kitchen, Rian and Shoo following.

"Sit there at the table."

Rian sat.

"Now don't worry. I've never done this before but how hard can it be?"

He realised that probably didn't inspire much confidence so he tried again.

"I'll cut a straight line at the back first, just to get rid of the length, then I can cut some more off to make to look good."

"Yoo caann make itt loookk goooddd!"

San wasn't sure if this was meant as an assertion, a question or a sarcastic comment so he ignored it.

He picked up a strand of Rian's hair, lowered it into the gap between the scissor blades and cut. Then he did the same with another and another. Confidence growing with every snip, it wasn't long before he was trimming a bit here and finessing a bit there and layering another bit somewhere else.

Soon there was a pile of cut hair on the floor and a very handsome, very *coiffed* Eyon sitting at the table.

"Well you look fantastic! Even if I do say so myself!"

"Reeelllyy? I willl go aanndd seee."

San was disappointed that Rian sounded so unbelieving and sceptical of his achievements.

But on his return from viewing himself in the mirror, San thought the Eyon looked taller somehow, almost as if he was standing straighter than before.

Without a word, Rian came up to him and hugged him tight into his feathers.

"Thannk yoo."

It was so softly spoken that San almost missed it and he felt a lump catch in his throat as he responded, "you're welcome."

"WOOF! WOOF," barked Shoo, who was now covered in snippets of hair, having been rolling about on the floor, making both San and Rian laugh.

Kitchen swept, breakfast was a lack lustre affair, since all that remained in the cold store was what he had rejected the day before. San placed Vinnbr's plate in front of her and watched her chew and swallow automatically.

The Eyon had been up before him and already plugged in when he first saw her. He wondered if she had even been to sleep. Or perhaps she had slept there, plugged in and with her eyes open. Just continued to stare at the rolling screen, her eyes reflecting the strange signs, whilst her brain shut down for the night.

He walked over to the large bed to check. It was made and he couldn't tell whether she had slept in it and remade it, or whether it was unused from the day before. OwnSan definitely slept. Not only had he seen this with his own eyes, and been witness to the hideous snoring that accompanied it, but he had had to deal with the consequently mussed up bed every morning.

A thought struck him then. Perhaps this Eyon was more tidy because it was a girl Eyon? Was there a

difference between male and female Eyons in that way?
He couldn't remember if any of his friends had ever
suggested anything about that, one way or the other.

He was on to the last bite of his food and feeling
relieved rather than disappointed about it. The hot
sandwich had filled him up, but it had been more of a
chore to chew and swallow than a pleasure. Perhaps that
was how Eyons perceived food.

"Do you enjoy food?" he asked Rian, suddenly
curious.

"Itt iss too bee eetenn. Itt iss neededd too sstay alive."

Just as he thought! "But it's not how you see your
food, is it Shoo?" he laughed, as Shoo looked up at him,
recognising his new name.

"You like your food *so* much you almost eat it
without tasting it, it's gone so fast!"

"Woof, woof," Shoo agreed, hoping that San was
offering another juicy morsel for his delectation.

But instead of a juicy morsel, San was holding the
kitchen scissors aloft, offering them to Rian. The Eyon
looked startled at first, reluctant to take the sharp
implement.

"I cann nott huurtt another..." he began, eyes wide
and distressed at what he presumed San was asking him
to do.

"What are you talk..." sudden realisation dawned on
San, "Oh, no, I don't mean you to *hurt* her...I want you
to cut the cable." He pointed to the thick black cable
which snaked out of the back of the machine and
disappeared into the wall at ankle height.

"I think if we break her machine, she will need to go
somewhere to get a new one, or fetch something to fix
this one." San explained. Rian sat still and quiet,

apparently waiting for the rest of the explanation of the plan. San sighed. He had hoped that Rian would immediately accept what he had just said, because the next part was where his plan fell apart.

"I think she will need to fly somewhere other than the store house to get what she needs. And I don't think she will want to leave us alone here."

"Oh!" as comprehension dawned, Rian's usual colouring came back to his face and he looked both surprised and relieved.

"Yoo thinkk wee cann essscape." Rian stated, looking less than convinced.

"Well, there's a place that the Pets get taken to, a factory...but I don't know what that is..." he felt the flaw in the plan was as high and wide as the drop from the cliffs itself.

"Facctorry. I havv neverr heard of that wword either." Rian either hadn't seen the flaw, the fact that she may decide to leave one or two of their little travelling band alone in the cave, if she even went at all.

San wondered if he should tackle that idea now or at the time of departure. He decided to leave it till the crucial moment. He had a gut feeling that if he mentioned it now, discussed the weight Vinnbr would be expected to carry, that the risk would be unacceptable to Rian. San was convinced that his friend would sacrifice himself, to let San have his freedom. And to him, that was unacceptable. Instead he talked through the other flaw.

"Of course since neither of us knows what a factory is, then it may not provide much chance of escape. But it's more chance than we have now, anyway." He hoped he sounded both confident and assertive.

"Telll mee whatt I should do."

It took only a few minutes to sever the wire but required some effort, with Rian having to use an almost sawing motion. As the blades finally came together, shedding the last of their resistance, San held his breath. At once there was a tremendous bang and a smell of acrid smoke in the air.

The effect was nothing short of dramatic. As if the cable had been an artery which fed her body, the severing of which now threatened her very existence, Vinnbr flailed around where she sat.

Rooted to the spot by the terrifying and grotesque scene in front of their eyes, both Rian and San had immediate misgivings. Both ran the same thought through their heads at precisely the same time: had this somehow injured Vinnbr? What had they done?

San managed to pull his eyes away from Vinnbr, to glance at Rian, his face tight with horror and anticipation. Somewhere Shoo was whimpering quietly. Vinnbr thrashed and twisted and then as suddenly as she had started, she stopped.

It was the weirdest thing San had ever witnessed. She just stopped, disengaged her talon and stood up as if absolutely nothing out of the ordinary had occurred.

Startled by this turn of events, San took a backward step, caught the back of his knees hard against the edge of her bed and flailed backwards on top of it.

Luckily Shoo wasn't lying on it at the time.

The initial sensation of falling rendered him fearful, but by the time he landed on the soft bed, after only a moment of flailing around, he was giggling at himself. The Eyon clearly didn't share his amusement.

Over and over again she inserted her talon into the resolutely blank screen, becoming more and more agitated when the machine did not whirr into life. Finally she seemed to accept that there was something badly wrong with it and clearly annoyed and impatient, began hopping and flapping around, anxious to go somewhere.

Perhaps his plan was working after all, perhaps necessitated by her machine blowing up, she would now have to take them somewhere. No words were spoken. It seemed as if Vinnbr was too agitated to give an explanation to Rian of what was happening and San suspected that Rian did not want to question her, lest he somehow give their plan away.

Clutching at his arm with one of her wings, she led him back over to the wardrobe. Suddenly the food he had eaten seemed to flip over in his stomach in a sickeningly queasy lurch. He knew would not be allowed to parade around dressed only in a top and underpants.

Reluctantly, he pulled the vile green dress off its hanger where he had deposited it the previous night. He shrugged it over his head and replaced the empty hanger on the rail.

But eager as she was to be off, something else had caught Vinnbr's eye. She hooked a vivid purple, red and black concoction off the rail and held it against him, measuring his size. He knew he would have to think quickly.

"HHHHJJJJJBBBBBNNN," she shrilled at him, thrusting the dress at him. He froze, panicked. "HHHHJJJJJBBBBBNNN," she repeated, waiting for his reaction.

"Shee waanntttsss…" Rian began but San interrupted him.

"I *know* what she wants, that's the problem!"

She seemed to prefer the horror of the new dress to the atrocity of the putrid green one. San was seriously worried. The green dress was awful in lots of ways, colour, style and size but this new one…well it was on a whole new level of awfulness.

He decided subterfuge was the only way to go.

"Oh, but I love this *one*," he cooed at her in what he hoped was a placating voice.

"Look how it twirls," he caught the sides with his hands and pulled the material out before pirouetting round to make the skirt billow out prettily, if that was possible with such a hideous garment.

From the look on Shoo's face, he would have sworn that if the little animal had been capable of covering his eyes with his paws, he would have done so.

"Yeah well, needs must Shoo, needs must!" he muttered.

Inside, he was mortified at having to perform these actions but it had the desired effect and the other dress was condemned back to obscurity within the wardrobe.

Again Vinnr's impatience caught up with her and she wasted no more time in turning her back to him, expecting him to hop on. If she had noticed Rian's new hair cut, she gave no sign of it.

San breath caught in his throat. Here, the vital part of his plan could so easily fail. He would have to be both assertive and convincing if he was to get them all out of here.

"She flew us all in here, so she can fly us all out," he said. He wouldn't leave either Shoo or Rian behind but he was worried about Vinnbr being able to carry their overall weight for any length of time. Rian's eyes clouded over with doubt and apprehension.

"Didn't your egg-mother fly you everywhere you went?"

In a way it was an unnecessary question as he already knew the answer. Rian could not fly. He had no wings, only arms.

"Yesss. Butt shee fleww mee separatelyy too herr Pett."

"But her Pet was a full grown woman and you are not a fully grown Eyon yet," San assured him. Rian understood what San was implying. It was a risk but the only chance they had.

"Shoo come here!" San called. Lifting him into his arms, he then wedged the small creature under the neckline of the dress, so that like San's own head, Shoo's head was protruding through, whilst his body was hidden. Shoo would thus be carried safely on Vinnbr's body without the need for San to hold him.

He wrapped his arms around the Eyon's silver feathers and was relieved to find there was still plenty of room behind him, for Rian to be accommodated. And as he felt his friend settle himself directly behind him, he noticed something strange. Where Vinnbr's feathers changed colour, where the gold and blue shot through the overall silver colour, the feathers seemed finer - softer and silkier. This was different to OwnSan, whose muted green and grey feathers, interspersed with swirls of gold, all felt exactly the same.

But in the grand scheme of things, he figured that the comfort of his Owners' feathers was really of no importance. What *was* important was to make sure they were holding on tight. Falling off an Eyon flying tree height is bad, but half way up a cliff - well that was another matter altogether.

However, he needn't have worried. Vinnbr didn't seem at all perturbed about carrying the extra weight. She angled her body, sort of hunching her shoulders and hip joints up, just so, so that her torso formed a cradle to keep them safe. He was more comfortable than he remembered ever feeling perched on OwnSan's back.

Vinnbr's flying expertise was clearly excellent and also far better than OwnSan's. She swooped out of the cave doorway in one smooth movement, wings beating furiously. Immediately, they were launched into devastatingly empty mid-air.

Unable to stop himself, San screwed up his eyes in terror and clutched more tightly to the Eyon's feathers. He could feel Rian's grip also tightening as he realised how far the potential drop was.

Shoo's reaction was even more extreme. Held safely but with no real sense of security, the poor terrified creature's body was wracked with extreme quakes and unfortunate emissions of gas, which billowed around the dress in a seeming attempt to be free.

San could feel Vinnbr's muscles and sinews all working hard to keep them in flight. Catching a current of hot air, the Eyon took full advantage of it, riding the breeze and climbing even higher in the sky, before dropping down again on the next cooler current.

This up and down movement was creating a strange sensation in the pit of San's stomach. It wasn't pleasant, but it wasn't entirely unpleasant either. His ears seemed to be popping in time to the beat of his racing heart and his stomach continued to clench and unclench.

"Wow, isn't this the strangest feeling?" he gasped.

"Hmmm Hmmm," was all Shoo could whimper in response, whilst Rian said nothing at all.

It wasn't until he wondered where the strange sound he could hear was coming from, that he realised he was giggling. He was enjoying himself. Still holding on, he dared to open his eyes.

He had never been flown so high before! The cliffs, themselves so high, were far, far below and now the doorways set in them, looked like tiny little holes, the size of ants. His stomach gave another huge lurch as Vinnbr swerved and curved round to face a new direction.

They had been in the sky for some minutes, yet hadn't actually got anywhere. It was almost as if Vinnbr was flying, just for the sheer sake of it, rather than to get to a destination. And then it hit San. She was flying like this for them! She was showing off and demonstrating what she could do! He just hoped that she didn't expect him to clap because there was no way he'd be unclasping his hands from her body, not at this height!

Time after time the Eyon performed amazing aerial stunts for their benefit. She swooped down towards the flat grassland on the top of the cliff in a nose dive, only to pull up at the very last moment. [The full effect of this was spoiled somewhat for San, when it caused Shoo to have a particularly violent gassy emission, against the side of his body.]

Then almost vertical, she rose high into the clouds, holding them firmly on her back by locking her hip joints over and around their legs. It must have been tiring for her but she kept it up. And each and every time, San rewarded her efforts with giggling and mock shrieks of terror.

Sometimes Rian laughed too but mostly he was silent, preferring to let San enjoy the thrills on his own.

Finally after several death-defying swoops where San was almost convinced they were about to crash, they once more climbed high into the sky and turned away from the city on the sea cliffs. He was disappointed that the fun had come to an end. It had been so unexpected and so out of character for an Eyon, that he had just immersed himself in it while it lasted. Shoo, on the other hand, or paw, as it were, was more than relieved and settled completely down.

For some time Vinnbr flew inland and San began to enjoy the journey and the sights. And after a while he began to recognise some areas and tried to map the landsape in his head.

"Isn't that the marsh lands I got stuck in?" he asked Rian as they passed overhead.

Rian thought it was, but perhaps a different part, as there was a wide and fast flowing river that they had never seen before.

Seen from above, the river curved and twisted at every opportunity, almost as if it were trying to lose something. In some places it was wider than others.

"Where does all that extra water go, when it narrows again?" San asked, knowing full well he was not likely to get an answer.

Assuming that the amount of water remained the same, did that mean then that where the river was narrow, it was deep and that conversely where it was widest, would that be the shallowest part? Of course the lake that he had nearly drowned in was deep, but only in the middle. Was this true of the river too, he wondered.

And if it was, how safe would it be to cross, if it turned out they had to, in orde to find a Human village.

It suddenly occurred to him that Vinnbr could be flying him back home to his forest. Back to OwnSan. Yet something told him this was not the case. They were flying back in the general direction from which he had come but ever so slightly off course. He didn't think this was because the Eyon was unsure of where to go to return him. He was now certain that even if she *had* stopped to consider where he had come from, even if she knew for definite, she had no intention of returning him. Her destination was elsewhere.

His attention was caught by a big clump of trees. Not big enough to be called a forest but dense nonetheless, with something not quite right looking about it. And then he knew what that something *not right* was.

"What *is* that?" he asked, trying and failing to get a perspective on it to enable identification.

"I donntt knoww," replied Rian in a tone that indicated he was equally perplexed.

The densely grown trees were interlinked by some sort of covered corridor so that the houses, and there were many *and* on several different levels of branches too, were all inter-connected. He had *never* seen anything like it.

# *Chapter 28.*

Sophia stood in the doorway, the sun behind her creating a strange effect with the light. She seemed to be outlined against the morning sun, yet herself be in darkness, her face hidden. Then she entered the hut. Her position altered, the sun fought its way past and around her to illuminate her features but still she was inscrutable.

"I have brought you both breakfast. I will say again that you are welcome to stay," she turned very slowly and deliberately towards Little who was sitting up rubbing his eyes.

"Both of you," she finished. Her tone was flat, emotionless and Loni couldn't tell whether she really meant this, or whether she felt she had to say it after the events of the previous night.

But all these thoughts were banished as Sophia looked at them and smiled sadly. Before they could respond, she continued, "but I know that you will not. That you cannot. And although I have my doubts about your safety if you leave, like you, I now believe that there is a purpose you are meant to serve." She sighed.

"And, may the sun in the sky help you, we *need* you to fulfil that purpose. If anyone can change the future, it is *you two*, 'Loni and Little of the Eyons'. *You* two who are now also 'Loni and Little of the People.'" She smiled sadly. "The People have asked that they be allowed to say their goodbyes to you *both.*"

So much emphasis was put on the word 'both' that Loni automatically reached for Little's wing, choking back a lump in her throat. Sophia too seemed full of emotion and her eyes were clear and honest as she looked from one to the other.

"The People are grateful for all you did and wish to make it known to you. Come, both of you, when you are ready." Setting down pates of food for each of them, she departed once more, closing the door softly behind her.

Loni was torn. Part of her was desperate to stay here in this village of humans. But what Sophia had said was true. She could not stay. *They* could not stay. Here, Little would be as out of place as *she* felt back home. She could not sacrifice his happiness for her own. She would die before she did that.

And also, they would never manage to change things if they stayed. Instead, her heart would break afresh every day, looking at and living with people she had been unwilling to help the best way she could.

Damned if she did and damned if she didn't stay, her heart sank.

This place wasn't right for her but it was the closest things had ever been to being so. But what did that mean to Little? She didn't dare ask him. He loved her so much, he wouldn't even hesitate. He would just do whatever he thought would make her the most happy. So she had to be strong for both of them.

That phrase resounded in her head and brought with it unwanted memories of the previous night. It had been what Sophia had said to Alzakery, that he had to be strong for both his own and Louisa's sakes.

'And look how that turned out' thought Loni sourly.

She passed one plate of food to Little and balanced the other on her knees. She chewed and swallowed, tasting nothing. Beside her Little was eating more silently than usual. It seemed that he had also been put off his food by recent events and could no longer enjoy it with his usual gusto.

Soon they had eaten their fill and prepared themselves for leaving. Loni felt grubby and was sure she looked it too. Her clothes were crumpled and dirty and very definitely the worse for wear. She wished the huts had a cleaning cubicle and longed for a hot steam. But as much as she longed for all that, she would have forsaken cleanliness forever, if she could have changed the events of the previous night.

Instead she made do with the tepid bowl of water and clean towel which had been laid out for her, by Sophia. It didn't get *all* the dirt off her but at least she felt a little fresher. There was a light knock at the door and once more Sophia entered, this time with clean clothes piled high in her arms.

"I have brought you these. They are not as fine as your own clothes nor as colourful but they are clean and dry and you are welcome to them. If there is anything else we can provide for you, please let me know," she held the clothes out to Loni.

Loni refused them graciously. "Thank you for you and your peoples' generosity Sophia. But I cannot wear these. I do not know what lies beyond here, but whatever it is, I must be dressed as I now am."

It was hard to explain what she was thinking and even harder to think badly of  Eyons, despite what she had learned. But she *had*  learned to be cautious.

"To wear these clothes would mark me out as different, *too* different and would draw attention to us and perhaps, eventually to you. I will not put you or your people in danger."

She hesitated a moment before continuing but ultimately it had to be said, had to be faced. "And perhaps we will meet the Eyons you speak of. What will happen if they realise we have been here? If they realise that we have spoken?" She was afraid to even think these thoughts but knew that it was something which had to be confronted, head on.

Sophia said nothing. Wise as she was, Loni doubted that it was something she had not thought through herself. Even so, she had offered Loni clean clothes. It was a brave gesture.

"If we do, I will not betray you. I promise," she finished. Little stood wide eyed at her side just listening. Loni knew it was a lot to ask, that he ally himself to her and these Humans, rather than his own species. And yet she knew that was exactly what he would do. And he would do it without hesitation.

Sophia seemed unable to speak, her eyes filled with tears. Leaving the clothes neatly on the ground, she left the hut without a further word.

Loni smoothed down her clothes as best she could. Perhaps the warmth from her body and the morning sun would smooth out the worst of the creases as she walked, although that was probably just wishful thinking. She pulled her fingers through her hair to detangle it, in a less painful way than using a brush, then used a wet corner of the towel to rub her teeth clean. Whilst she did all this, Little merely ran his wings over his feathers, redistributing his body oils evenly and keeping himself waterproof.

It didn't take very long to do, but she was aware that she was dragging it out somewhat. She ran her hands through her hair one last time. Finally, she knew they could put it off no longer. Standing, she drew Little close to her and gave him the biggest, tightest cuddle she could. Heart pounding she grasped the door latch and pulled.

A light drizzle of rain fell. Too fine to be seen, it nonetheless soaked the ground and clung to every surface. The whole village stood there, waiting in the rain for her and Little to make their appearance. They stood in family groups, husbands with wives, sons and daughters all together, holding hands.

Hair and clothing wet, with no protection from the rain, they stood still, silent and waiting. Loni looked from family group to family group. She tried to memorise the common look of each one, how this eye shape went with this hair colour in one group and that eye colour with this mouth shape in another.

Yet it was the things which her brain wasn't actively focusing on, that it took in the most. How this wife held her husband's hand. How that son clung to his mother. And how that father's hand rested protectively on that daughter's shoulder. Her eyes captured it all and her brain stored it.

But it was one person in particular who caught Loni's eye.

Alzakery stood slightly to one side, his son wrapped up against the weather and securely cradled in his arms. Seeing Loni, he approached her and the villagers parted to let him through.

"Thank you for what you did," his voice broke as he struggled to get the words out. The bereaved man turned to Little, so that he was included in these thanks.

"I know you tried to save Louisa but it could not be done. But without you, *both* of you, I would surely have lost Callum too," his voice was raw and sincere. He bowed his head in a deep nod of respect before stepping back out of their path.

"The sun brought you to us. I pray that the sun will be harnessed in the sky and keep you from rain. And may you go in peace, Loni and Little of the Eyons. Loni and Little of the People."

Eyes swimming with tears, Loni managed a choked response. It wasn't quite the traditional wording that he had spoken, but it wasn't far off either. Planting a kiss on her fingertips, she then transferred the kiss to baby Callum's forehead and made a silent promise to herself.

This child should herald in a new dawn. This child, his life so hard and cruelly won should bring an end to the carnage and terror of the past. She and Little just *had* to make it so.

And so with the tears still wet on their faces, Loni and Little bade their farewell to the People. The weight of their pain was too much to bear and they could not stay.

In their hearts, the villagers understood. One by one they wished them well. Loni *felt* their words as much as heard them.

Sophia busied herself, giving out orders for fresh food to be fetched and well wrapped, for them to take on the next part of their journey. Her eyes were still red from crying and her face tear stained, where the tears had made tracks down her cheeks, before drying.

But there was a subtle difference in her body language and it was reflected in how she stood now. Holding herself erect, she seemed taller than she had before, almost as if some heavy burden had been lifted from her shoulders. Which in a way, Loni guessed it had.

Scuttling chickens and dogs from her path, she reached forward and embraced Loni and then with only the slightest hesitation pulled Little into the embrace also.

"We have lost so many over so long a time, that our hearts will bleed forever. That will not change. And yet you have given us such solace, such hope, that I pray that you may find the answers you seek and in doing so, bring about a better future for us all. May the sun always shine for you and the land provide. Go with our blessings and our love," she kissed them both. "And remember that there will always be a home here for you, should you want it."

Turning to Loni and releasing Little from the embrace she said softly so that no one else could hear, "I have searched your features Loni and you are unlike us here. I wish I could tell you that I recognise you as one of us, but I'm afraid I do not. Your skin is darker than ours and your eyes a shade I have not seen before. I fear there are many peoples like us across the land and I hope you find the ones to which you rightly belong."

"I wish that it was not so, but I see the truth of your words with my own eyes," Loni sighed. Her heart felt fit to burst with pain and sorrow.

"I don't know where we are headed Sophia, and I don't know what we will find when we get there but I do know one thing. Something has gone wrong somewhere. There is a saying "two wrongs don't make a right" but here it seems that two rights have somehow made a wrong. In my heart I know that Eyons are not bad but they have done a bad thing to you and your people."

She turned to Little and looked him straight in the eyes before continuing. Although he could not understand everything, she felt she had his approval and agreement for what she was about to say.

Taking a deep breath she continued her pledge.

"I promise to try to change things for the greater good of all. I give you my word, Sophia." She felt Little squeeze her hand lightly with his sharp talons, trying to make a point but without hurting her.

She understood and amended what she was saying, "*we* promise and *we* give you our word."

"ESSSSS, ORRDDD," Little added, to make sure that Sophia knew he meant it too.

Loni made the promise solemnly and as she said the words, she locked them tight in her heart for safekeeping.

# Chapter 29.

A light drizzly rain had begun to fall as they approached the interlinked tree house but San paid it no notice. He was too amazed by what he was experiencing to take any more in.

Vinnbr flew right in, landing on a huge platform at the entrance to the giant house. She angled her torso, shunting her hip joins downwards and outwards, allowing them to slide easily off her back. Extracting Shoo from the dress proved to be more difficult however and San was surprised at the amount of patience Vinnbr exhibited as he and Rian tussled with the little creature.

"Come on Shoo. LET GO!"

Afraid to be separated from him, Shoo had repeatedly dodged San's attempts to dislodge his head from the neckline of the dress they both wore.

"You can't just hang there, and I can't carry you everywhere."

Shoo still refused to budge. San was now becoming exasperated with the animal.

"I feel like some kind of two-headed monster with you there like that!" he pleaded, attempting to wrench the creature out from underneath, bottom first. All flailing legs and lashing tail, he deposited Shoo back on the ground and turned to Vinnbr.

Nudging them forwards with her wing she half pushed, half dragged them along the corridor to where it opened up into several different rooms.

The corridor was wide enough for them all to walk side by side, with Shoo in between them but the floor of it had a different feel to that of the tree houses he was used to. It sort of swayed, as if it was not entirely fixed in position, as if both ends were anchored to something else but the mid-section hung loose.

"Grrr," Shoo growled softly at the moving floor, clearly distrustful of it. San felt like joining in.

It made him wonder what would happen if a really big gust of wind came along. Would the corridor come unhinged at one end and everything and everyone in it, be hurtled to the ground? Would they lie there whilst the gale caused the passageway to lash at the ground like an angry snake, crushing all in its path?

Most of the doors leading into the various rooms were ajar, allowing San to see straight in. He didn't even try to hide his amazement. Even if the Eyons had been inclined to notice, they wouldn't have been bothered by his reaction anyway.

He couldn't believe his eyes. There were machines everywhere, and in every room. Huge machines that whirred, with moving parts that rapidly zoomed up and down. Small ones that clonked and shuffled bits sideways. And some that were silent.

He felt Shoo jump in fear at the sight but the creature made no noise. Instead he slunk even closer to San's legs, trembling and resolutely avoiding looking at the Eyons.

And there were also giant versions of the machines that both Vinnbr and OwnSan used at home. The screens scrolled as rapidly as the smaller versions he was more accustomed to but these ones also emitted a strange bleeping sound that San had not encountered before.

And there were Eyons everywhere. Some tended machines that spewed forth cloth, whilst some gathered the material up. Others fed this material into yet another machine, which seemed to produce finished articles of clothing.

The combination of bundles of cloth and flamboyantly lustrous feathers, produced such a riotously coloured scene, that it almost hurt his eyes to look at it. Stripes and spots merged with solid colours to give an overall 'streaky' effect, as if all the colours were bleeding into one, or trying to!

Being hurried along still, San passed another doorway. Here the machines appeared to produce pieces of flat metal and plastic. These raw materials were then subsequently fed into other machines and turned into kitchen utensils and any number of common household things.

"Spoons, colanders, forks," San's mouth seemed committed to try to keep up with his brain in identifying all the things it saw. There were things which looked suspiciously like the knobs of the steam enclosures and these were only *some* of the things he could identify. There were many, many more things being produced, that he couldn't put either a name or use to.

Here, the Eyons lent their colours more effectively, providing a colourful antidote to the burnished steel of the machines and their produce, lifting the image from being stark and grey.

The rooms themselves were vast and spanned more than one level and every chamber had the same layout. There was a ground floor, packed with working machines, which was overhung on all but a central open area, by three layers of balconies running all the way around. So that, even those working on the very top level, could look down and see those below.

Using the open space as a flight zone, Eyons flew up and down everywhere, from one level to the other. And on every level, there were huge, hulking machines.

Shocked to the core, San realised that he had never once given though to how and where all the *things* he used on a daily basis were made. Or who made them.

What was even more peculiar though, was seeing the Eyons working. Working together, yet separately. One fed a machine with raw material, another collected the end result. Neither spoke to the other, nor made eye contact over the hissing pieces of metal. It was almost like they were machines themselves.

San felt his jaw drop in amazement but Vinnbr seemed not to notice. He locked his gaze with Rian. Rian too was astounded at the sheer scale of the place and the production which went on within it.

"I nevverr knew abowwtt thisss pplace!"

Something in San's mind clicked into focus and he wondered where all these Eyons had come from. It was something he would have to ask Rian about later. For now, they had more immediate problems to deal with. Hurrying them past several of the doorways beyond which her fellow Eyons worked, Vinnbr finally stopped before a door which was painted in a rainbow of colours.

This was the only door which had not been allowed to retain its natural wooden hue and therefore clearly special. San felt his apprehension mount as he followed her mimed directions and pushed the door open wide enough to peer inside.

The air in the room was different. In the corridor, the smells and scents of machine oil and hot plastic, merged and mingled with the cold metallic tang of pressed metal. And all of this was overlaid with the subtle aroma of powdery papery skin, covered with dry dusty feathers.

But inside the room, there was no mistaking the change of aroma. Here, as he held open the door just a fraction, just enough to get a sensory flavour of it, he smelled the all too Human fragrances of sweat, boredom and conversely, excitement. Small snuffling sounds came from the region of his knees and he knew that Shoo was also aware of the different smell.

San recognised that strangely evocative scent which was a mix of anxiety, nervous energy and desperation. He had smelled it many times before but he had never once recognised it for the raw emotions it really contained.

On the edge of these two worlds, one Eyon, the other Human, is where he would have stayed, if he could. He would have used the time to try to metaphorically reach inside his head and grasp the strange kaleidoscope of images, thoughts and feelings, that had begun to form and attempt to twist them into some semblance of a meaningful train of thought. He would have raced the ideas up and down inside his skull, attempting to establish what was really going on, and *why*, and *how,* it had all come about. Unfortunately he didn't have the luxury of time.

Instead, Vinnbr, tiring of his reluctance to do what was expected of him, yanked open the door to its full creaking width. Patting him briefly on the head, she gently pushed San through, whilst keeping firm hold of Rian and preventing him from entering. Then she turned away, clasping Rian's arm and taking him with her.

It was so quick, that there was no chance to *think* anything let alone say anything. Only the expression on Rian's face betrayed his surprise at this development.

Shoo, carried along by San's momentum, sought refuge in the space between his legs and the heavy door, shielded from sight and unwelcome attention. San watched Vinnbr and Rian depart and the door close softly behind them, before the heavy silence in the room made him turn around.

He felt the gaze of at least fifty other Pets, as all eyes turned on him, the newcomer to the playroom. Not a single one of them seemed in the least familiar from his communications across the cliffs. He might have been mistaken, but he was sure that he had gotten a fairly good look at all of the heads that had stuck out of the caves. And these were completely different Pets. From some other place!

He smiled tentatively, but it did nothing to ease the tension. There was an air of aggression here that he hadn't encountered before and he didn't quite know how to diffuse it.

Unseen behind him, Shoo also seemed to pick up on the atmosphere and his shivering intensified, causing the door to emit a small rattle as it banged against its frame.

The smile froze on San's face. No one smiled back. Board games were instantly forgotten, winners were no longer interested in their victory, nor losers in their defeat. Instead everyone was captivated by the sight of the raggedly dirty boy, dressed in the horrible, too-big, green dress.

# Chapter 30.

It was the river which halted Little and Loni's progress. Not because they couldn't get over it, for that was easy. True, it was too deep looking to wade through and too fast flowing to swim through but they would just fly over it. Or more accurately, *Little* would fly them over it. But Loni was worried about how tired he was becoming.

At first it had been horrible, leaving the village behind them, not knowing which direction to head in, the rain drizzling down upon their bare heads and beading onto her clothes and Little's feathers. But after a while it had seemed more cathartic than anything else, as if the rain was washing away all the pain and grief.

The air was warm, with no chill to it, so it wasn't an entirely unpleasant experience. And although it probably made her even more dishevelled and dirty looking, there was also something rather beautiful about this rain. It was somewhere between a fine mist and light droplets. Individual drops couldn't be felt or even really seen, it was only as they collected up into larger pools of liquid that they had any impact.

Even then, Little wasn't bothered by the rain. In fact the raindrops seemed to virtually bounce off his oily feathers rather than soak into them. It was only where he had torn his feathers out, that the rain seemed to have any impact. And these bald patches were soon almost entirely covered by the surrounding dampened feathers pressing down and spreading out.

Loni had watched, fascinated, as the drizzle gathered on his plumage, the moisture holding in place, sparkling like tiny jewels, before quiveringly running off. And as it did so, it joined with other streams of liquid making their way down his body, back to the ground.

"I wish I could look that lovely when I am wet, Little," she teased him. It was hard to make light conversation after all they had learned but to change things, they had to go on. And they couldn't go on if they were bound with misery and despair.

"LONEEE ALLIISSS LOVVELLIIII."

"Well, gee thanks for the confidence boost but I guess we both know I don't always look lovely!"

She hesitated before voicing a thought but something had occurred to her. "You know that eventually the sun will soak the water back up and it will be held as clouds ready for the next rain."

"ESSSS AAAAIIINNN, ETTT, OTTER," he had clearly made the connection between rain being wet, being water but she feared her train of thought was too sophisticated for him. In her head, there was an undeniable feeling of natural inevitability about the whole cycle. She wondered if this was how the villagers had come to view the Eyon raids – just another self-perpetuation of the cycle of life.

"AAAIIINNNN WAY," Little held his wing outstretched, talons held upwards to indicate the rain seemed to be drying up. In the distance a rainbow formed, its colours dazzling against the pale sky. Little noticed it first, grasping Loni's arm and pointing with his other wing.

"JJJJYYYYYBBBFFSSSS!" he screeched excitedly, "JJJJYYYYYBBBFFSSSS, JJJJYYYYYBBBFFSSSS."

"Oh *rainbow*," Loni interpreted.

"ORRRIINNNBBBOOW!" Little repeated.

"No. *Rainbow*," Lani explained.

"NORRINNBBOOWW," Little tried again, still mashing the two words together.

"Rainbow…*rain…bow*," said Loni slowly, realising her previous mistakes.

"RRRAAAAIIIIINNNNNBBBBBOOOO," stated Little slowly and precisely.

They had seen rainbows in the past, but this one seemed brighter, and bigger and bolder. Loni thought that it was probably just that here the landscape was uninterrupted by trees, which made it seem that way. But a small part of her mind disagreed. That part said that this rainbow *was* brighter *and* bigger *and* bolder. And after everything she had seen and heard recently, she certainly wanted it to be so. She wanted it to represent hope, a new start. But she feared that it was *only* a rainbow.

She smiled at Little and nodded to indicate that she had seen it.

"People say that you can wish upon a rainbow, Little," she said wistfully. Of course the people from her home had also said children were handed over to be Pets and that Human villages were always at war with one another…and these were clearly lies. Or if not lies, then stories made up so long ago, that no-one knew how untrue they were. For a moment she felt that coppery taste on her tongue again.

"IIISSSHHHH!" he replied.

Then when she seemed to still be lost in her own thoughts and not understand that he wasn't just copying her, that he wanted *her* to make a wish he repeated himself.

"IIISSSHHHH. OOOOOO IIISSSHHHH OOOOWWWW."

This time Loni understood.

"No, Little. *I* won't make a wish now, *we* will!"

It suddenly seemed like a really good idea.

"EESSSSSSS!" Little was nodding emphatically, causing the remaining droplets to be shed in an arc of water, which unfortunately alighted on Loni.

She brushed her damp hair away from her face and wiped her hand across her eyes, flicking away the accumulated rain. She turned to Little and took both of his wing tips in her hands.

"We wish for a way to make things right," she thought about the best way for that to happen.

"To make things right FOR EVERYONE, EYON AND HUMAN!"

She raised her voice and shouted her wish, shouted it to the sky and the sun and most of all, to the *rainbow*.

"EEESSSSSSSSSS!" Little took his cue and shouted too.

Loni smiled at his boundless enthusiasm and pulled him down to sit beside her on a large flat rock. Faced with the prospect of having to use what remained of his strength to get them over the river, it seemed sensible to stop for a brief rest and some food. The grass was too wet to sit on but the stone appeared to have already mostly dried in the warmth of the sun.

The river was a beautiful shade of blue, with swirling water in some places, where it passed over rocks and stones on its way and a perfectly smooth mirror in others. Wild flowers lined its banks, their red and yellow and purple hues a dazzlingly lovely sight. Moisture from the recent rain lay imprisoned within the petals and glinted out at them, twinkling in the warm sunlight. It seemed like a better place than most to have a rest.

She shared out some of the food the villagers had given them, making sure that she gave him enough for his big Eyon body. Luckily, Little was so absorbed in his own share that he didn't notice that she took only a small amount for herself.

A dragon fly hovered over the river, presumably looking for its next meal, whatever that was. Loni pointed at the insect.

"Dragonfly. Dr..aa..g..on..fl..y," she pronounced slowly, for Little's benefit.

"Dddddrrrrggggggffffllll," he tried hard to repeat. Then slightly better, "ddrrggggffll."

"That's it, you're getting the hang of it. And in your language?" she asked, pleased with his progress.

Little shrugged his shoulders, his wing tips slightly raised in an 'I've no idea' sort of look. Loni wasn't sure whether it was because he was young that he didn't *know* the words for some things, or whether Eyons just didn't *have* words for everything, or things that didn't matter to them.

If anyone had asked her before she had found out what she had, she would have said that she thought most things didn't actually matter to the Eyons. But everything at the village had proved otherwise. If Eyons cared about one thing, then that one thing was certainly getting hold of Pets. And keeping hold of them!

Why would that be? And none of it tied in with the image of the solitary, peaceful Owners that she knew and loved. Had OwnLoni herself gone to some village and snatched Loni? It was impossible to imagine that happening. Or had some other Eyon taken her, then passed her on? Did that mean that there were two kinds of Eyons, one peace-loving the other fearsome? And was there some difference because of the machines?

She snuck a look at Little out of the corner of her eye. She couldn't even raise an image of a fierce and violent Little in her *mind*, let alone her heart. Once more the image of the machine sitting waiting in its own small cardboard box came to the front of her mind. What if ultimately that was the choice? What if there *were* only two ways for Eyons to live...either hooked up to machines and together with but distant from their Pets...or no machines but fierce and terrifying? What if *that* was the real choice?

She knew the argument was flawed. She didn't know for a fact that there were two types, or even that if there were, the fierce ones didn't hook up but it was a possibility. And after all they had seen and done, she wanted to ensure that she carefully considered any and all possibilities.

And if it were so natural for Humans to have children, then why did it never happen to Pets? Back in the village she had learned about how families lived together …mother, father and children, all in one hut. It was an alien concept to her, and as such should have been so foreign as to feel weird and yet…and yet it had seemed perfectly *right*. Not even just normal but *right*, as if anything else could only be wrong.

Absently she touched the triangular markings on her arm.

"Where did I come from Little?" she asked him, knowing full well he could not provide an answer. And she had other questions too, ones that she dared not ask even herself. What had happened to her family? Would she ever even find out? Did they wonder what had happened to her? Or did they too believe, as Sophia's people had, that the snatched children were eaten in some kind of victory supper? Did they still cry themselves to sleep?

A thought struck her, the impact of it causing her heart to jolt and her breath to catch in her throat. Had her parents gone on to have more children? Had they perhaps had older children when she herself was snatched? Did she have brothers and sisters out there somewhere? Did she look like them? She tried to imagine her own face on another body, older or younger. Taking the thought to its natural conclusion, she realised that there could be a whole family somewhere just waiting and praying for her safe return. But where?

Now that she had realised this, it was yet another purpose to be added to her list. Now she had to prevent Little being hooked to a machine, stop the Eyon raids *and* find her family! Any one of these things could take a lifetime to achieve…but all three put together? Well that was just epic.

She stole another sideways glance at Little. He too was lost in thought, his features slack as he concentrated on whatever was going on inside his head. Loni guessed it was fairly similar to what she was thinking. It was almost inconceivable that she was *not meant* to be with this baby Eyon, to raise him and to love him. Yet the truth was undeniable. The truth was that she should be living with her own family, mother, father and brothers and sisters, if there were any. And not with an Eyon.

What would happen if she found her family? Would they be as accepting as Sophia's people? Or would the rage in them be worse, as they recognised her as one of them? Would the pain be too deep, the affront too personal, to be swept aside? Would they harm Little? She could not let that happen. She *would* not let it happen.

Her heart's desire was to put everything right for everyone. But the further they travelled and the more they learned, it was beginning to look more and more unlikely. The truth was, that much as she wanted her family, they were *strangers* to her and the familiarity of her love for Little would outweigh the potential for love from strangers any day.

Taking another small bite from her food, she munched on a juicy strip of chicken thoughtfully. Little had wolfed his down as rapidly as ever but even though Loni had less to begin with, she had managed to eke it out. She was trying to fool her stomach into thinking it was full, by chewing each bite at least a hundred times.

This turned the chicken into tasteless mush, so that by the time she did swallow, it was enough to make her heave. But either way, eating slowly and/or feeling sick, it had the same end result. Neither her mind nor her stomach wanted any more filling.

The last strip of chicken would be her undoing she feared. Nudging Little out of his private reverie, she nodded towards the remaining piece of chicken.

"Go, on Little, you have it. I'm full up!" she smiled. It didn't even touch the sides of his throat, it was snaffled up so fast. Loni giggled. How could anyone *not* love Little?

Lunch over, they made the short flight over the river and trudged onwards. Only when Loni had to transfer the sack with their meagre food supplies to the other hand, or over the other shoulder, did they stop for a rest.

They had been gripped by a sense of urgency, which although unspoken they had somehow wordlessly agreed to act upon. Eventually a forest appeared on the horizon, the trees grown thick together and lush. As they walked Loni tried to make a plan with Little.

"When we get there, just act normal. They will wonder who we are but they won't suspect we have run away, why *should* they? We just have to act normal, ok Little, do you understand?" she turned to him and grabbing his wings made him stop, facing her.

"Little is a big Owner," she hoiked him up to stand taller and straighter. "I know that back home you are too young to have a Pet but things might be different here." She pointed to herself and stooped down a little, trying to look smaller, "and I'll try to look younger." She tried to angle her arms into her body, so that the triangles were not clearly on display.

"I've no idea what they'll think of us. That's if they think about us at all, which they probably won't. Come on."

"EAAATHERSSS!" he reminded her.

"Oh, yes, your missing feathers! Look, smooth them down over the bald patches," she patted them down as she spoke. "There! They are pretty much covered up. I don't think anyone will notice."

"CRRASSHH INNNN TREEE?" he suggested, eyes wide.

"Won't they wonder how you crashed into a tree whilst flying?"

"SNEEEEEZZZZEEE. BIIIGGGG SNEEEZZEE!"

"Yes, good idea. If anyone asks, the story is that you were flying and you had a giant sneeze, crashed into a tree and lost some feathers." She smiled at his inventiveness.

"Anyway I don't think anyone will notice and if they do, they probably won't bother to ask anyway."

Loni hoped that what she had told Little turned out to be the truth. But in her head, she wasn't so sure. What if these were the fierce Eyons? What if they caught and hurt her...or even more unthinkable, hurt Little for colluding with her? She felt the colour drain from her face but kept her expression light, as much for him, as for any strangers who may be watching.

There was no point in approaching cautiously as they wanted to appear open and above suspicion, so they walked straight through the nearest trees and into the enclosed circle formation of "Low Forest."

The sight which met their eyes was not at all what either of them had expected. Instead of a calm serene scene, they were confronted by a horde of Eyons frantically running around, seemingly searching for something, a huge pile of discarded protable machines lying abandoned to one side.

Low bleeps issued from some of the machines, as if in their haste to put them down, some of the Owners had not even bothered to switch them off. Comparable in size and shape to the ones she saw everyday back home, they looked strange only in their abandoned state. As if in a trance, Loni noticed that one or two had cracked screens, as if in the haste to set them down, they had been placed less than delicately.

A huddle of Pets sat on the ground, whispering together.

Fear shot through Loni's heart but she squeezed Little's wing tip to reassure him. They were searching for *them*. OwnLoni had somehow sent a message here and now they were going to be returned to her. They would find out no more truths nor be able to do anything about them.

Everything was lost.

# Chapter 31.

S an's mind raced.

"WHO are YOU?" The owner of the shout had a face which matched his tone of voice, hard and loud. He pushed his way to the front of the room, shoving older and younger Pets aside without any regard to their welfare.

A small table crashed over and all the cards on it fluttered noiselessly to the ground. The two old men who had been playing there, hurried to pick up the cards, before they were crushed underfoot by the man who now strode towards San. A young boy, not able to move out of the man's path with enough alacrity, was shoved roughly aside and sent spinning into another boy, both boys landing in a heap on the floor together.

"I said WHO are YOU?" the man demanded. Close up the man didn't look any nicer. He had moved so close that San could not only tell the colour of his eyes, but count the number of red veins that stood out in the whites of them. Not to mention the throbbing of the veins in his neck or the tide of foamy spittle which lodged at both corners of his mouth.

Funnily enough, San wasn't in the least intimidated, which he suspected was the effect the bully was trying to achieve. He'd certainly managed it with all the other Pets, by the look of it. Not a single one moved or said anything. And whilst he was aware that all were watching him, none of them would meet his eyes. He wasn't sure if they were afraid, or ashamed of their fear, but the result was the same.

"I am San. Who are *you*?" he called the man's bluff and looked him right in the eye. As the man was at least a good head taller, and probably about twenty years older than him, this meant that San had to angle his head upwards whilst almost standing on his tip-toes. It was a bit unfortunate but he didn't think it really put him to much disadvantage. In fact, depending on how you chose to view it, it perhaps made him all the braver, although Shoo silently quaking behind him did not inspire much confidence in the idea.

"I am Will, that's who I am!" angry face bellowed, his complexion seeming to grow at once redder and darker as his temper rose.

"Let me tell you something *San*," he managed to sneer the name out like it was a dirty word. "Have you ever heard the saying 'Where there's a Will, there's a way'? Well that Will is ME! And that way is MINE! Ok *Sannie*, you understand me?"

The younger Pets all knew what was expected of them and as one they sniggered at the implied reference to San wearing a dress. Only the elderly Pets looked on blankly, indisposed to help San but unwilling to collude in the bullying either.

San took a deep breath ready to respond. And then his inner voice spoke up. 'Why bother?' it said. 'Why waste breath on this idiot?'

He had to agree, the voice was right. So, he simply turned around, scooped Shoo up, grasped the handle of the door, yanked it open and walked through.

He half expected to be hoisted back through the doorway and told that Will hadn't done with him yet. But the door swung shut and stayed that way.

Where was Rian?

San peered round the first door he came to. There were Eyons everywhere and on every level but none of them were Rian. He tried the next door and the next, conscious that at any moment he could be noticed and apprehended.

And what if, when he did locate Rian, he turned out to be on one of the balconies with no way for San to reach him, or for Rian to get down? Would he even be able to catch Rian's attention?

There were three doors left to try. Two close together and one on the opposite side. Acting on pure intuition, San peered around the one which stood alone, Shoo still quaking silently in his arms.

His intuition proved to be correct. He had found Rian. And he wasn't on a balcony.

The only problem was that he was on the far side of the room, separated from the door by several large machines and at least four Eyons that San could see.

San had to think quick. Pulling off one shoe and the sock underneath it, he then rolled the sock into a ball, before pulling the shoe back on. Then making sure to aim carefully, he fired the rolled up sock into a large whole in one of the machines off to his right.

The missile hit its intended target and with a loud metallic groan, the machine ground to a halt. At once, the Eyons closest to the door hurried off, to deal with the stalled machine and Rian was alone in his corner.

"RIAN! RIAN," San half called, half hissed, trying to get the volume correct to reach only the right ears.

Rian's head snapped up and turned towards the doorway. Casting a fake nonchalant look at the assembled Eyons hovering over the ailing machine, he ambled towards where San had stood just a moment ago, before ducking back behind the door.

San waited what seemed to be an eternity before Rian appeared before him.

"Come on, let's go!" He turned round and began walking towards the exit which would lead them from the corridor back to the outside.

"Saann!"

He heard the call at exactly the same time as his brain registered that he was walking alone, that Rian wasn't following. He retraced his steps.

"Come on!" he urged.

But his heart recognised the look on Rian's face, even if it did not want to acknowledge it.

"Please Rian, please!" he begged.

Rian shook his head sadly, tears rimming his huge eyes.

"I haavv foundd aa pplace heerr wwhere I caann haavve aa purrpposse. I amm acceppttedd here, myy armss lett me doo some of the things the other Eyons cannot doo. They arr grateful forr mee here."

San had picked up on the phrase 'other Eyons' and understood its significance. Without remarking on its use, he understood that Rian was *finally* thinking of himself as an Eyon, finally finding peace within himself. San was both ectastic for his friend and devastayed for his own loss.

"Iff I go with yoo to findd a Huumann village yoo willl nott stay there, willl nott learn whatt yoo need too learn, because of mee."

San knew that his friend spoke with brutal honesty but his heart was wrung out nonetheless. "No, Rian, please!"

"Yesss ittt isss ttrrue Saann. Andd I willl havv a good life here with Vinnbr. Wee cann care for each other. Shee hass no Pett aandd I cannot havv a Pettt.." He paused, biting back the emotion which began to overwhelm him. "Buutt I cannnott expecctt yoo too stayy. I willl misss yooo," he reached out a hand and stroked Shoo's furry head. "I willl misss yooo botth."

Hard as it was, San had to accept Rian's decision.

"We will miss you too, my friend. But I am glad that you have found a purpose." He took a huge gulp, swallowing back the tears that threatened to fall.

Then unable to stop himself, he flung himself and Shoo into the big Eyon's body in an embrace.

"Goodbye, Rian. I understand that you cannot come any further with me and I wish you well. If it be fate's decree, then we shall meet again. I hope that it is so."

"Farewelll my Humann friend Sann. Mayy fate carry yoou with care." The Eyon folded his arms tightly around San and Shoo for a moment before stepping back. Stepping away from them.

"And you Rian. May the fates carry us *all* with care." San struggled to get the words over the huge lump which had suddenly reappeared in his throat. Eyes glistening wetly he turned away.

Only when he reached the external doorway, did he dare to turn around and look back. And he hoped that what he saw wasn't just his imagination, hoped that the friend standing there, really did stand more erect and straight and proud.

Then he opened the door and walked through it and out onto the landing platform beyond. From there, Shoo stuffed once more into the dress alongside him for convenience, it was an easy climb down to ground level.

"There's just one slight regret," he told the captive Shoo, its face level with his own.

"Woofum."

This variation in response seemed to be due to the creature's relief that San had rescued him and caused by an attempt to wash San's face with his tongue and bark at one and the same time.

"Vinnbr. She's still in mourning and I think this will hit her hard. I mean she seemed like a good Owner. And if I'd been …well…a normal Pet I guess, it would have been ok. But she's got Rian now and together they'll be fine."

He laughed, "and I'll miss all the flying stunts! Though I guess you won't, will you Shoo?" He smiled, dropping the last few feet to the ground.

"Woofum."

Carefully extracting Shoo once more, he ripped the horrid green dress off and tossed it on the earth where it belonged. It wasn't an entirely wise decision, as a light drizzle of rain still fell, but he couldn't bear to leave it on. Aware that the longer they stood there, the more exposed they were and the more likely recaptured, he tried to refrain from wasting time stomping on it.

But the temptation proved *just a little bit* too great as he felt himself give the stupid old dress one enormously powerful kick. Shoo joined in too, sharp white teeth ripping at the hem and pulling it free of the rest of the garment. The dress took the full force of their fury, and billowing on the slight breeze, wafted elegantly upwards ever so slightly.

It was just enough. The material snagged on the lower branches of the tree, all spread out, almost as if the person inside it had just vanished in a puff of smoke.

San stifled a giggle. "It's funny but it might also get us caught."

They would have to make a hasty retreat. He looked around and had no idea what direction to take. The river he had seen was to the right and the Sea City behind him. That left straight ahead or to the left. Since he had tried to take a straight route on his journey so far, deviating from this could lead them round in circles. They would *have* to continue straight on.

They ran full pelt for as long as they could, before slowing to a sprint, then a jog, then reluctantly, a fast walking pace. It was tiring and he suspected it wore him out faster than it did Shoo, but they had to put as much distance as possible between themselves and the huge factory. His body was cold and wet but at least the exercise warmed him a little. Shoo seemed fine, invigorated even, by the running they had done.

And then the strangest thing happened. They walked out of the drizzle.

One moment it was still alighting on them, each new drop blending into the previous one, the next it wasn't. But it didn't appear to have stopped. Instead it was like a curtain which separated the land. The rain continued to fall, just beyond where they now stood, looking back at it. He took a small step back the way he had come and extended his hand across the invisible barrier. Rain washed his hand and wrist but didn't cross the line.

"Well look at that, Shoo. Isn't that just the strangest thing to behold?"

He realised there had to be someplace where the rain stopped, the clouds not extending any further, but he had never experienced it. Nor possibly ever would again, he thought.

The rain began to ease off, the misty droplets becoming finer and less regular. And it was replaced by another of nature's glorious wonders. A shining rainbow.

He had never seen one such as this before, where he could see where the arc terminated at both ends, far in the distance.

"You know, there's a saying that there's a pot of gold at the end of a rainbow. Does that mean at both ends? Or just one? And if so, which end? And how can you tell which is which? Life's just a big mystery isn't it Shoo?"

The little creature looked up at him taking in his every word.

"Why would anyone be interested in a gold coloured pot anyway? See, Shoo there's yet another mystery!"

They weren't headed in the direction of the rainbow – either of its ends, so he'd probably never know. His legs found their own steady rhythm and not having to concentrate on his route, his mind began to churn up other ideas he had previously just accepted. Not only did he not know how new hatchlings originated, he also didn't know where new *Pets* came from.

"There had been one time last winter, when the air was becoming colder and damper by the day. Two new arrivals had appeared in the same week, only a few days apart."

Talking to Shoo wasn't as good as talking to Rian had been, as it didn't give him any direct answers but he had found that it helped clarify his thinking and it was certainly preferable to walking in silence.

"One was little girl of two years." The triangles had looked clear and freshly marked on her arm. "The other one was a little boy, a bit younger. He was a cheery little thing, and all the female Pets fussed and chattered over him. But the girl was different."

San remembered how huge her eyes had been as she had looked around at her new surroundings. They had been a striking shade of dark green and when she had turned and fixed her gaze on him, he had been reminded of the forest, on a hot summer's evening, when the trees wore their luxurious thick green foliage.

He had smiled warmly at her, but her gaze had remained blank. Instead she had pulled a faded brown patch of blanket closer around her and jammed her thumb in her mouth. But she had kept her eyes fixed on him.

The Pets had sat in a wide circle thinking up names for the newcomers. San had suggested "Forest" for the girl on account of her eyes and this was warmly received and unanimously agreed upon.

The boy had sat on the lap of one of the women as the discussion progressed, playfully tugging on her hair and completely oblivious to the fact that he was the focus of so much attention. Forest however, had refused such comfort and instead sat very straight and ever so slightly out of the circle.

It was only by accident that the boy's name had at last been agreed upon.

One of the older Pets had suggested the name Ross, just as the boy gave a particularly huge tug. The woman's head had bobbed so sharply up and down, it had seemed she was giving such vigorous approval, that the whole circle had burst out laughing. And so the boy had been named.

For a moment San's reverie was interrupted as he was forced to focus on his current situation. He had come to the edge of a wide lake, beyond which he could see a large hill on the other side. It was too large to swim across and he didn't fancy re-enacting any of his near drowning episodes of late, so he curved his path to go around it.

"It didn't take long for Ross to fit right in, but Forest took much longer. She had seemed nervous and afraid for quite some time." San paused to think about this statement.

"It seems strange now but somehow, it didn't at the time. And no-one mentioned or questioned where they had come from, or even why."

"Woof."

"I know! I mean it was just accepted. Just another part of a Pet's existence."

"Woof."

San had the odd sensation that this was beginning to become a real two-way conversation.

"And I was one of the very ones who hadn't given it a moment's thought. Until now."

"Woof!"

"Shoo are you understanding anything I say or is it my imagination?"

"Woof." Tail wagging and responding to his name being said. Shoo gave an extra, "Woof."

"So is that a yes or a no?"

"Woof," replied the creature, regarding San very seriously.

"So I take it that's either, neither or both," San laughed. "Let's face it I might as well be talking to the grass as you, if I want a real response. But you're company anyway."

Excited by his tone, Shoo began leaping around and jumping up on him as they walked.

"No jumping. Save that energy. Who knows when we might need it," San admonished gently.

They arrived at the foot of the hill on the other side of the lake, much sooner than he had anticipated. There was no way of knowing what lay behind it, so mindful of their last capture, he approached with as much stealth and caution as was possible.

Luckily there were many bushes lining the side of the hill and so hiding behind them and dashing from one to the other, and carrying Shoo again, he zigzagged his way up to the top, heart hammering in his chest.

At the brow of the hill he managed to find a little thicket of bush. Unfortunately it was a thorny one, but he forced them into the midst of it anyway. His top was snagged several times, but luckily the thorns, whilst embedded in the material, were not large enough to really scrape his skin and Shoo's short fur did not seem to get tangled easily. His clothes were already ragged and torn and he was filthy so what difference would it make?

From this vantage point he could see a fair distance in every direction. To one side of him lay the lake and behind him was the river, too wide and fast flowing for him to cross safely.

But what caught his attention lay directly before him, off to his right a little. It was a collection of houses, the like of which he had never seen before. They were all on the ground. Not a single one was in the trees. In fact, that was the oddest thing of all…there *were no* trees nearby. Could this be exactly what he was looking for? A Human village? No, he realised that was just wishful thinking. It was to quiet, too still and too well tended to be a place where war torn survivors lived, ate, slept and did battle. The houses did not look particularly strong, didn't even look as if they were meant to withstand force. Nor were they damaged in any way that he could tell. This was just another deviation from the tree houses, but it would still be Owners and Pets who lived in them. Perhaps this was where the Owners from the huge work place, where he had left Rian, lived with their pets?

There was no one around and perhaps that too made sense. If they *were* the ones from there, then perhaps this place was empty. On the other hand, that didn't mean that there was no one around at all, did it?

Filthy, ragged, missing his trousers and in the company of a possibly never-seen-before creature, there was no way he'd go unnoticed. And that was fine if it was a Human village but it was not. He was sure of that.

Craning his neck, he looked further afield to what lay behind the collection of strange treeless houses. He could see only grass beyond. So how were he and Shoo to get down the other side of this hill without being seen?

They weren't. But the solution to the problem wasn't too hard to find. They had walked and walked and been flown and escaped and walked and walked some more.

He was exhausted. It didn't matter that it wasn't yet night, he would simply lie down here, in the shade of the thorny bush and go to sleep and Shoo would sleep with him. Then when they awoke refreshed and cool in the dark, they would skirt past the village and be long gone by the time morning came.

But the mind is a law unto itself and once it has imprisoned an idea, it will not easily relinquish it. And so he slept. But not well. And as he slept, the rain began again. This time with renewed vigour.

# *Chapter 32.*

Loni held her breath as a particularly large pink and gold Eyon, rushed towards her, squawking wildly. They had been recognised!

She prepared herself mentally to be apprehended... but the still shrieking Eyon, rushed past her and disappeared through the trees behind where she stood. What was going on?

She felt Little pull his wing tip from her hand and only belatedly realised that she had been squeezing it *too* tight. Wordlessly they exchanged glances. He was mystified too, even though he must have understood what the screeching was about. Clearly, he hadn't been able to put it into context. Nor did he have the time and privacy to explain what he could to Loni.

Just ahead of them sat a large group of Humans, huddled together and talking earnestly.

"Whatever's going on, they'll know what it is. We'll go over and try to find out ok. Just don't say anything ok, Little."

"EESSS, OKK LONNEEE."

"Say *nothing* Little, not *even* that!" she hissed at him, trying to talk from the very corner of her mouth, so that anyone watching would not clearly see them having a conversation.

"EESSS, OKK LONNEEE."

"Little that's not funny. Stop it now!"

She was concerned about how these Pets would accept a baby Eyon sitting with them, but what else could Little do? There were no other young Eyons in sight, and back home - funny how long ago that life seemed now - he was always by her side. But that was there and this was here and things could be very, very different from one place to another, as she had already discovered.

So, inwardly taut with suppressed anxiety, Loni strove to keep Little calm and appearing nonchalant, they strolled over to the assembled group.

Quietly and trying to draw as little attention to themselves as possible, they found a gap in the circle and slotted themselves into it. Strangely, the Pets shuffled themselves around to accommodate them, yet no-one questioned them about who they were or where they had come from.

It seemed that the current situation these Pets had found themselves in, was just too unique and too startling, to cope with any thoughts of anything else. Loni and Little settled themselves on the ground with the other Humans and sat quietly, listening to the whispered conversations.

What she found out was even more startling than anything she could have imagined. A boy called San had left his Owner and now both Pets and Eyons were frantically worried. It was the sole topic of conversation.

Where had he gone and *why*? Loni wondered if exactly the same thing was happening in her own forest right this very minute. Wondered how OwnLoni was feeling, how she was coping.

This was too great an opportunity to be missed. She would have to find out what had motivated the boy. But she would need to be patient, attentive and most of all, subtle.

"Did anything strange happen before he disappapeared?" she asked the group, trying to tone down the excitement in her voice. It was one thing to be equally excited as they were but quite another to be more than that.

"Well he did almost drown but Jed saved him and he seemed fine," responded the woman on her left side. Loni burned to find out who this Jed was but strove to be subtle.

"What was he doing before that?" she enquired in what she hoped was a logical line of exploration. "Just talking to Jon, I think," responded the woman. Loni thought quickly. She couldn't ask who Jon or Jed were but she clearly needed to speak to them. Because there was a distinct possibity the boy had found something out, or that he knew or suspected   something so profoundly disquieting, that he had been forced to escape.

"Jon!" Loni called, feeling Little tense with apprehension at the unusual turn of events. Loni kept her voice short and sharp and only at mid volume, as if she were indeed calling to someone she knew, yet her eyes scanned the crowd, seeking the person who would respond to the name.

A young face turned in her direction. "Yes, what?" he asked, seemingly unperturbed that he did not know her.

In some ways her luck had held. There were so many Pets here, so many more than at her home, it was not that obvious that she did not belong here. Each person probably thought she was just a Pet they hadn't spoken to before now, hadn't noticed before.

"Did San do or say anything strange?" she asked.

"No, he was just the same as always." He turned back to the person at his side to continue his conversation. No lead there then. Perhaps this Jed would know more.

"Where is his Owner?" she asked, afraid to use the term OwnSan, in case they did not name their Owners in that way here.

"That's OwnSan over there," a woman with thick brown hair interspersed with grey streaks, gestured towards an Eyon at the edge of the clearing, unwittingly giving Loni the answer to what he was called. Not even bothering to lift its head up, the Eyon opened his mouth and shrieked, "EEEEKKBBRR, EEEEKKBBRR," before once more becoming silent and still.

"He's just stood there, poor thing, ever since *the disappearance.*" She used such a heavily significant tone of voice for the word 'disappearance', she managed to make it sound as if she believed he had just vanished in a puff of smoke. For a moment Loni stared at her. Was it possible she was making light of it? But the woman, solemn brown eyes etched with deep set wrinkles at the edges, seemed straight faced and incapable of humourising the situation.

Loni glanced surreptitiously at the indicated Eyon. Hunched over, sort of huddled over his own feet, he looked not small as such, but rather *diminished*, as if he'd been squeezed into a smaller space than he would usually take up.

And he was shivering. Even from this distance, she could see his body shaking. He stood alone and separate. And miserable.

A cold band tightened around her heart and she had to gulp down thoughts of OwnLoni once more. Going over to console this unknown Eyon was not an option. She couldn't risk bringing any attention to herself and Little but that knowledge did nothing to remove the bitter taste of sorrow in her mouth.

A light feathery touch to her palm confirmed that Little was thinking the same. She was glad of his comforting and offered her own back to him, grasping his proffered wing tip in her hand. But she was careful not to meet his eyes. It would be their undoing if she did.

It struck her as slightly strange that not one of the Pets could suggest a reason why San would leave, or imagine how he could have got down from the tree house on his own. Loni looked around her. The trees were *high* but they were all densely packed with branches and foliage. It wouldn't be too difficult to climb down, as long as you were brave enough.

Only one Pet seemed unconcerned about the situation. He sat slightly apart from the others and took no part in the conversation. Instead, he listened intently, a dreamy smile on his face, his hands working deftly to twist blades of grass together in a thin chain.

Neither old nor young, he had a sort of ageless look, as if he combined the wisdom of age with the hope of youth, within his bones.

But there was something about the way he sat there, a kind of coiled look, as if at any moment he would be prepared to spring up into action. Even stranger, was that he occasionally seemed to be stifling some inner mirth, only just seeming to prevent gales of laughter escaping from within him.

Instinctively Loni knew that this was Jed. And she also knew just by looking, that he held a large chunk of the puzzle. She consciously focused her attention elsewhere, and strove to piece tighter the little bits of gleaned information she already had whilst trying to work out a strategy to approach the man.

Not only was San the *same age* as her but by her best reckoning, he had left his home at about the same time she and Little had left theirs. How weird was that? Was it just coincidence or was it more than that?

But it was a real possibility that he had not intentionally left, as he appeared to be rather stupid, having nearly drowned himself mere hours before he disappeared.

Conversations carried on around her but she listened with only one ear until something unusual was said, something that so nearly echod her own internal thoughts, that she felt herself stiffen involuntarily.

"Perhaps he has been 'taken' against his will?" suggested a young woman who cradled a three year old girl on her lap, her tone of voice suggesting that the comment had not been completely serious. There followed gentle laughter from the crowd at such a ridiculous idea.

The young woman spoke again, this time to the child, a soft smile on her face, "sorry, Forrest, they don't like your idea. Never mind."

Loni could see that the woman held the child in genuine affection and had not meant to hold her up for derision. But she also saw the naked look of anger on the child's face, her deep green eyes narrowing and her mouth tightening in temper.

And there was something else too. The idea the child had proposed was so close to the truth of the origins of all the Pets, Loni had to wonder if it was mere coincidence. Could the child have known something the others didn't? Did she remember something?

Loni would have loved to question her about it but it was neither the time nor the place. And anyway the girl was only three years old! Would it be fair to confuse and scare her with talk of what she remembered? Probably not. The fairest thing would be to leave the girl alone. Nothing could be gained by upsetting her.

In the meantime, Loni took a good look at the assembled faces, comparing them to the families she had so recently seen at Sophia's village. Would the girl who had been taken from the short family with the large noses, be about the same age as the girl now sitting to the right of Little?

She had the right sort of nose and seemed small for her eight year markings. Did the boy with the piercing blue eyes and raven black hair come from the family who had lost such a child, six years ago? Or was she mixing up the features and years of raids?

It was difficult to keep all the information straight in her head and she was trying so hard. Only one thing was sure. All these Pets had come from *somewhere* and if it wasn't Sophia's village, then it was somewhere else!

"There's something about you. Something…*familiar*." The gruff but whispered voice in her ear, made Loni nearly jump out of her skin.

Reflexively she squeezed Little's wing so hard, that for a moment she actually felt the tiny delicate bones beneath his thick feathery down. He made a small sound of pain and Loni immediately released him. But she didn't turn to look at him to check he was ok. She didn't dare. Her attention was completely riveted by the previously coiled up man, who now crouched beside her. She was astounded that he had moved so close and she hadn't even noticed.

He repeated himself, this time without the pause, obviously expecting a response from her.

"There's something about you. Something *familiar*."

Her mind went into overdrive. What could she say? What should she say? This was the very man she had planned to seek out. But now that he had sought her instead, she became tongue-tied with the fear of charging ahead and scaring him off.

At her side, Little also kept quiet. He had realised that the best way for him to act, was as though he were oblivious to everything, just as everyone would expect him to be. So he sat and tried to look as if he were focused on internal thoughts, and he *listened*.

In the end Loni didn't *need* to say anything as her interrogator carried on, "do you know who you remind me of? No, stupid question, of course you don't. Well, I'll tell you. You remind me of San, that's who. *San, the boy who has just escaped*".

Involuntarily Loni's eyes opened wider and she felt, rather than saw, Little stiffen at the remark, at once understanding the implication. This man didn't believe San had just wandered off. He realised the boy had escaped. Just as *they* had.

The man had stopped talking for a moment and appeared to be analysing her reaction to his words. Satisfied with whatever he saw there, he briefly glanced around. Loni followed his gaze. Only herself and Little were listening to him. All the others were engaged in their own conversations and oblivious to what was going on with her.

"You are Jed, aren't you? The man who saved San? I've been wanting to talk to you about…" Loni had to stop herself from gushing at him, so anxious was she to hear his side. She swallowed the impulse to prattle on and instead stopped so that he could explain in his own words.

Nodding silently to affirm his name, Jed took time to settle himself comfortably by her side before continuing. His tone of voice was almost casual but the gaze he locked onto her eyes, was not in the least. Instead it held her prisoner, demanding complete and utter truth.

"I have never seen two Pets who look so alike and I have lived many summers. *He* has gone and yet now *you* are here, a stranger in our midst and with a baby Eyon as companion. Things just keep getting stranger and stranger. I think it's time you started talking," he paused for breath. His eyes crinkled up at the corners as he smiled at her.

"By the way, please to meet you…?" He held out his hand and trailed off into request.

After only a moment's hesitation Loni took it. "I'm Loni." she stated simply. His hand was narrow and slim fingered but the grip was strong and warm and Loni knew she had made a friend. Quietly and careful to keep her voice low and her tone light, Loni told him everything she had learned. Jed let her talk, never once interrupting or asking for clarification. He just listened.

Amazingly, although the information must have shocked him, he didn't seem all that surprised.

"I suspected some of it, but I'd never have thought that there were Human villages so close to here. Thank you Loni, you have given me lots to ponder over. Let me tell you now what I think."

And he did.

Unlike Jed, Loni couldn't just sit silently listening and repeatedly asked for things to be clarified or explained further. Periodically without turning towards Little, who sat quietly beside them, she tried to explain Jed's ideas and theories more fully.

On the whole his ideas weren't as mind blowing as they once would have been to her. She had already witnessed with her own eyes, families living together. It was what he said about a connection between her and the missing San and images carved in some kind of necklet thing, that boggled her brain and forced her to sit open mouthed for at least a minute, whilst the idea sank in.

# *Chapter 33.*

In San's sleep, the recurring dream revisited him. Only, this time it was different. *He* was the same in it and so was the woman, but for the first time he became aware that they were not alone. There was someone else there, perhaps *even more* than one - but certainly at least *one* more. And some of them were monsters.

He was holding someone's hand – not an Eyon's with thick sharp talons, but a small and delicate hand. A girl's hand. He didn't know how he *knew* it was a girl's hand - he couldn't see her - he just *knew*. And in the dream she was squeezing *his* hand, just as tightly as he was squeezing hers.

And the dream revolved, as dreams sometimes do; images turning upside down and inside out. Familiar things change into unfamiliar, so that even when something is recognised, its dreamscape is so altered from reality, that it becomes almost unrecognisable. Perhaps the reason lies deep within the subconscious. Perhaps the mind, ever aware of its own frailties, seeks to bury that which it cannot accept. Only the heart, which sees with a deeper eye, can see beyond this, to the kernel of truth within.

His heart ripped at the hard shell of the dream, splintered it to fragments and discarded them in the dust, seeking only that one kernel of truth.  His hands clenched and unclenched in his sleep, as his mind and heart fought. And he was there in the dream, fully there as he had never been before, every sense burningly alive.

Heavy rain washed down upon them. It had never rained before in the dream, but only *he* was wet. He could feel the rain on him, soaking into his hair and body. Yet the woman in the dream was completely dry. He became aware that he was crying.

His hands, momentarily freed from their internal battle, reached up to his face and wiped away the tears. They fluttered over his closed eyelids and even in the dream, he paused to wonder how his eyes could be closed, yet he saw so clearly. Something in his mind clicked and he became aware that he was dreaming. For just a moment his mind hovered on the edge of sleep, trying to tip him into awaking.

Anchoring himself to the dream world was imperative! If he woke now, he would know no more and understand no more, than he had before. He closed his eyes more tightly and willed himself deeper into the dream. He hooked his attention to the image of the woman in front of him. Hooked it in tight and fast!

Something was blocking his view. He tried leaning to the side but he was held firmly in his own position by an unseen force. He was clasped tightly but not cruelly. No pincers dug sharp into his flesh, nor ropes bound him with unnecessary force. Whatever restrained him was strong but gentle. And then the thing which blocked his view moved.

He saw the woman, teeth bared in a ferocious snarl as she fought with the monster who stood towering over her. Like watching poured water swirl into a glass, the images behind it distorted through the swirling liquid, he was forced to wait till the image was still, to see the true picture.

The woman tore at the monster with her bare hands, feathers clutched in handfuls and ripped from its body. A carpet of bloodied feathers covered the floor. It reminded him of the leaves in autumn but with more spectacular colour. Reds and greens and blues and silvers.

Against his will, his eyes focused on the minutiae details; the bent and warped quills and the crushed look of the silky strands. He tried to raise his eyes, tried to look away but couldn't. He was soaking wet. How could tears make him so wet, so drenched, soaked to the skin?

The feathers held his attention still. But it was of no real consequence, because his heart stripped away the final layer of covering over the knowledge it already knew. Like cogs on a wheel, the truth just slotted into place and the wheel turned once more.

The woman reached for him, her eyes beseeching…and it was a mirror of his own eyes he was looking at, the shape and colour so familiar. Arms outstretched, she reached for him but was held back by the large Eyon in her path.

Frantically the woman grappled with the Eyon, her eyes now seeking something on the other side of the creature. San followed her gaze but he already knew what he would find.

His eyes followed the line of his outstretched arm to his wrist, and on to his hand, where it met another hand, another arm. Ever so slowly his vision travelled up the length of the arm, to the shoulder and on to the face. Eyes wide in shock and horror she stared at him with a young version of *his own face*. It was her face ...and identical to his.

He felt his mouth open involuntarily, as his jaw dropped. Matched in height and build and features they stood locked together in part embrace. He looked down at their joined hands, fingers laced together and locked in place. Until their hands were forcibly ripped apart.

And he and the young girl were carried off in opposite directions by the Eyons who had been restraining them. His empty fingers flexed in the air but she was beyond his reach. He opened his mouth to scream and the sound he produced was unfamiliar to him, the voice young and immature. But he screamed anyway.

The girl was screaming too, her rhythm a split second behind his. The sound was so similar to his own, that at first he mistook it for an echo. Somehow their rhythms synchronised and the two separate screams mingled together, as if emanating from one sole voice, the pitch and timbre identical.

Her voice grew fainter. Soon her screams were but a faint memory in his ear and in his brain. Yet they were indelibly inscribed on the very muscle of his heart. And then he was alone, without her and without their mother.

He awoke drenched in a cold sweat, his fingers sore and muddy. The sun had been replaced by the moon in the sky and it was raining. Cold hard rain, unlike the drizzle from before. Deep trenches had been dug in the now waterlogged earth where his nails had clawed, his hands trying frantically to hold on to the girl in his dream. Rainwater had pooled here and was even now soaking into his sleeves.

Pulling themselves out from the bush was a lot more difficult than climbing into it had been. The ground was slippery with mud and he was cold, wet and miserable and still without trousers.

But there were houses down on the other side of this hill and there would be clothing there. Certain that no one else would be around this late and in this weather, there was not much need for caution. But neither could he just run down the hill. The rain was torrential and the grass was treacherously slippery. He would have to be careful that he didn't slide all the way to the bottom and break a leg in the process. Very carefully, Shoo padding along silently beside him, he began his descent.

# *Chapter 34.*

Loni and Little were eager to leave Low Forest but they waited for the right moment. The daylight was dying and as it did so, both Eyons and Humans alike had come to the same realisation. The missing boy was not going to be found that day. Nor was he likely to be found in the approaching darkness of the evening. This shift in focus brought with it a curiosity about the strangers in their midst.

As Little was too young to be an Owner, Jed managed to fob the Pets off with some story about how Loni's Owner had heard about the missing boy and had come over from their home far away to help with the search. Inevitably, there were lots of questions then, about where they had come from and how similar it was.

There were also some observations that Little seemed unlike other Eyons. But no one seemed quite able to put their finger on in what particular way he was different, even though he sat in their midst, unlike any other Eyon. Loni tried hard to keep to the truth as much as possible whilst keeping it vague, as she thought that was the least likely way of tying herself in knots and getting found out. So she simply said that he was, "a bit different", which they seemed to think meant that he was too stupid or something to be like the other Eyons.

She suspected that they would never guess that he understood a lot of what they were saying. He was proving to be very skilled in the art of looking disinterested. Besides, it was so far removed from what they knew of life, it was unlikely the thought would even enter their heads.

Even Jed had been confounded by the news that Little had mastered the art of Human speech. Perhaps that was a slight exaggeration, but she was so proud of him and wanted to make it sound even more extraordinary!

It was surprisingly easy to lie to these Pets, who had no knowledge of what lay behind their little corner of the world. Loni wondered what their reaction would be, if she actually told them the truth. What would she say?

'Oh I guess none of you know this but you have all been stolen from your families! You, the boy over there, I think I may have met your sister, her name is Annabell, if I remember correctly. You look like your mother but you have your father's curly hair. And you – yes you, the girl sitting there animatedly talking…are you aware that your father died last summer. You are the spitting image of your mother and she told me losing you just broke his heart. He kept on breathing for some years but really he was dead from the moment you were gone, she said.'

Could she say any of this? No, of course she couldn't. The truth was too bitter. She couldn't even sweeten it in any way. She couldn't tell them where they had come *from* without telling them how they had been taken.

She couldn't shock and devastate like that. And what would it achieve? What would they do with the knowledge? Would they walk off into the night the way both her and San had done? Would they rebel against the Owners who cared so much for them? Or would they remain here, sticking to their routine and what they were used to, day in and day out? Would they outwardly stay the same whilst a light went out forever in their hearts?

Perhaps there would be a number of different but equally devastating reactions. But only one thing was for certain, it was not her decision to make. Only one person had enough vision and foresight to make that decision. Jed.

She could trust Jed's judgement. He knew and cared for these people assembled here. When the time was right he had promised he would break the news to them gently and individually.

"They will take it hard, I think. Most of them have never considered where they came from."

He had looked at her intently then and she had felt his unspoken question.

"No, I'm sorry Jed, I saw no one who looks like you there," she said quietly and then realising how sad that sounded added, "but of course that goes for nothing…there were so many…"

He interrupted her, not unkindly.

"Do not concern yourself Loni. I have 45 triangles. The chances of my mother and father still being alive are slim at best. I know that. I just hoped…maybe…that there would be someone…" his eyes had crinkled into a smile but there had been a faint glimmer of suppressed tears. She had felt his pain, it had been so similar to her own thoughts, her own pain.

He had moved back to his original position in the circle, to make sure no unnecessary attention was drawn to her and Little. She was sad to see him go but agreed it was for the best.

Alone again with Little, in the midst of all these strangers, she felt the weight of the knowledge she held, and the responsibility it thrust upon her. The first step is aways the hardest, she thought. They had taken the first step when they had left home. But now another first step was waiting to be taken. A step so precarious, that if misplaced, could topple their world on its face. Yet without that step, this world would never be able to run, to feel the freedom it deserved. She gathered her courage up.

"Do you think," she faltered, directing her suggestion to the grey haired woman who had been so sympathetic towards OwnSan. She was the most likely candidate for accepting what she was about to say. "Do you think, that as we are all here, I mean the Owners and the Pets," she tried to keep her voice sounding as if she was just this very moment having the idea, instead of thing it through for the past half hour.

The woman listened patiently. "I was just thinking that we might as well all eat together. I mean it's late to all go home and start cooking now. Perhaps some could cook and others clear up? And that way we could stay together …and maybe find San?" Of course, she didn't think this would help find San in truth but it would hopefully serve two other purposes. Firstly it would let her and Little be fed and keep them inconspicuous.

And secondly and more importantly she hoped it would force more interaction between the Pets and the Owners, not just their own Owners but the wider community of Eyons. Because if this woman could be sory for OwnSan, then surely the other Pets could too and if they could do that, could show that...

It was only one small change, one small step but it was a step nonetheless. And like a real step does, the balance would shift, perhaps only slightly. But it would shift and with it, there would be that desire for another step, another shift in balance to maintain the forward motion.

"That's a very good idea!" The response was so immediate that the woman rose from her position and called a large group of older Pets around her, before coming back to her former position.

"Some of the Pets who enjoy cooking will make the food, and us others will clear up afterwards," she smiled at Loni before turning her attention elsewhere.

It didn't take long for the air to be filled with the aroma of delicious food. The conversation had moved somewhat, having exhausted the riddle of the missing boy for the time being.

Loni watched how the food production had been organised. A table bearing ladles and stacks of bowls and spoons had been set up just behind her and three men stood attentive there, ready to dish out the food as it arrived. But it was the way that it arrived which was the most surprising.

Backs padded out with what looked like sheets to protect against spillages and burning, a procession of Owners flew large covered tubs down to the waiting men. The men simply untied the binding ropes and removed the hot steaming food. Tub after tub was desposited, all from the same treehouse where other Pets had cooked the delicious smelling dish.

Loni smiled her acceptance as she was passed a steaming bowl of food. Her first impulse was to pass it immediately to Little, but on glancing briefly at him, she found he was also being given a huge bowl. The smell was mouth-watering. In fact it smelled so wonderful that she seriously doubted the taste would match up, so high had her expectations been raised.

Fortunately, she was wrong. She lifted the spoon to her mouth and delighted in the fabulous taste and texture dancing on her tastebuds. Luck was definitely on her side. With food this tasty, the perfect time to slip away would be after the supper. Just slip away when everyone was fed and relaxed.

One by one the Owners approached the circle of Pets. Loni could feel Little tense at her side, as he waited for her cue regarding what to do. Unsure herself, as to the correct course of action, she decided the best policy was to wait and see what happened.

Hesitantly, the Eyons made up a second circle behind the Pets. It was so similar to the circle she had sat in at Sohpia's village, that Loni couldn't help but make comparisons. And there were many to make. The Eyons sat down in particular spots, and without acknowledging one another, waited to be served. Even those who had so recently been working at the food delivery, having now been relieved of their duties, sat silently and unmoving.

Loni assumed that each Owner sat behind his or her own Pet, but the second circle was wider than the first and gaps where created where Eyons had not yet appeared. But what was most striking was the way they sat – closed off and separate from one another. They were close enough to reach out and touch one another, talon to talon, even across the gaps. Yet it was as if some invisible yet nonetheless impenetrable wall separated them from each others' view. Even so, Loni instinctively felt that the very first baby step on the path of change, had already been taken. She could expect no more right now.

Only OwnSan sat apart from the circle. Unable or unwilling to move from his self imposed vigil, he was oblivious to the others around him. The old woman with the greying hair approached him with a bowl of food and tried to prise it into his grasp. But there was no muscle tension there and his wings merely fell to his sides whenever she let them go. Undeterred the woman continued for some time before giving up.

Finally placing the bowl on the smooth ground, in front of the distraught Eyon, Loni thought the woman would simply walk away then.

But instead she surprised Loni with her actions. She grasped the Eyon in a big hug, smoothing his disarrayed feathers down and holding him tight for several seconds. Only then did she release him and turn towards the circle where Loni sat. Another small step had been taken!

Never before had Loni witnessed such a thing – a Human showing affection to any Eyon who was not their Owner. Quickly her eyes darted round the circle. Who else had witnessed this display of empathy? No-one, not even Little, whose eyes were fixed on his food. On returning to the circle, the woman slotted neatly into a gap between two other old women and began conversing animatedly.

Loni tried to watch them whilst not *appearing* to watch them, but it was difficult. What would happen when all the Eyons had taken up their places and sat down? Surely the gap behind her and Little would stick out like a sore thumb?

Little must have been thinking the same thing because he slowly began to shuffle backwards, trying to take up the empty space behind her. Loni wasn't sure if this was a good or bad idea. There was always the possibility that this would make things far worse. Perhaps as it was, the Eyons wouldn't really notice them. But if Little sat with the adult Eyons, there was a real chance he would blow their cover if questioned. Even though it was unlikely that they *would* question him, it was a risk she was not prepared to take.

Calmly and quietly she placed a restraining hand on his wing, her eyes flashing him the message : 'stay put'. He got the signs and immediately stopped shuffling. Taking her cue to make themselves as anonymous as possible, he buried his head in the bowl of hot food and ate as quietly as was possible for him.

Storm clouds gathered overhead and the day shook off the last of the daylight, shrouding itself in a sudden darkness. Now, the only light was the flickering of the bonfire set in the middle of the inner circle. Loni stared into the flames as all around them everything changed.

# *Chapter 35.*

San realised that it wasn't quite night but it was dark
and it was wet. His legs were stiff and aching but it
was his knees which hurt the worst. The hill was steep
and he had to walk down it sort of angled backwards, to
hold on to his centre of gravity and stop himself from
falling and rolling all the way to the bottom. It was an
awkward way to walk and put too much pressure on his
joins but he had no choice.

His back ached too, but luckily that particular ache
did not last long and he soon got into a steady, if not
graceful, pace of walking again.

Then, as his brain began to connect fragments of the
dream into a coherent whole, he forgot about the
mechanics of walking and moved on automatically. His
mind was whirring almost as fast as his mother's
spinning head in the nightmare.

Up close, the village looked even stranger than it had
from the top of the hill. The rain drummed on the little
roofs with such a din, that it would obscure any noise

that he might make but he still needed to be as silent as he could. He had to locate the store house. He was desperate for new, dry clothes and something to eat. Studying the houses, he realised there was no obvious reasoning as to which hut was the store. They were all of a similar shape and size.

Rain beating down hard on his head and dripping into his eyes made it hard to think coherently. Shivering with a mixture of cold, fear and excitement, his teeth were chattering so loudly he couldn't even hear himself think! Then it came to him, what he should do.

All he had to do was listen in at each hut and try to peer through any cracks in the wood. A faint glow from a scrolling screen, the slightest hum of an Eyon machine or any other manner of normal everyday noise would indicate habitation. Only the store hut would be empty, and so would be in darkness and silence. It seemed like a foolproof plan.

Approaching the first hut, he put his ear to the door at the point where the hinges met the wall. There was no need to look for a light coming from this one! The snores from the sleeper inside were more than enough to indicate that it was inhabited. Disappointed, but relieved that he'd had the good sense not to just blunder in, he moved on to the next hut.

From this one, which looked identical to the first, there was no noise. Excited, he pressed one eye to the crack in the door jam. The door was quite a tight fit in the frame and he couldn't see in but there was just the faintest glow of light. He moved on to the next hut.

As before, he listened in for a few moments. No sound. No snoring, no shuffling, no talking. He put his eye to the hinge side of the door. No light! Was it possible that the resident Eyon had gone to bed?

No, he didn't think so. This was it!

"Stay here Shoo and be quiet but if someone comes, growl really quietly." The thought for a moment before adding "BUT NO BARKING," in a hissed whisper.

He knew Shoo didn't understand but it made him feel better to do it. He watched, surprised, as Shoo sat down on his haunches and prepared to wait, as instructed.

San hesitated only a minute or two, his hand steady on the door, before he opened it and slid silently in. It was dark inside, perhaps even darker than outside, where at least he had had the glow from the moon to help him. Inside there was nothing.

Moving blindly, his foot caught on something on the floor and he accidentally sent it rattling across the room. It was only as it whacked against the opposite wall with a clang, that he realised the house was not unoccupied after all!

His eyes, beginning to adjust to the lack of light, dimly made out the shape of a young woman asleep in the middle of the floor. Cushioned by a mattress of soft straw, her slumber was deep and undisturbed. If he had taken one more step, he would have walked right into her.

He stood very still and held his breath. Surely she would wake up and see him there. Or perhaps disoriented from her sleep, she would assume the noise to have been made by her Owner. Or, she would think it had been in her dream and go back to sleep. Or, the missing Owner would walk in at any moment and catch him. Or...

It occurred to him that while he had been standing there perfectly still, for several minutes, thinking about what *may* happen, none of the things actually had!

The woman had not moved or stirred in the least.

His eyes had grown more accustomed to the gloom now and he was able to see more clearly. He looked at the stillness of the woman and the unnatural way her body lay in perfectly straight lines. There was a strange smell in the air too. Sort of metallic and cloying. It reminded him of a cross between the smell of the machines at the place he had so recently escaped from, mixed with the smell of the meat from the cold store room.

He took one nervous step towards the woman. A small hole in the centre of the ceiling was positioned directly above her face. The hole was slanted he noticed, rather than straight up, and thus prevented the rain from pouring in, unless of course it was blown by the wind, in that same direction. Yet some moisture had accumulated there and had fallen onto the woman, giving her face the appearance of being suffused by tears.

Even in death he could see how beautiful she had been and indeed still was. Her hair was long and dark and framed a delicate but nicely proportioned face. She looked peaceful and unafraid, as if she had drifted off to sleep never to wake up.

What he couldn't understand were the circumstances of her death. Young people didn't just die, did they? Ok, so he had nearly drowned himself in the lake recently, and then there was the poisoning episode but that was best forgotten really. Anyway, those had been accidents and could have happened to anyone, even if they did usually happen only to him.

But this didn't look like an accident. She couldn't have fallen from a tree because there weren't any here. Nor was it likely that she had drowned, as she didn't look bloated or water-logged. She didn't look hurt in any way. She just looked exactly what she was - dead.

His thoughts were interrupted by a low whining and frantic scraping of claws on wood. Shoo had clearly tired of being sentinel. Or more likely had become too afraid to stay there alone. San hurried over to let him in before he woke everyone up.

Nose to the ground Shoo followed some scent which led to the dead woman. Startled by his discovery as much as San had been, he gave a little yelp and backed off.

"Could she have died from some illness?" San carried on, answering his own question. "Unlikely. I've never heard of a disease for which there is no medicine."

It was a mystery. Had it also been a mystery to the inhabitants of this village?

"Do you think she cared for her Owner all day before dropping down dead? Or had there been some indication, some sign that she had not been well?"

Now Shoo didn't even bark in response, the situation felt even more eerie. "And what does it mean if they knew she was unwell but couldn't make her better? Could it be contagious?"

He took a step backwards without even realising it. And then common sense stepped in. Surely if what she had died of was infectious, they would not have laid out her body in this manner, would they? No, this dead woman would do him no harm, neither intentionally, nor unintentionally.

It was also a mystery why she was placed here and in this way. "Why hasn't she been laid out in the Tree Of

The Dead? Uh, ok, stupid," he chided himself, "there *are* no trees here!"

"In my forest we place our dead in a special tree house at the edge of the forest. It's peaceful there and calm. And it means we never roam far from where we lived," he told Shoo.

He stopped, realising suddenly what he had implied. "Except that's not true of me. Maybe I'll never be put there now." His eyes welled up with tears of self-pity for his future dead self. Sensing his upset, Shoo came close and nudged him with his nose.

"Thanks, Shoo, I know you care about me. I care about you too," he sniffed loudly.

He looked at the way the woman's hands were folded peacefully across her chest, the fingers slender and elegant. Her hair long and sleek, appeared to have been freshly washed and brushed and looked to be arranged so that it fanned beautifully around her.

Her clothing, of a rougher material than he had encountered before, also seemed clean and freshly donned. *After* she had died? Had someone washed, cleaned, dried and changed her? *After* she had died?

And then he noticed the flowers. Bunches of them had been placed by her feet, so that viewed from the right angle, it would appear that she was walking on them.

"Walking on a carpet of flowers," he whispered wonderingly. Buds were also entwined into her hair – little delicate flowers, as delicate as the woman's own features. He was amazed at the care and attention that had been lavished upon this Pet. It was certainly not the norm.

Shivering partly from the cold and partly from the shock of finding a dead woman, he needed to be on his way quickly. Fortunately there was a pile of clean clothing on the other side of the hut, although disappointingly there was no food anywhere that he could see.

Then again, with a dead woman in its midst, who died of who knew what, would he have been inclined to have taken any food from here anyway?

It was slim pickings too from the pile of clothes. From the four pairs of rough trousers he found - most of the items were skirts and dresses - only one was any good. One pair were way too big, another way too small and one had holes everywhere and were well worn. He had no idea why this pair were even being kept.

He pulled on the one pair which fit best and replaced the others as carefully as he could. The material was scratchy on his skin but it was better than nothing.

He looked for a shirt or replacement top, but there were none to be found. It was only then, that he realised the world was quieter than it had been before. The rain had stopped and with it, the drumming of the raindrops on the roof. Either the storm had dried up or it had blown away to some other place. It was time to leave.

If only he had realised then that he was leaving the very place he had been seeking. A village of Humans.

# Chapter 36.

Loni wasn't entirely sure whether it was the sitting in a circle, or the eating communally which made the difference. Or was it perhaps sitting in the warmth of the flickering fire, whilst storm grew overhead, which did it?

Was it the shared worry about the missing boy, all alone in the dark, that seemed to be working to bring the Eyons together? Was it a combination of all these factors? Or was it the fact that for once the Eyons had been separated from their machines for a considerable period of time?

There was no way of knowing. The only thing she did know was that the chain of events she had put in motion when she suggested the communal eating was speeding up. The notion that she had held that if she could just start to get these Humans and Eyons to co-operate better, then everything else would surely fall into place. Co-operation would foster communication and maybe, just maybe, life would be changed for all.

But it was the speed at which the events were happening which was astounding. In her mind she had thought it would be like a tap drip, drip, dripping, till eventually the whole sink overflowed. But it was not. Instead it was like a little crack had appeared in the bowl of the sink, which under pressure had widened to a huge fissue, before completely cracking in half.

And at first the change had been so subtle that she had barely noticed it. Just a slight nod of the head from Eyon to Eyon; the merest indication that they acknowledged one another. No eye contact, just that nod.

And then the strangest thing happened. One Eyon passed a comment to another, sitting next to him/her and got a response. The particular Eyon in question looked neither male nor female so she couldn't be certain which it was. Loni watched the situation unfold before her eyes.

From the way the Eyon spoke to its neighbour, whilst holding aloft a spoonful of food as if for examination, Loni surmised the comment was about the food. And to her eternal amazement, the response it provoked, also entailed that Eyon to hold his/her food aloft for a second, before wolfing it down. Had they actually *tasted* the food before throwing it down their throats? If they had, it was certainly a new development!

Beside her, Little still slurped noisily at his food. He was certainly enjoying his portion. Loni tried to close her ears against Little's racket and the conversations around her. Her attention was riveted on the two Eyons.

Their conversation becoming more animated, she saw them angle their bodies towards one another to facilitate the flow of their chatter.

And then, even though Loni hadn't thought this possible, things got even weirder. First the Eyon who had initiated the conversation turned to the Owner on his/her other side and drew this one into the situation, by once more holding his/her spoon aloft and commenting on it. Then the one he/she had initially been talking to did the very same with its neighbour!

Now there were four Eyons holding an animated conversation. But even four animated Eyons screeching and shrilling didn't drown out the noise of so many Pets talking animatedly. Nor did six Eyons, or eight. But the noise was growing.

Loni looked around her. She squeezed Little's wing and indicated with her eyes, the direction he was to look. She felt him immediately sit up straighter in amazement when he realised what was happening.

She caught Jed's eye from across the circle. He had noticed too. Of course he had. He held his hand up to her, the palm towards her and fingers splayed and she recognised what he meant. 'Wait five minutes then slip away.' She smiled softly at him, a thank-you for all his help. What would become of him, of these people, when they knew the truth? Like a stone set to roll down a hill, she suspected there would be no stopping it, until it was ready to stop. And just like that rolling stone, the truth would smash into everything and everyone in its path, oblivious of the rights and wrongs of it.

She trusted Jed's judgement but even so, she feared for him. Would the Owners become angry or even vengeful with him? Would he be in danger? And even if there was no trouble – where would *he* go? Would he spend the rest of his life wandering, in search of his family?

These things were all beyond her control, but it didn't stop her from being concerned about them. And the Pets *had* to be told. Painful as it would be for all concerned it would be the only way to stop the raids. Permanently.

Pulling her attention back to the Eyons, she noticed most of them were now talking to one another. For some this seemed easier than for others, especially for the females who were less hesitant and generally had longer periods of speech, but all were making the effort.

Like a forest fire, the conversation had spread and now the noise level was so high, that the Pets could not fail to notice. There was a sudden reversal of noise, as almost simultaneously all Human conversation died. Instead they all sat open mouthed staring at their Owners, amidst the growing babble and racket of Eyon speech.

And that was exactly when Jed turned to his neighbour and made the comment he had suggested earlier to Loni.

"Don't you think San looks like that girl Loni?" he asked innocently. And as the only Human voice, it cut through all the noise and racket of the Eyon conversation to strike deep into the thoughts of the assembled Pets. Now, questions would be asked. And Jed, who already knew most of the answers, would have to steer both Pets and Owners towards a greater understanding.

Loni and Little took their chance and shuffled backwards, right through the gap behind them, where no Owner sat. They shuffled away from the fire and the light and into the darkness beyond. No one stopped them or cried out or even noticed.

Once they were fully in darkness, they dared to risk standing up and walking away. And when they reached the edge of the forest, they kept on going until they were out of sight, never even daring to look back. It was only when she let out a huge breath, that Loni realised she had been holding it in, in the first place. In all honesty she had expected to be found out or called back or grabbed or *something,* but nothing happened. Nothing.

"What do you think about what Jed said, Little? I know you were listening."

Little remained uncharacteristically silent.

"You know how much I love you and I always will. It doesn't matter if this boy looks like me or even whether or not he *is* my brother. Even if he has a necklet that shows the two of us, me and him together. *You* are my brother *too. You* are the one I have grown up with – the one I have *watched* grow up. Nothing and no-one can change that. Do you understand?"

She pulled him close to emphasise the truth of her words.

"ESSSS ITTLLL UNNEERRRRSSSSTTTAANN," he replied then more quietly, "Ittlll luvvv Lonneee."

"And Lonneee luvvvs Ittle too," she smiled, copying his sounds as best she could before reaching up to give him a great big kiss on his soft Eyon cheek.

The sky above them was dark and thick with black clouds. It was only a matter of time before they broke and the rain came. The ground was unfamiliar to them so they walked slowly and held on to one another for safety. Loni wasn't sure if they walked into the rain, or whether it just started up. Only one thing was for sure. It was no light drizzle.

Thick, heavy droplets struck her with such force that she wouldn't have been surprised if they had left some mark where they landed. An indentation on her skin or a bruise perhaps, so show the ferocity of their fall from the sky. In her mind, the lashing rain was a punishment for her, an advance payment on the misery she would cause with her revelations. The misery that had to be caused to set the truth free and change the world.

In a way it was a silly thought but her heart clung to it nonetheless. And strangely it made her feel a tiny bit better. She would take her punishment and accept it as her due but she would still herald the truth because that's exactly what it was – the *truth*.

Her hair was soaked within a matter of moments and even Little's waterproof feathers seemed to be taking a real beating in the torrential downpour. Battered down by the force of the rain, his feathers clung to his bony frame, the normally silken fronds bedraggled and matted together. She just wished poor innocent Little didn't have to suffer the sky's punishment too!

Heads bowed in cold, wet misery, they trudged onwards. The combination of darkness and driving rain, made it almost impossible to see where they were going.

"I just hope that we're not going round and round in circles here," she shivered.

"NOOO ISSSSS OOOKKKKK."

Loni wished she shared his confidence in their orienteering ability, she was sure that they had passed the same distinctively shaped tree at least twice.

It wasn't long before she was soaked through to the skin. Her clothes clung to her both uncomfortably and restrictively. Every step she took resulted in her having to pull the wet clothing from her legs, where it clung and hindered her movements. Then at the next step, it would slap back to where it had clung before, so that she had to drag it back off her once more. Not only was it tedious and uncomfortable but it served to slow them down considerably.

The driving rain also took away their option of Little flying them somewhere. The wet weight of them combined would just be too heavy for him to carry. Yet, brave soul that he was, he had offered to do this. Loni loved him even more for this gesture and it was because of that love that she would not take him up on the offer.

She wondered if wet feathers had quite the same restrictive effect as wet clothing, but didn't feel inclined to try to explain what she meant over the noise and misery of the storm. She supposed in some ways it was worse for Little. At least she had shoes. He on the other hand, or foot if that were more appropriate, was barefoot. Her feet were squelching, but his slapped down into muddy earth with every step. Surely that was worse? And of course he was still missing some feathers.

She wondered how Sophia's people were faring in this weather.

"At least there was a step into the hut, remember?" she asked Little. His blank look suggested he didn't have a clue what she was talking about.

"The huts, they each had a step leading up to them, remember? You don't think that the rain is heavy enough to flood them do you?"

She kind of expected Little's oft shrieked 'don't know' for a response but none was immediately forthcoming. Instead, he seemed to be deeply considering the comment before responding.

Feet still slapping in the mud, he wallowed right into an exceptionally large puddle as face turned towards her own, he finally responded to her question.

"DOOONNNN   TTTHHHIINN    SOOOO.
SSSTTEPPPP  TOOOO HEEIIGHT."

She was astounded by how his speech had improved
but automatically informed him of his mistake. "You
mean it was too *high*. Height is what the thing has, high is
…well what it *is*."

Even to her own ears, that didn't sound much of an
explanation. But how did you explain the difference
between high and height? Anyway, what was important
wasn't the semantics of the actual words, it was the fact
that he was right.

The step to each hut had been quite high, so as long
as the rain didn't last for days, then the people should be
ok.  Flooding wasn't something she had ever had to be
concerned about before, living in a tree house.

She realised that the knowledge she had gained had
made a fundamental shift in how she would forever view
things. She wasn't sure if that was a good or bad thing. It
was just one more thing that she had no control over.

After what seemed like a very long time, broken only
by the occasional bit of conversation, they came across a
few trees set close together. There were not quite enough
to make a forest, so it was unlikely that anyone lived
there, but it always paid to be cautious.

Approaching carefully, they scanned both the trees
and the surrounding area for any signs of habitation. But
there were none. No tree houses, no ground huts.
Nothing and no one. Except the trees themselves and the
shelter they could offer. It was too good a chance to turn
down.

It took three attempts for Little to get them into the
protective shelter of the branches. He was tired and he

was sore where he lacked feathers but those weren't the only problems.

On the first attempt, Loni had literally just slid right off his back after climbing on, landing splat on her bottom in a patch of mud and splattering them both. It seemed that the combination of wringing wet feathers and soaking wet clothing produced a sort of slippery slide effect.

"OHH LONNEEE DIRRRTTTEEEE!" Little had screeched in mock horror and to which Loni had replied, "BUUUTT ITTLL DIRRTTTEEE TOOO."

Even in the middle of a storm, soaking wet and miserable, they had found that hilarious. It had taken more than a couple of minutes of sniggering before they were able to wipe themselves down as much as possible and try again.

The second attempt was no better. This time Loni made sure to hold on very, very tight, whilst Little angled his body to cradle hers. He wasn't fully grown, so there wasn't as much space on his back as there would be with an adult Eyon, but it was enough. Loni felt secure and was sure that this time she would manage to stay on.

He had lifted his wings high above his shoulders and brought them down fast to his sides, as usual. But his wings were so wet, that instead of the light tap they usually made against his torso, they had made a horrible wet whacking sound. And as they had whacked against his body, they had jettisoned all the rain stored in them, in a wave of water. That had been funny too, but less funny than the failure of the first attempt.

It struck Loni that she ought to be concerned. Perhaps Little's strength was failing him. Perhaps he was just too tired. Either way, it was bad news. And if that was the case, things would only get worse. They needed to shelter in the tree. They *had* to get up there. Funniness left the situation and was replaced by desperation, as she realised the gravity of their circumstances.

If Little did become weak, here in the driving rain and with no Eyon medicine around…She couldn't complete the thought. She wasn't sure if her mind wouldn't let her heart continue with the train of thought, or whether it was vice versa. Either way, she banished it before it reached it's natural conclusion.

Faced with two failures, Little was clearly determined to get it right the next time. He motioned Loni to stay where she was then moved away from her. He shook himself and flapped his wings several times, trying to dislodge as much water as possible before returning to her. Loni held her breath in fear and anticipation.

"Ready?" she asked hesitantly.

"EDDDDYYYYY."

A crazy voice, reeking with a desperation she could taste, sounded off in her head. 'Hold your breath and make yourself float on his back, like a balloon,' it said to her. She knew it was crazy, but she did as the voice bid anyway, just in case!

This time they were successful and flew straight up to the thickest branch they could find. Only when they were up there, sitting firmly on the branch, did she dare to let out the breath. And she did so silently. She didn't want Little to know how scared she had been. Or have him feel that she had lost faith in him. Because she hadn't and she never would!

Sitting on a narrow branch wasn't ideal, nor was it very comfortable but it was certainly better than being out in the rain with no shelter. They huddled together for warmth and rested as the storm continued to lash at the tree. It almost felt as if the rain were a living being, intent on their destruction. And that it was angry at the tree for harbouring them. She knew this wasn't true, but it didn't stop it feeling that way.

A shiver ran up the length of her spine and pinpricks of premonition ran across her scalp. Or perhaps it was merely the water draining off her hair which made it feel like that. She huddled closer to Little and wrapped her arms around his wet feathers. It wasn't going to help either of them dry but it gave her heart comfort to do so. In return, Little rested his head on her shoulder and waited for the storm to pass.

# Chapter 37.

S tealthily, San and Shoo left the village, just as they had entered it. He wondered if taking the trousers could be classed as theft. He was aware of the concept of 'stealing', but it had never been relevant before.

"How can anything be *stolen* when it's all there, free for the taking?" he enquired of Shoo.

His hand automatically reached down to squeeze the fabric. These trousers didn't look the same as his own, nor did they *feel* the same. But he had seen with his own eyes how and where all these things were made. Unless of course that was only *one* of the places where things were produced! He paused to consider this new idea for a moment.

"Perhaps it is only *my forest,* where the Owners work, plugged into their machines. Perhaps it's unique and different to everywhere else! Maybe every other Owner in every other place, goes *out* to work somewhere."

"Woof."

Yet he couldn't understand how the system worked. Did they all work towards a common goal, a shared need, like players in a team of softball?

It seemed strange to think of Eyons having some sort of shared vision. Even if that were the case, since this was a separate place to his home, did that mean he had stolen the trousers after all?

He continued to mull these philosophical questions over as they left the village far behind them and entered the long grass. The blades of grass were still wet from the recent storm and were so long that he was getting soaked once more just by walking through the field.

Even though it was still dark, he could tell by the way it crushed heavily underfoot, that the grass wasn't springing back up after they passed. Instead, it seemed to surrender under their weight and lie flat and defeated on the sodden ground.

This worried him immensely, as he was sure that they must be leaving very visible tracks through the field. Like a thread unravelling from a spool, they were leaving a trail which anyone would be able to follow should they be so inclined. And *he* had left not one but two Owners now!

Two Owners who may well be searching from him right this very minute!

Then again if no-one was actually *looking* for him, there would be no reason to think anything of it, even if one of the Eyons *did* come across it.

"A trail leading from one place to another would not be suspicious in itself, would it?" he enquired of Shoo, who deemed to give no response this time.

And it was a long way from both his own home *and* the place where they had escaped from Vinnbr. He just hoped they would come out the other end of this soon, onto a flat plain with no other signs of habitation nearby.

Then again what if they did? What if that was exactly what he found? "What if there is nothing and no one beyond this field? What will we do then?"

They couldn't keep on walking forever. He thought about his reasons for leaving home in the first place, the search for the truth. Was he any closer to finding it? His dreams had revealed so much, but would that have happened anyway, even if he had stayed with OwnSan? Or was it the leaving which triggered the vivid memories?

And now that he knew some of the puzzle, would he recognise the rest of it? He was filled with self doubt. Would he notice the right signs, would he be observant enough, strong enough, brave enough, to act upon them?

He certainly hoped so, but right now he had no choice but to continue walking. It was either that, or turn back and retrace his steps to get home. And he wasn't sure that was even possible. Even if it was, it wasn't really an option. To have turned back now would mean that he had forsaken the truth, that he had opted for the easy answer.

To have come this far and then give up – that was almost unthinkable. To have left OwnSan to fulfil his quest, quell his curiosity about the neclet and what it meant and why he had it,was one thing. But to be viewed as having done it on some whim, some flight of fancy…well that was completely unacceptable. It brought dishonour to them both, as though the bond of love they shared was worthless. And it wasn't. This was just something he had had to do! Therefore it had validation.

Arguing with himself over these thoughts, he plodded onwards, Shoo trotting along quietly at his heels. Finally, they reached the other side of the long grass. There was just enough light to see the glinting of the lake on his left hand side.

"It must be absolutely huge," he sighed. "Just as well that we didn't try to swim across." Although they wouldn't have been much wetter if they had, he reasoned.

Suddenly the air was rent with a sound like the clapping of thunder. It was so sudden and so loud that he physically jumped, startled. But what made it worse was the proximity of the noise. Its 'WHOOP, WHOOP, WHOOP' was so close, he couldn't identify if it came from just in front of him, just behind, or slightly to either side. The noise was *just there*! Bewildered that there was going to be another storm so soon after the last, he didn't immediately recognise that sound for what it really was.

He scoured the sky for shards of lightening. The last thing he needed was to get struck by one of those, he worried. A huge bolt of lightening flinging him to the ground just as he finally found what it was he was searching for, would be the final straw.

"Doesn't lightening always accompany thunder?"

He thought it did. And which came first, the thunder or the lightening? He knew there was some counting thing you could do to tell you how close the storm was, but that didn't seem relevant as the noise had been so loud. It had to be right above him.

Perhaps that was to be his fate after all…perhaps he would be annihilated by the storm, just swallowed up in the enormity of it all.

Scooped into the sky on a shaft of lightening, burned to a cinder and then casually tossed into the lake to cool off, his charred and blackened skin causing the lake to hiss and spit steam at the storm…

But no lightening flashed in the dark. Instead what he saw filled him with more dread than even forked lightening could ever have done.

Flocks of Eyons filled the night air. Their wings beating in perfect synchronicity, they flew in formation, making an inverted V shape.

Their individual colours muted by the dark sky, they appeared at once both sinister and dangerous. It occurred to him belatedly that it was the beating of their wings that he had heard, not thunder! Shoo shot behind him, cowering down, hidden in the long grass.

They passed not quite overhead, but slightly to the right of him. Was it possible that they did this all the time, after their Pets went to bed? No, he was sure they didn't. There was some other reason for this behaviour and whatever it was, it was unusual.

He stood, unnoticed and unobserved and watched. Keeping in formation they flew, till they were merely little dots in the sky.

"That's about where that village is," he whispered. "Are they heading for there?"

But even as the words left his lips, almost as if he had somehow summoned them, he saw that they were turning back, swooping and keeping to the same formation as before. But they had moved over in the sky a little bit. If they kept the trajectory they were on, they would be directly overhead in only a few minutes.

They would find him. He was absolutely convinced of that. And they were looking for something, or someone. They would see his trail and follow it to where he now stood. There was nowhere to hide and no way of covering his tracks. He watched them, terrified as the specks in the sky grew ever closer and larger.

"Oh no!"

Then he had a stroke of good luck. Something interesting must have been spotted on the other side of the field, for one or two of the Eyons broke off from the group, swooped down and alighted on the ground. He didn't know what they were looking for, or even whether or not they had found it. All he knew was that those particular two Eyons soon returned to the sky, empty taloned and still looking.

Then a different Eyon swooped down at another spot, and another and another. All resumed their flying after only a moment of two but the formation had been broken and was not realigned.

Closer and closer to him they flew. The distance between each Eyon was now twice as wide as before. Whilst this was good, it was obviously not good enough. The Owner on the very far side would undoubtedly spot him. It would be flying virtually straight over him and couldn't fail to see him. There was no point in even trying to hide. He shut his eyes and waited, his clenched teeth still managing to let loose the quietly repeated, "oh no, oh, no" on and on.

Louder and louder came the sounds of beating wings. Not perfectly timed any more, they overlapped and double beat with each other in a melee of sound. He felt the air above and around him stir, as it was disturbed by the huge flying bodies overhead.

The long grass bent in the breeze created by the huge Eyon who now hovered above him. He could feel its presence and its eyes boring into him. Terrified, but unwilling to go to his fate with his eyes shut in a cowardly manner he opened them.

But the vision which met his eyes surprised him. Feet not touching the ground it just hovered there in front of him.

A fully grown female, her black and white feathers looked worn and faded, whilst the smattering of purple that swept across the black and white, looked unusually dull and lifeless. It reminded him of ripe bruises on tired flesh, as though the Eyon had been through some trauma which had sapped all the vitality out of them. But the most startling thing of all, were her eyes.

Red rimmed and bloodshot, it was clear that they had done a lot of crying – and recently. He realised that he hadn't even been aware that Eyons *could* cry. He knew Rian could but then Rian was different in so many ways. He recognised the expression on her face too, a strange blend of bewilderment and hurt.

And there was also something else. A glimmer of hope in her eyes, which had initially flared bright, before turning to despair. Whatever it was she was searching for, it certainly wasn't him. She had looked at him, her eyes wide and growing wider and wider - and then all the hope had gone out of her, just like a light being turned off.

"GGNNNCCCHHHBBBB."

The word came out wrong sounding to San's ears. Muffled and half chocked out on the back of a sob, it had no meaning to San yet was clearly meaningful to the Eyon.

"Ggnnnccchhhbbbb," she repeated softly and longingly.

She raised a wing tip, its talons fatally sharp and ever so gently placed it under his chin. Lifting his face up so that she could see it fully, she bent her head to the side, angling it first one way then the other, as she scrutinised him.

One wingtip still holding his head aloft, she used the other to trail a path across his face. From the middle of his forehead he felt the talon sweep around his left eye and onto the curve of his cheekbone before following the length of his nose and traversing over his closed lips. He held his breath.

"Ggnnnccchhhbbbb." This time there was no mistaking it, it was an anguished cry. Heart felt and heart rendered, it trembled from the Eyon's mouth and hung in the air between them.

A drop of moisture landed on his upturned face and settled on the join where his lips met one another. Unbidden, the moisture trickled into his mouth where he recognised its salty texture. It was a tear! A tear that had fallen from this Owner who now held him captive. There was something so pitifully sad about her, so desperate and lost, that his heart went out to her. For an instant neither of them moved.

A look passed between them, something unspoken but which felt strangely like recognition. Like him, she was searching for something. And like him she could not settle for less than that which she sought.

'Perhaps we're not that different after all' he thought. Then, as suddenly as she had come, she was gone. She just left him standing there. No cries to alert the other Eyons, no victory shrieks. She had seen him and let him go. For whatever her reasons, she had kept his secret.

He turned to watched her rejoin her flock and deliberately steer them away from his path, angling her body towards them. He felt a surge of gratitude towards this unknown Eyon who had held his fate so clearly in her wings.

The flock surged first one way then another as they disappeared into the distance. He held his breath and counted to ten, waiting for them to reappear as they had before. But this time they were gone. Perhaps they had returned to where they had come from. Or maybe they had moved on to conduct their search elsewhere.

Or maybe, just maybe, the Eyon who had seen him, was diverting their attention deliberately, to give him some time. Either way, he would be wise to avoid the direction they had taken.

So calling Shoo to him from his hiding place, San made the decision to continue to skirt the edge of the lake to see where it led.

Which was just as well, as unbeknownst to him, if he had continued on his course straight ahead, he would have found himself in the midst of High Woods where all hell had broken loose in the search for the missing young Eyon and his Pet, Loni.

# *Chapter 38.*

L oni and Little waited in the shelter of the tree till the worst of the rain had fallen. Huddled together for warmth and comfort, they had dried off slightly where their bodies met but were as wet as ever on the other side.

"Come on then Little, best get walking again, I suppose."

Little, for his part looked less than thrilled at this idea. But as usual he followed Loni's suggestion as if it were an order and hopped them both back down to the ground.

It was still dark and their path was as unlit as before. They could only just about see what was ahead of them, everything else was shrouded in darkness.

Perhaps there was a kind of fundamental truth about life itself in that, she thought. She wondered what Little would think of that idea and decided to try to find out.

"You can't ever tell what's ahead, can you?" she asked him.

"NOOOOO. ISSSSS ACCCCKKK!!!" was his semi-unintelligible response.

"What?" she queried, needing him to explain.

"ACCCKKK. ACCCKKK!" he screeched, then seeing her confusion, tried harder, "AAACCKK."

Loni got it this time. "Oh, *dark*. Yes it is dark. But that's not what I meant."

Little interrupted her, "AARRCCKK, AARRCCKK," he practised.

"Yes, I *know* it's dark. But what I mean is, you never know what's ahead of you in life. I mean look at us. Who would have thought we'd end up here, like this?"

Even in the dark she caught the glimmer of fear in his eyes and immediately saw his misunderstanding.

"Oops, sorry Little. Didn't mean to scare you there. I didn't mean we were gonna be here forever when I said 'end up here, like this'. I meant...I mean..." for a moment the words failed her and she became twisted up in trying to explain.

"I mean I didn't know that we were going to leave, but we did and now I don't know where we're headed..." Somehow she didn't think she was really helping to alleviate his fears.

Perhaps that was the whole point though, she mused. She thought about poor Louisa and all her suffering. Would she have even risked having a baby, if she had known the birth would kill her? Maybe there were some things it was better not to know. Maybe if we knew how things would turn, out we would be unable to carry them through. But it would sure make the decision process easier, she figured.

It was only when they got to a smallish lake that the night seemed to have lifted a little and there was a bit more light. They stopped to take stock of their bearings.

"I'm fairly certain that ahead and to the right is the direction we've already been. Behind us is Low Forest where we've just left." Whirling round, she indicated each of the directions. "And over there looks swampy, which only leaves that way!" she pointed ahead and to the left.

"ISSS OTTERR."

"You think its getting hotter? Really?" Loni wrinkled her nose at the idea. "I'm still a bit cold."

"NOOO LONNEEE. OTTERR, OTTERR. LOTTSS O OTTERR!" Little insisted, pointing to assist his meaning.

"Oops sorry, you mean water, don't you? Well, we'll just keep to this side of the lake." She cast him a sneaky sideways glance. "Keep working on the words Little, you'll get there…" but she was giggling and she knew that he had realised she had deliberately misunderstood him. It was her payback for all this times he had done it to her.

Onwards they trudged and when they met the river again, it seemed only sensible to cross it again, in the same manner as before. So hoping onto Little's back once more, Loni took a ride over the river. Except this time he didn't just fly over to the other side but continued flying for quite some distance. She guessed he felt better and stronger after their rest in the tree, but even so, he couldn't keep it up for long.

Yet they had covered a considerable amount of ground and luckily had seen something strange, which they might have otherwise blundered unknowingly into.

Just to their left, was what looked like a normal everyday Eyon forest. Except that it wasn't.

With a bird's-eye-view from the sky, both Loni and Little had noticed that this one was different. The tree houses seemed larger than normal and were interconnected, as if you could walk from one to the other, all the way around.

Trying to convey her confusion to Little, whilst travelling on his back was tough but somehow Loni managed it and Little's response although somewhat alien to her, seemed to indicate that he was at least surprised if not also confused by this strange set of buildings.

By mutual consent therefore, they had avoided the strange forest. Something about it was so different that she worried it was where the fierce Eyons came were. They had started a change in San's village but she feared that they were not ready, not yet strong enough, to do the same with warrior Eyons. So instead, they followed the edge of a huge lake that lay on their right hand side.

Tired herself, Loni was worried that Little would become too exhausted after all the flying he had done earlier. So after finding a particularly lush patch of grass, she pulled Little down beside her and they snuggled up to sleep once more out in the open. Little, as usual didn't take long to drift off but Loni was kept awake by strange thoughts.

Everything felt different inside her head. Hopefully there were answers ahead, revelations and solutions. She just prayed she would recognise them! And with that thought, her mind drifted off into a long, deep slumber. She didn't even feel Little's body toss and turn as he dreamed about his missing Egg-Mother, nor feel the tears which streaked his tired face.

# *Chapter 39.*

The morning sun had been a welcome sight to San. At the very least it signalled that the strange and difficult night was over, and that they had put some distance between themselves and all the places they had passed through.

Initially, he had gloried in the warmth of the sun, enjoying how the rays of light had seemed to lick at the exposed skin of his arms, illuminating the fine hairs and making him feel more alive, than he had the previous day. Even Shoo seemed more bouncy than usual, displaying a spring in his step that made it seem like the world was a better place.

"The world is a *strange* place though really, isn't it Shoo?"

"Woof|!" neither agreement nor disagreement.

"I mean, there you were, alone in the swamp, and I'll never know where you came from. I was wandering alone since I left OwnSan. And then there is Rian, who was *choosing* to be alone, because it was better than being taunted all the time. Is *that* our destiny? To be alone?"

Catching the note of sadness in San's tone, Shoo let loose a low whine rather than his customary bark.

It cast an ominous feel to the heat from the sun as if, under its direct glare, all San's worries and fears would come to life. He hoped fervourently that the feeling did not turned out to be a presentiment of things to come.

Intensifying its heat, the sun was blisteringly hot. It was beating down so hard on his exposed head, that when he saw the huge stone building ahead, he didn't believe his eyes.

"Is that a real place, Shoo, or am I daydreaming? Has the sun fried my brains?"

"WOOF WOOF WOOF."

From the frantic yapping, San correctly deduced that Shoo was excited, which in turn, meant that the building was very, *very* real!

"Glad you think so too, Shoo." His tone was light and jovial now, despite the heat. "For a moment there I even wondered if I HAD been struck by lightning last night and that all this, was a pain induced electrical hallucination."

The sun was so hot, the very idea of cool shelter was enough to get him speeding over to the shade of the building.

He was aware that it was unlike anything he had ever seen before. It was this very unusualness which worried him.

"So far everything unusual has landed me with a problem…but staying in the sun any longer isn't really an option!" he pronounced. So they approached boldly.

"Anyway," he reasoned to Shoo, "pretty much *everything* I've encountered in the past few days has been unlike anything I've ever seen before."

He carried the thought through to its logical conclusion. "So in a way, the very fact that it *is* unlike anything I've ever seen before, kind of makes it normal!" It was a rather warped way of thinking but it worked for him.

"WOOF."

"I'm glad you agree."

★★★

The sun was hot and it was this heat which woke Loni and Little. Her face felt dirty and dusty but more worryingly it felt hot. Too hot. Little also looked hot and flushed. She supposed he was probably worse than her, being almost completely covered in feathers. They would have to find some shady place soon or they would burn, if they didn't die of heat stroke first.

There was nowhere to shelter in their immediate surroundings. Their only hope was to find somewhere ahead where they could rest, away from the powerful glare of the sun.

"If we can find somewhere to rest whilst the sun is at its hottest, then we can start out again when the temperature cools down."

"RRESSST,                          OOOOLLLL OOOOOWWWWNNNNN!" Little panted beside her.

Neither of them had the inclination to discuss what would happen if they didn't find some shelter soon. It just wasn't an option.

"In the meantime, let's have a quick paddle in the lake to cool down," suggested Loni.

"NOOOO IMM! ITTLE NOOO IMMM!" Panic was written all over his face.

"You don't need to be able to swim, just dip in your toes, sorry talons," she instructed and couldn't help but laugh at his blissful expression as he followed her advice.

"Better yes?"

"ESSSS! ESSSS! ESSSS!" he sighed, still careful to stay only talon deep in the water.

After a quick paddle and drink from the lake, which didn't look all that clean or taste it either, and a hurried something to eat, they resumed walking. Well at least she didn't have to worry about their food rotting in this heat, she thought, as there wasn't enough left to last much longer anyway.

Unsure whether it would be a worse fate to starve to death, be poisoned to death by eating food which had turned bad in the intense heat, or dying of sunstroke, she didn't at first notice the strange building.

They had been walking for some time and she had become so lost in her reverie that she had almost arrived right in front of it before her addled brain seemed to recognise what it was.

Even Little had been quiet. She remembered him chatting away to her in half Eyon, half Human, at the start of the day, but at some point he had fallen silent. Whether that was due to a lack of response from her or because, like her, he was conserving his energy for walking she was unsure.

But now with the building directly ahead of them, they could not fail to notice it.

"What *is* that?"

Loni wasn't even aware that she had spoken out loud until she heard Little's answering, "DOHH OHHH!"

They exchanged knowing looks of caution, but both were too curious, not to mention hot and desperate, *not* to explore it and anyway there was no-one around, Eyon *or* Human.

Besides something in the very most inner core of Loni gave a huge lurch and a million butterflies took flight in her stomach.

"Well, whatever else it is, it's shelter...and we're desperate, so let's just go in. Ok? What do you think Little?"

"OKKK LONEEE."

"OK then Little," she smiled her very best smile at him and linked her arm with his. For some reason it seemed completely the right thing to do – enter this strange place braced by each other's support.

Was this place somewhere she had been looking for all along? But hadn't even known it? Were there answers contained within these walls? Answers which would show them how to change things for the better for Eyons and Humans alike?

Did it contain something she had been drawn to by fate and destiny? She didn't know for certain but there was the strangest feeling that wouldn't go away.

So they approached boldly.

★★★

San and Shoo had walked almost all the way around before finding the entrance, a huge open doorway set into the stone wall. There were no windows and no other entrances or exits, only the one that they had found. The building was strangely tapered as it rose to the sky, so that wide as it was at the bottom, it seemed to end in a point at the top, on all four sides.

It appeared not to go straight up, but instead each wall leaned in towards the other three, all the way up, closer and closer until they met.

In addition to that, as if that wasn't strange enough, the walls were made of something other than wood. He wasn't sure what it was, but it somehow reminded him of the cliff houses he had seen so recently.

Except it didn't seem to be one continuous piece of rock.

Instead, it appeared to be a multitude of rocks, which had been joined together to form the structure. Each rock was flat and smooth and sort of rectangular shaped. But the strangest thing about it, was the uniformity of the blocks of rock. They were all identical to one another.

His eyes scrutinised the towering wall above him. Identical blocks of rock stretched to either side of and above his head, the rows becoming narrower and narrower as they reached the top.

Heart hammering with excitement, he went inside. Unusual smells immediately assaulted his nostrils and seemed to captivate Shoo, who rushed around in a frenzy of sniffing. San recognised the scent of decayed wood and damp musty earth but these had been largely overlaid but other unidentifiable scents, almost animal like, in their wild and uncontained muskiness.

Perhaps a wild boar had used the building as a den recently but there were no animals present now. Other than Shoo, that is, who was now doing some sort of weird rolling thing on the ground.

"Whatever you're doing, can you stop it now please?" coughed San through the flurry of dust and dirt that Shoo was kicking up. Shoo completed a final roll then reluctantly got back up and strolled over to San.

"Wow what have you been rolling in? YOU STINK SHOO!"

But Shoo didn't even condescend to whimper, all he did was loll his tongue out at San as if he were laughing.

The building seemed larger on the inside than he had thought it would be.

He was starting to become accustomed to the unusual air and the smelly creature at his side. There was no point in trying to hold his breath as he investigated his surroundings.

As wide as the building was, it seemed to be equally matched by its height. Shafts of light shot blade-like through gaps, where rocks or the unidentified substance used to join them, had weathered away and provided some illumination but he still had to strain his eyes to see.

It was the smallest piece of wood jutting out from the stone, high above him, which at first caught his attention. Following an imaginary line he traced the beam to all three other walls, where he could only just make out similar remnants of wood. There could be only one purpose for wood strung across, from one end of the building to the other three.

"That used to be a ceiling. Or a floor! There was an upper level here once," he told Shoo. Then, thinking about the Eyon place he had just escaped with its many levels, he continued, "perhaps even more than one upper level."

To add fuel to his theory, there were bits of wood and other materials in random piles on the floor. Whatever there had been up there once, it was long gone now and all that was left to show for it was this rotten debris.

Eyes still fighting to adjust fully to the gloom, he went to take a closer look.

★★★

Now Loni was hurrying Little along. They were so close to finding what they were searching for, she just *knew* it. They rushed through the entrance to the strange structure and stopped dead. There was a boy there. And a dog. A boy and a dog together!

His mismatched trousers and top, spoke volumes to Loni in an instant. She recognised the similarity of the top he wore, to her own, the material finely woven and finished. And she recognised the rougher finish to the trousers and how they sat, not quite fitting right on the boy's frame.

Most importantly she realised the significance of the difference in the two materials. And the dog was young, not much more than a puppy really, she thought, comparing it to a mental image of 'Blissen' from the village.

Looking roughly the same age as she herself was, Loni didn't really need to glance at the triangles on the boy's arm for confirmation of his age. But she looked there anyway. Unconsciously she held her own marked arm aloft as she did so, displaying her own triangles for his inspection.

The amount of triangles they each displayed was identical. Yet that wasn't even the most astonishing thing.

Little began to squawk comically, pointing to Loni, then the boy, then Loni again. It seemed that, amazed as he was, he had forgotten how to communicate to Humans. Or perhaps he had chosen to hide this ability.

What shocked Loni was her similarity to the boy who now stood open mouthed before her. Their hair colour was identical, as was their eyes. But it was the matching dark skin tone paired with the wide mouth and nasal bridge that clinched it.

Loni held her breath as she stared at the boy and the boy stared right back at her. It was like looking in a magic mirror, she thought, one where you were a girl looking in at it but the reflection returned to you, was that of a boy. A boy wearing her face. Jed had been right, they *were* almost identical.

For a split-second she wondered why the other Pets from San's home in Low Forest hadn't noticed or mentioned it. But really she knew why. Even if they *had* noticed, they would have turned a blind eye to it. They would not have wanted to know about anything that might have upset their happy ignorance. Until of course, Jed had forced them to think about it. She briefly wondered how that was going there.

"San?" she asked him, her voice quivering with suppressed excitement. It had to be him, who else could it possibly be?

"How do you know my name?" he asked her quietly but without moving an inch from where he stood.

Instead, he seemed to be straining towards her, from his neck upwards, almost as if his feet were stuck immovable and against his wishes, from where he was.

Pulling Little towards her, she grasped his wing before she began. It was imperative that he knew she still loved him and that he was still a part of her, regardless of what was about to happen.

She felt a shiver run through him and realised that he was excited but apprehensive. There was no doubt that he would be worried about where he now fit in. But she just hoped that he would realise that he still fitted in *exactly* where he always had – at her side.

She took a deep breath and introduced herself and Little quickly, before telling how and why they had left their home, how they had travelled across the land and how they had come to hear of San's escape too. It all sounded a bit garbled, even to her own ears and probably wasn't making much sense to him. She tried again, starting slow and concise but couldn't keep it up for long.

Loni felt the whole story of her and Little gush forth from her, she just couldn't hold it back. Trying to tell it in a methodical way, from start to end, was hard, as her emotions were so jumbled up in her heart and head. Several times it occurred to her that she had missed a bit out and had to backtrack to fill that bit in.

She told him about the villagers and the Eyon raids. It was just as difficult to recount it, as it had been to hear the story in the first place.

San's eyes filled with tears that mirrored her own, and she hastened to explain how distressed Little had been at the discovery of what his species did to her, or rather, their, species. All the while her voice rose and fell, speeded up as she reached an exciting, exhilarating part of the tale and cracked with emotion as she relayed their devastating discoveries.

"I guessed it could only be you," she finished breathlessly. "After all, how many stray Pets can there be, roaming around? But I don't know how or why I was drawn here. Or how I can change things for other Pets".

Her throat was raw with so much talking but she was relieved to finally get it all out. She just hoped it had made sense to the boy, who all the while she had been talking, had stood only a short distance from her …but a lifetime away.

San approached her quietly and took her hands in both of his.

"Look at me Loni. Don't you remember me at all? Don't you remember how we held hands so tight, even as the Eyons tore us apart. Don't you remember *our mother* screaming? Don't you remember her clutching for us, fighting the Eyon who held her back?" he paused to look at her, tears streaming down his face.

It was eerie to look at him…so like her own face…so well known and yet unknown at one and the same time. His voice trembled as he locked eyes with her and said softly, "and then there is this." In one quick movement he removed the necklet and placed it in her palm.

Her eyes were drawn to the carving displayed there. The crude engraving which symbolised them as individuals, whilst also being two halves of one whole, cut roughly in half. She knew what it meant. Her hand rose instinctively to her throat, where she suspected that once, long ago, the missing half had hung. Lost now and forgotten as having ever existed, she wished that it were not so, wished she had that half to join to this, but it was gone.

"Loni, I am your brother, but also more than that. Born of the *same mother* at the *same time, I am your twin.*"

The force of his words, even though somewhere really, really deep down, she had already known and accepted the truth of them, were earth shattering.

Loni's knees buckled at the back and it was only the fact that her hands were so tightly held, which kept her from falling to the ground.

She listened intently whilst he explained all about his dreams and how as soon as he had laid eyes on her, everything had fallen into place and he had remembered her fully. And as he recounted his own tale, Loni's mind pieced together fragments of her own dreams and glued them to the holes in his.

I have something to show you over here," he pulled her towards the far corner of the building. His hands felt so right in hers, so perfectly normal that she didn't ever want to let go, yet she shrugged free of one of them, so that she could clasp Little with it instead.

Walking as a threesome, with Shoo glued to his side, San led them to a pile of rubble over in one corner of the building and pointed upwards.

"I guess this was once some kind of way to get up there, to what was an upper level, before it rotted away. If you look carefully there are still some bits of wood up there. I found this on top of all the rubble. It was wrapped in oilskins and looks in pretty good condition." He paused before carrying on.

"Like you, I feel we were brought together again for a purpose and I think this has something to do with it."

He handed her what seemed to be a collection of papers, all fixed in place and joined together inside a hard cover. On the front it had huge red letters :

To Whomever Comes After :

A Brief History Of Mankind To The Year 2050.

Whatever had been written there was unknowable to her. Instead of meaning, she saw a collection of signs and symbols, none of which she could read.

"Do you understand any of this?" she asked San and Little in turn. Neither of them did.

All San knew was that the mysterious object was called a 'book'.

"There's nothing else in here. I've looked. Only the Book," said San.

"Then the book is *also* what we've come here for, apart from to find each other," replied Loni with certainty.

And with that, she carefully put the heavy book in her bag and taking San's hand in one of hers and Little's wing in the other, she led the procession out of the temple - for that is what the building was - and on towards the huge purple hued mountains far in the distance.

For a moment, the quartet of two Humans, an Eyon and a dog stopped simultaneously. A light refreshing breeze had sprung up from nowhere and seemed to carry their names on its tongue.

"What was that? Did you hear it?" asked San breathlessly. Little and Loni nodded, yes they had both heard it too and even Shoo gave an extra loud 'woof'.

For a moment they thought of the Owners they had left behind and pledged in their hearts to someday return to. But their quest was not yet complete.

"It was our destiny calling, that's what it was," smiled Loni as they started walking again.

"ESTINEE!" proclaimed Little.

"Woof, woof."

And the book with the huge red letters, remained firmly closed in Loni's bag, its secrets whispered only to the wind.

For now.